PICKUP NOTES

PICKUP NOTES

JANE LEBAK

Philangelus Press
Boston, MA USA

Also by Jane Lebak:

Seven Archangels: An Arrow In Flight
Seven Archangels: Sacred Cups
Seven Archangels: Annihilation
The Wrong Enemy
The Seven Angels Short Story Bundle
The Boys Upstairs
Honest And For True
Forever And For Keeps
Half Missing

ISBN: 978-1-942133-19-3
Library of Congress Control Number: 2016933558

Cover: C.K. Volnek

DEDICATION

For Thomas

ONE

Bach hated me, and I didn't blame him. After the thousands of horrible mistakes I'd made playing his pieces, he had to be lurking somewhere in the afterlife plotting one lady musician's untimely demise. I'd bet he'd do me in with a method that involved rosin, bow hair, and maybe a music stand flying out of the dark.

He hated me, and yet I loved him. I was flying up the scale as I played Kodály's viola-solo transcription of the Fantasia Cromatica, a nine-minute piece that made it sound like I was going down in order to go up again, eight-note clusters that took me in a little back-and-forth so that each time I ended up one step higher than the last, and then I'd repeat the whole thing all over again.

I'd propped the sheet music on top of my dresser using the library's copy of *The First Man in Rome*. I'd never nailed this piece the way I wanted to, but oh, the tension and the pauses, the climbs and the hesitation before the repeats. It was a rhythm like breathing and life, and it took everything out of me to keep my fingers flashing over the right places on the fingerboard.

With my arm cocked all the way under the instrument, my wrist twisted at an angle that would make most orthopedists shriek, but that's what I had to do to hit the highest notes. And then I'd stretch out my arm again and let my fingers race down the fingerboard toward the scroll so I could plummet those sounds back to a low C, the lowest a viola could go.

Throaty. Beautiful. It was precision and it was hunger. It was glory and it was yearning.

It was also really, really difficult, so when I screwed up one of the runs, I stood for a minute, breathing hard. I'd try it again from the top. It wasn't like Bach could hate me any more, right?

In the next room, my apartment door opened.

All the hairs raised on my neck. I was the only one in the building. At least, I'd thought I was. My grandparents had left an hour earlier to go bowling, as I'd discovered when I'd dropped off the rent check on their table. No one should have been here, and certainly no one should have climbed up to the attic I called home.

I replaced my viola in the case, calling, "Hello?"

I stepped out into the kitchen and found my sister, of all people. "What are you doing here?"

Viv looked momentarily startled, but then she forced a laugh. She swept her gaze around my kitchen, like the British Queen inspecting preparations for a royal ball, her chin high as she studied the chipped dish in the rack and the cracked linoleum. She couldn't have missed the overdue bills on the table, festively dressed in their pink envelopes and so very politely referring to me as Josephine.

She folded her arms. "I always forget how you live like a rat."

While all my apartment's inadequacies piled up in my head, Viv strode into my bedroom where I hadn't made the bed or put away my laundry. She shook her head. "If this is the best you can do, you should be the one living at home with Mom."

She was only three inches taller, so it made no sense to feel tiny beside her, ever the "little" sister. But with her dancer's body that hadn't changed even after having a baby, she illustrated the difference between "slender" and "skinny." Add in her unpilled sweater and brand-name jeans, and well, you get the picture. How could brown-eyed-brown-haired-and-starving compete with blonde-and- curly-haired-and-limber?

She lifted the book off my nightstand and smirked. *Northanger Abbey.*

I took it from her and shoved it in my jeans pocket. "Where's Zaden?"

"Mom took him to the park so I'd have a few free hours."

I snorted. "And you came here? Your social life sucks?"

She grinned. "I'm apartment hunting."

She let that hang.

Apartment hunting—?

My fists clenched. "The hell you're getting my apartment. If you recall, you forced Mom to kick me out when you wanted my room for the baby. Besides—" Please don't let my voice break. "—I live like a rat."

She laughed. "*This* place? Why would I want this? I'm here to see everything I *don't* want."

If there were justice in the world, even a tiny thimbleful of justice, lightning would have struck through the window and left a pile of dust I could have eliminated with one whirr of Grandma's mini-vac. *Viv? Huh, no, haven't seen her for weeks.*

I frowned. "Are you also ready to get a job?"

Her eyes flared. "I have a job!"

Returning to the kitchen, I called over my shoulder, "Holding the door so Mom can load drapes into her car is not, in fact, a job.'"

Viv's voice flattened. "What would you know about having a job? Is your squawking viola putting food on the table?"

I pivoted. "My music's fine."

"I can see how fine it is. What's it like being a failure?" The Queen of The Low Blow raised her eyebrows and pointed to the peanut butter jar on the counter. "Oh, wait, it *is* putting food on the table, although not jelly too."

"Get out of here." I edged her toward the hall, but she still wore that smirk. "We're supposed to starve for our art, don't you remember? Some things are more important than jelly."

As soon as she hit the hallway, I slammed the door.

What the hell? I paced to my room and folded my half-load of laundry. *Strutting into my apartment and pretending she wants it and telling me I've failed—like she's such a success?*

Jeans. Sweatshirt. Socks, balled. Underwear. Another pair of socks. And Viv. In my head: Viv, Viv, Viv.

Damn it, I *would* make it as a musician. No, my string quartet wasn't playing Carnegie Hall, and no, we wouldn't get a record deal, but that didn't make us failures. And someday my family would come hear my quartet in concert, and then they'd realize what I'd worked for.

A text came in on my phone from my quartet's first violinist.

Hey, Joey, how can you tell a viola is playing out of tune?

Oh, do go on. How can you tell a viola is playing out of tune?

Thirty seconds later, the next text arrived: *The bow is moving.*

So funny, Harrison the Ever-Helpful, and also ever-ready to remind me that violas are the dumb blondes of the orchestra, and we even have our own blonde jokes. Or viola jokes.

When I finally finished cleaning, Viv was gone, but she still wouldn't clear out of my brain. *It must be nice to have Mom for your own personal banker. How's it working out, using up the unlimited minutes on your cell phone?*

When the hurricane in my head reached Category 5 and I still hadn't won the argument, I went back to my bedroom and picked up my viola. I cradled it in my hands, then pressed my lips against the tense strings and let the smell of wood and rosin surround me.

I let off a long breath.

That. That was life, right there.

Then I noticed the time. *Oh, crap!* I hid my viola in the back of my closet under the eaves, then yanked on three layers of my warmest clothes. I grabbed my jacket and raced down the block for the bus.

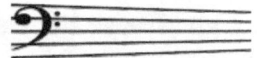

After I arrived at work with sixty seconds to spare, I donned the cornea-frying yellow vest that was all the rage in Nowhere. Cue the applause: I worked as a toll-booth operator.

That's what you got with a BA in music, funded entirely through student loans. And whoa, the day I got that first loan statement in the mail, payment due on receipt? I applied for every job I could. Down at city hall the guys gave me a good ribbing when I mentioned playing the viola. "Why are violas bigger than violins?" said the guy behind the counter, and as I folded my arms, he guffawed, "They're not! It's that the violists' heads are smaller!"

Despite my small head, or maybe because of it, I got the job. And it was fine with me. Standing in an upright coffin? Fine. Inhaling exhaust fumes? Fine. Paying off my steep loans? *Perfectly fine by me.* I could have done a lot worse.

At the time clock, our security guy pointed to the conference room. "Ted wants everyone in there."

You might think (as I did on my first shift) that these talks would be about security, accuracy, or arm position to prevent repetitive strain. And if so, you'd be as wrong as I was.

In a room crammed to critical mass with reflective yellow, Ted preached as if Jesus Christ had just saddled his horse. "You have to remember—" He always shouted like he was competing with the tunnel traffic. "You have to remember you're the last faces the drivers see as they exit Brooklyn! A positive interaction will last all the way to Manhattan."

As his words thrummed on, on, on like a drum machine, I fingered the third movement of Mozart's "Dissonance Quartet" against my upper arm.

Ted raised a fist. "We're going to increase traffic through our tunnel and show up those folks at the Manhattan Bridge and the Queens Midtown Tunnel!"

Speaking for my glassy-eyed coworkers, a *reduction* in traffic would be more welcome. Thank goodness the city had disapproved Ted's request to select a random operator to wave at passersby suited up as Batty, mascot of the Brooklyn Battery Tunnel.

Thus infused with goodwill, I headed out to become a human vending machine. I clicked on the space heater beneath the register and tuned the radio to the classical station. (A customer complained once about the offensive music. What's offensive, you ask? Dvorak.) I set my cell phone face-up on the counter. Everything was in order.

Well, one more thing. Last year I bought a bobblehead of J. S. Bach, and I plugged him into the radio so he could bob in time to the music. The Bach-Bopper cost fifteen bucks I should have spent on, you know, food, and the dude ate batteries, but whenever he started dancing, I giggled.

Then I opened my lane and it was eight bucks. You want to go leave the borough and you don't have an EZ Pass? Eight bucks.

Half an hour into my shift, I got something else: a text message from my favorite cabbie. "What lane are you on?"

Between vehicles, I replied, "3, outbound."

Every lane was in operation, and when the traffic report came on, I got to hear about us. *Outbound on the Brooklyn Battery Tunnel, expect fifteen-minute delays.* I had a ton of cars in line. Well, more than that. Four cars is a ton. I'd calculated that on my first night.

After traffic came weather (Cold? In February? Never would have guessed) and next came Mozart's G Minor symphony. *Yeah.* I could do anything while listening to that.

My plastic Bach agreed as he dipped and pivoted.

Deep into the rush hour, I hadn't shut my window for forty-five minutes, but I'd fully warmed up: the greeting, the pay-out, the send-off. The smile I forced for most but which came naturally when a driver was cheerful despite the backup. I recognized some regulars, like the woman whose 1985 hair and eyeshadow were visible from six cars back, who sometimes handed me a package of M&Ms with her toll. In the past I'd gotten hellos, cups of coffee, pamphlets asking if I'd found Jesus, and business cards from drivers asking me on dates.

An SUV lurched to a stop in front of my window, the driver's face purple. "What the hell took so long? I've been in line twenty minutes!"

The first thing that popped into my head was, *The radio says fifteen.* What I actually said was, "I'm sorry, sir."

He slammed his fist into the dashboard, and I jumped. "How long should it take to get money? Five seconds? Why'd it take so long?"

I don't know. Why is it taking so long to complain?

Behind him, someone slammed the horn and didn't let up. Startled, I looked up to see a yellow cab.

I grinned. My favorite cabbie.

The guy in the SUV shoved me his money, and I punched the button for the toll arm. "Thank you, sir."

Tires squealing, he launched onto the BQE, no longer my problem. Heaven help the other drivers.

Pulling up, my favorite cabbie met my eyes, his mischievous brown ones almost hidden beneath his Yankees cap. The same Mozart played from his radio as from mine. Third movement, minuet.

"Thanks." Biting my lip didn't hide the compulsive smile. "My hero."

The cabbie averted his eyes. He had an EZ Pass unit, so he didn't need to wait in traffic. But he kept the unit shielded for trips through the BBT, and he always handed me a yellow sticky note with his toll. His hand brushed mine, and calm spread through me like when I touched my viola.

I glanced at the note. A hedgehog behind the wheel of a

taxi, profanity symbols over the roof. I stuck the sketch to my window.

He had a passenger, so he only winked before pulling through. Between each of the next five vehicles, I looked at his drawing. "Don't swear too much," I whispered to the hedgehog. "You'll get tipped better."

A salt-spattered Ford Fiesta came into my lane, and the woman stared at me. No payment. Just...watching. Ah, my favorite: drivers who took a swat at the city government by being a pain to the lowest-paid employees.

"That will be eight dollars, Ma'am."

"That's robbery," she exclaimed.

You mean, "Highway robbery."

I gave the automatic, "I'm sorry."

The woman pointed to the bar. "Then let me through."

I frowned. "If I do that, I'll lose my job."

She tossed her head. "I refuse to pay."

Looking in her eyes, I saw... I don't know what I saw, except that this woman's smirk, the way she expected to get whatever she wanted, her disregard for the drivers behind her... It told me that to her, I was no one.

Trying to control my voice, I said, "I'll just call security, then." And I pushed the button.

The siren sounded, and lights rotated on top of my booth.

The woman's mouth opened. "What are you doing?" She grabbed a bunch of coins and bills from the console and hurled them at my window. A quarter struck my arm, but most of the coins ricocheted off the glass and two bills fluttered to the pavement.

While I plastered myself at the far side of the booth, she shrilled fifty names at me, names I could hardly hear over the ringing in my ears. *Bitch. Idiot. I'll get you fired.* Were the other operators staring? The other drivers? But what could they do? She was right on the other side of the sliding door, and I wasn't allowed to leave the booth. I had nothing in here to defend myself. Just a radio playing a symphony Mozart wrote in the last years of his life when he was hemorrhaging money and couldn't find a way out.

Security arrived in the form of Walt, a guy twenty years and fifty pounds my better. She gave him a mouthful while he kept pivoting his glance between us. Afraid my legs would crumple, I wedged myself up onto the stool. He was going to take her side and I'd get a write-up and Ted would put me on admin leave and I'd end up bankrupt. But wasn't the whole exchange on camera? How soon would a panel review the tapes? Or was it cheaper just to replace the grade-three civil servant?

The woman ended her tirade with, "And then she threw my money back at me!"

I struggled to speak but in the end could only shake my head.

With a lack of hurry familiar to anyone who's ever worked for city government, Walt bent to pick up the bills and every last one of the coins. He counted it and handed back some change. Shaking, I put up the gate, and while he supervised, she flipped me off and pulled through.

When he turned to me, I almost expected he'd pat my hand the way my grandfather used to. "Full moon. All the crazies come out." And with that, Walt headed back to the office.

I deposited the money in the register. A minivan pulled in, handed over the toll, and rolled out. As the radio played the final notes of Mozart's G Minor symphony, Bach slumped, his dance ended. I glanced at the clock, wondering how much longer I could keep this up.

TWO

Our scene: a black-tie wedding at Manhattan's University Club, a banquet hall with mile-high ceilings, two thousand pounds of crystal dangling over our heads, and sound-swallowing acoustics. Breathtaking, gorgeous, and home to the reception of many a blushing bride.

Tonight's bride was blushing courtesy of the open bar.

"You have to play 'Hotel California'!" She kept shouting her demand right into our first violinist's face, and this time she added something that's made me want to wrap a C string around my own neck too many times. "It's my day!"

Her day. Well, her evening. Judging from the flush of her cheeks, tomorrow wasn't going to be her morning, so she might as well live it up tonight.

Rational conversation hadn't helped. Harrison had already protested four times that we couldn't play it. That we hadn't practiced it. That we had no sheet music for it. And had she failed to notice string quartets make classical music?

We'd stopped playing, but we were still entertaining the crowd. Gone were the clinks of silverware and the thrum of conversation. Who wouldn't be fascinated by a three-sheets-to-the-wind bride and a baffled quartet with no guitars, no drums, and no singer? They probably thought it was the most outrageous thing that ever happened at a wedding, but they didn't know about the time a chipmunk got into the church and hid beneath our client's bridal gown.

Although come to think of it, the chipmunk wasn't screaming that any high school garage band could have managed this very simple request. The chipmunk also hadn't threatened to stop payment on the check.

I glanced at the cellist on my left, wearing a tuxedo now that he wasn't driving a cab. Shock had replaced the mischief in his eyes.

The groom dragged over the emcee, shouting, "Make them do it!"

The emcee leaned closer to Harrison. "Can't you try?"

Harrison hissed back, "Are you out of your mind?"

Ah, the permanent standoff. Harrison wasn't going to play and the bride wasn't going to back down and the emcee wasn't going to stand up to her. That left us how many options? So I tucked my viola and bow against my side. Approaching the bride, I pitched my voice low like my instrument. "This is such a beautiful wedding. Let's take a walk to the head table. You can show me the cake topper."

The bride swung to glare at me, and her anger drew all the air out of the hall, leaving me unable to breathe. "Don't you dare tell me what to do! If I want to hear about hotels and eagles, I'm going to have it!"

I stepped backward, only to have the bride grab the scroll of my viola. I yanked away, but she said, "Now play it!"

That's when our second violinist took the floor. With her height enhanced by her floor-length sheath dress, Shreya raised her violin with authority.

Me? I authoritatively fled.

I had no idea what Shreya planned to do, but with her black hair loose to her waist, she would look pretty darned good doing it. And then, to my surprise, she played eight bars of the usually-done-on-guitar riff made famous by the Eagles.

Seeming too small for his tuxedo, Harrison whispered, "Oh, God."

Hands clasped, the bride nodded: do it again.

Shreya laid bow to strings and repeated the riff, this time going all the way through. I detected subtle differences between the first and second attempts, but I didn't think the bride could have, even if she'd been sober, nor that she'd have cared. Shreya was improvising, in other words. And just like that, we were flying without a net.

I caught Harrison's eye. Did panic harmonize with horror? For all I knew, Harrison might have been the only one in America who'd never heard "Hotel California." But we already had our heads in the guillotine, so I raised my viola. If Shreya could fashion a performance out of a drunken bride's demand, surely I could pick up the key and fake it.

After all, the joke goes that in order to imitate a violist, you only need to hit a lot of wrong notes in the low register.

Once I started, Josh our cellist laid down rapid bass notes on my other side.

After Shreya ran through it a third time, she gave her head a good shake. Then clamping her violin between her chin and shoulder, she raised her left hand to yank off the black-haired wig, revealing a head of ultra-short blue hair.

The bride squealed as Shreya resumed playing, her hips never still, her violin so in motion that I couldn't believe it stayed aloft. Partners, she and the violin fully inhabited the space of the music. Beneath the chandelier crystals were the bride all in white and Shreya all in black, the bride still and Shreya in motion, the bride alone but Shreya and her violin together.

God, she's good. I scanned the guests to see if anyone else recognized the magic, but no. At setup, the events manager had said the bridal party arrived drunk to the ceremony, and most of the guests hadn't taken long to follow suit.

The groom stood slack-jawed while several groomsmen cat-called, and that's when the bride snatched the emcee's mike so she could warble on about Califo-o-oornia. Rather than change key to follow her, Shreya kept repeating the riff. The videographer wore the world's wickedest grin as he encouraged the bride to mug for the camera.

Ever our heroic leader, Harrison set his violin on the chair and laid his arm across the bride's shoulders, guiding the mike toward himself. Finally. This was fun and all, but maybe he could stop this Titanic from sinking not only itself but our quartet's career.

"Thank you very much!" He sounded enthusiastic rather than horrified, and it stopped her mid-lyric. He guided the mike free of her hands. "Let's have some applause for our bride Melissa and her stunning performance!"

Stunning. Unintentional irony was not Harrison's strong suit, but it got applause. Heaven help our reputation. Worse, if the bride woke up tomorrow and remembered any of this, that check would end up bouncing harder than a home run whacking the upper deck at Yankee Stadium.

Heart thrumming a staccato, I glanced sideways, and this time Josh caught my eye. He winked. I snickered.

Cocking her head, Shreya sauntered to her seat, flashing us a grin. It was as if she'd said, *We're a team.* We might be a newish quartet, but it'd take more than one wasted bride to knock us to the ground.

Struggling to relax my shoulders enough to play, I looked to Harrison for our cue.

Only then did I see Harrison still standing with the mike, and what he held in his hand. Before I could react, he earned us the eternal enmity of Miss Manners and anyone else with good taste. "If anyone wants to buy a copy of our CD, it's on sale tonight for fifteen dollars!"

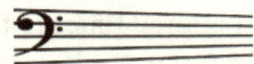

By the time I turned on my computer the next morning, still pajamaed and sleepy-eyed, Harrison had sent ten messages.

I sighed as I walked away. The world had not yet, and still has not, produced enough coffee to cope with Harrison, but I'd give it a try.

While pouring my coffee, I glared sidelong at the computer, which should have blushed for allowing all those emails through. Once I read them, I risked learning our other clients had heard what went down and re-booked actual professional quartets. The longer I delayed, the longer we were kind of like Schrödinger's Cat (Schrödinger's Quartet?,) neither dead nor alive.

What did I really want to do? I wanted my viola. If I could, I'd close my eyes, draw a mellow tone from my instrument, and then with the wood vibrating against my shoulder and jaw, play until I forgot the world.

The problem was, good as it would feel, I couldn't hide from reality forever. And if I left Harrison to deal with things on his own, I'd hate the results.

I returned to the creaky wooden chair, tucked up my slippered feet in defense against my cold apartment, and wrapped my warm mug in my palms. Thus fortified, I read Harrison's messages, all ten of them—all about the same lunatic notion.

My voice cracked. "Harrison, you idiot—what are you doing?"

Destroying us. Pretty much.

Whenever Harrison got an idea, he explored every iteration, the logistics, and the overall applications. And he documented it. Texts, phone, email. Whatever was closest, he'd grab that device to send his most current snippet of a thought. When he first floated the notion of a string quartet, I heard from him a hundred times in four days, roughly five times our contact the rest of the time we dated.

And now our fearless leader wanted to take Shreya's solo from last night, weave it into something perfectly respectable by Mozart or Haydn, and turn it into a frankensong.

I couldn't bear it. I hit reply and typed, "Tell me, when

did you lose your mind?" but then deleted it. As soon as I sent it, he'd know I was awake and start phoning.

Last night delighted him, clearly, but it made me cringe. Shouldn't someone of his background know you do not hawk CDs at a wedding? Have them available, yes. Advertise them: hell no. But Harrison had blown me off with, "We sold five, didn't we?" and then launched into how we should transmute the sound of Shreya's improv into cash.

I didn't mind money. In fact, since absence makes the heart grow fonder, I was quite taken with it. But there were limits.

By the fifth email, I couldn't stomach my coffee. I had less chance of stopping this than derailing a train with my bare hands. He meant to drive us into some weird hybrid genre, and then who'd hire us?

No, get calm. All wasn't lost: Shreya hadn't replied, and the scheme hinged on her. Maybe she'd tell him to take a flying leap.

In the middle were three messages that didn't involve rock music. Josh had sent a reply to only me: "I don't get it. Do you think Harrison's excited?"

Finally, some sanity. I emailed back, "What tipped you off?"

After that, a joyous message that should have opened with a blare of trumpets, from a potential client who'd called three days ago. Subject line: Meeting. Body of the email: a bride and groom wanted to discuss their wedding. Today, at lunchtime. Harrison had replied, "Absolutely," and then sent a separate email to me: would I mind coming? *Yes, Harrison. I always go along with you.*

Another client had sent a final playlist for a wedding in two months. In addition to the ubiquitous Pachelbel's *Canon in D Minor* and the "Ave Maria," she'd requested Beethoven's Fifth Symphony.

I laughed out loud. Don't get me wrong: I love it too, with those opening notes that have captivated everyone for two hundred years as the sound of Fate knocking at the door. (*Da-da-da-DUMM!*) But it was a symphony, for crying out loud. Had she failed to notice she'd hired a string quartet?

Harrison had CC'd me on his reply to her too. Good. Let him explain the difference between four string players and a symphony orchestra—except he'd approved the bride's entire song list. Even Beethoven's Fifth.

After blinking three times to make sure he hadn't suggested we play a medley of songs from the Fifth Dimension (oh those "Wedding Bell Blues!"), I picked up the phone. Yes, there was voicemail. No, I didn't listen. Harrison answered before it rang twice.

"Are you out of your mind?"

"Hi, Joey!" Was that raw, unrefined cheer I detected? It stood in counterpoint to my raw, unrefined shock. "Isn't this the best? It's going to get us a lot of attention."

He was lucky we weren't together in a locked room. "We're playing *Beethoven's Fifth Symphony*?"

My voice should have carried musical notation, like *outraged-issimo*.

His musical notation would have read, *whatever*. "Oh, that. Josh can arrange something."

I said, "Can Josh arrange for an additional seventy-two musicians, because—"

"Anyone dumb enough to ask a string quartet to play a Beethoven symphony is going to be dumb enough to believe we've succeeded. We'll lift the main theme and a few of the melody lines, pass them around for five minutes, and we're good."

I started pacing. Clearly further protest would fall on deaf ears.

"They don't listen anyhow." Harrison totally missed the irony. "It's not as if half the guests will know what the full symphony sounds like. Maybe they've heard part of the first movement on Loony Toons. *Da-da-da-DUMM*." Remember about Fate knocking at the door? Someone please keep it closed. "I'm not going to say no to a contracted client."

I glanced at the Pay Later folder, which encouraged me to shut up and cash the check like a good girl.

Harrison said, "We do the "Ode To Joy" all the time, and that's part of Beethoven's Ninth, right? Right. Have you read my email about the fusion project?"

"Some." Then my brain twigged to what he'd said, and my voice rose half an octave. "It's a project?"

"Yeah! We can start by—"

"Wait!" I found myself by the door, one hand on the knob. It wasn't as if I could flee, so I really must have been trying to lock out Fate. "You can't just plunge forward! We're a quartet—there are four of us!"

"Well, yeah." He sounded amused. "That is kind of the point."

"So you can't drive us alone!" I went into my bedroom and grabbed the blankets off the unmade bed, tugging them tight. "We have to agree to this!"

"Of course we'll all agree." Harrison's idea of informed consent: he informed, you consented. I smoothed out the comforter. He said, "Quit panicking and trust me for once."

"But—"

"You didn't believe me that the quartet would work out, and hasn't it?" He paused for effect, and I straightened my pillow. "You need to start trusting me sometime before we get married."

"I'm not marrying you, Harrison." But my voice had keyed down a notch. An in-joke. We had a history. Maybe our quartet had a future too.

"Well, I wish you'd trust me anyway." That was the first time he sounded concerned. "I want us to succeed just as much as you do. Okay?"

I wanted to believe him. I wanted it because I needed us to survive. "Okay." I glanced out the bedroom window at another line of row houses. "For now. We'll talk it out at practice."

THREE

Only Strings was the smallest shop in Manhattan, the size of my grandparents' kitchen. In a brownstone on a side street off Fifth Avenue, parallel rows of fluorescent bulbs illuminated wall-to-wall compartments of strings: only strings. Violin, viola, and cello strings. Harp strings. Piano strings. Harpsichord strings. Arvin didn't stock kite string, maybe because he'd run out of compartments. Have you nurtured a lifelong desire to study the zither? Arvin could string it.

I was second in line. The first customer said, "Do you sell guitars?"

Arvin didn't look up from his paper. "No, sir. We're Only Strings."

Before the rebuked customer realized he'd been dismissed, the phone shrilled. Arvin answered with, "Only Strings, may I help you?" A pause. "No, ma'am. We're Only Strings." He hung up.

I'd first met the owner when he delivered a lecture to my college music theory class. Our professor had introduced this brick-like man with thinning hair as an expert historian of stringed instruments, but instead, head barely clearing the podium, he delivered a ninety-five minute monologue about *strings*: materials used for strings, a thousand instruments with strings, different methods of vibrating a string (striking, bowing, plucking) followed by the construction of strings, the manufacture and distribution of strings, and disadvantages of certain types of strings. He recited the favorite strings of every classical soloist since Ditters von Dittersdorf in the late 1700s. If he had index cards, he never referenced them. After fifteen minutes, as Arvin gave instructions on how they gutted sheep in sixteenth-century Italy, I snuck a look at the professor to find her gaping. And right then, I'd have followed Arvin anywhere.

At the end of the lecture, I broke three years of collegiate silence to ask two questions: did he have a business card, and what was his favorite music?

His reply? "I don't really listen to music. I just love strings."

As a bonus, his shop was five blocks from Harrison's apartment, perfect for an early-morning stop.

My turn. I stepped to the counter. "I'd like a tuna melt on wheat bread with a thin slice of swiss cheese on either side, but not too much tuna."

Arvin began saying, "No, ma'am—" before recognizing my face and busting up laughing. Looking away, he said, "Good grief, Joey, for a moment I thought you'd taken the prize for the dumbest customer of the hour. Corelli Alliance medium violas?"

"The usual." The usual in two senses: at sixty bucks a pop, restringing the viola meant I'd dine on ramen noodles for a week.

He zeroed in on a drawer the size of a CD without needing to look at the packets. I handed over my credit card and tried not to notice the total, then shoved the receipt in my wallet for taxes. Most days, the credit card hung out in a Mozart CD case while Beethoven guarded my ATM card. In real life, either of those guys would have bankrupted me in a heartbeat, but walking around without a credit card kept me from impulse buys.

My nose wrinkled. "Have you also got a tire iron so I can beat sense into Harrison?"

"Sorry, doll. Only Strings." Arvin tucked my strings into a paper bag and creased the top shut. "What's he doing?"

"New direction for the quartet."

"Decent music for a decent price. That's a good direction." Arvin paused. "He hasn't been in since December. Tell him to get back here before his E string snaps during a bridal march."

That happened once, but Harrison covered. He wasn't like Paganini, the violin-stuntman who used to cut three strings and play an entire concert on the G alone. But I suspected Harrison practiced sometimes without touching the higher two, just in case.

Now for the next stop. I let myself into Harrison's apartment, serenaded by an awkward version of "Twinkle Twinkle Little Star." Harrison sat on a folding chair before the seven-foot windows while a boy played a violin shorter than a loaf of Italian bread, the acoustics augmented by hardwood floors and lack of clutter. Totally, totally cute.

Silent as a cat, I removed my coat and boots, straightened my beige sweater, then slipped into the kitchen to turn on the tea kettle. I'd dressed up a notch because of the client meeting, but that didn't mean anyone should look at me.

A woman read a book on the couch, inadvertently coordinated to match the décor. Or maybe intentionally, since you couldn't miss the color theme. Red, white, and black. I imagine the day after renting the place, Harrison must have taken a cab to Ikea, found a lamp he liked, and then dragged around one of those flat carts in search of things it matched. Gleaming black coffee table? Check. Even the tropical fish beneath the incomprehensible oil painting complemented the scheme. Maybe he recruited students that way too. "Ma'am, I was wondering if you've ever considered violin for your child. For starters, your ebony hair matches the couch."

Leaning forward at the end of the piece, Harrison

corrected the boy's bow hold while cheering him on. *That was so much better! I can tell you practiced hard this week. Now here's what I want you to work on for the next few days....*

The boy clutched his eighth-size instrument with a strangle-hold, bouncing on his toes while standing eye-to-eye with Harrison.

After he saw them off at the door, Harrison joined me in the kitchen. He pointed to the milk and sugar I was adding to the oversized mug of Earl Grey. "Is there any other torture you could inflict on that poor defenseless tea?"

I rolled my eyes as I stirred. "You were good with the kid."

"So listen." I might as well have remarked on the atomic weight of neon. "We'll call it *string fusion*. My brother is investigating how we get permission from the copyright holders, and—"

I waved him off. "Wait until Josh and Shreya get here. The whole thing's a bust if they don't agree."

Only momentarily troubled, Harrison steamrolled on. "They'll like the idea. You're the only one down on it. I'm thinking we're—"

"Oh, for goodness sake!" This must be how it felt to get trampled to death by guinea pigs. "Quit it!"

By the time I finished my tea, Josh and Shreya arrived, and Harrison had the living room set up with two more music stands. As he retrieved Josh's practice cello from the closet, Harrison blathered about rights and permissions, and I set my mug in the sink next to his breakfast dishes, hoping he wouldn't give me a migraine. Was it too much to ask that a string quartet could play actual string quartets?

When he once again called it a *project*, I turned back to the sink. Hot water. Bubbles. Lots of bubbles. Clean dishes. No one can argue with clean dishes. The world would stay sane if only I put everything where it belonged.

After I set the last dish in the rack, I went out to find Harrison facing me with a haggard look. "Have you heard about the tragedy? A car with three violists plunged into the Hudson River!"

Ah, that joke. "And the tragedy was that they could have fit two more?"

His eyes brightened. "Rats, you heard it already?" He turned back to Shreya. "I can't stop thinking about that song last night."

Taller than me by five inches, Shreya looked better on a bad day than I'd look after a makeover. With angular cheeks, nutty skin, and dark eyes, she had no need to buzz-cut her hair and dye what remained electric blue: she'd have attracted attention anyhow. She only ever said the hair was "to match my violin," which for the record was light maple and not blue spruce. Harrison once called her the anti-Joey, since I dressed to disappear and performed with my frizzy brown hair in a bun.

She shrugged. "Sometimes you've just got to make a noise. Even if it fails."

Josh said, "Well, you s- s-" He blinked, then gathered himself. "—saved our bacon."

"Maybe our hummus," Harrison shot back. Shreya was vegetarian.

Josh laughed.

Although last night both guys wore "the musician's uniform" (tuxedos) today they could have auditioned for Clash of the Closets, Harrison arrayed in his LL Bean and Josh in beat-up denim with his New York Yankees cap pulled low over his eyes. Josh was over six feet, Harrison a bit under, but they weighed the same, giving Josh that "starving musician" aura. Without the cap, Josh had black hair that curled whenever it got too long, whereas Harrison trimmed his brown hair every couple of weeks.

I looked around to find Shreya studying me. She asked, "Are you okay?"

I looked at the floor. She'd done something fantastic last night, and I should be grateful. "You were marvelous. Where did you learn to do that?"

She shrugged. "Practice."

I forced a smile. "I practice too. I couldn't have pulled a guitar riff out of my pocket."

"It's not that impressive. Improvisation is just another skill to practice." She shrugged. "I used to screw around doing exactly that. It's doable. You ever try?"

I was about to answer when Harrison said, "Okay, guys, let's get started. Mozart's not getting any younger."

"Now that would be a trick," said Shreya, and I laughed.

Josh looked up. "Oh, good. I was afrrr-raid you'd forgotten how to do that."

I stuck my tongue out at him. He grinned.

Already tuned from the lesson, Harrison gave us an A, and we tuned to him.

Shreya said, "Can we go over the first movement of the *Dissonance Quartet*?"

Harrison said, "I'd like to see you do 'Hotel California.'"

I said, "And I'd like to win the lottery. Let's do real music first. We could tinker with the fusion all day, but right now, Mozart is paying the bills."

He shrugged as he got out the score. Sure, because it was a big favor to let our quartet play quartets.

Harrison raised his bow, and he started with the motive, followed by Shreya. I followed before they were completely done, and as I worked through the phrase, Josh joined. We split off into four branches, the sounds coming up when I knew they would and sometimes surprising me with how we overlaid one another, enhanced one another, contrasted. Harrison's line, Josh's, Shreya's, mine—a dialogue, a community, a tug-of-war.

This kind of conversation was a comfort: scripted, controlled. No need to listen behind the words to figure out what people were really saying. You knew what you were saying was good enough, because Mozart or Haydn said it was good enough, and you could trust them. No second-guessing, no judgment. A classical quartet was the perfect friendship between instruments.

As if driving a car, I had four checkpoints: the music stand, Harrison and his cues, Shreya on my one side, and Josh on the other. Shreya moved even while seated, but now that I'd seen her dancing I wished I could free her from that chair. On my other side Josh's fingers changed the tone of such an impressive instrument with so little pressure. I loved the fluid motion of his hand during a vibrato, the way he smiled while coaxing that instrument to emote. And there I was at the center, concentrating so hard to nail the tough parts while staying in the rhythm of the piece as well as my own personal rhythm: upbow, downbow, check the music, watch Harrison, watch Shreya, watch Josh, watch the music again.

Then the movement ended, and I trembled because it had been here and it was over. I returned to myself again, but I couldn't remember the intervening time. These moments— these too-few moments with a viola and a bow and a universe of sound—these were reasons I could stand in a toll-booth, could shiver through nights in an attic apartment, could face down my bank balance every month.

If you took that away, I'd die. It was all I had.

Me and a musical phrase, an instrument singing with three other instruments in its mellow tenor while the cello gave the bass and two violins worked as alto and soprano. Four instruments, one song, one quartet playing in a key that unlocked my soul.

It felt smooth. It felt natural. And in other ways, it felt like a back-alley fight with the composer.

Today after the first take, we backtracked to hammer on one section where Shreya always sped up because her line was difficult, and I did the same because my line was just as tough; by the end of that passage, we'd all be playing double-time. Through all this, Josh got stuck alternating two notes, and Harrison wasn't playing at all.

"Wouldn't it be nice," Harrison muttered as he got out his metronome, "if we could all just learn our stuff and let it fly?"

Shreya said, "And people wonder why the Beatles broke up."

Harrison laughed. "We're fine. We're like family."

Quartets had to be closer than family. Whenever we prepared for a performance, we had to live in each other's heads to adjust to the unexpected. And that was thrilling too, when Harrison cued us with the slightest of motions and I could read his mind for what he wanted.

An hour later (really? an hour?) I felt breathless as we completed a run-through of the fourth movement. Intoxicated by the ending, I just wanted to start over again, to make a fleeting sound permanent.

Instead Harrison set his golden-brown violin upright in his lap. "That was awesome! Now, let's talk fusion."

Fighting disappointment, I reached for the flannel cloth in my case. As I wiped down my viola, taking care for the distressed parts, Harrison reviewed all the points he'd emailed over the past twelve hours. That a thousand string quartets in Manhattan compete for the same hundred weddings every weekend. That for most customers, one string quartet sounded just like the next. That people would remember the really cool wedding where the musicians didn't play the same old stuff.

As proof, Harrison said, "Remember the Creighton wedding?"

Josh burst out laughing, and I flinched.

Shreya said, "Um, no?"

I shook my head. "You should get down on your knees every night and thank God you weren't with us yet."

Josh flashed a smile that made his whole face brighter. "The D- D- deejay didn't show up, so guess who they asked to play the rrr-reception?"

Shreya shrugged. "Big deal."

Harrison snorted. "I'm not heartless. I only charged them

double."

I said, "And afterward, we modified our contract to include overtime."

"Hell yeah," Harrison said. "But back then we had barely three hours of music we considered performance-worthy."

Shreya's eyes flared. "And you had to play a four-hour reception?"

Josh turned serious. "We p-p-panicked."

I said, "Harrison made the decision to recycle."

She said, "And—?"

"No one noticed!" Harrison laughed out loud. "They kept eating their trout almondine, and we got our check."

"But even if your premise is right," I said, "that doesn't mean your conclusion is."

Harrison held out a hand to stop me. "You want proof the product is good? Let's hear Shreya do that again."

She played it through, much smoother than last night, and I closed my eyes to savor her power.

Harrison turned to me. "How could we let that go?"

The tension spread from my gut to my shoulders. "But how many riffs would convert to violin? And wouldn't any sober bride who wanted 'Hotel California' book a cover band?"

Harrison beamed. "We'll make rock music more legit."

Josh said, "Other gr-groups do this. I looked it up on—" He blocked, then blinked. We waited out the stutter until he shifted words. "I Googled it."

Harrison leaned forward, his violin cradled in the crook of his elbow. "I Googled it too. What you find is other quartets doing arrangements of wedding-esque songs like 'Fields Of Gold.' *We'll* fuse harder rock with Mozart or Haydn quartets."

Shreya said, "The Trans-Siberian Orchestra does it better."

Harrison ran his fingers over the violin's F-holes. "They've taken classical music and worked high distortion electric guitars into the melody line. I want to replace the first violin line of a standard quartet with a recognizable rock riff. Mozartian rock!"

You had to hand it to Harrison. He could sling around the word *Mozartian* as smoothly as I could the word *pizza*.

I forced a laugh. "Okay, so we blend 'Hotel California' with *Dissonance*, and the exact location of Mozart's grave lights up the world's seismographs when he rolls over. Then what? We sell brides a half-baked version of 'Hotel California'?"

He pointed toward Shreya's violin. "I refuse to call *that* half-baked. That's deep-fried musical gold. She handles that guitar riff and suddenly it's violinistic!"

Yeah, that's a word too.

Harrison went on, "People recognize those songs, and that's why we'd do it. How many brides have we interviewed who feel totally outclassed by chamber musicians?"

I paused.

A certain kind of bride seldom signed the contract. Nervous, she'd show up at lunch with her mother or the groom's mother. She'd scan our song sheet with a vague incomprehension, then pass it to her equally-baffled companion. Classical pieces have titles like *String Quartet Number 8 in E Minor, opus 59/2* rather than "Bridge Over Troubled Water." Those brides, if they booked us at all, wanted us for the ceremony and never the reception.

"Think accessibility," said Harrison.

"Oh..." For the first time, his plan made sense from a marketing perspective. He wanted an entry to classical music for people who think it's what you hear at Carnegie Hall if you earn seven figures. Or what you were supposed to have for your wedding. You don't have to enjoy it—you just have to do it.

That was us: the dental-floss of the musical world.

On the other hand: "We can't afford to lose the clients we've already got. Won't this hurt our musical credibility?"

Harrison sighed. "The way it hurt Bond's?"

"Bond is locked into techno-dance classical."

Harrison's face sagged in mock sorrow. "And sobbing every time they cash a tremendous royalty check, do you think?"

Josh said, "You don't ne-ne-need the money."

Harrison looked stung. "I want us to succeed."

Josh raised his eyebrows. "Then it's not about the money."

Shreya said, "It's a way to get our name out there."

And what would they add after saying our name? "Think about the time commitment to come up with enough of these."

Harrison waved a hand, as if he could write a check and order thirty-six-hour days. "Not a big deal. The rock tunes are simplistic. Josh can arrange the music and manage the transitions into the real pieces." He looked back at me, which helped because for a moment I wasn't sure he remembered I existed at all. "You know, some of Mozart's stuff was considered lowbrow in its time."

"What the hell is that supposed to mean?" I walked toward the windows, frowning. "You're not listening. If we fail—if this ends up sounding like crap—there's no room for error! We could lose everything."

"No, not everything." Shreya laid a hand on my shoulder as she passed me en route to her violin case. "We might make ourselves sound like idiots, but even that might help us stand out."

I looked to Josh, but I wasn't getting any backup from him.

The last holdout, I walked to the couch to set my viola in its case, then zipped it shut. I shifted my weight and stared at the area rug with its swirling black and muted red.

"I need to think about this." I bit my lip. "I'm not convinced."

FOUR

Five minutes to noon, my laptop bag and beige sweater and I accompanied Harrison to a hotel lobby. Our fearless leader had us meet clients in hotels instead of coffee shop lobbies on the grounds that we'd have an easier time finding one another, but I bet he thought he looked better in the artificial living-room décor.

Clients believed we met to assess their needs and hand off our sampler CD. In reality, Harrison wanted to sell, sell, sell. I'd have rather said bye-bye-bye, but I accompanied him because, although terrific at smooth-talking a signature out of a nervous couple, Harrison didn't always remember our limits and would cheerfully offer the moon on four strings.

He and I looked good together, both a plus and a tragedy. While Harrison belonged on the front of a college recruitment brochure, I owned exactly two outfits suitable for meeting clients. I tamed my hair with a hair clip, applied make-up as if performing, and carried the laptop case. Harrison did the talking while I stood a pace behind looking professional.

I spotted our quarry first: their uncertain scan of the lobby, as if the normal humans were worried the musical humans might be performing right there, just because. I nudged Harrison, and he approached them, wielding an

31

old-money handshake bestowed only by breeding.

I sized up the bride because different brides required different tactics. Confident brides wanted relaxed musicians. Timid brides required hand-holding. And on the other extreme, you got the Bridezillas, the ones for whom every detail had to be perfect. With them, you had to sound uptight so they knew you had your act together. I hated those brides' picky demands, although I didn't hate cashing their checks. Last year Shreya had spoken with one of these, then came back with her verdict: if Christ had turned water into wine at this woman's wedding, she'd have been totally put out that it was a Shiraz and not a Merlot.

I couldn't make a determination on first glance, so while we walked to Panera, I did the one thing I knew would make engaged couples talk. "How are you doing on the wedding-planning?"

And instead of getting a list of gripes about the dress, the ring, the attendants, and her father who didn't want to wear tails on his tuxedo, I got a glare at the ground. "I hate it. I hate every minute of this stupid wedding thing."

I said, "Um—"

Harrison said, "Are you sure you want to be talking to us?"

Oh, great, jettison our next paycheck. The groom said, "Chrissy's mother is making it difficult."

"Difficult?" The bride tossed her head. "I don't even know where to begin—everything is, 'Oh, that's not how Aurelia did it!' Because for the rest of eternity, Aurelia's wedding is the pinnacle of how weddings should have been, because of course Mom went out and planned her entire wedding and Aurelia did everything Mom wanted."

I said, "Aurelia's your sister?"

"Yes, and if she crashed her car into a bridge abutment, it would be the loveliest wreck you've ever seen, and I should have one just like it."

The groom snorted. I could already predict that if we

signed this client, it would be the *mother* on the phone, demanding to hear us rehearse and asking for our exact shade of concert blacks. Our first Momzilla.

The bride fumbled in her wallet for a fabric swatch, a glossy magenta that careened toward the brink of violet. "My mother wants *this* color for bridesmaid dresses, and she wants the tablecloths to match, but the caterers won't match it because, get this, they don't want fifty tablecloths that make people go blind." I think there were tears in her eyes. "And in the middle of everything we had an infestation of fucking spiders in my apartment—like, a thousand of them, these stupid little white spiders crawling all over everything. And I'd be squashing them while my mom is on the phone telling me to call back the caterer and demand fuchsia table cloths. I thought this was supposed to be *my* wedding."

I whispered, "Oh my God." I could just imagine if I ever got married. "Why don't you elope?"

Harrison said, "You don't get presents if you elope."

I nearly swung the laptop case right at his skull because you can't call a client greedy and expect her to stay, but the bride chuckled. "Yeah, pretty much. And everyone expects a big wedding. Like Aurelia's. So we'll go through with it." She closed her eyes. "Although if I see even one more spider, I'm going to run away and never come back."

At Panera's crowded counter we placed our orders, thankfully on the quartet's dime rather than my own. Harrison offered to carry my lunch while I staked out a table.

I opened the laptop and checked my email. One of the messages had a semi-familiar name, and the subject line "Hotel California."

The room tilted. Already? Word had gotten out already?

When I opened the email, though, it was a message from last night's videographer. "Great job! This was so awesome you have to have it, but don't spread it around because I'm risking my neck getting it to you."

Very funny. Although—and here I sneaked a glance at the

couple we were courting—maybe some mothers-of-the-bride did own a guillotine.

Regardless, I opened the video to find three minutes of footage, starting with a drunken bride bellowing at Harrison. I hit pause.

Harrison was still at the counter, so I fished out my headphones. Then, holding my breath, I clicked play. This was going to hurt; the only question was how bad.

I expected humiliation, so I surprised myself by laughing. Harrison was totally flummoxed when the bride charged in and interrupted Beethoven. Typical Harrison. He shouldn't have tried to reason with her. If he'd talked crazy back, maybe she'd have behaved.

The camera didn't have a good angle on me or Josh, but Shreya was right beside Harrison for the eruption of Mount Bride. When the bride went for my instrument, Shreya's expression changed completely, from startled to angry to—determined?

Now that was odd. And pretty cool.

Scratch that: she was more than determined. By the time she stood, she was no longer Shreya. The first go-around seemed tentative. Then the wig came off and she cut loose, and her focus transformed to joy. I wasn't imagining things last night: she did dance. She loved every second of it. To be that good—wow.

It cut off before the bride started singing (thank goodness) so I dragged the video back to Shreya's first riff, her bow mid-retake. I studied the layout, the ferocity in her eyes, the duo of black- and white-clad women at the center of a banquet hall, one spinning magic from the memory of a song. For the first time I thought maybe Harrison was right, that we could spin money out of magic.

The bridal couple returned, and I shut the laptop.

As they settled down, the bride across from me and the groom diagonal, the groom said, "So...what do you play?"

At my side, Harrison handed them our song list. They

scanned it like a menu in Russian. Awesome. We were about to lose a client.

The bride's cell phone went off, and she fished it out, laying her purse alongside her tray between her and her groom. And as she rolled her eyes saying, "Yeah, Mom, I'm meeting the musicians now..." I noticed movement near the strap. A tiny white spider.

No, two spiders. Crawling out of her purse. And getting near her food.

She snapped shut the cell phone, and before she could put it back in her bag, I leaned forward. "Okay, so you saw the song list and it made no sense, right? Well, it's not supposed to."

She looked me in the eyes, and I stayed forward so she didn't look down to see two spiders, start screaming, and then forever associate our quartet with arachnids. "Quartets perform a special kind of classical music called chamber music." Come on, think, Joey. Think. Keep talking. "It was written by composers like Mozart and Beethoven for in-home performances among friends, each instrument taking a solo part. In some ways, it sounds like a conversation."

The bride smiled. "That's pretty cool. You can make the instruments sound like friends talking to each other?"

"Absolutely! And it's the different combinations that make things so exciting!" I didn't look away from her eyes. "The first violin and the cello, or the viola and two violins, or all four of us playing in unison. Think of all the ways you can churn things up because different combinations highlight different features. The mix-and-match game is a quartet at its best."

She hesitated. "What about when you're at your worst?"

I snickered. "We sound like you and your mom."

She laughed out loud, and I relaxed a bit. Okay, so this was a timid bride after all. "There are four of us—you know, the quartet part. Um—" The stupid spiders were up on her tray now. "So your basic chamber unit is the string trio: a violin, a viola, and a cello." I had no idea what the groom was doing, but she was still looking me right in the face. *Please don't look down. Please don't look down.* "From there, you can go ahead and enhance it with something to take the difficult parts: an oboe quartet is an oboe, a violin, a viola, and a cello. With a flute quartet, you add a flute." I smiled at her. "Would you care to guess the special instrument in a string quartet?"

She giggled. "Another violin?"

I pointed right at her. "Bingo!" Take that, Momzilla. Your daughter is going to be a great bride, even if the tablecloths don't match. "That's why there's a first violin and a second violin. The first violin is the leader, giving the cues but also getting the most difficult parts. Usually it's playing highest, so you hear it best."

The bride frowned. "But you said it's like a group of friends."

I'd almost forgotten Harrison was there until he said, "We are friends, but a quartet needs someone in charge."

The bride reached for her bag to put back her phone, so I stretched across the table and took the song list from the groom, cutting her off. "A lot of our songs are modern, as well, just arranged for a quartet." I pointed to "The Entertainer" and "Eleanor Rigby."

I couldn't keep leaning over the table forever, and those spiders were dangerously close to her sandwich.

Our fearless leader then said, "You know, we need space for the computer," and so help me, he dropped a napkin onto the tray, right over the pair of spiders. He cleared her drink and sandwich off the tray, then lifted it (spiders and all) and took my tray and set it on top of the other, like a spider sandwich. I stood her purse upright, hoping that would deter any remaining explorers, and as he left, I said, "Thank you."

He tossed over his shoulder, "That's what fearless leaders are for."

I glanced at the groom, who was smirking. Great. He'd

seen the things too. But at least she hadn't.

I set the computer further forward, but I couldn't think of what to do with it. The bride dropped her phone back in her purse, then took a bite of her sandwich. After she swallowed, she said, "Okay, I figured this was all stiff-stuff, because Aurelia had a quartet. But you make it sound almost fun."

Harrison returned in time to say, "We can go one better than Aurelia. For a fee, we can work your special songs in with our repertoire."

I glared at him. He flashed me the adorable smile that meant he knew I wanted to club him to death with a panini.

The bride looked puzzled. "You could play 'Lady' by Styx?"

Harrison said, "Not just play it, but weave the main line into one of these quartets."

I cut off Harrison by saying, "We can't guarantee any specific song at this point."

He leaned forward. "She's too modest. Since this is our specialty, I'll tell you that of course we can."

Oh, for crying out loud. There was being friendly to a timid bride, and there was insanity. "We'd have to look over the music first to make sure we could arrange an adaptation that would do justice to the wedding you're planning."

The bride's phone rang again. "You mean the wedding my mom's planning," and she took the call, so I opened the laptop and found a thirty second clip of "Lady." As I suspected, helicopter crashes sounded more violinistic.

The bride said, "Mom wants to know if you can play the 'Ave Maria.'"

I snickered. "If you ever meet a wedding quartet that can't play the 'Ave Maria,' it's because they're living under a bridge with their hats out for spare change. I can play it in my sleep."

She said into the phone, "Yeah, Mom, they can do it. No, you can't talk to them. They're really busy," and then hung up on her.

Our henpecked bride was already looking bolder. "Okay, so let's let's back up. You can take 'Lady' and weave it into something done by Mozart? Not just play it, because I have to be honest: those versions sound lame."

"I think it will sound lame anyhow," said the groom. "Sweetie," and he turned to the bride, "if we're going to have someone play 'Lady,' why not a cover band with electric guitars? Or a DJ?"

She glared at the table. "Aurelia didn't have a DJ."

The groom laughed, and that was the sound of an unsigned contract. "Honey, go one way or the other. Either get a string quartet to play whatever it is they play, or tell your mother to jump in the river and have what you want. You know I'll support you."

My heart pounded. "Why not have both? For the rest of the evening, you could have a full complement of Haydn, Beethoven, and Mozart, but your first dance can be to 'Lady.' Aurelia won't know what hit her."

The bride looked at her groom. "You know, you're right. Why is my mother dictating everything all of a sudden? We can get a DJ and just have what we want. She's going to complain anyhow, so she might as well complain about things we enjoyed."

I exclaimed, "But—"

The bride picked up her purse and looked at me. "I'm sorry. We shouldn't have wasted your time, but you were really helpful."

Harrison said urgently, "You know, if you listen to our CD—"

"Before you go," I said loudly, interrupting Harrison's interruption, "watch this."

I had left the video open in my web browser, poised right after the drunken bride backed off. I clicked to start and handed over the laptop.

Despite the volume of all Manhattan at lunch, the speakers did their job. As Shreya's riff skirted the edges of my hearing, the bride's pupils widened. At the point when Shreya began dancing, the groom's mouth opened.

Harrison murmured in my ear, "What the hell?"

The groom said, "She's astonishing."

I beamed. "That's Shreya Ramachandran, our second violinist."

The groom's head shot up. "Second violinist? But you said—"

I jerked my thumb toward Harrison. "He's the first." Folding my arms, I probably looked confident. Or something. "You can hear we don't sound ridiculous. Why would we promise what we couldn't deliver?"

Well, for the money. But with their wedding a year away, surely we could cobble together something.

The bride looked up from the screen. "Why'd she take off the wig?"

"Working the crowd." I had no idea why Shreya pulled off the wig. Who knew what Shreya ever thought?

When the video ended, I pulled back the laptop so the bride couldn't hit replay and see we'd pulled this out of a top-hat like a magician's rabbit. She looked up, taken aback, but I only clicked the laptop shut. In the marketing books they said keep 'em wanting more. Now it was a necessity.

I put steel into my voice. "And that's the kind of violinistic rock theme we fold into a traditional Mozartian quartet."

Dear God, Harrison had infected me. I'd said both *violinistic* and *Mozartian*.

The groom said, "Okay, I'm convinced."

The bride bit her lip. "I still don't know. I mean, my mother—"

Harrison picked up her fabric swatch. "You know, you were talking about the details. Let's blow your mom out of the water. For a small fee, our second violinist will dye her hair to match."

Yeah. That bride couldn't get her signature on the paper fast enough.

Harrison was ebullient. "I can't believe you did that!"

Me, not so much. "And I can't believe you did that." We walked toward the subway, my brain terribly conscious of a three hundred dollar check in my wallet. "You're out of control!"

He snickered. "How is that any different from changing our song list?"

My voice edged toward outraged. "How is selling Shreya's body different from playing Henley instead of Haydn?"

"She dyes her hair blue. Why would she care?"

I handed him my phone. "Want to find out right now?"

I wouldn't cash that check before Harrison consulted her, that was for sure.

When he didn't take it, I muttered, "I notice you didn't offer to dye your own hair."

"And I notice you suddenly became the biggest champion of string fusion."

"Don't you even—?" My voice broke, and I stopped to face him. Pedestrians parted around us like a stream around a boulder. "Without clients we aren't a string quartet. I'll go along with you, but we have to do it right. We can't count on Shreya to pull us out of the fire whenever things get hot."

Of course, Harrison didn't look at all contrite. "You need to trust me that this will work."

"I don't need to trust you." I folded my arms. "I need the quartet to survive."

FIVE

The Saturday after our first stay at the Hotel California, we were booked for a dignified evening wedding.

Per usual, Josh decided to drive rather than entertain the whole subway system by lugging a cello while wearing a tuxedo. Also per usual, he offered me a ride.

I knew what to expect. I accepted anyhow.

It wasn't that he sweet-talked me into it. He could have sweet-talked me into anything if he wanted to, but he never tried. No, he just went with the straight-forward, hesitant, "You want a lll-lift?" and then a soft, almost shy, "I'll p-p-p-pick you up at five-thirty," and I said yes.

Like a gourmet wine-taster, after seventeen years I'd learned to identify and even predict Josh's three different stutters: blocks (when the sound wouldn't form), repetitions (*s-s-s-sandwich*), or prolongations, when he'd drag out a syllable (*sss-sandwich*). Back when we used to talk on the phone for hours, I'd find myself thinking in his stuttering rhythm, and I'd have to remind myself not to do it out loud. I didn't know how he'd react, if he'd think I was making fun of him. He'd certainly be justified.

The sound itself was pretty cool, especially when he was relaxed, almost soothing in the way you could take your time and really listen. What unnerved me were the things they call stuttering "secondaries," the way someone who stutters does things he subconsciously associates with speaking fluently. When Josh blinked rapidly or twitched his head to the side, those things that made people stare until I wanted to melt into the floor—those were secondaries. He avoided eye contact, but I'd learned it wasn't that he didn't want to look at me: that was just something most stutterers do.

For the most part, it wasn't a big deal. He said what he needed to say, hesitant and never quite looking at you. He sang without a problem. Reciting in tandem with someone else, he was fluent. Sometimes he and Harrison, going over a difficult section, could say the notes for each part in time to each other, and Josh never stuttered. Although anxiety itself didn't cause stuttering, when relaxed, he stuttered less.

And when he drove, he swore fluently.

At exactly five-thirty he pulled up outside my house in a scuffed black Jetta with the logo missing. A perfect gentleman, he even opened the door. He looked good: tall, trim, well-tailored, and with that sudden look-away that made him seem coy. He waited for me to buckle in before turning on the engine, and he offered me the choice of radio stations.

He checked for oncoming traffic, and when all was clear, he slammed his foot dead to the floor, launching the car to the speed limit and beyond.

I clutched the door handle and shut my eyes.

Josh never noticed when I did that. After years of splitting the cabbie work with his dad, it was instinctual to ignore his passengers, and ignore me he did. He also ignored the laws of physics. We approached escape velocity while ascending the entrance ramp of the Gowanus Expressway, a thousand feet in the sky.

To the driver in front of us, he snarled, "The one on the right! That's the one that makes it go forward!"

It never did any good to ask Josh to ease up. In the past,

he'd taken that as a challenge, and it left me longing for the days my nearly-blind grandfather weaved all over Flatbush Avenue in a Buick the size of a tugboat.

As soon as Josh found room, or maybe even a few seconds before, he cut to the left to pass the guy, immediately forgetting him in order to concentrate on the next car, which by sheer coincidence also went too slowly. "You'd think he's dragging a couch." He gripped the wheel, growling, "Hey, guy, I know you're in a Chrrr-ysler, but it can do better than that."

A car passed us. Josh muttered, "Mmm-maniac."

Shooting through the Brooklyn Battery Tunnel, the engine sound screamed off the white tiles like something out of *Star Wars*. I told myself it would be okay, no really, although I pulled my viola to my chest to shield it with my body. He was a grand-master driver who hadn't been in an accident in the last three hours. I meant, years. It had been three years since his last fender-bender, and even then he'd been rear-ended.

To his credit, we arrived faster than if I'd taken the train, but I couldn't kiss the ground because Josh thought that sarcastic.

"I'm nnn-not that bad," he said as I shut the door.

In the midtown church, a florist's crew worked at turning the place a violent pink. It was six o'clock. Harrison and Shreya had already arrived.

Harrison glanced up. "You look awful. Did Josh drive?"

"Hah." Josh set his cello on the floor and removed his jacket. "Really n-n-n-not that bad."

We stashed our jackets and cases in the sacristy, tuned, and sought out last-minute instructions from the wedding coordinator. The officiant was a young priest whose voice had already softened to a texture I'd transcribe as *subito piano*, and he paused to admire our instruments.

"Don't be too pleased with mine," Harrison told him, frowning at his violin while adjusting the micro tuner on the tailpiece. "The A string keeps going flat."

I said, "Give it time. It's cold."

"It's had enough time," he snapped. "Yours isn't complaining."

The priest grinned. "Should I pray for it?"

Harrison muttered, "If you think that'll work better than threats to turn it into toothpicks."

This was one reason to ride with Josh: heat in the car. Like any piece of wood, string instruments expand and contract, and very few couples get married in a hermetically sealed vault in the heart of a museum. Our best compromise was getting them to room temperature.

Ignoring Harrison's endless re-tuning, I stood to play a three-octave C scale. At the end, I scanned the frescoed ceilings, listening as the notes died away. "Awesome! These have to be the best acoustics we've ever played."

Harrison looked up. "You and I should get married at Carnegie Hall."

"Except I'm not marrying you, Harrison." I projected to test how far it would carry, and sure enough, the wedding coordinator turned from halfway across the church. Every decibel worked for you in this building.

Modern churches annoyed me, with their dead spots where you'd play as loud as you could but no one could hear, where there'd be no air and you had to rearrange the chairs five times to find the spot where you could breathe again. But this one? Gorgeous and functional, like playing inside a musical instrument.

Shreya adjusted her seat, then stepped back to study our placement. "This will do. I guess I can stay."

I tugged at the edge of her black hair. Our blue-haired beauty once again wore the wig turning herself into a professional, although I guess at some point she'd have to become our magenta-haired beauty. "I'm surprised you showed at all."

Her eyebrows shot up. "Hey! I wouldn't skip a performance

unless I was bleeding to death!"

I laughed. "Oh, good. I was afraid Harrison's deal would drive you away."

More puzzlement. "What deal?"

Harrison looked up from his violin. "Yeah. Um, I didn't get a chance to talk to her yet..."

Josh stopped tuning. Shreya took a step nearer to us. "What's going on?"

Harrison looked at me. "Don't be a coward. You tell her."

My fearless leader. Fighting a grin, I said, "That bride we booked last Sunday was very...particular...about color coordination."

Shreya's eyes flashed. "She wants an all-white quartet, and a brown-skinned Indian woman ruins the decor?"

I smirked. "Oh, far, far better."

Harrison plucked his A string. "They couldn't have cared less whether you were white or Indian or Martian. You're the reason they booked us at all."

Dead silence. I bit my lip, struggling not to laugh. Shreya looked from me to Harrison, then back to me. "And that's because—?"

Oh poor Harrison, having to confess. "Because Harrison took note of how particular she was about color coordination and made her a teensie little promise."

All four of us clustered. My voice wasn't as steady as I wanted because I was still fighting giggles. "She wants your hair dyed to match the bridesmaid dresses."

Stepping back, Shreya interrobanged, "What?!"

Josh burst out laughing, and then I was in stitches too. "Oh, it gets better!" I couldn't help myself. The two violinists were glaring at each other. "Harrison offered it as a perk."

"She wasn't going to sign us!" Hands raised, he backed away as Shreya stepped toward him. "I didn't think you'd mind!"

"You didn't think I'd mind? And what color is my hair going to be?"

I sing-songed, "Fuchsia!" The acoustics carried it all the way through the church.

Before Shreya could react, Josh muttered, "Thank God it's not p-paisley."

I laughed even harder. The wedding coordinator and the priest were staring. Harrison offered a weak smile.

Josh turned to Harrison. "Should I p-paint my cello?"

I said, "How about concert magentas?"

Josh said, "Music printed on p-p-purple paper?"

I looked at him. "We could dye our bow hair too."

Shreya stood with her eyes closed, but her shoulders shook with helpless laughter. "Fine. Fine."

Harrison forced a used-car-salesman smile. "See? It's not so bad."

"Dude—?" She shot him a look over her shoulder. "It's called a wig."

I took my seat, huddling over myself to stifle the persistent giggles while Josh kept shooting me glances that triggered another bout.

I looked up to find Harrison standing over me, and as I was about to make a joke, I stopped. I'd expected his wounded puppy look, but instead—coldness?

Well, he couldn't fire me right now. Most brides could count to four. "What?"

He murmured, "You enjoyed that far too much," and before I could respond, he leaned closer. "Don't do that to me again."

He turned his back and checked the tuning of his A string.

I hunched over myself, afraid to look in case Josh was staring at me too, or Shreya. I blinked hard, tried to straighten my sheet music only to drop it all. I thrust it back onto the stand, then did scales with my eyes closed, listening to the perfect intonation. C scale. G scale. A-minor scale. It would be okay.

Harrison didn't say anything else to me. Shreya and Josh had fallen quiet.

Six-thirty. Our package started with music for the guests half an hour before the wedding, long enough for a Haydn quartet.

Between movements, Harrison adjusted his A string.

"Give it a rest," Shreya murmured. "It's good enough."

"Good enough isn't perfect."

Shreya shot back, "Perfect is the enemy of good enough."

Unsure if Harrison were still pissed, I tested the waters. "What if I garrote you with your own A string? Will that be good enough?"

"Only if it's in tune when I die." Harrison plucked the string again, but he didn't sound angry. "Maybe the bride will be a little late."

We proceeded to the second movement. As usual before a wedding, they were more interested in catching up than in the musical ambiance. We were background, like the stained glass windows. Musical wallpaper.

By the time we finished the quartet, the priest and groomsmen had gathered at the front (along with, I presumed, the groom). Next, a larger group of guests would fill in during the final five minutes, and then we'd begin. We played a shorter piece.

Seven o'clock. We looked for a signal to seat the families, but none came. After a quick check of the A string, Harrison started the air from Handel's *Water Music*.

It ended. Still no signal. Harrison selected another short piece. We played through. Seven fifteen.

My brain itched with a realization: only now had the church begun to fill.

Our contract specified the start time at seven, yet most guests only arrived at seven twenty? Had the bride told us the wrong time? But no, the wedding coordinator had prepped for a seven o'clock wedding, and the groom, who ought to know, had arrived for seven.

Seven thirty. Harrison laid his violin across the seat. "Shreya, take a solo."

I grabbed the sleeve of his tuxedo with a questioning look.

"I'm talking to the groom. That bride better show up or the check won't clear the bank."

I looked down to hide the grin. Only Harrison.

Shreya gave an Irish melody that set the hair on my neck straight up with its subharmonics. Perched at the edge of my chair, I alternated between watching her and watching Harrison conspire with the groom, who then flagged over the best man and the priest. A cell phone came out of the groom's pocket, and when Harrison returned, Shreya finished up.

So—did we still have a wedding to play? Or were we going to improvise, like the time the bride bolted?

Harrison held up the music for Mozart's quartet *The Hunt*.

My eyes widened. A thirty-five minute piece?

Mouth set, he nodded.

Before I could ask whether the bride had fled, the priest took the lectern. "May I have your attention, everyone? We've heard from the bride, and she's running a little late."

Harrison didn't appear as unnerved as I by the guests' knowing laughter.

The priest continued, "While we wait, please relax and listen to the Boroughs String Quartet. We'll begin as soon as she arrives."

Harrison leaned close to me. "Quit looking terrified. Hell yeah we'll give them a concert. At three hundred bucks an hour."

Well—yes and no. While our contract did stipulate that rate of overtime, who goes to a ceremony mentally geared to play for hours? At a reception we'd at least get a break in the middle. But by forgetting to show up, the bride had us playing indefinitely and, after an unspecified time, needing to sound fresh for the ceremony when everyone (i.e., the check-signers) would be paying attention.

On the other hand, those pink envelopes on my kitchen table would encourage me to make my best effort, so up went the viola, and I awaited Harrison's cue.

Mozart should have written a longer quartet because he finished before the bride came, so Harrison indicated the Beethoven string quartet that had gotten interrupted at last week's wedding. Oh, for heaven's sakes, another thirty minutes? She was an hour late already.

Between two movements, I glanced at the guests expecting to find them mingling, but instead of the sides of their heads I saw faces. Without a wedding to distract them, the guests had begun focusing on the only entertainment in the church. They were staring at me—at us, but at me too. I bet they saw my goosebumps.

Harrison noted the same thing: the faces, the stillness. Between movements two and three, he stood, announced what we were playing (when had he ever done that?), and thanked them for their patience.

And then, ever classy, he reached into the jacket pocket where he kept our CD.

Scrambling up, Shreya grabbed his arm before he could speak.

Silence ruled. It was the longest hour of my life, the moment her dark eyes bored into his hazel ones. Harrison appeared puzzled. Shreya whispered, "Not in a church."

Defiant, but comprehending he was outgunned, Harrison shrugged, and they both retook their seats.

At eight we sat through another announcement that the bride was finally on her way this time. Beside me, Josh gave a rueful chuckle.

Before the priest stepped down from the lectern, Shreya stood for a solo rendition of "Waiting For A Girl Like You."

The crowd laughed, and the priest laughed, and Shreya laughed, and I wanted to run. Grab the viola and run as fast as I could.

And then so help me, Shreya gave a recognizable bit of Chicago's "Does Anybody Really Know What Time It Is?" Louder laughter, followed by applause. Someone called, "Can you do 'It's Too Late'?" and Shreya obliged.

Harrison's eyes went as wide as stopwatches. He did the exact opposite of what I wanted to do: he strode to the mike. "I'd like to introduce Shreya Ramachandran, second violinist for the Boroughs String Quartet!"

She stepped out from the chairs as someone shouted "Time In A Bottle—?" and she played thirty seconds of Jim Croce.

Heart pounding, I turned to Josh for reassurance, but given his own wide-eyed stare, I might as well have asked the church mouse. Between this and the "Hotel California," our reputation was down the toilet. That wedding coordinator would never recommend us again. Once she started chatting up her coordinator friends over margaritas, we'd be forever remembered as that grandstanding quartet who lost their minds.

Shreya worked the crowd. Harrison mentioned our name every single time he could. He introduced me and Josh and even took a couple of digs at the viola. ("You guys have heard violins but not violas, right? That's because modern recording techniques remove all the extraneous sounds.")

He urged me to take a solo, but it felt like the floor was made of ball bearings, so he took one himself.

At nine-thirty the wedding coordinator gave a signal that deserved accompaniment by bells like Armistice Day: at last, for real, like seriously, here came the bride. Harrison and Shreya shared the mike as they thanked the guests for their patience.

And then, having already played for three hours, we began the real work.

After the ceremony I was spent like a one-dollar bill. Whenever I moved, pain shot up my left arm and across my shoulders. In a room off to the side of the sanctuary, I rubbed my shoulder, then worked my fingers along my neck. Yehudi Menuhin said a violinist has to be in excellent physical condition because you need to hold your arms above your heart. He didn't even play the viola, which weighs more, has a heavier bow, and requires more pressure on the fingerboard.

I stopped only when we were approached by a beigeish creature, half sequins and half pearls: the mother of the groom. Oh, good. Payment for the overage.

Then I noted the tightness of her mouth, the steel of her eyes.

Harrison approached the woman, but she refused his handshake. In a thin voice, she said, "We only authorized you to play. No one told you to make a spectacle of yourselves."

My mouth opened. A spectacle of ourselves? With a bride three hours late to her own event that at its best was little more than pageantry?

Harrison's eyes widened. "I'm sorry. We made the best of a bad situation."

The woman stared down Harrison, then glared at Shreya—who had the flattest expression I'd ever seen—and then gave me a once-over as if I weren't worth crushing beneath her glittery taupe pumps. I couldn't breathe.

With the air tinged by the hint of Obsession, she said, "You had no right. None at all."

An apology lodged in my throat. I couldn't get it out, but I couldn't force it down either.

She turned her back to rejoin the bridal party.

Then I realized: all that, and we weren't even going to get paid?

We four stood in silence for nearly a minute. Finally it was Shreya who broke it. "What crawled up her ass?" She put a hand on Harrison's shoulder. "At least you got your wish. The violin warmed up."

"Thanks. Why isn't the universe listening as closely when I ask for more clients?" He returned to his chair, then wiped down his violin with a cloth to remove four hours of rosin from the belly. "What did she expect? The bride was on California time, but *we* ruined the wedding?"

"But you know—" and I got up close to Harrison, "they didn't ask for us to put on a show. When we booked them, we never said we'd start taking requests off pop radio."

Harrison frowned. "You were onboard with the fusions."

"*They* weren't onboard with the fusions!" Behind me, Josh closed the sacristy door. Good—they'd already heard enough from us. "Bait-and-switch happens to be pretty damned unprofessional!"

Shreya said, "Joey, I was the one—"

"You weren't the one who grabbed the mike and opened your big mouth!" I didn't take my eyes off Harrison. "Shreya gave them a snippet. You spun it into a concert the bridal party never intended!"

Harrison folded his arms, one of those poses where you just wanted to hit him because he looked so damn confident. "They never asked for it because they never dreamed the bride would go for an Olympic gold in the fashionably-late competition."

Behind me, Josh said, "It's okay. It's d-d-d-done."

"It's not done!" My voice broke. "He screwed us over! We're not going to get paid because of him!"

Josh touched my arm. I jerked away from him.

"We'll be okay," Josh said. "It's j-j-j—" He shook his head. "Just one wedding."

I clenched my fists. Reputations were made and ruined one wedding at a time.

Harrison said, "They'll pay up. Remember that pretty little contract my brother designed? An hour in small claims court will get us a check."

Shreya said, "I'm sorry, Joey. The whole situation was just so ridiculous, I didn't think. I whipped off the one song, and then it snowballed."

Harrison pffed. "I'm not sorry. The guests loved it, and

if anything, we've proven we can do what I said. Imagine if we'd had pieces already practiced."

I rolled my eyes. "Weddings are not about us."

Harrison said, "I don't see why they shouldn't be."

No, of course everything should be about Harrison.

I sat with the viola case on the table in front of me, draped my arms over it and laid down my head, then kneaded my neck and upper arm. God, it was late. Not by my regular schedule—at ten-thirty I'd be only halfway through my shift. But it felt like the day should have ended by now.

Then, gentle pressure: Josh behind me, massaging my neck and back. I closed my eyes and let my shoulders melt so he could work out the tightness.

Harrison said, "Hey, Josh? Come take care of me next?"

Josh laughed. "Bite me."

Shreya chuckled. I couldn't find the energy.

A click as Harrison snapped the clasps on his case. "Well, if the groom takes after his sweet mom, maybe the couple deserves each other." He put on his coat. "Are you guys starving? I am."

Harrison had no problem thinking about food five minutes after the world ended, so he suggested a mid-priced restaurant he knew nearby. We locked our instruments in Josh's car and went on a hike.

Once we were seated and with menus in-hand, Harrison said, "This one's on the group," and I let off a breath. I could order more than water and a cheese sandwich.

"I hope the server comes soon." Shreya fingered her earring while taking a pass over the menu. "I'm tired of waiting for people."

"I should have known." Harrison drank some water, then turned to me. "Do you remember when we booked this one?"

Seriously? This exhausted, I wouldn't have remembered interviewing this bride while she juggled torches. "Enlighten me."

"The one we met at her office."

My eyes flared. Her! She'd invited us for 10:30. We'd arrived to learn she wasn't in yet for the day. Cracking her gum, the secretary said, "She's running late," with the same tone you'd use to say water is wet. After twenty minutes, I voted to leave, but Harrison stayed because we'd had a contract drought. After that we heard nothing for so long we assumed she'd signed different musicians, and then one evening I was stunned to find in the mail, of all things, a signed contract and a check.

I frowned. "Wasn't she someone your mom knew?"

Harrison leaned forward. "Her father? Is an executive for an *airline*."

That did it: we laughed so loud heads turned.

Shreya asked, "Which airline?" and I replied, "Any of them!"

Harrison said to me, "Are you going to be late for our wedding?"

"No, because I'm not marrying you, Harrison."

"Damn." He looked so disappointed that my heart dropped. "You'd show up on time."

The waiter arrived. *Hello I'm some unforgettable name may I take your order.* Harrison: barbecue chicken sandwich and a Coke. Shreya: Vegetable minestrone and a garden salad, just bottled water.

And then Josh: "I'd like a hamb-b-b-b—" He gasped, and his voice dropped to barely audible. "Ham-bur-ger. And a C-c-c-coke."

I flushed right to my ears.

The waiter smirked. "And do you want fry-fry-fries with that?"

Josh looked up, pale.

Still glancing over the menu, Harrison said abruptly, "You know, I'd like to change my order. Cancel the barbecue chicken sandwich, and instead bring me the manager."

The waiter dropped his pen. "What?"

Icy-hard, Harrison stared the waiter dead in the eye. "I

said, fetch me your manager, unless I should head to the kitchen to get him myself."

His voice had dropped an octave. The last time the world heard that tone was John Jacob Astor on board the *Titanic*. The waiter backed away from the table.

My vision speckled. Harrison felt fifteen feet away from me. "What are you doing?"

Settling his napkin on his lap, Harrison shrugged. "I'm going to give the waiter the opportunity to brush up on his job application skills."

Josh shot back from the table. "D-d-d-don't!"

Harrison's eyes glinted. "I'm not letting him get away with that."

Josh grabbed his jacket. By the time I got out of my chair, he'd already left.

On the street, I jogged to catch up. "I'm sorry."

He hunched his shoulders, and I hurried to keep pace.

Eventually he had to stop for the Don't Walk at the corner. While a dozen cars whished by on the wet pavement, I tried to touch his forearm. He just jammed his fists in his pockets.

This sucked. We were already tired—why'd the idiot waiter have to do that? How hard should it be to get a burger?

"He's j-just a jerk." Josh stared as if he could see the subway through forty feet of concrete and earth. "He shouldn't lose his job."

We shared a sphere of silence amidst the cars and pedestrians. I didn't know what to say. I hadn't known in first grade, hadn't known in second grade, hadn't known when I destroyed things for us when I was sixteen. Right now, guess what? I still didn't know. I'd never know.

The light changed, and Josh turned uptown. Ah, heading toward his car.

I didn't know what to say, but silence felt wrong. Was this anger or humiliation? If it was embarrassing just sitting beside him, what was it like that whenever you opened your mouth, you risked some stranger making you his personal entertainment?

My phone buzzed with an incoming text. Shreya. "Manager groveling."

"Good," I muttered. I texted, "H got waiter fired?"

She texted back, "Manager looks pissed."

A moment later, a text from Harrison. "Come back."

Easier said than done. "Josh, the manager is on his knees in tears. Do you want to go back?"

He shook his head, then pointed to me.

"Not without you."

He turned aside, but I caught his expression: shame and frustration together.

I texted Harrison, "No."

As I turned to Josh, I struggled to think of something comforting. "You can't help what other people think."

Josh pulled out his phone and texted me, "Why can't the jerks be tagged so we know in advance?"

My phone buzzed again. Harrison: "Where are you?"

Then Shreya: "Wait for us. We're coming."

Josh's phone buzzed, but he looked only at me.

My arms ached, but how could I hug him when I knew too well which of us had been the jerky sixteen-year-old?

"You're only the catalyst." I squeezed his hand. "You never asked for this, but you show us who people really are."

SIX

I awoke on Harrison's couch, my neck stiff but my hands fingering the "Ave Maria."

I groaned. "Oh late bride, you are a pain in the shoulders."

I heard a chuckle across the semi-darkness of the living room. Shreya.

"What's up?" I murmured, searching for a clock. It was a little before eight.

"Going to church," she whispered. "Keep sleeping."

I stretched. "I had enough of churches last night."

"I can't get enough of them. Back in an hour."

The door clicked. I lay with my eyes closed, playing the "Ave Maria" against my right arm and soothing myself by imagining notes under my ear, a vibration against my collarbone.

Church. I'd figured she was Hindu. But then again, Shreya told us nothing about her life, not even where she lived.

After last night's debacle—debacles—we'd made a command decision to barricade ourselves at Harrison's and drink ourselves silly. You know that old joke? "Two musicians walk past a bar, and—hey, it could happen!"

Harrison sent us upstairs with his keys and his violin, following minutes later with two six-packs of Arrogant

Bastard. He'd had the first bottle open before he reached the couch and two pizzas delivered before we polished off the first six-pack.

My joints creaked as I hauled myself toward Harrison's coffee maker, a device with more blinky-beepy bits than R2-D2. When it humored my best guesses by producing a brownish liquid, I cleaned up the pizza boxes and transferred a bunch of empties to the sink. That done, I turned to find the person responsible for many of them.

"Morning." Harrison had a scratchy just-awake voice, and he squinted as if pained. "Thanks for making coffee. Shreya left?"

"Went to church."

"Really?" A grimace overtook his face. "Maybe God will tell her where we should seek asylum."

"Canada." I gathered four mugs. "You want to test whether the stuff I made is actually coffee?"

He settled on the stool alongside the island, forehead resting on his hands. "Right now the headache and exhaustion are numbing me." His shoulders dropped. "I'm sorry, Joey. For a lot of things."

I tried not to laugh. "You're hung over."

"I'm sorry about that, too."

I smirked. "What do you have for breakfast? Should I get some bagels?"

"At least you've got a full-time job." Harrison hadn't left Harrisonville yet. "Keep the sweats until I see you again." Then I got goosebumps as he met my eyes. "It's surreal, waking up to find you in my kitchen, wearing my clothes."

That was the hangover talking, nothing more. Biting my lip, I walked back to the living room. "Do you mind if I get my email?" At the very least, I needed to send an invoice to our time-challenged clients. If we had to battle to the death over money, we might as well declare war before breakfast.

"Go ahead." Harrison pressed his hands over his eyes. "I'll call my students. They'll need another violin teacher after I flee the country."

I logged into the guest account. "What time do they start showing up?"

"Nine-thirty is the earliest."

About to remind him we weren't actually fleeing the country, I realized no, it was that he couldn't very well teach with a semi-sleeping quartet lying around his apartment.

I kept our invoice online as a Google doc, so while Harrison talked to somebody's mother, I plugged in three hours at the contracted overtime rate (you've gotta love a total like that) and created an aesthetically pleasing paper shakedown. En route to emailing it to our client, though, I got hijacked: the quartet's Gmail account had ten unread messages.

Ten?

The spam filter must have failed. When I checked the subject lines, though, they weren't about drugs to enhance our "performance" but rather questions about booking performances, two requests to hear our demo, and three questions about availability on specific dates. One couple even wanted to meet.

What the hell?

On the seventh message I got a clue: "I saw you mentioned in the *New York Times* Fashion and Style section, and after I looked up your website—"

The New York Times?

I spun toward Harrison, huddled at the counter with a case of early-morning stares. "What have you done now? Why are we in the *New York Times*?"

Wide-eyed, Harrison chose to stall. "What?"

I turned my back and typed into the address line. Jerk. I bet he put us on the cover as the string quartet that will eventually do half-assed renditions of perfectly good pop songs.

"We've got ten emails from people who saw us in the *Times*, and— Oh my God."

The *Times* website had loaded, and when I searched on "Boroughs String Quartet," I found us. Right there. Us. In print.

"Don't do this to me. What does it say?" Harrison leaned over my shoulder. "Oh, shit."

Trying to ignore the warmth of his hands on my shoulders, I highlighted the important paragraphs.

On Saturday evening, Ron Estes, son of Broadway actress Angelica Majeur, married Regina DeLay, daughter of City Council Member Sheila DeLay, actress in several off-Broadway produc- tions, including the award-winning Honest And For True. *Outdoing anyone's standards for "fashionably late," Regina arrived at 9:30pm for a seven-o'clock wedding.*

The unexpected stars of the evening were the Boroughs String Quartet who with unparalleled professionalism gave an impromptu concert until the bride graced everyone with her arrival.

Although their lineup began with well-executed but stodgy quartets by the standard names of classical music, after the first hour they delighted the guests with by-request renditions of popular songs.

Guests enjoyed plenty of laughter and several jokes at the expense of the violist. When the bride arrived, her guests were unanimous in regretting that it had to end. As Regina entered, the musicians resorted to the very-predictable Pachelbel's Canon.

Regina's dress was designed by—

Harrison kept whispering, "Oh my God—" and then a little later, "Oh my God," putting his verbal acuity on a par with mine.

"Apparently we're professionals," I murmured as I sent the article to the printer. "Who knew?"

"Do you know what this means?" Harrison whispered, as if in a museum. "We can double our prices."

My head shot up. "Are you nuts?"

"Maybe triple!" His fingers clenched on my shoulders.

"You don't understand how some people think. They can't hire Joshua Bell to serenade their trip down the aisle, but they can and will book a string quartet because it appeared in the *New York Times*. We're positioned for a massive upgrade in our clientele."

He began pacing as if he were ready to jump out of his skin.

And me? I couldn't have left the chair right now even if the apartment were on fire. "But our skill set hasn't been upgraded, and our repertoire is being downgraded!"

"They loved the pop stuff."

Of course they did. The music on high-rotation for three hundred years was stodgy, and Mozart, the original party animal, was moldy. But "Hotel California"? Only the best for our highest-paying clients.

Harrison had a head of steam by now, his train of thought thundering along the rails of inevitability. "Okay, so you revise our website. Put 'As Seen In *The New York Times*!' on the front page and anywhere else you can. Link to it, pull a couple of quotes, especially at the top of the testimonials page."

I sighed. "I created the website. I think I know how to update it. I'll mention it in our Craigslist ads too."

I glanced up to find Josh in the hall, looking at me in Harrison's clothes at Harrison's computer. I wrapped my arms around my waist and angled aside. He snapped to, then gave me an inquisitive look.

"Last night's wedding got a review in the *Times*."

Josh's eyes widened.

"They said we handled the chaos professionally." Harrison looked ready to climb the ceilings. "I think I'll have some coffee after all!"

I for one knew how to capitalize on it: I copied the front end of the article along with the URL and attached it to our invoice in the email to last night's bride. Let her argue with that. If she were as prompt coughing up a check as she was for her own wedding, we might see a green Christmas.

Holding a mug, Josh watched over my shoulder while Harrison kept ruminating, and by the time I hit send, Harrison was at maximum intensity. "We've definitely got to record a CD of fusion mixes!"

The world disappeared in a high whine.

No, not a CD. Anything but a CD. I'd rather perform naked than record a new CD. Naked and on fire.

As Harrison seized the laptop and parked himself on the couch, I turned to Josh, who was studying me again. I looked away. "How are you doing?"

His shoulders slumped. "I'm f-fine."

Shreya returned with a box of donuts. Harrison thanked her with, "What a professional thing to do!"

She looked at Harrison as if he'd lost his mind, so while Josh investigated the donuts, Harrison told her about the article.

I went to the kitchen to grab a chocolate glazed donut. If a CD was going to kill me, I might as well be fat and caffeinated.

Like me, Shreya wore Harrison's clothes. She said to Josh, "Hey, are you okay about what happened at the restaurant?"

His flinch made my heart twinge, but he covered. "St-still stings. But he's nnn-not the first idiot I've dealt with."

Shreya had gotten more of an answer to that question than I had because one of the previous idiots Josh dealt with was yours truly, in an act of breathtaking idiocy that will stand tall on a pedestal in the annals of idiotic things the world's idiots have done.

Shreya chuckled. "I'll print you a business card saying, 'Yes, I stutter. Give me a burger and no one gets fired.'"

Josh pulled out his wallet and handed her a different business card.

To Law Enforcement and First Responders:
My name is Joshua Galen. I am diagnosed
with stuttering. When I talk, I may:
  • Repeat sounds
  • Elongate sounds
    • Be unable to speak at all.
I would like to cooperate. Please do not
assume my trouble speaking is suspicous
behavior. Thank you.

Shreya blinked. "Okay...that's different."

Josh flushed. "I got pu-pu-pulled over once."

I stopped myself before saying, "*Only* once?"

He bit his lip. "It didn't work out so well, so I ma—" I could tell he blocked on the rest of the word because he blinked rapidly and twitched. "I made that card."

Shreya frowned. "Why would a stutter be suspicious behavior?"

"You've seen the mmm-movies." Josh nodded. "We're all a bunch of sss-psychos and drrr-rug users."

I felt cold, but Shreya sounded breezy. "Silly me. I forgot about your psychotic drug-use." But then she paused. "Hey, you want some unsolicited advice? Tell the idiots to fuck off."

Josh said, "How?"

She said, "It's not just idiocy. What you're dealing with is prejudice."

You know that moment where you screw up during a concert, when it seems like everyone turns toward the viola to see who ruined it all? When every other musician inhabits a sphere of perfection while you, and you alone, don't know what the hell you're doing? And there's the spotlight, the kind you don't want, glaring in your eyes while you try to pretend everyone didn't hear the clunker note you just made? Yeah, that.

Josh had the decency not to look at me, but the room grew a mile long.

Shreya continued, "These folks don't single out Harrison

or Joey, right? When someone treats you like shit, it's no different from someone hating me because I'm from India or because I have blue hair, and I don't let them get away with it."

Shreya took a seat, and Josh joined her, as if listening to the pied piper. "Okay, then. How do you not lll-let them get away with it?"

Shreya glared. "By being in their faces. I demand to be treated right. A lot of 'Excuse me?'" She accompanied that with raised eyebrows and a glare ferocious enough that I nearly apologized. "A while ago I realized that when I let people walk over me, it's the same as saying they're right. But what if I decided there was no shame in being female or being Indian or having blue hair? Same deal: decide for yourself there's no shame in stuttering."

Josh frowned. "It's that easy?"

"Not at first, no." She bit her lip. "This one guy always bitched how my parents were job-stealing immigrants. They just took it for ages, but you know, we're American citizens too, so I told the guy to shut his fucking mouth. He left us alone after that." She leaned forward. "Tough as hell, but I pretended it was easy, and I kept doing it. Harrison beat me to the punch last night, but I'd have done it standing and looking a lot more menacing."

I smiled to myself. A golden retriever puppy mouthing a teddy bear would look more threatening than Harrison—although come to think of it, last night he had looked pretty damned intimidating.

Josh was still frowning.

She muttered, "Besides, any self-respecting individual in the food service industry knows you don't harass the people paying your tip."

Huh. Did she have a day job as a waitress?

"Hey, that was fast." Harrison looked up from the computer as if no one else had been speaking. "We can get in the recording studio by Thursday."

I splashed hot coffee over my wrist when I yelped, "What?"

He waved down whatever would have followed. "Relax. There's no way we'd be ready by Thursday. But Jenny from the studio happened to be online and said she'd get us a block of time just about whenever we want."

Oh yeah—I'd forgotten all about Jenny from the studio. Couldn't she have volunteered for the first manned mission to Saturn?

I blinked hard as I reached for a napkin. "I don't think we need a CD."

"We don't," Shreya said. "What we need is to build our customer base."

Was that the sound of an ally? Really?

Harrison said, "We can do that with a CD."

Shreya picked up a chocolate glazed donut and broke it in half. "You're not getting it. No one makes money off CDs. You're thinking CD because it's pretty and it scores a quick fifteen bucks." She pointed her half-donut at him, and I marveled at how much nicer she'd said that than when our original second-violinist said the same—moments before becoming our ex-second-violinist. "You've got to think longer-term. The point is to have a reputation. And to have a reputation, we need wedding guests who remember us for more than an hour."

"With a CD in their hands," Harrison replied, "they'll have a way of remembering."

For heaven's sake, did he not even listen? I said, "How many of our last CD have we sold?"

He opened his hands. "You're the business manager."

"Over a year, maybe fifty. It's not worth the effort."

Undeterred, Harrison said, "But we also give them to potential clients. Our fusions will be so innovative that they'll need to hear them to understand."

Next time I should talk to the donut. At least when it ignored me, it would be sweet.

Harrison said, "Plus, brides talk to other brides. They'll hand the thing off to each other."

The coffee tasted like nothing, and I set down my mug to stare at the table. *Hey, donut? I really don't want to go through this again.*

Harrison looked to Shreya. "You'll figure out which solos we'll work into other pieces. Josh, I know this is going to be tight, but you'll have to arrange them. We'll record piecemeal as we get them polished. Most of the pop tunes seem simplistic, so it shouldn't take as long to get them ready as something by Mozart."

Shreya said, "We should keep them to five minutes at most."

Arrangements. Practice. Studio time. Graphic design. Layout. Copyright. And tension, endless tension.

Harrison turned toward me. "Joey, I'm sorry, but we have to do it quickly."

I couldn't meet his eyes. The last time I'd refused to give Harrison what he wanted... Well, he'd dumped me. How many violists did he have on speed-dial?

Josh said, "Why quickly?"

"Because in addition to wanting a group mentioned in the *New York Times*, some of these people have the attention span of a magpie. You can't build publicity on nothing. That late bride gave us a gift, and we need to pounce on it."

He made sense. But still, couldn't I just grab my viola and go play for a while? Shut his bedroom door, leave them to hammer out the details, then come back with my head cleared to find out exactly which way the train was going to derail?

Harrison looked back at me. "You get the worst job, I'm afraid. You'll need to write press releases and publicity material."

Writing publicity for a CD I didn't think should exist. "That's all?"

He feigned a smug smile. "Well, it's only fair because the

viola doesn't have to play any real music."

I gave a half-hearted glare, but he raised his hands in self-preservation.

Great, the puppy-dog eye defense. I took back my coffee, the realest thing in the room. "You win." My throat tightened. "So which songs do you think we're unleashing on which defenseless quartets?"

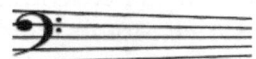

A stack of CDs had sat on my desk for a year. The group on the cover no longer existed.

Fifteen months ago, I'd stupidly thought song samples would help clients make up their minds. Ever practical, Josh recorded a performance and burned the tracks to CD. At the next client meeting, I handed one over.

On the way home, Harrison hit the ceiling, one of the few times I'd seen him truly angry. Sure, he'd been aware Josh was recording, but our intentions had gone straight over his head. That's why, in general, it paid to listen.

His verdict: "If we're going to put ourselves out there, it damn well better be the same quality as the Orion String Quartet."

I said, "The Orion String Quartet has a record label and a budget."

It will surprise no one that he ignored me. For the second time in my life, he said words I'd come to loathe: "Begin as you mean to go on."

By the next week, Harrison had booked a recording studio. As a neophyte quartet, the expense wiped us out. No salary for a month, and man, that hurt. Josh patched together a cover using a pretty font and our brochure photo. It looked okay, and with no money for graphic design, we voted three to one to keep it. Harrison insisted he'd pay for a professional cover himself.

Peter Merced, our original second violinist, had gone along until then but went head-to-head with Harrison over the cover. The argument erupted for the fifth and last time during practice, with Peter calling Harrison an arrogant jackass who stuffed his pillow with twenties.

"You don't care about the music," Peter hollered, violin case in one hand and the doorknob in the other. "You're a smug rich brat playing with his little string quartet, wanting a pretend CD so your rich Mommy and Daddy can flash it to all their rich comrades."

Josh pursued him down the hall while I yelled at Harrison to go after him and apologize. Harrison only stood with his arms folded. You can't bring someone back: I knew that even before Josh returned empty-handed. Josh tried again that night, attempting to talk Peter down while taxiing passengers around Manhattan. (Wouldn't you have loved to be in the back seat for that?)

He failed: Peter had shaken the dust from his feet, done with Harrison, done with petulant brides, done with string quartets. Last I heard, Peter went to play for a Broadway musical.

An all-around lovely experience for no one. Yet Harrison wanted a repeat.

Perhaps it was shock that made me follow when Josh offered a ride. Perhaps the idea that Josh might talk sense to Harrison blinded me to the more sensible thing I could have done, which was to take the subway to Brooklyn. Or walk.

As we pulled onto the street, I said, "Look, about this CD—"

Josh cut me off with a profanity-ridden description of the truck blocking the intersection, and that made up my mind: waiting was good. I'd wait until there was no chance Josh would drive right through the lobby of a skyscraper because I'd infuriated him by mentioning Peter.

We pulled up in front of my house with me discreetly checking my extremities to make sure all remained attached.

Keeping the engine idling, Josh finally no longer resembled the Road Runner's hyperactive cousin.

I said, "About the CD—are you okay with that? After what happened last time?"

Josh's fists clenched on the wheel. "Like anyone ever stopped H-Harrison?"

"Yes, we can stop Harrison. He can't record a CD if you and I fail to show up."

"Knowing H-Harrison, he can pull another cellist out of his top hat, and you don't even need a viola nowadays because you can just use a ...washing machine."

Ah, that joke: the only difference between a viola and a washing machine is vibrato.

I shook my head. "He won't replace both of us if we fight. What if he gets bull-headed with Shreya and she walks? Then where are we?"

Josh said, "I hope she d-does threaten to walk! It's not like you or I had any effect last time."

I said, "But Peter left!"

"And did that change anything? No!" Josh got more fluent as he got angrier. "He got everything he wanted. He got the CD, and he got a new second violinist to boss around. He probably counted that a straight-up victory."

I recoiled. "But—"

"I was one step away from lll-leaving myself." His eyes stood out as his cheeks flushed. "I was waiting for just one more thing, one more push, and I was out the door. Only Peter left first."

Oh shit, oh shit, oh shit—and I'd set him off again. I whispered, "But you wouldn't!"

He slammed his fist into the seat. "I hate the way he says things you can't fight at the moment, like he's the authority on the way the world works!"

My heart raced. I had no clue how to stop this speeding train. "He just wants us to succeed."

"Succeed?" He glared at me, and I recoiled into the

door. "What the h-hell good is 'success' if we're a bunch of sss-sycophants who just do whatever the hell he asks? He's condescending and sarcastic to you, ignores Sh-reya when she disagrees, and when did he become the authority on publicity?"

I was shaking. "But—"

"But what? I recorded a whole CD, and what did he do? Not good enough. I designed a cover, and what did he do? Not good enough! It's never good enough! It's always just one more thing, one more, one more! Does he think it's possible one p-person can always be right? Really?"

I said, "But he doesn't—"

"We are not his property!" Josh was breathing like he'd just run a mile. "I still haven't forgiven him for railroading us."

Vision blurring, I wrapped my arms around myself. "I'm sorry."

Whipping his head away, he glared out the windshield.

"I'm sorry. I shouldn't have brought it up." Yeah, thank heaven I didn't start this while driving.

Then, silence. Nothing from him. Nothing from me. Him still breathing hard, me still trembling. And I couldn't even reach across to touch him because of the instrument case in my lap, the steering wheel across his, and two decades of history dragging behind us like a hundred-car freight train.

I tightened up around myself. "So should we push back?"

"Forget it."

I'd seen Josh do this before, seen him stockpile until he detonated. Like uranium where it's stable until it reaches critical mass, and then you get the whole blast at once.

"I can't just forget it. You haven't forgotten."

Josh shook his head. "You'd be surprised by the shit I can get past even though I remember it j-just fine."

And because I had to go to work, and because I couldn't tell what would happen if Josh took it to Harrison and our first violinist couldn't work together with our cellist anymore,

I took the only course that made sense. I capitulated.

I gave a lame, "Maybe this time it won't be so bad." So much for recruiting an ally.

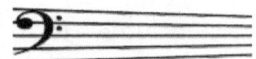

That night at the toll-booth, I waited for a lull in traffic so I could do two jobs at once. My mom always griped how owning your own business takes over every part of your life. This held true for the quartet. When we weren't practicing or performing, Josh was creating musical arrangements and Harrison or I were dealing with clients. And as the business manager, I'd gotten saddled with generating publicity.

They'll give even a violist a library card. Two years ago, I'd checked out *The Idiot's Guide to Public Relations*, and since then I'd cobbled together press releases for our first CD, our change in lineup, and anything else I could think of. I passed them on to thirty-five email addresses for New York/New Jersey newspapers. And then they'd get deleted.

That, apparently, was the point of a press release. The book described a "news hole," where a newspaper first lays out the ads and next fills the remaining empty spaces with articles. If they had an opening three column-inches long and your press release happened to fit, they might run it. Kind of like a publicity lottery.

Tonight, between cars, while my plastic Bach danced to Samuel Barber, I prepared to alert the media about our mention in the *Times* and subsequent trip to the recording studio, and heaven help me, our availability for interviews. As if. But it sounded good, and we were all about sound.

As an expert multi-tasker, I also spent quality time wishing I could put Harrison on a barge and push him out to sea. And that's when I got The Gentleman.

Every business must have its version of The Gentleman, that particular customer who excels in his particularity. In my case, his effect was enhanced by a spineless manager who caved in a stiff breeze. The sight of The Gentleman's black Cadillac engendered in me an urge to put up the toll arm, pay his fare myself, and cower under the register.

The white-haired Gentleman took a good fifteen seconds to lower his window (with a manual crank because his Caddie was of the "tanks with hood ornaments" vintage). After extracting his wallet from his breast pocket, The Gentleman unfolded it and selected a hundred dollar bill.

Signs at every lane stated we don't accept bills larger than a twenty.

I said to The Gentleman, "Have you got anything smaller?" He looked placid. "No, I haven't."

In the past, Ted's only response was, "For God's sake, just take the man's money! The customer is always right!" Thus Herr Bach watched me pull four twenties, a ten, and two singles from the register.

The guy had to have a problem, and with that much money you'd think he could hire a psychiatrist to solve it. ATMs didn't spit out hundreds, so he must be getting these babies from a bank. But if he was at a bank, why not get twenties? I thought at first he was counterfeiting, but the bills passed every test.

A guy that ancient might remember when New Yorkers rebelled against rising tolls by paying with pennies, backing up the lanes for hours. Was this an aging hippie in his final civil protest?

As I handed back his change, I noticed the security guy sauntering over. Was he curious as to the delay? Or bored and looking for some reason to keep his job?

The Gentleman replaced the bills in his wallet with care that none should wrinkle, returned the wallet to his breast pocket, raised the window (another full fifteen seconds,) and idled beneath the toll arm.

Walt watched him go. I showed him the hundred. "Could this be counterfeit?"

He held it up to the street lights. "How should I know?" He handed it back.

Thank God for our security force's investigative prowess. I slept at night knowing Walt protected us.

I needed to work on my press release, but as this was the most excitement he'd had all evening, Walt didn't leave. With a glance at my Bach bobblehead, he said, "You still play that big violin?"

Stifling a grin, I said, "Yeah."

He said, "Why?"

Was his real question how I could cram more joy into a life so fulfilled by my full-time job?

Walt went on, "I had to take piano as a kid, and I hated every minute."

Another car came through, so I did something unusual and performed my job. After it left, I said, "It's like touching something bigger than you are. It's making something. Haven't you ever wanted to make something?"

He leaned against the side of the booth, arms folded. "I like cooking."

"Did you ever draw? Or build with Legos?" Josh and I spent a hundred hours with his brother's bucket of Legos. "Haven't you ever wanted to make something that would last?"

He shrugged. "Music doesn't last. You stop playing and it's done."

I got the next car's fare, then took my time slipping it into the register. "We made a CD, so that will last. You want to buy one?"

He said "Maybe sometime" with a tone that meant *Never*. "I'm not a violin person."

I figured as much. "Well, if you know someone who wants players for a wedding, I'll cut them a deal."

He said he'd keep that in mind, and maybe as bored with me as I was, he left.

I had a trickle of cars, never few enough to finish my press release, so with Bach glowering at me for my lame defense of his life's vocation, I thought about what I should have said.

He was right: music wasn't transferable. When I put down the viola, the music stopped. If I didn't practice, I'd lose my skill. A painter doesn't need to practice for the next viewer to see the same landscape, but a friend can't pick up my viola and hear my music. Even worse, when I pick up my viola, the only music it plays is my own.

I miss my grandfather. My viola was once my grandfather's viola, and now that was all I had left of him. Memories of long afternoons, me studying in his kitchen while my father's father played in the living room, the viola's throaty tenor singing tunes so familiar I knew them without ever knowing them. In that ordinary world I first came alive, first looked up to find the horizons were further than the walls of my home. I could touch fire. I could cup it in my palms, heat and light together, and enkindle the world.

In those days I'd close my eyes and become someone else, and my grandfather and I would play together to forge something between us that was real, that was more than just an old man and a young girl and two wooden boxes, more than just eight vibrating strings.

And that breathless moment when he pressed his viola into my smooth hands with his knobby ones and said, "This is yours; this will always be yours," and for the first time I found a way out. A way up.

Yet twelve years later my grandfather's songs were as faint in my mind as the spice of his aftershave, and I'd never hear them again.

Some say violins and violas remember their owners, that they reverberate with melodies of the past. Maybe. Maybe over time the vibrations formed patterns in the wood, and maybe the sound keeps trying to work back into them.

I'd tried so often, to reconstruct my grandfather's songs brought with him from Greece. As a kid I didn't need to know their names. They were "that one" and "that other one," and if he owned sheet music, I never saw it. He must have learned from his own grandfather, only unlike me, he paid attention.

Sometimes when I played late enough that my fingers were inaccurate, alone with the mute on so my mother's mother wouldn't hear, I'd find myself hungering to follow one note with the wrong one; in those hours, the "right" notes sounded awkward, and I wondered if the viola wasn't trying to soothe itself with musical comfort food, longing for the century-old pieces it sang every day under my grandfather's fingers.

SEVEN

Tuesday morning, as I replaced the mop in Grandma's closet, I looked up to find my mother and sister, with my nephew in tow. Viv said, "Still living on food stamps?"

I shut the closet. "Better than welfare."

"Josie, don't be rude. She's your sister." Mom dropped her coat on the kitchen chair. "Where's your grandmother?"

"Living room." Mom could have heard the TV if she'd listened; in fact, she had turned before I finished. "Hey, Mom?" My heart thrummed. "My quartet got mentioned in the *New York Times*."

I don't know what I'd expected, but some kind of reaction. Instead she waited, and I just babbled. "We were playing for a wedding, only the bride was late. Like really late, more than three hours. And we kept playing the whole time."

My mother's brow furrowed. "Why would that have made the *Times*?"

Viv said, "It's in the science section. *Shitty Music Fails to Kill Wedding Guests*."

Bitch.

Mom said, "Vivvy, hush. Your sister always wanted to get things done for herself. Let's hear what she did."

It was an opening. "It was in the fashion and style section.

It was a high-end wedding, and the bride being so late was unusual enough that we got mentioned."

My mother seemed even more confused. "A high-end wedding hired your quartet?"

Viv said, "Atonal music is all the fad."

I clenched my teeth so I wouldn't shoot back a nasty reply.

Mom looked at Viv. "Honey, don't be jealous just because you can't do those things. Come on."

She left to find Grandma. As I realized I was being dismissed, I said, "Would you like to see the article?"

"I suppose." In the door, Mom paused. "It's very good you have connections, you know. People are judged by their companions."

Yeah, but they kept me around anyway.

I got out the vacuum, and Zaden started climbing the pantry shelves. I said to Viv, "You might want to get him out of there."

"He's fine." She folded her arms. "When are you moving back home?"

"Fifteenth of December in twenty-never." I glanced at the clock. "What are you doing here, anyway?"

"Grandma's watching Zaden while Mom and I go shopping." She waited, but I refused to ask why she needed her Mommy to go shopping. Instead I vacuumed the hallway.

Fifteen minutes later, I returned to the kitchen to find my mother rifling through some envelopes. "Oh, honey, the mail came. Why is the phone company putting your bill in a yellow envelope? You shouldn't get behind on those things."

I snatched it from her.

"Don't be so sensitive."

I plucked a credit card offer from Viv's hands. "Thank you."

Viv said, "Are you as late with the rent as with everything else? Poor Grandma."

Forcing a smile, I glanced at Grandma, who seemed uncertain. "Grandma's fine. You're the one going shopping with Mom's money."

Mom said, "Don't be so negative just because you've always been the independent one. I'm buying fabric for a client."

Viv looked miffed. Busted.

I got back upstairs to find my apartment unlocked and a Matchbox car on my kitchen floor. They'd taken my milk.

I slammed the door and locked it, for all the good that would do. Grandma had the key, and anything Grandma had could be in Viv's hands in minutes.

Well, except for the apartment. Grandma knew damned well she'd become the unpaid baby sitter the hour Viv moved in.

When the front door slammed, I looked outside as Mom and Viv got into Mom's silver Accord. I returned to the basement to throw in a load of Grandma and Grandpa's clothes and take up mine from the dryer. They too had left before I returned, probably taking Zaden to the park so he could unleash his destructive power on the swings.

I trudged back to my apartment, but instead of folding laundry, I played scales. Up, down, up again, all the notes where they needed to go. Then, warmed-up, I launched into some Bach.

Bach is awesome. My instructors all said you should play Bach every day: it's precise and mathematical even as it's lively and compelling; it keeps your fingers nimble; and it engages your brain. I'd been learning Bach pieces since Suzuki Method 1, and this morning I started running through them all, sometimes breaking off midway to begin another. I mixed two by accident, the first half of one and a chunk out of the middle of a second.

While playing, I closed my eyes and imagined myself a team with the instrument. Back in high school, I made the mistake of telling Josh the viola and I were best friends, and he wrote back, "Some friends. You aren't even on a first-name basis."

I replied, "What good is naming something that doesn't come when you call?"

Josh said, "Do it anyhow."

I strung Josh through three emails before finally giving a drum roll and its chosen name.

"Woody."

He retorted that Woody sounded like my new boyfriend. Or rather, my "bow."

I never called the viola Woody, not in public. But sometimes the name slipped out: "Come on, Woody, you know that was supposed to be a C-sharp."

Today, unfortunately, none of the notes wanted to come right. Music might be a team sport, but one of us didn't have her head in the game.

I shuffled through my music, longing for something slow and powerful and brilliant, but nothing filled all my requirements: I wanted a melody to straighten the twisted mess that was my life, to put everything in the right places, to give back something I never had but still felt stolen.

Needing to play something, make something, I did more scales. *Make me forget. Take me away from here.*

My cell phone rang. Harrison. I didn't answer.

Two rings later, I changed my mind. "What's up?"

"We may be booking an event in ten days. I know you'll crab at me because it's short notice, but I want to do it anyway. Can you play on a Thursday afternoon?"

I said, "Okay."

Silence.

He must have expected a fight, because he sounded tentative. "We could do this playlist in our sleep. No Beethoven symphonies."

Again I mm-hmmed him.

He said, "Well, okay, then. I'll talk to you later," and cut off.

I held on to the silence a few seconds before tossing the phone on the bed. Back came the viola.

It took an hour to two hours of practice every day to stay on top of my skills. My grandparents' neighbors never complained, although to be honest they may never have heard through the walls of a pre-WWII building. When my grandparents were home, though, Mom said they wanted me to use a mute.

Only now, free to play loud and unmuted, I crouched at the edge of my bed, eyes shut as hard as I could. I tried to breathe deep, too aware of the tension up both arms and across my throat.

I set the bow in its slot without loosening it and left the case open, sheet music scattered on my bed. I covered the instrument with the silky viola blanket I bought Woody last year even though I hadn't bought a new blouse in two. I imagined Woody thinking, *I survived World War I, and I need a silky blanket?*

I turned on a Green Day CD for the noise I couldn't produce myself, and I straightened a couple of things in the apartment. My apartment. Mine. Not my sister's.

With the kitchen still half-dirty, I turned on the computer to find email at the group account, a thread of messages between a corporate address and Harrison, the whole arrangement conducted in the last hour. On opening the messages, I found an enquiry from the Executive Assistant to the Vice President of Something about a retirement party. Harrison set up a phone call with the secretary, and then a final message, maybe twenty minutes ago, in which Harrison had emailed them a contract. Just like that, we were booked for two hours in the middle of a Thursday afternoon.

Holy cow. That happened quickly.

Based on the email exchange, a corporate gig was little different than a wedding, although my heart skipped at the price-per-hour Harrison quoted—and it stopped when our liaison agreed. Even with the economy in the toilet, some corporations didn't hesitate to treat themselves to whatever they wanted.

Whether we were worth that much... Um, yeah. Harrison thought we were; them too, or they wouldn't have paid. But of course the most this executive secretary (or her boss) could have heard were the clips posted online.

The air felt thin. What was going on? We weren't any different than a week ago, and yet people wanted us. We named a bold price...and clients forked it over. We had a corporate client, and that vaulted us into a different category.

An alert popped up on IM. Josh.

"Harrison called," he typed. "We added a retirement lunch gig."

I typed back, "Saw the emails."

His reply came quickly: "You gonna quit your day job? {grin}"

My reply: "It's a night job."

And from him: "If Harrison keeps jacking up the rates, you could buy a Stradivarius viola."

Or a Starbucks coffee. "I'm fine with mine."

Then, after a pause, he sent, "What's wrong?"

I typed, "??"

He typed, "You're upset."

I typed nothing at all. Just rested my fingertips on the keys.

His message appeared: "You want to come here? Have lunch?"

And while I was typing out, "I don't know," his next message arrived: "I'll cook for you there. Expect me in twenty minutes."

I blinked. "Are you sure?"

"Sure. Hang tight."

He signed off. I re-read the chat trying to figure out where I'd tipped off Josh to something I hadn't admitted to even myself.

By the time he arrived, holding a white paper bag, I had the apartment straightened via the industrial-strength cleaning power of I-have-a-guest-coming. He'd decided against cooking. "Didn't want to poi-poison you on the verge of—" He blocked, then backed up and retook it: "Verge of success."

I'd already started to relax with him near, and I met his eyes with a smile. "You've never poisoned yourself."

He looked worried. "I've come close."

He made me sit at the table, like Princess Joey The First. Out of the bag with a flourish came deli sandwiches and bags of chips. He winked at me, putting some of that performance magic into it so I'd laugh, then produced two packets of Land O'Lakes mint-flavored hot chocolate (ooh, seventy-five cents a packet) and a plastic baggie with marshmallows.

While the tea-kettle heated, he set the table. "Now—" He blocked on the next word, then said, "Shit," and shook his head. "Now—" He blocked again.

Could I understand why he didn't want to say it? Yep. I didn't want to deal with me either. "Now why am I being a unbelievable grouch?"

He shook his head. "Not grouchy. Just—" This time he hadn't blocked because he didn't look frustrated. "Tense."

He laid out napkins, dispensed chocolate powder, and poured water into the mugs while steam frothed up like Vesuvius giving a rumble. The round table barely accommodated two place settings, but it was what I'd found in the apartment on move-in. Any closer and our knees would have touched. The chair legs squeaked on the faded linoleum whenever we moved. He wouldn't meet my eyes.

I pushed back to go to my spice cabinet, and he said, "No." He pointed to the sandwich, so I opened the wrapper. He'd bought me a ham and cheese sub, lettuce and tomato, no pickles, and—

I grinned. "You remembered the oregano! I knew there was a reason you rocked."

He flushed and looked aside.

We ate without words, just the crinkle of wrappers, the clink of spoons against mugs, the fizzle of whipped cream firing from the canister. But as we ate, I realized: the last time Josh had ordered something, the waiter made fun of him. Yet today he'd ordered two different deli subs with an assortment of condiments, including oregano. Had he stood at the case, staring through the Boar's Head olive loaf wondering whether he'd make it through the word "pickle"?

My throat tightened. "Thank you. For lunch."

He didn't look up, just smiled self-consciously.

I added, "You're right. I was tense."

A smugness came to his eyes. I tossed my wadded-up sandwich wrapper at his head, but he batted it away with a "Hey!"

While I cleared the table, he said, "Is it the new clients?"

My eyes narrowed. "I hope they're deaf. Right now, I can't even play."

He frowned. "Have you tried Bach?"

I bit my lip.

"Even Bach won't help? M-Must be bad." He frowned. "Hotel C-C-California?"

I flicked water at him from my wet fingers.

He chuckled. "Okay, okay. But it's got to be bad if Bach can't help." He shook his head. "Poor Woody."

"Hey!" I spun, eyes wide. "I thought you'd forgotten!"

Smirking, he cocked his head, a dare to stop him. "I saved that email. It's good blll—lackmail."

"I'll kill you." I wrung my hands dry with the dish towel. "You're right here in my kitchen with all these knives."

Josh said, "Most of them are a hundred years old."

I nodded. "Blunt and rusty. It would probably hurt."

He didn't appear concerned. "You'd have to t-testify why at the trial, and then Woody would be in the public record."

My shoulders slumped as I gave a mock sigh. "Well, you've got me there."

When I realized how intently he looked at me, my breath caught. I paid careful attention to draping the towel on a cabinet knob. "Um—so—I don't suppose you brought your cello."

By the time I turned back, he was avoiding my eyes.

I brought my viola to the living room, and Josh pretended to be my instructor. First scales, then bow exercises, and finally a few different vibratos.

"You haven't forgotten how to play." He looked relieved. "Even though a violist doesn't need to know all that much to begin with."

I pointed to my head. "The trouble's in here."

He grimaced. "I nnn-know the feeling."

He asked for my crappy viola, the one Dad picked up secondhand from a student supply shop. I was mean to it, though. I'd stolen its case to house my grandfather's, leaving it in Grandpa's century-old coffin case with rusty hinges and bow mite carcasses. As for the instrument, it stretched my strings. Always in plain sight on my book shelf, it had an ultra-shiny Student Viola appearance, plus enough dings to make you think the instrument had a penchant for taking the fight outside.

But most of all, it was a decoy. Mom thought that was the instrument I played professionally, and I let her keep thinking it.

Josh tuned it, wincing at the sound. The strings of a viola are the same as the strings of a cello, only an octave up, so he began one of our standards without needing to do the mental translation I did when playing a violin. I joined.

In unison, we played through. He missed a few notes because he wasn't used to the viola, but it was otherwise passable.

"Whoa," Josh said. "You really can fake viola by playing sss-slow and hitting a lot of wrong notes."

I poked him with my bow, and he laughed.

We used to know a couple of viola-cello duets, and we messed around with what we remembered. Finally I dug out some solo music to play in unison.

The next time I noticed, we'd played a full hour. I hadn't

been able to do it alone, but with Josh, I'd managed to get my mind off the world. I almost wished we hadn't succeeded, though. Although we were both relaxed and ready to really start, the rest of the world would have thought (strangely enough) it was time to head to our respective jobs.

At the front door, I squirted water from my bottle into a bowl behind the trash cans. There was a stray cat I kind-of cared for. I also left a handful of food on the ground.

I said, "Thank you. I'm glad you came over."

Josh averted his eyes.

I looked up from the bowl. "Do you ever wish something really frustrating in your life would just go away?"

After a long pause, he replied, "Yeah. I do."

EIGHT

Let me tell you two ways to screw up a relationship.

The first way is to email your friend—your buddy since first grade, the guy you ate every lunch with in grammar school and whom you've exchanged letters with every week since—and mention the upcoming high school dance.

Sure, you know he stutters. He was the one who gave you your nickname, since he always tripped over the "s" in "Josie."

And sure, for years after his parents divorced and his dad moved him to another neighborhood, every so often you'd see him at your recitals or at his, and you'd remember, yeah, he does that thing with his voice, where his mouth zips ahead of his brain, and you get a couple of pickup notes before the word starts.

But you don't think about that when you say, "Hey, want to come?"

Because your friends want to meet this mysterious guy who sends actual in-the-mail letters and whom they sometimes scrawl notes to in the letters you write back, this Josh Galen who calls you Mrs. Galen. They don't know you both hid from the same bullies who called him Gay-gay-galen and used an even worse name for you. They just think you were friends. They've seen his stick-figure cartoons hanging in your locker, remnants of the days you used to draw in each others' notebooks at the rear of the classroom, and they don't know—you wish you could tell them but you don't—how on the last day of sixth grade before he left for a performing arts middle school, how he struggled to speak and couldn't get out anything at all while you sat on the swings. Finally he gave up and handed you a note that said, "Will you be my first kiss?"

And when you said yes, he leaned forward and gave you a peck on the lips, a touch that burned a line all the way to your stomach. You saved the note in your grammar school yearbook.

Now you're both sixteen, and he says sure, he'll come to the dance at your school. That's how to screw up a relationship.

Because when he gets there, he stutters. And when he blinks or twitches, your friends stare, and you're embarrassed. No, you're more than embarrassed. You're totally ashamed because they don't hear the intelligence and they can't see the mischief. Instead someone laughs, and one of your classmates whispers, "What's wrong with that freak?"

He tries to put his arm around you, and now your friends are laughing at *you*.

That's when you say you're sick and you want to go home, and you won't talk to him on the way back to your house because you don't want him to talk either. You just want the night to end. And when you get home, he tries to hug you, but you won't. You tell him not to bring you inside. You slam the front door and run all the way to your bedroom.

Then you don't email him for a few weeks. When he finally emails you, it's sterile, just a forwarded joke. Replying, you never mention what happened, and neither does he.

Congratulations: you may now live the rest of your life knowing you were ashamed of your best friend. And based on how things cool off on his end, he lives the rest of his life knowing it too.

Here's the second way to screw up a relationship:

On our first date, Harrison and I were cuddling on his couch, bored with our rental movie, and he breathed into my ear: would I prefer something more exciting? And yes, I had something much more exciting in mind. We downloaded sheet music and played violin-viola duets until midnight.

As he walked me to the subway, he said, "That's not how I envisioned spending a night together."

I shrugged. "In my limited experience, playing music is better than sex."

"Ouch!" His eyes fluttered with the wounded puppy look that's saved his life many a time since. "Maybe the problem was your duet partner?"

I laughed. "I never found it to shut off my brain the way music does."

At the subway, Harrison kissed me good night. "Maybe if I put on some background music...?" and I replied, "We'll have to find out."

Harrison and I had met three weeks earlier in an orchestra run by a steel-haired conductor in possession of a whip-like sarcasm: "Oboes! What the hell is going on there?" "Flutes, you remind me of the Beatles—they also haven't played together since 1970!"

One afternoon, preparing for a Tchaikovsky symphony, I asked a question about the viola part. She snapped that the second-chair violist shouldn't dare bother the conductor with the kind of minutiae the first chair should be taking care of. The first chair was a really nice eighty-year-old man who should have retired around the time I'd graduated grammar school, and he gave me the wrong answer—as we learned after the next take. Glaring with those armor-piercing eyes, the conductor unleashed enough vitriol to poison the whole section. The first chair violist let me take the hit while I quivered, small and useless and worthless, as she cataloged every last one of my musical faults for the entire orchestra.

Afterward Harrison secured us a booth in the corner of a nearby restaurant. He tried to tell me I should have been first chair but no one could bear to let the old guy go, but I could see right through that. So then, with me cuddled against him fighting tears, he nuzzled my neck and whispered the plan he'd devised after our first date: a string quartet. No yelling, no venom. A cozy group. On the back of the sheet music for *Tchaikovsky's Fifth Symphony* he jotted notes on everything our string quartet could become.

I went home that night with an unfamiliar feeling: hope. We'd make this work. We'd recruit two more players, then someday have brochures and a playlist, and maybe even clients. I daydreamed my way into tolerating that horrible orchestra, propping open a little escape hatch in my mind.

Meanwhile, authorized by my "I guess so," Harrison lured Peter and Josh onboard within two weeks, and our first client signed a contract five days after that. We were in it together now.

In the mornings, I'd awaken without that crushing dread of yet another day with no money, no joy. Harrison took charge, and I felt nothing but relief. I couldn't believe he'd even have taken a glance in my direction, but the fact that he liked me—that he was building a future with me? Really? Viv told me about guys who nail-and-bail, but Harrison was building a foundation. Had I wandered into a Jane Austen novel? I mean—his family had money from way back, but their current family portrait featured a lawyer mother and a doctor father, plus their three heirs—the oldest daughter a doctor, the middle son a lawyer.

And bringing up the rear, Harrison Roosevelt Archer, the caboose child in a family where both parents ended each day knowing their heritage had been handed down. They indulged his every whim. I'd always loved the stories about how as a child Felix Mendelssohn was given his own orchestra to conduct, and Harrison would have gotten one too if he'd had half a mind to conduct.

Instead, starting at age three, he took violin lessons, and he never stopped. Whatever he wanted, the checkbook opened. Summer at the music camp? A Juilliard education? A Stradivarius? (Okay, not a Strad, but his two-hun-dred-year-old violin appraised at well into five figures.) Whatever you want to do. Just do it with excellence.

So Harrison excelled. For him, starting a string quartet based on little more than a one-night-music-stand wasn't scary at all: he never considered it might fail.

Besides, if he crashed and burned, you can extinguish a lot of flames with a trust fund—or whatever you have if your moneyed family is distantly related to an ex-president. (I never probed his finances, but he didn't afford that apartment on a music teacher's income. And later on, I knew how much he got paid by the quartet because I was the one who paid him.)

One night he took me for sushi, and afterward to his apartment to (theoretically) listen to quartets. Ten minutes later we lay entangled on the couch, hardly listening analyt-ically...if at all. Harrison in those days showed a romantic energy I found startling in its gusts, as if he spent all his time thinking about me until we were together, and then he wanted to do all the things he'd thought about. After the CD ended, he turned on a performance DVD until I needed to go home. We didn't watch much of that either.

Brushing the hair back from my cheek, he murmured, "You could stay. You'll only be coming back in the morning anyhow."

We had planned tomorrow to "conduct" musical business.

I feigned confusion. "You're trying to save me the train fare?"

Serious, he nodded. "That's a lot of money."

I kept my tone academic. "I think you want to hook up."

He took that for permission, saying "Maybe a little," and

kissed his way up my throat.

I shifted away. "What if I get pregnant?"

He nuzzled my ear. "I'd take care of you."

I ran a hand through his hair. "Really? You'd rearrange your life to include child support, Sunday visits, the whole fatherhood thing?"

His lips brushed my neck. "Anything you wanted."

I whispered back, "You are such a liar."

He burst out laughing. "I love you!" He pulled me close for more teasing, but no matter how good he smelled or how much I loved his arms around me, I insisted no.

Later I kept asking myself why, but I only came back to this: fear. Not afraid of sex, but afraid of him seeing me, afraid of him having all of me in front of him. He had everything. It made no sense he'd be interested in me. I didn't trust him, not yet, not with my heart, not with so little time as collateral.

Pouting, he got out the instruments and we played together, me asserting this was better than sex anyway and him insisting he had insufficient data for a proper comparison.

At one o'clock he said, "Really, Joey, stay. I promise not to hassle you." He paused, then added, "Although if you change your mind and tear off my clothes, I swear to put up token resistance for a tenth of a second," and he was so genuine that I laughed. Yes, I'd stay.

We joked around, the way we did so often back then ("I only own one pair of pajamas, so we'll have to share") and in his bed we cuddled. With his breath against my neck, I could imagine this was how eternity felt, wrapped in the rhythm of someone else's existence.

Just like in a chick flick, I woke up alone. I found him in the kitchen, already showered and dressed, brewing a pot of coffee. He tensed as I wrapped my arms around him, and instead of kissing me, he gentled me back.

I said, "Is something wrong?"

He wouldn't meet my eyes. "Are you okay with eggs for breakfast?"

I felt cold all over. "No. Talk to me."

He said nothing for the longest pause in history. Then, not raising his eyes, he tried to hug me, and I shoved him away because I realized we were breaking up.

He appeared shocked as I glared into the face of a guy who'd only yesterday said he loved me, and here on the cusp of hearing that he didn't really, I struggled not to lose it. What the hell happened? What about our quartet?

He said, "Joey...I'm sorry."

I folded my arms. "Is this because I turned you down?"

He looked aside. "No. I mean, I was disappointed, but then I was lying awake, and I started thinking—thinking about Josh and Peter coming over later today—" The hollow in his eyes pitted me at the core. "We need to be professional."

"What do Josh and Peter have to do with anything? Unless—"

Unless he didn't want to admit—admit to them—

Harrison wouldn't meet my eyes. "You have to begin as you mean to go on."

—because he could do better—

Voice raised, I struggled to react to what he'd said rather than what he hadn't. "You and I began this group because we were dating!"

Harrison flushed. "But dating—it never ends well. What if we wind up hating each other? We'd be stuck working together anyhow, like Fleetwood Mac."

"Who then produced the top-selling rock album in history because of it—and recorded seven more albums!"

Harrison laughed. "And where are they now?"

"They performed at a presidential inauguration! I'll take that!"

Why the hell were we shouting about Fleetwood Mac? But it hurt less than having the real fight. My mother showed me long ago that if you scream about dish towels, you never have to admit out loud that you're unloved.

He sounded desperate. "A sub-group within the group

creates factions, and factions affect dynamics. People take sides. To go the distance, we all need to be equal partners. That means we have to be professional. About everything."

I said, "Will you listen to yourself? It's not about power dynamics!"

He folded his arms. "Do you want to be second-rate? Because for me, that's not good enough!"

That was when my heart stopped. If I pushed, he was going to go all the way and say it: I wasn't good enough. I was the disposable one. The viola joke. And now that I'd said no to Harrison, Harrison was going to get rid of me.

Fighting tears, I couldn't talk. I'd maybe get out a squeak and I'd never hang on; I'd fall to pieces, and I didn't want him to see that. I didn't want him to see me naked, and if I cried in front of him, that was the worst nakedness.

I fled his kitchen and slammed his bedroom door.

Not good enough. Not good enough.

I yanked on my clothes, but it took three tries to button my blouse.

Once dressed, I ran out of energy. I dropped to his floor, back to the bed, knees up, face cradled in my hands. He didn't want me. I wasn't good enough. Not as a musician. Not as a girlfriend. He was embarrassed to be seen with me both personally and professionally. By breaking up, he could make me leave. He'd get a new violist and a new girlfriend, and they'd all move on. But what about me?

No. Stop. Think. I had things I could do. I could manage the finances, and I could design the website. I knew how to pay taxes and get licenses. I could be useful. No one ever noticed the viola part. I could stay if I didn't cause any trouble. Keep my head down. Just keep doing my job and at some point things would be okay. That would be good enough.

I forced myself to a stand and folded his pajamas, tucked them under his pillow, made his bed, put everything where it belonged, and then returned to the living room.

Harrison slumped on his couch, staring into the fishtank.

"There's your viola. Are you leaving?"

Damn him.

"No." He'd have to work harder than that to get rid of me. "We're going to be professionals."

That's how we decided. We wouldn't mention our brief relationship to Josh or Peter. We'd pretend it never happened at all.

An hour later, I commandeered our meeting and forced a host of decisions. A name, a repertoire, a group website, a list of contacts. I didn't think of the nevers: that we'd never kiss again, never spend hours on the phone, never make love.

Josh finally asked if I'd washed down a handful of amphetamines with five espressos.

In my peripheral vision, I saw Harrison glance up, but I didn't turn my head. "We need to get everything in the right places if the group is going to succeed, and I'm going to make sure it happens."

So you see, there are two ways to screw up a relationship. You can be ashamed of him. Or he can be ashamed of you.

NINE

During practice, my cell phone buzzed. I glanced at the number, then gasped. "It's the *Village Voice!*"

While the other three stared, I fielded a request to interview us.

"Your press release got us interested in a series of articles about survival as a musician in a city full of musicians," the reporter explained in a cigarette-worn voice. "I want to interview the four of you prior to your gig for the Manhattan International Group, then send a photographer to capture you playing."

Violin upright in his lap, Harrison mimed that I should tell him what was going on while Shreya did the same, and Josh, standing by the kitchen with a can of Coke, just looked shocked. It was too many people demanding my attention, and I blanked. "I— I think that would be fine."

Harrison hissed, "What is it?" while the reporter asked in my other ear when and where we could meet. I told him to hold on while I checked.

"I caught you all together?" He laughed. "I should go meet you now."

No, Harrison would have ripped off my head. Actually, he might have invited the guy over. Both options sucked.

On the other hand, I didn't want Harrison to blow an aneurysm, so I told him, "It's an interview request."

I didn't get to finish. Our fearless leader snatched the phone, introducing himself as he disappeared down the hall.

Shreya's eyes were huge.

Josh was pale. "I can't."

I blinked.

"Interview." He tried to speak, then blinked quickly enough that I recognized a block. "I- I- I- I—" His face reddened, and he gulped air, then tried again to talk.

He looked scared. And then I realized why. Of course a reporter who wanted to talk to *us* would be talking to *Josh*. And Josh stuttered: right now he was thinking he'd stutter in front of the whole world.

"You don't have to," I blurted.

"Hey!" Shreya stepped close and cocked her head. "It's a reporter. Not a subpoena. Besides, I'll talk to him first. Terrify him with the blue hair."

I rolled my eyes. "The *Village Voice*, remember? He'll be more offended by my brown hair."

Harrison burst into the kitchen. "How's Monday?"

Josh was shaking his head. I jerked my thumb toward him.

Harrison said, "I'll handle that. I promised I would." He looked from me to Shreya. "Monday? Ten-thirty?" When Shreya shrugged, he confirmed it, then hung up. Then he shouted, "This is so cool!"

Ashen, Josh said, "I c-c-c-can't—"

Nonchalant, Harrison handed back my phone. "I'm not asking you to talk to him. We'll think of something, but whatever we come up with, you won't have to talk."

My hands shook as I put the phone in my pocket. "And what do we say to a reporter?"

"We talk about whatever he feels like asking, that's what." Harrison beamed. "You've seen interviews with other groups. How did you guys meet? When did you start playing violin?

What's the difference between a violin and a fiddle? Where do you see yourself in five years?"

Shreya said, "Huh. Where do we see ourselves in five years?"

"On the cover of *Rolling Stone* fighting off crazed groupies," Harrison said without missing a beat. "You'll run your own music school. Josh will be fighting six paternity suits, and Joey will be moonlighting with her own viola-based girl-band."

I snickered. "And you?"

"I'll have launched a red-hot solo career that stuns—ow!"

I applauded Josh's direct hit on Harrison's head with a pretzel. Harrison rolled his eyes and picked up the pretzel to deposit it in the trash.

I said, "What do you wear for an interview?"

Harrison opened his hands. "Wear what you would to a job interview."

Small problem there. "I took my civil service exam in torn jeans and a t-shirt that said 'The Party's Over.'"

Harrison blinked. Hah—stopped him cold. "Oh. Yeah, not that. Try *casual afternoon wedding*."

So the same boring outfit I used for meeting clients.

I said, "And if they twist everything to make us sound terrible...?"

"We're not politicians." Harrison spread his hands. "There's no such thing as bad publicity. If they paint us as hateful kitten-killers, then at least they stirred up controversy. In fact, it's better if they do because then people will remember. Trust me. This is going to work out great."

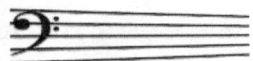

I kept thinking of a reporter saying, "Ms. Mikalos, how did you end up with the viola?"

The answer wasn't easy, not like I imagine Harrison's

would be. *Gee,* he'd say, *I started getting season tickets to Carnegie Hall when I was three, and when I was four my chauffeur would take me from preschool to the conservatory....*

But me, I guess it starts in fourth grade when I didn't realize you shouldn't pry apart frozen chicken with a steak knife. One stupid mistake later and I'm scrunched on the floor with a three-inch gash in my palm. I couldn't reach my parents, couldn't remember the number for Viv's dance studio, so I called Josh. His dad flew right over in five minutes, and he raced me to the ER to get stitched up while Josh and his kid brother tried to put direct pressure on my hand because Josh saw it on a cartoon. Like two hours later my dad came for me, and Ed escorted him out in the hallway.

I have no idea what he said, but that night Mom confiscated my house key. After that, I got picked up from school with Viv and got benched outside her dance class. When the other moms asked about my bandages, Mom said, "Little Miss Independent got herself in trouble again," and they would glance at me, shocked, and change the subject, like it was too embarrassing.

The first day I read a stack of Baby Sitter Club books in the corner, and a couple of the moms talked to me. But on the way home, Mom was furious. "At home you never need anyone." She glared at me in the back seat while the light turned green. "Over there you're bothering everyone." So I tried not even to talk anymore.

After a week of this, Viv bitched during Sunday dinner about having to be *a whole half-hour* at the doctor to get my stitches removed.

Rubbing my brand-new scar, I snapped, "Like it's a picnic to sit forever while you pretend to dance."

Mom said, "Josie, quit starting trouble. Vivvy needs us."

I slumped in my seat, glaring at my drumstick.

Across the table, a clink as my grandfather set down his silverware. "Why are you going with them?"

I drew figure-8s on the table cloth with my fingertip. "Grandpa, I have nowhere to go."

He didn't say anything else, so it was a shock when he fetched me from school Monday in his menthol-green Duster that reeked of vinyl and gasoline. He brought me to his airless house, where the dust made my eyes water, but it beat the dance studio by a mile. I cleared debris off on the counter so I could make toast. He boiled water and unearthed some yellowed tea bags. I chatted with him while I did my homework, then watched cartoons. He drove me back home at six.

It was like a party—and I'd get to do that every day! Grandpa, driving his brontosaurus to the school, and me, getting swallowed up like in a cave while my friends all stared—and seriously, I don't think any seventy-year-old man ever learned so much about the fourth grade as he did by the end of the month.

But the important part: I practiced my violin there (back then I played violin) and he gave pointers. I couldn't figure out what he meant, though. He kept talking about positions. He kept adjusting the way I held the bow. He said I rosined it too much, which in retrospect he did have a point about. When you play, it shouldn't make a cloud.

After one frustrating Friday, he brought me home Monday to find his windows open, the air crisp, the counters cleaned—and on the table, a black coffin case.

I crept closer. "I didn't know you played violin."

"That's a viola." He patted the case. "I haven't touched it since your grandmother died."

Ten years.

Grandpa unsnapped the rusted clasps, worked the hinges open, and pried up the lid to reveal the world's most amazing work of art. It didn't gleam like my half-size. Timeworn, the finish caught the mellower tones of light, golds and oranges I'd never seen until just then. He turned it over so I could trace my fingers over where the wood grain fanned out like a flame. He muttered in dismay at the bugs clinging to the bow hair. But me, I cradled that "big violin" and raised it, sighted along the belly. In a moment that divided my life like a crease down the center of a book, I fit my cheeks into the waist and pressed my lips to the rib, nose above the F-hole, intoxicating myself on the perfume of old wood and powdered rosin: the scent of time.

Then the viola's sound enveloped me, a throatiness I'd never drawn from my violin, the soothing depth, the purr of a contented cat as the instrument sang under my grandfather's hands. Who knew wood and metal, hair and chalk could create a voice?

I switched instruments. I never looked back.

On interview day, Harrison and Josh wore Oxford shirts and ties. You couldn't beat a guy in a tux, but standing together, they came close. While I was admiring them, I noticed Harrison looking me up and down, so I turned to Josh with a comment about the weather. Except he was staring, probably terrified, and when he focused on my face I had to repeat it.

Shreya? Wore a gauzy grey skirt and a burgundy silk blouse with a gathered scoop neck and an empire waist. She'd dusted her blue hair with glitter.

On arrival, the skinny flannel-shirted reporter shook Harrison's hand, then got one look at Shreya and couldn't take his eyes off her. Immediately he wanted to take her picture. He said he wanted a picture of the group, but really, he wanted her.

He chatted while positioning us for the photos. His blue eyes lively, he moved the couch away from the wall, then arranged Josh and Harrison on either side of me, seated, with Shreya poised on the arm. He said, "I can't decide which you look better with," and Harrison said, "Me, of course. Everyone looks better with me," and we laughed. Me too, but it stung.

Through all this, Josh said not a word. So far, all he'd done was shake the reporter's hand, nod, and pose. I wasn't sure we'd pull this off, but Harrison had formed a plan, and I'd move more than couches to make it work.

When we settled for the interview, it was the reporter on the leather chair, Harrison on a folding chair, and Shreya, Josh, and me on the couch. Harrison had choreographed the seating so we'd "naturally" fall into position to bury Josh. Harrison had his violin on his lap, and as he spoke, his fingers stroked the scroll or ran along the F-holes.

The reporter started a digital recorder. Fingers poised over the laptop, he said, "Let's start by telling me about yourselves."

Harrison introduced all of us by name and instrument, making sure to sandwich Josh in the middle.

The reporter frowned. "Help me out. What's the difference between a viola and a violin?"

Harrison said, "The viola burns longer," even as Shreya said, "No one cares if you spill beer on a viola."

The reporter looked up, wide-eyed. I gave him a mild, "The viola is the butt of a hundred jokes, and the violin isn't."

Chuckling, the reporter leaned back. "I like you guys. How long have you been playing together?"

Harrison seized control of the interview, although every so often Shreya or I interjected with a clarification or a contradiction. Josh sat back while I perched on the edge of the seat, and Shreya used her hands as she talked. Overall (to no one's surprise) Harrison proved the most effusive, riveting the man's attention on himself. Violinists lived for a hit of the spotlight.

The reporter said, "Where do you see yourself in five years?" and Shreya cracked up.

I said, "Harrison wants us on the cover of *Rolling Stone*."

The reporter shook his head as he typed.

Harrison said, "Really high caliber weddings."

Shreya said, "I see us moving up from weddings to concert halls."

I shrugged. "I'd like to quit my day job."

The reporter glanced at Josh. "And you?"

"You'll never quit your day job," Harrison said to me, then turned to the reporter. "Ask what her day job is."

"Hey, not fair!" I flushed. "He doesn't need to know that!"

"I think it would make a terrific story."

"I think you're out of your mind."

Harrison faked a sad look. "What if it kills you?"

I mimicked the look. "I hope it does."

The reporter sounded amused. "What is your day job?"

I exclaimed, "No comment!" And Harrison snickered.

The reporter said, "It can't be that bad, can it? But fine, let's talk about your fusion mixes."

See? That was Josh right out of the crosshairs. Go us! I said, "Shreya does an awesome version of 'Hotel California.'"

"Um—" Harrison's demeanor changed in an instant. "I forgot to tell you guys: their agent got back to me this morning. He said no." His cheeks pinked. "No rights." Then he looked up. "We'll find something else. Don't worry."

The reporter hummed. "Can I hear it anyhow?"

Harrison handed Shreya his violin, then asked the reporter to shut his laptop and turn off the digital recorder.

Shreya checked the tuning while I opened my laptop to bring up the video. "She improvised this whole performance."

After the video finished and the reporter was saying, "Wow" and "that was terrific," Shreya played the riff. He fell silent.

She'd changed it again: this time she played the final guitar part, and she used the entire length of the fingerboard to keep all four strings ringing, doing as much string-crossing and position-shifting as humanly possible—and maybe some that wasn't.

I knew the song was about being suckered into a place you could never get away from, whatever you wanted to interpret it as. They say it's marriage or the California lifestyle or materialism—but damn, the way she did it now, you could feel the chains around you, the way the notes formed prison bars and kept ringing with one note not gone yet before the next took over, as if you'd never forget the song the way she played it, never hear it any other way again.

For four minutes, but maybe it could have stretched into eternity, Shreya captivated the reporter in a private concert, her motion and the magic that gathered for her and an instrument.

When she finished, the reporter sat open-mouthed. What's the sound of one reporter clapping? This.

Taking back his violin, Harrison said, "It's a shame. But we've already gotten the rights to two songs, and more will come. Plus, we can still perform it live."

The reporter reached for his computer. "Well, you never know. You may get the rights eventually."

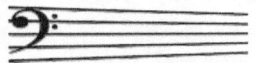

On Thursday, Josh and I took a service elevator to the corporate luncheon's function room. I'd learned right away that some of these places didn't want the feet of the hired help gracing the same carpet as their guests, so we got the conveyance with the metal gate. In our prep room, we found Shreya straightening her wig in the mirror.

"It's like you're two people." I removed my jacket and tried to ignore the thought of all those highly-paid men who'd be following our songs with their critical ears and frowning eyes. "What's going to happen when the *Voice* prints you with blue hair in one photo and black in the other?"

"They'll cope." She gave her head a shake. "As long as the people signing the checks don't have a problem, we don't have a problem."

"They might not have a problem with blue hair at all."

"Harrison would rather not take chances. Except for magenta." She grinned. "Apparently magenta's fine."

Josh said, "But why dye it if blue might get you cr-riticized?"

She shrugged. "After a while, don't you get sick of people's attitudes? Enough to dare people to show who they really are?" She studied him. "Have you ever deliberately stuttered, just to see how someone would react?"

Josh started. "I nnn-never tried, no. But maybe I should just start t-t-talking and letting everyone deal with it."

"Do it!" Shreya's eyes brightened while I fought disbelief, as if she'd suggested we all get comfortable with wetting our pants in public. "Since it's going to happen anyhow, and there's nothing wrong with it, quit hiding and just let it happen. Or would you rather get to the end of your life and say, 'I'd have tried that, but I might have stuttered'?" Shreya turned. "And here's our fearless leader."

Harrison shambled into the room looking as if Death was holding the door.

"Oh my God," I gasped, and Shreya exclaimed, "But wait, Josh didn't drive you!"

Josh muttered, "I'm not-not-not that bad."

Harrison set his violin on the couch, then dropped beside it. Laying his head against the cushions, he gasped, "I'm dying."

I pressed my wrist against his forehead. He had a fever of about a hundred and ten. Shit.

Harrison gripped a travel mug, and he roused himself enough to drink from it. Then he pulled off his coat, handed it to me, and lay prone.

Oh crap, oh crap, oh crap. "Have you taken anything?"

He choked out, "I'm mainlining Motrin."

Shreya's eyes were wide. Josh bit his lip.

Shreya's verdict: "We're screwed."

My mind raced. "Who can we call?"

We had a roster of replacements in case someone was sick, hurt, dead, or pissed off enough to perform in Broadway musicals. But not fifteen minutes before a performance.

"I can play," Harrison rasped. "I just won't sing."

I wasn't sure in what universe Harrison could play, but we were about to find out. I tried to sound glib as I paraphrased Isaac Stern. "Keep that thing tucked under your chin, and you won't have to sing."

He should have laughed. Instead he closed his eyes.

With start time breathing down our necks, Josh and I checked the setup. I tried stacking music for us all, but I dropped the papers and Josh had to help. In ten minutes, we'd be playing for seventy-five stuffy executives, minus a violinist.

Back in the prep room, Harrison was out cold while Shreya played warm-ups. Sitting on the floor, I tuned, and then because it felt wrong not to, I tuned for Harrison. The A string behaved; maybe his violin was worried.

Like most musicians, Harrison had trinkets in his case. Behind the second bow he kept a family photo with worn edges and a Carnegie Hall ticket stub, but nothing more. It shouldn't have surprised me. My case contained viola detritus (an old C string, a cracked bridge, fossilized rosin) and a red feather I'd found on the sidewalk before one of my recitals. In the compartment with my real rosin, I kept a black and white photo of my grandfather, a candid shot where he looked serious. I also had a dried flower dating from our grammar school's first public performance. Josh's father had brought me a corsage, and I'd saved the carnation.

Shreya settled beside me, murmuring, "Are we now a string trio?"

I pitched my voice to match. "We can daisy-chain a bunch of solos and maybe play a few pieces in unison. You can't play two violins at once, can you?"

She smirked. "If only I'd brought my other violin."

I struggled to keep it light. "The one that matches your hair?"

The banquet manager knocked. They were ready to let in the guests, and music should be playing as they entered.

Our dead man arose from the couch.

"What are you going to do?" I asked. "Cough in tune?"

He rolled his eyes, but even that pained him. "I can play. Trust me." Then he broke up coughing.

We wouldn't work the crowd now. Playing before anyone even entered, we took up our role as background music. With all these half-listeners, maybe no one would care how we sounded. Although they'd notice if Harrison collapsed.

We began with the first movement of Mozart's string quartet "The Hunt." The hall was smaller than most wedding receptions: eight tables set for ten, plus a dais with a microphone stand. The burgundy carpet and padded chairs possessed excellent acoustic-destroying properties, but banquet rooms don't care about acoustics because the musicians aren't booking the location. At least this place didn't have drapes.

Maybe Harrison had a point: if I ever got married, I should do it at Carnegie Hall.

Speaking of Harrison, with the violin tucked under his chin, he pretended to be alive. He gave our cues. He was on tempo. Though pale, he wasn't ghostly.

After we finished the movement, we broke while the company president gave a welcome, and diners behaved like a good lunch crowd: eating, conversing, laughing. No one looked in our direction. Perfect. Harrison didn't topple, so we kept playing.

After Mozart came Beethoven, and following Beethoven were speeches. The banquet manager dismissed us to the prep room.

Harrison handed Shreya his violin and collapsed onto the couch.

I checked him again. Still white-hot.

We dug into our "vendor meals." The guests dined on whatever costs forty-five dollars a plate; the musicians got hamburgers and fries. Well, half of us. Shreya had a salad. Harrison had nothing.

Sitting with my back to the couch, I said, "You going to try eating?"

He murmured, "This is how I wanted to die, with my bride at my side."

Josh chuckled.

"There's nothing wrong with you, Harrison." An air of menthol ghosted Harrison, the scent of too many cough drops in too short a time. "You want more tea?"

I opened his thermal mug and got a silly smile: chicken broth. He took a little, then flopped on the cushions. I spread my coat over him.

A dutiful quartet always aids its fearless leader: we plundered his meal, Josh nabbing the extra burger, Shreya stealing his salad, and all of us splitting his fries.

"You think we can finish without him?" Shreya said.

I rolled the edges of my hair between my fingertips. "I don't want to mess with things. It's only half an hour, so he has to survive just one more piece. We'll play something we know by heart but most people aren't familiar with, so they won't notice any mistakes. You'll have to give the cues."

Shreya recoiled. "You think I can?"

I stared at the floor. "You've got a better shot than him."

When the banquet manager fetched us, I dropped a hand on Harrison's shoulder. "They don't pay if you die before the gig ends."

He pushed off the couch, looking miserable and a bit dizzy, so I picked up his violin. He straightened his hair, braced himself, and headed back out.

As we sorted the music, a woman in a business suit approached. "I'm Michelle Emmetts. I had spoken with Harrison Archer."

He shook her hand, sounding raspy. "Thank you for

having us today."

She said, "You guys are wonderful. Now that the boring part of the lunch is over, we'd really like it if you enlivened things with requests and the fusion mixes."

Worry stabbed through my heart. But Shreya said, "Absolutely."

Harrison looked to me. "Can you do the announcing?" He turned back to the executive secretary. "My voice is shot."

Her brow furrowed. "You sound as if you need to be in bed with some tea."

"The show must go on!" That smile was undiluted bravado, but she didn't realize.

A photographer set up in the corner while the banquet manager liberated a microphone. Terrific. I'd forgotten about the *Village Voice*. They'd capture every instant of our demise.

Harrison was whiter by the second, so I pushed him into his chair. We huddled.

"There's no way he can do this," I whispered.

Josh said, "Tell them n-n-no."

Harrison rubbed his temples. "We are not telling them no. I can do this."

"You're going to drop dead," I hissed.

Shreya said, "No, Joey, I think we can pull it off." Her brow furrowed. "We've practiced the 'Hotel California' mix. We'll lead off with that." Shreya's steely eyes gave me a sense she knew what to do, and I tried to focus on her. "I'll take requests. I can whip stuff off the top of my head and do it solo. We've only got to hold out for half an hour. Can you do introductions?"

Nauseated, I nodded. But what else was there? Josh wouldn't take the mike, and Harrison couldn't. Nerves or not, I'd have talk.

Shreya gripped my arm. "Even if we fail, we're going to make a whole lot of noise doing it. They won't shoot you." A pause and then, "They might hit you with a slice of seven layer cake."

I couldn't even laugh. People were already watching and we hadn't even begun. My vision sparkled.

Harrison sighed. "I'm sorry."

I snapped, "Quit being sorry and just sit there before you collapse."

When he didn't give me any flack, I felt bad. I also fought the urge to check his pulse. But he had a fever; if he were dead, surely he'd have reached room temperature?

Shreya took the mike, and her posture changed. So did her attitude and the tilt of her head. It hit me in an instant: she'd worked crowds a lot—not just for a late-bride concert. "Now that the talking is over, how about we make Beethoven roll over and give our honoree a lively send-off?" She raised her violin. "Because some places you can retire from, and some places you can't possibly escape."

She ripped off the riff to "Hotel California," then launched into the piece as practiced over the last couple of weeks.

She stood; the rest of us sat. As she moved with the violin, a thing of beauty in both appearance and sound, she transfixed everyone's attention.

The practice paid off. We moved into the fusion, into the Beethoven, back out into the fused part, and again to Shreya's solo. She was right: Harrison screwed up a few times, but no one knew those parts, so no one cared. Her cues were awkward, but Josh and I compensated. Meanwhile the photographer canvassed the room to get shots of Shreya, and I struggled not to listen for Harrison's violin.

She took us through an extra repeat of the theme before calling it quits, then bowed. The guests applauded.

She turned to me, and I tucked my viola against my side to approach the mike.

"Well—" You know how Shreya was totally comfortable doing this? Now they'd get the other extreme. "Since you've been listening for an hour, do you know the definition of a string quartet?" No one answered, thank goodness, which would have thrown me off. "One good violinist, one pretty good violinist" (I pointed to Harrison and Shreya in turn), "one failed violinist" (I raised my hand and they chuckled), "and one person who hates violinists" (Josh saluted), "all getting together to talk about how much they loathe composers." General laughter. My first public viola joke. "Your soloist is Shreya Ramachandran, the pretty-good violinist. If you have a request, let us know, otherwise you'll be stuck with a bunch of stodgy quartets by dead Europeans."

I turned to Shreya. "Is the 'Hotel California' located on 'Baker Street'?"

"Why, yes." She grinned. "I believe it is."

As I returned to my seat, Josh flashed a thumbs-up. I shuddered because the longest six hours of my life had ended.

Shreya started our somewhat-practiced Baker-Street-Mozart fusion, her violin taking the part of the saxophone solo.

Twenty minutes remaining.

We got a request from the honoree, a dedication to his wife: "Danny's Song." Hey, 1971 called and said we could play her theme! It had a violin line, thank heaven, even though it was more fiddly than violinish. Shreya made a few mistakes, but not terrible for setting a bow to strings and letting fly. After a minute, she segued into a movement from Handel's *Water Music* we'd played often enough that Josh and I did it from memory (although it took Harrison a few measures to catch on) and every so often she worked the theme back into the piece.

While she soloed, I glanced at the guest of honor, a round-faced man not much older than my father, seated beside a wispy woman in a lacy blouse. He held her hand. You could almost hear the words from Shreya's violin. So sweet. I wonder if my grandfather felt that way about my grandmother.

Meanwhile Harrison looked like we'd need to carry him out. His pallor scared me even more than his labored breathing. After a look, Shreya opted against a final request and started the Pachelbel Canon, even though most of the time she claimed she'd prefer to eat fire ants live.

After it finished, I took the mike and thanked everyone. Then I held Harrison's violin as he struggled to his feet. He shot me a meaningful look, and I whispered, "No CDs. Move it."

He was alive enough to glare.

In the prep room, he went prone again. Josh said, "I'll dr-drive you home."

"Thanks." Harrison massaged his temples. "I'm nearly dead anyhow."

He ruined the effect by coughing and then flinching with his hand pressed to his ribs.

A knock came at the door. The guest of honor had approached, and he shocked me because he was only my height. Again I thought of my grandfather.

"I wondered if you had a moment." The gentleman had a warm smile and clear blue eyes, a softer voice than I'd expected. "Would you happen to have a CD?"

I fished one out of Harrison's bag along with our business card and a couple of flyers. I didn't ask for money. "I'm glad you enjoyed the performance."

He handed me a twenty. "It was a wonderful send-off. Is this enough?"

Shreya dug in her wallet to find a five. I wasn't sure why she bothered. He seemed young to retire, but maybe these executives went on permanent walkabout once they had a small mountain in the bank.

I smiled. "Well, you'll have plenty of time to listen to it, relaxing at home."

His response sounded measured. "My wife and I are looking forward to some time together, yes." He squeezed my hand. "Thank you." He went to Shreya and Josh, then Harrison, who hadn't quite managed to stand, and shook their hands too. "It really was splendid. I'm sorry you had to work while sick," he said to Harrison. "I know how hard that is."

The door clicked when he left. Josh handed Harrison his coat, then lifted both Harrison's violin case and his cello. "Come on, fea-fea-fearless leader. Let's get you home."

TEN

The phone rang at eight Wednesday morning. That must mean Harrison was finally feeling better, which also meant it was time to kill him. Poor baby, stir-crazy after canceling his whole week to nestle in bed guzzling NyQuil, but still, he knew I went to bed at three, and this was just too damn early.

That's when I remembered: Wednesday! The *Village Voice* would have printed.

And it turned out not to be Harrison anyhow. "Guess what?" sing-songed Josh's voice.

My heart raced. "You have the paper?"

"Dad left a stack on the k-k-kitchen table."

Josh's Dad rocked. "Is it good?"

"I haven't checked. You want me to rrr-read it to you?"

I curled under the covers. "Yeah, go ahead."

Eyes closed, I listened to Josh describe two pictures, one of us arranged on Harrison's couch and another of Shreya performing at the retirement party.

"Mmm." I shifted the phone to get more comfortable. "Don't stop."

About three paragraphs into the story, my mouth tingled and I couldn't focus. Not because I was falling asleep, but because the more awake I got, the more I realized what I was hearing. They said we'd share an article with three groups, yet instead the Boroughs String Quartet was hogging several dozen column-inches all to ourselves in New York's largest entertainment weekly.

This wasn't just a mention in a wedding write-up. This was us, larger-than-life. Heck, after hearing it, I wished I could hire this group.

We were, they claimed, "evangelizing chamber music" by "rendering it accessible." We'd shattered the public perception of classical as something for sherry-sipping septuagenarians who wouldn't recognize Darth Vader.

Josh burst out laughing, and I exclaimed, "What? What?"

"Guess what?" he said. "I'm mysterious."

"Get out!"

"Dead serious. Cellist J-j-j-j-joshua G-g-g-g—shit." He'd never gotten out his whole name in one shot. "...me.... is a mysterious man who maintains a silent presence in the background."

"Deep," I said.

"Very."

He kept reading, and the occasional stutter gave me time to linger. Call waiting beeped, and I ignored it to keep hearing him tell me about ourselves.

When he ended, I said, "How does it feel to be mysterious?"

"If I told you, I wouldn't be mysterious anymore."

"Touché." I chuckled. "I guess a sharp reporter notices when someone doesn't utter a single word during an hour-long interview."

"Can't fool the prrr-ress." Josh prolonged the word so he purred it.

"Lucky," I said. "Women throw themselves at the strong silent type."

Josh laughed. "As if. They always go for our 'good-looking, enthusiastic f-f-f-first violinist.'"

The article barely mentioned me, par for the course, although it mentioned the viola jokes.

"I keep getting call-waiting." I rolled over in bed. "Twice in three minutes. Harrison?"

"Bet on it. He beeped mmm-me too."

"Let him sit. Actually, let him phone Shreya." I stretched, arching my back. "We ought to celebrate."

"Come over," said Josh. "I'll make breakfast."

It took thirty minutes to shower, dress, and get to the place he shared with his dad. Josh met me on the front stoop, then unburdened me of a bag of donuts and handed me a copy of the *Village Voice* before I even got into their apartment.

I re-read it standing over his kitchen table. We were right there in front of us: the mysterious cellist, the invisible violist, and the two sassy spotlight-hugging violinists. The struggle to survive as a musician, the magic of pulling "Hotel California" out of a hat, the birth of a new repertoire, and our determination to carry on despite losing our keystone song.

"This is—" I turned to Josh to find his eyes bright. I didn't know what to say. "It looks *real*."

He knew what I meant.

While I unzipped my jacket, I noticed a small animal nosing around the baseboards. "Oh! I finally get to meet them!" I crouched, holding out my hand, but it ignored me. Josh always had a pet. When the last hamster had died in January, he'd picked up a pair of hedgehogs.

I hunted for a place to pet the thing where it wouldn't stick me. "What did you name them?"

He paused. "They won't c-come when you c-c-call."

I said, "And—?"

He went to the table and typed into his laptop: "Stradivarius" and "Shostakovich."

I winked. "The match for Stradivarius ought to be Guarneri."

He grinned. "I n-n-need the verrr-bal exercise."

I tried to touch it again, but it waddled away. "What do they eat?"

"Insects. Mealworms."

"Bow mites?"

Josh shuddered. I laughed.

Beside the laptop he had the conductor's score for Beethoven's Fifth Symphony; on the screen was Sibelius, our music notation software. Oh, yeah, that stupid bride wanted it done as a quartet.

While he tended to breakfast, I checked it over: he'd dismantled the symphony into the motive (*Da-da-da-DUMM...*) and barely anything else. Think of what you'd find on a crank-driven music box that said "Beethoven's Fifth." Josh was enough of an arranging genius to generate four lines and three minutes of this, and as Harrison said, the bride wouldn't care. If she wanted something this ridiculous, she wouldn't know why it was ridiculous when we played it, even if Beethoven's ghost broke a viola over my head. But if Harrison wanted to play this ever again, I'd feed him his rosin cake.

The coffee maker beeped. Josh took a bowl of beaten eggs from the fridge, plus butter and mushrooms. I set the English muffins in the toaster while he cooked omelets and fried bacon. I put away his laptop but kept the newspaper out, and while we ate, we looked it over again.

I frowned. "I'm not happy about them saying we don't have the rights to 'Hotel California.' People might think it's bait-and-switch."

Josh shrugged.

"We should write the reporter a thank-you note." I looked up. "That's what you do, right?"

"Yeah, because I majored in pub-publicity."

Josh's father Ed emerged from his bedroom, asking about all the fuss, then roaring with laughter and clapping him on the shoulder. "You guys did terrific. I've got to read it!"

That wasn't like him. "I thought you brought it in?"

"I wanted you guys to have the honor of reading it first." He beamed. "But I could barely sleep. I wanted to wake Josh up!"

Josh watched him read, grinning the whole time. "You, mysterious?" Ed exclaimed. "I've seen more mysterious things in the back of the fridge!" When I giggled, Ed sighed. "I'm real proud of you." He turned to me. "I'm proud of you too. You guys worked real hard for this."

"It's not the Nobel prize in music." My ears burned. "It's good, though. We might pick up more clients."

"I'll bet you get a million!" He slapped Josh's back. "I'm getting ten more copies and sending them to your grand-mother, Aunt Connie and Uncle Jake, Aunt Donna, Andrew, and some to save." He took another look at his son's picture in the paper. "Say, did you guys leave any breakfast for an old man who only plays the radio?"

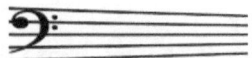

By eleven o'clock we'd arrived at Harrison's. I had seven missed calls, three resulting in voice mail requests for more information. Josh took care of my jacket and viola while I transcribed names and numbers and mentally blocked Harrison's nonstop commentary. If our headline had bumped shoulders with a Mars landing, world peace, and the discovery of an infinitely renewable natural resource whose only byproduct was champagne, he wouldn't have noticed.

Shreya had a brilliant idea: "Perhaps we could practice?"

Grumbling about how of course we were going to practice, Harrison dragged his monologue right out to the living room, and I imagined the sound distorting like a train whistle blaring off into the distance.

Harrison said, "So Joey, now you can quit your day job and marry me."

"Perfect," I called back, "except that I'm not quitting my day job, and I'm not marrying you."

"Glad you agree." He cocked his head. "When will you quit?"

"When we earn enough that I won't be kicked onto the street."

Shreya looked up. "I thought you lived with your grandparents."

I shrugged. "And—?"

She started. "They'd kick out their granddaughter?"

"I rent from them." Her eyes widened, so I added, "Harrison may have jacked up our rates, but we're not self-sustaining, even if we all move in together and share a toothbrush."

We started with fusion mixes. After the second, Josh and Shreya discussed altering the arrangement to evoke the viola and cello voices.

While they talked, Harrison murmured, "Why'd you have breakfast with Josh?"

What was his deal? "To celebrate the article."

His eyebrows shot up. "Celebrate?"

"Yeah, he carried me to his taxi and played the *Jupiter Symphony* while ravishing me in the back seat." Find dagger, insert into ribcage. "Oh, wait, he didn't. He made coffee and eggs." I sighed. "I get those mixed up."

Harrison looked pained. "I'd have made breakfast."

How dare he? "That would be unprofessional."

He turned away. Good.

Shreya said, "I think we've got it," and wrote a prompt on my score while Josh crossed out several measures on Harrison's.

Our dynamic had changed with the fusions, with Shreya's violin taking the virtuosic material, in effect making Harrison the second violinist for the duration of her playing. At some point maybe we'd call her our fearless leader-ess.

Since none of us wanted a ringtone concerto, I found three more missed calls after practice. I sat again copying information from voicemail so Harrison could call them back.

I had my viola in one hand and cell phone in the other, about to leave, when the phone rang again. Unknown number. To save Harrison a callback, I answered. "Boroughs String Quartet, home of the 'Hotel California.'"

Shreya rolled her eyes.

"Who am I speaking to?" demanded an older female voice who did not sound amused by my brilliant greeting.

Fine, I could play that tune. "Josephine Mikalos, the violist. How may I help you?"

"I'm Annette Tilton." The woman's voice had the sharpness of a carving tool slicing the F-holes out of a violin body. "I'm the intellectual property attorney for The Eagles, and you can consider yourself served with a cease and desist order."

The blood drained from my head, and I stood in a vacuum.

She kept talking, but it made no sense. I registered the word lawsuit, the words "copyright infringement," and a demand that we take down our video. She went on about her client being in a bad position and proper channels and she knew my type and we'd be in court so fast our heads would spin.

Even as Shreya rescued my viola from my limp hand, Harrison grabbed the phone from the other. "Hello? Who is this?"

Josh guided me to sit on the couch. Shreya whispered, "What's going on?"

My voice cracked. "We're being sued."

Harrison had begun arguing, but I couldn't think. She knew my type? What type? And why would she get our website suspended? What defamation of character? What had we done?

The last thing Harrison said was, "You know what? From this point, we'll conduct all conversation through our attorney."

He hung up, and then his shoulders slumped.

Josh said, "What the hell is going on?"

Harrison offered a weak, "The Eagles have landed?"

No one laughed.

He recapped for Shreya and Josh, and for me too, since the conversation had crumbled in my head: we were on the hook for defamation of character, and they wanted to file suit against us for copyright infringement. She wanted our video off the internet, and she demanded we cease talking about her clients in public.

Josh sat nearer to me on the couch. "Are you okay?"

"But—" I closed my eyes. "What video are they talking about?"

"I'm as clueless as you," Harrison said. "I made sure the reporter wasn't recording when Shreya played for him."

Josh said, "Maybe the videographer from that first bride? But he sp-specifically told us not to, and I can't imagine the bride did."

"Why are we being stupid?" Shreya woke up Harrison's computer and gave the question to Google.

We got a page full of hits, the top site being the *Village Voice*. The online edition had a subheader: *Eagles Say No Violins*.

Reading over Shreya's shoulder, Josh breathed, "Oh shit."

Shreya clicked over to the *Village Voice* page. It had a sidebar: the mean corporate attorneys and the big-money entertainment industry were standing in the way of four vibrant local artists.

Like a fairy tale, except my money was on the fire-breathing dragon.

My vision went spotty as Shreya clicked the video box.

"That's—"

"I know." I needed to sit. "That's the retirement luncheon."

On screen, a miniature Shreya played the "Hotel California" fusion, gorgeous with the long-haired wig and her eyes closed as she bowed the violin. The camera followed her, only occasionally panning over the rest of us. She was the one with the melody, the beauty, and the hypnotic motion.

Harrison said, "Damn, but you're good. I wish I'd been alive to see that."

I gave a nervous laugh.

Josh said, "They didn't t-t-take down the video yet."

"I doubt they will," Shreya said. "They had every right to record it."

"That's what I get for performing while dead." Harrison frowned. "I didn't check for cameras."

"You check for cameras?"

He nodded. "How else would I know where to look?"

"You're hopeless." I tried to sound breezy, but it failed. "Hopeless" described me better than Harrison.

Harrison's voice was tentative. "It might work out."

I strode right in front of him. "We're getting sued! Didn't you hear that? How on earth is that supposed to work out?"

"I don't know," Harrison said, reaching for his own phone. "That's why I'm going to call my brother and ask."

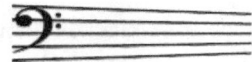

At times like this, it was handy to have two attorneys who took our first violinist's calls.

Shreya lifted my grandfather's picture from my viola case. "Which composer is this?"

I forced a smile. "Zachary Mikalos. He composed me."

"Father? Grandfather?" She studied the picture, then studied me. "He looks like you. Same expression." She replaced it, then tucked my viola under the blanket. Picking up Harrison's iPod, she said, "Anyone up for the Mendelssohn Violin Concerto?"

Josh said, "Whose?"

Shreya clicked through, reading off the soloists. "Heifitz. Anne-Sophie Mutter. Hilary Hahn. Joshua Bell. Itzhak Perlman. Yehudi Menuhin."

The clicking sound made my hair stand on end. I just wanted everyone to be quiet while Harrison found out how bad it was going to be. Instead, Josh said, "Early Yehudi

Menuhin, or late?"

"Late."

Josh looked puzzled. "He doesn't have I-Isaac Stern?"

Oh, for pete's sake... Why wouldn't everyone shut up?

Shreya clicked back through up the playlists. "Sorry. I missed him."

This was why we'd get away with Harrison's scheme of covering things that never should have been covered by a string quartet: in classical music, everything is a cover. We don't have recordings of Mozart performing Mozart's string quartets. He copied out the notes and then (he wrote to Haydn,) "sent them out into the world." That's why you can have fifteen interpretations of the same score.

Still, the conversation needed to end. "Do Hilary Hahn." Then I lay down beside the speaker, eyes closed to let the orchestra's sound engulf me.

At the table, Harrison read his notes back to his brother, recapitulating one line at a time the venom of the nastiest woman alive. Every word felt like a burn.

The music, though, the Mendelssohn could soothe anything, and I let it.

Would have let it. Josh said to Shreya, "I sh-should know this, but where did you learn violin?"

Yeah, so much for soothing the soul with music and lawyers. Shreya had dodged that question during our interview. Josh hadn't been our only mysterious one.

Shreya's eyes widened, but she laughed. "Same way you guys did? Started taking lessons in someone's living room and went from there."

I rolled over so my chin rested on my forearms.

Josh said, "But you can pull a rock s-song out of your head and translate it to the fingerboard while you're dancing."

At the table, Harrison laughed at something his brother said. That was a better sign than if he hunched down whimpering, but it felt like heat up my spine.

Shreya shrugged. "I already said you can practice improv.

Figure out the key, do the scale, and those notes are your likely suspects. Pick out the lowest and highest notes, and that's your range. Practice a couple of hours with the radio." She forced a smile. "And anyhow, didn't Yehudi Menuhin say you have to move while you're playing?"

Josh grinned. "Y-Yehudi MM-Menuhin in his wildest dreams didn't move the way you do."

Shreya's laugh sounded forced. "Thanks. How did you start the cello?"

Josh missed her change-of-subject maneuver. Or maybe he didn't and just wanted soothing through pointless conversation. Far be it from me to steal his novocaine. "We were in third grade when we started orchestra. She got a v-violin, and they gave me a cello I didn't want."

My head snapped up. "You didn't?"

He shook his head. "I wanted a trrr-rombone. But I—"

I couldn't tell if he'd blocked or wasn't finishing the sentence. He didn't look blocked.

Harrison walked to the kitchen. "So a venomous phone call is SOP?" A soda can hissed as he popped the top. Then, "Can you be that much of a jerk too? Because if yes, I'm so getting you a better Christmas gift." More laughter.

How could he laugh when someone wanted the quartet dead? Why wasn't he screaming?

Shreya said, "So your school didn't have trombones?"

"By the time I was—" Here Josh did block, blinking. "— able to ask, the trombones were gone. The saxophones were gone. Cello was the only thing left."

I stared at my hands.

Shreya sat back. "Fortunate for us, I guess. But wow. I had no idea."

No, neither had I.

Now that he said it, though, I remembered how we'd been crammed into the band room while Mr. Mendelson demonstrated the instruments. How there had been no organization, kids raising their hands and yelling out instruments, then being brought to the storage closet to grab something.

And how when I'd looked at Josh, he'd had a wide-eyed strangled look, his ears red and his hands shaking. I'd only shot up my hand and shouted for a violin.

Harrison and his phone took a trip down the hall. "No, we did not know we'd been videoed." Then, "No, we're not hosting the video on our site." And then, "Of course we didn't lie to the newspaper. We're not *that* professional!" followed by more laughter.

I never understood how Harrison could joke about life and death. Yet it didn't sound forced to him at all, as if a lawsuit was only a game of badminton, whacking around a string quartet like a shuttlecock.

Turning back to Josh, I tried to steady my voice. "I should have done something."

He gave me a little push. "Yeah, you should have k-k-k-kicked Mr. Mendelson in the head until he bought another trrr-rombone."

I wove my fingers together. "Well, maybe not that."

He gave my arm a squeeze. "It worked out fine. Usually a trrr-rombone doesn't blend so well in a string quartet."

Shreya added, "I could say the same for a viola."

Josh laughed, but I must have looked murderous because he quit it.

Behind me, Harrison said, "So there's no such thing as bad publicity?"

As if. Of course there was bad publicity. Bad publicity got you sued.

I was done at that point. Done like an overcooked hamburger—done with the small talk, done with regrets from third grade, done with Harrison laughing at the guillotine. Done, done, done. So I put my head right into the speaker and listened to Yehudi Menuhin, admired the way he did the runs and how he entered that cadenza and totally owned it, and how Mendelssohn could break your heart without knowing it but only because he didn't know you'd be listening in two hundred years. *Molto appassionato*, it said for the first movement. *Very impassioned.* He'd written a melody that wrung you out like a wet handkerchief, and right now, with a lawyer set to wring us out too, listening physically hurt, but the music expressed the desperation.

When finally I looked up, I found Harrison on the couch, his brows an inverted V as he watched me. I pushed onto my elbows, then sat, lightheaded. Shreya paused the iPod.

For once he avoided theatrics. "We'll be fine. It might get hairy, and we might get more phone calls, but we didn't do anything wrong."

"I knew that!" I scrambled to my feet. "But if we have to defend ourselves in court to prove we didn't do anything—"

"It won't get that far. Assuming they even file suit, we'll get dropped and they'll go after the paper. The paper didn't print anything factually incorrect, so again, there's no question of libel. We're not making money off the video, so there's no copyright infringement."

I raised my voice. "And defamation of character?"

"I'm quoted as saying it's all right that corporate denied permission. That's not defaming anyone."

"That's not the point!" I strode toward the couch, and Harrison jerked up his gaze from his notes. "I'm not worried about being wrong! I'm worried about paying an attorney a hundred dollars an hour I don't have in order to tell a judge the things you just said! Your brother can't represent us, can he?"

"He's not the right kind of attorney, no. Neither is my mother." Harrison shook his head. "There's only so much I can say. Ninety-eight percent of that phone call was bluster. The other two percent is unlikely, although possible."

"I have a question." Shreya sat on her heels alongside the stereo. "How likely is it that other record labels will deny permission based on what appears to be a very public hissy-fit?"

Harrison's shoulders slumped. "I don't know. This wasn't

my idea. We have to work forward from here, that's all."

"Begin as you mean to go on," I said. "And apparently we mean to go on getting assaulted by lunatics who are over-wrought about who mixes their crap with Beethoven."

I grabbed my coat and viola, and Josh joined me. The last thing I wanted was to stand in a toll-booth taking people's money and people's attitudes, but after that caliber of crap had hit the fan, it seemed more necessary.

All the same, I didn't need to hear another eruption from Mount Lawyer-Bitch. I scrawled my passcode on a piece of paper and handed it to Harrison. He, he of all people, looked glum. "I'm not taking any calls for the rest of the day. Go ahead and check my voicemail every couple of hours and listen to her threats." I turned off my phone and shoved it into my pocket. "You talk Lawyerese to the woman, because I can't."

"I have your whole private life right here in my hand." His tone didn't match the snark—he was really off-balance. "If Prince Charming leaves you a voicemail, I'm deleting it because you're supposed to marry me."

"Go ahead." I rolled my eyes. "I get three or four of those every day."

On the street, Josh and I in separate silences threaded our ways through the pedestrian traffic, Josh in the lead and me trailing. A subway train blew by underneath, blowing a gust of air up my legs, just like the way that lawyer had blasted in without warning. Damn it.

We turned in at Only Strings. Arvin was dealing with a would-be customer.

"Do you have any peg compound?"

"No, sir. Only Strings." Arvin looked past him. "Josh! Joey! What can I get for you?"

Josh raised a hand, and Arvin said, "D'Addario Helicore cellos?"

The customer said, "You have a picture of a violin on the door, but you don't have peg compound?"

"No sir," Arvin tossed over his shoulder as he pulled open a drawer of cello strings. "Only Strings."

I offered, "You can pick up peg dope at Marty's Music three blocks up, on Sixth."

The customer looked puzzled. "But this store is—"

I nodded. "Only Strings."

He left, muttering, "Only in Manhattan."

Arvin rang up Josh. "How's it going?"

"The *Voice* screwed us over."

Arvin looked up. "That was a nice piece. One of my customers even mentioned you because I've got your flyer up."

I glanced at the bulletin board, sagging with flyers from every musician in Manhattan. "Really?"

Arvin shrugged. "Why not?"

Far be it from me to gainsay Arvin. "The newspaper guy talked about us not having the rights to 'Hotel California,' and now we're getting sued." I glared at the cash register. "I want to strangle him."

Arvin handed me a coiled guitar string. "That'll be six-fifty."

I glared at him until Josh burst out laughing.

Everyone was a comedian. "Would you do the hit for me?"

"Sorry, doll. Only Strings." He smiled. "It's not that bad. All this publicity and maybe you'll get the rights. The video's online? I've never heard you play."

Behind us, a customer entered. Josh said, "It's all Shr-reya. She's good."

"Keep making noise. Remember, you're a musical family, and people fight like hell to protect their own." Then he turned to the new customer and corrected her that no, he sold Only Strings.

Out on the street, Josh called his father to coordinate a taxi-swap. I rubbed my hands together and breathed into my fingers. Trombones. Josh. The muted kid who ended up hauling a cello to school, although sometimes he'd carry my violin too, the way he'd carried Harrison's last Thursday. The fifteen-years-ago strangled look that I'd only now decoded as, "I want something so badly it hurts, and I can't say a thing." Shouldn't I have recognized it?

Who knew if he'd have made as amazing a trombonist, or if he'd have ended up playing cello anyhow? Maybe Fate had better things in mind for Josh than he had for himself, and maybe Fate made it all work together for him because he'd never have made it happen on his own. If he hadn't been afraid to speak, or if the school hadn't had only two trombones, or if the music teacher had been organized enough to lead starving wolves to fresh meat, Josh wouldn't be here right now.

When he got off the phone, I said, "You could still take trombone lessons."

He shook his head. "I messed around with Stuart Carignan's once. It wasn't all that great." His mouth curved mischievously. "You can whack the guy in front of you, but not much more."

I stared at the pavement.

"You okay?" He put his hand on my shoulder. "No, you're not." He blinked, then gave a little head-shake. "Don't worry about the lll-lawyer. It'll be all right."

And you got your law degree where? But that wasn't right. He wanted to help. He just didn't know what else to say.

His cheeks flushed. "They can drag us into court. They can't take our mmm-music."

Why was he so sure? There were a dozen ways, from court orders all the way to damage penalties that would require selling our instruments. "And what if they do? That's what scares me."

"Don't let it." He put his hands on my shoulders and lowered his head toward me. "You're a musician. I'm a musician. We'll p-play. That's what we do." And then, after a hesitation, his hands tightened. "The best music the quartet plays... is something no one can steal. It's ourselves. It's the four of us."

ELEVEN

At two in the morning I returned home, my thoughts firing in random directions. What waited for me: email threats? a subpoena? If a subpoena, maybe they nailed it to the door, and then I'd get in trouble for the hole in the woodwork.

No, my grandmother would have intercepted that. I'd find a thick envelope in the middle of my table, a note in her loopy script on a yellow sticky note. "Josie, a nice gentleman brought this. Please bring up my laundry before going to jail."

In the absence of a process server sitting on the stoop, I checked behind the garbage cans to find that my stray kitty had finished all the food. I added some, then refilled the water bowl from my plastic bottle. I clicked my tongue against the roof of my mouth.

My breath was visible in the chill. Shortly a shadow brushed my leg, followed by a petulant meow.

"Yeah, you're suffering," I whispered. "Most cats get fed during the daylight. Deal with it."

I squatted beside the cat. In the streetlight I couldn't make out his tabby stripes, only the white on his paws and his nose. He growled at his food, terrifying the kibble awaiting its quietus.

When I extended a hand, he skittered away. "Silly thing. I've been doing this for a year. I'd have eaten you by now if I wanted to."

Grandma hated cats, always had, saying they'd pee on the tree. She'd have pitched a fit if she realized, but because I was the one dragging the trash cans to the curb and back, she never saw the bowls. I stashed the cat food in the entryway in an unlabeled Rubbermaid container alongside the shovels and rock salt.

A car passed. I tensed until it turned the corner, but the cat kept eating. I touched his flank, and he leaped away, then glared and returned.

"Have you ever been sued? I imagine it's scary. What if I can't afford your food any longer? You'll have to eat pigeons."

The prospect didn't worry the cat as much as it should.

"They won't send me to jail. But if I stop feeding you, maybe they've won. Maybe I should run to Canada with my viola the way Harrison suggested." I grimaced. "This whole situation is his fault. Who thought it was a good idea to mix classic rock and classical string quartets?"

At least the cat didn't pretend it was a good idea.

I forced a smile. "But hey, there's the definition of optimism: someone suing a violist."

Hah, I made my own viola joke.

I stood, and the cat bolted.

I found no subpoena nailed to the door, nor a letter with ten fancy names. Emboldened by that, I should have checked my email, but the thought turned my stomach. Instead I turned on the shower and plugged the tub drain.

Boiling in the hottest stream I could stand, I thought again about my joke. Harrison once quipped that the first rule of law is not to sue broke people. By that measure, my student loans immunized me against lawsuits for the next sixteen years. The quartet's pocket-change wouldn't pay the opposing attorney to do more than write a draft of a nastygram (maybe that's why she phoned?) and beyond that, yeah, they could force us into bankruptcy. We'd have to dissolve the quartet, but they'd never collect.

Some victory. "You lose: we're dead."

The *Voice* might also get sued, but bet me the *Voice* had twelve attorneys on salary. I think even the garbage man had his own attorney nowadays.

By the time I stepped out of the shower, leaving the water trapped so the heat wouldn't go down the drain, I'd rehearsed the argument inside my head eight times. There was no way out: we'd end up in court over something spewed out to fill "the news hole," and just like that, we were sunk. Because before they realized we had no money to take, we'd have spent it defending ourselves.

And what would I do then? My sister was gunning for my apartment, and my grandparents wouldn't allow me a safety net. What would happen once the attorneys sank their teeth into my wallet and gave it a hard shake? Move back with my parents and...oh, God, Mom would take my viola. I'd never be able to hide it there. If that lawyer wanted to crush me, she could.

It was all so fragile. Mom said I was independent so often I never realized just how easy I'd be to destroy.

In my pajamas, I turned on the kettle for cheap hot chocolate, but then what? During toll-booth lulls I'd finished my library book, and none of my DVDs appealed.

After the kettle whistled, I poured the water into the powder and gave in to the necessary: I checked my email. A dozen new ones appeared.

The first was from Shreya: "Joey, this stinks. I'm not sure if it's as good as Harrison says or as bad as you say, but it stinks. We'll get through it, though. Even if we have to relocate to India, hey, I've got family there."

I didn't reply.

Nothing from Josh, whom I assumed was still driving around Manhattan. Josh had sounded so certain we'd be fine. His assurance had carried me all the way to Brooklyn, but then I'd stood in a toll-booth for eight hours and the worries came even faster than the eight dollar tolls.

Harrison had emailed too. "Joey, when you get this, call me. It's nothing bad, but I want to talk."

Yeah, because if it was great news, he'd need to deliver it via voice to cushion the blow? That "it's nothing bad" brought all sorts of catastrophes to mind. He might as well have said, "Call me so I can pop out your heart with a corkscrew."

Instead I went to violinist.com and scanned the forums. Only when I kept thinking of the sword hanging over my head did I finally reach for my phone, avoiding a look at how many calls I'd missed.

Harrison's voice bubbled out at me. "Did you see it?"

I hesitated. Then, "See what?"

"You have to go back to the *Village Voice* article and read the comments!"

I shook my head. "I can't."

"Read the comments, Joey."

"Just tell me."

He sighed. "I'm promising you it's not bad. Okay, fine. Here. 'You guys rock.' 'Shreya Ramachandran is God.' 'They need to sell this stuff.' 'I hate classical music but I like them.' Yeah, some are negative. Some people don't like the idea of doing classic rock with violins because it'll ruin the rock songs. Fine. But no comments about whining crybabies, and the *Voice* hasn't taken down the video. And trust me, their lawyers began billing hours the second that attorney called."

I didn't answer.

"Meaning, that attorney hasn't got enough in her pocket to take us to court. We did nothing wrong, and they know it. All the paper did was piss off an attorney or two."

"And a group of living music superstars."

Harrison said, "But we'd already been denied permission, so what can they do? Deny it again? We're no worse off than before."

He had a point.

"I told you to look. I'm your fearless leader. Do it."

I opened up the article, then clicked the video so Shreya played while I read the comments.

Halfway through, I said, "Not bad."

"Yeah, not bad. Shreya is some guy's deity, and that's not bad."

A few responders called Shreya's blend an abomination, plus a few comments about corporate rock. Some saying they hated the song in both versions. But most were approval.

"The question is," I drawled as I logged into Gmail, "whether any of them feel like propitiating the deity."

Ah. Fifteen emails.

"Apparently yes."

"I didn't check the group account," Harrison said. "How is it?"

I read them to Harrison. Ten were raves. Five were event enquiries.

"A family reunion. That's a first."

Harrison sounded awed. "I wonder what we charge for that."

"Not as much as for weddings. Music is in the optional category for a reunion."

"I'm not so sure. If they're asking—"

"We'll quote them our pre-jacked-up wedding rate and see if they need smelling salts. Period. Corporations don't care about saving money. Neither do brides. Families do."

Harrison sighed.

I smirked. "Unless they're Rockefellers."

"I don't recognize the name," said Harrison, "but I can ask my parents."

"Google them. Aren't tax returns considered public record?"

Harrison laughed out loud. "Wow, that's mean! I wish I'd thought of it. And no, they're not unless you're president of the United States of America, whose name I do happen to recognize."

I bit my lip. "But it'll all be for nothing once some lawyer swoops in and snatches everything."

"It's not going to happen."

"You don't know that!" My heart pounded. "You don't understand! I'm working around the clock to survive. I don't have rich parents who will pick up the pieces when some judge torpedoes my life!"

"Joey—"

"Don't *'Joey'* me! I'm out there every night to pay off loans I took out six years ago, and when I'm not paying off those then I'm paying off my day-to-day upkeep and the rent my grandparents keep jacking up, and I'm always paying off everything, but I can't keep making it work if they take money I don't have!" My vision was blurring. "It's all payback and maintenance, and the only thing I have going into the future is the music, but they're going to take it—"

"Don't you dare wig out on me!" Even as I'd gotten more shrill, he'd gone deep, commanding. "I need you to keep it together. You're the one with the business sense. Stay grounded."

I closed my eyes. "But—"

"There isn't a 'but.' Quit freaking out on me!"

I fell silent, clutching the phone so tight it hurt. I couldn't let go.

"Don't be scared. That's what the lawyer wants. If you ever hear from her again, tell her she's supposed to talk to me. That's why people have fearless leaders, right? To handle nasty attorneys."

My heart banged so hard I thought it might quit. I tried taking a deep breath, but it caught. That woman, her voice, her disdain—

"Joey, you need to get calm."

"I know." That would have sounded better if my voice hadn't cracked mid-word. "But she was so angry."

"They're paid to act angry." His words were breezy. "Do you know how angry you could sound for half a million dollars? I mean," he added, "for fifty bucks an hour, you sound almost like a musician."

"And you almost sound like you're not a jerk."

He laughed out loud.

I rubbed my eyes. "Can your brother do that? Sound like a disgusted hellbeast scraping mud off his shoe?"

"Is that how she spoke to you?"

"Like I wasn't fit to answer her call."

"Well, she's not fit to rosin your bow. They study for years in law school just to sound nasty."

The memory of her voice felt like a punch to the gut. "She graduated top of her class."

"That doesn't mean she's classy. It's going to be okay." A pause. "We've got to respond to all these emails."

I frowned. "Tonight?"

"Well, tomorrow. I was already asleep. I don't know how you keep these hours."

"I need to. Besides, I don't teach violin to preschoolers at nine in the morning."

"When we get married," and Harrison sounded cheerful, "I'll want you coming to bed with me."

I sighed. "I'm not marrying you, Harrison."

By the time I got into pajamas, my brain had geared down. I fell asleep thinking about family reunions and Only Strings.

The next morning, Viv banged on my door way too early and strode into my kitchen before I could spring out of bed. "I'm taking milk for Zaden!"

You'd think Grandma would have figured out by now that Zaden wanted something other than skim. Well, for that matter, you'd think I'd have figured it out and started buying skim myself, but I hated the taste.

When I didn't hear my door slam, I came out to find her standing over the table, grimacing at the *Voice.*

"What?" I said.

No answer. I pushed past her to the coffee maker.

"Why are you in the paper?"

I blew at my bangs. "Where have you been, Viv? I'm in the paper all the time."

She went back downstairs, leaving the door open. I kicked it shut.

Five minutes later, I remembered she'd hijacked my milk, so I got dressed, poured black coffee, and went downstairs. As an afterthought, I grabbed the newspaper.

At the kitchen table, I found Grandma and my mother complaining about one of my great-aunts. I milked up the coffee and then waited, pulse pounding.

Grandma looked up. My voice came a little too high-pitched: "I wanted to show you that my quartet got into the paper."

Mom nodded. "You told us about that."

"This is a new article. That was about a wedding. This is just about us." I put it onto the table, but my mom was adding more sugar to her coffee. I edged it closer. "See, we've got a photo and everything."

Mom looked at Grandma. "It's so nice how she made that band with her goth friends."

I forced a smile. "It's not goth. They're concert blacks."

Grandma's eyes widened. "Is your group really doing that well?"

The disbelief on her face left me nauseated. "Well, yeah. This is a huge opportunity."

Mom shrugged. "What is this paper? I've never heard of it."

"Mom, it's the *Village Voice.*"

From the door, Viv called, "It's a free paper."

Mom nodded at her. "Oh. So not like a real paper."

No, only the number one entertainment newspaper in

New York City. If Viv had gotten into the *Voice*, Mom would have wallpapered my grandparents' living room with the article.

Grandma handed the paper back. "So...money isn't an issue for you?"

Great, was she about to jack up the rent again? "Money's an issue for everyone." I went to the door. "Hey, Mom, can you bring a copy home to Dad?"

Mom looked at the article, and she frowned. "You've been doing this for two years now. Shouldn't you be more...I don't know, successful?"

I said, "It takes time. You know that. Most weddings are booked fifteen months out, so we need to build a client base."

Mom shook her head. "I always thought you were the one who'd make it on your own. If you'd just gotten a real job, you wouldn't have to take money from men in the streets at night."

I totally needed to update my website bio: *Violist Joey Mikalos, goth strumpet of the tunnel.* "I prefer the jobs I have, thanks."

"You shouldn't be too proud to ask for help. Vivvy couldn't make it on her own, but you're just so stubborn." She pointed to the picture, then looked me right in the eyes, and for the first time it felt as if all her attention rested on me. "Is that the viola your father bought?"

I tried to sound smooth. "What do you think? I don't have a real job, remember. A new viola would cost tens of thousands of dollars."

I braced for the accusation sure to follow my non-denial, but instead she dropped the paper back onto the table. "Oh, I wouldn't know. All these instruments look the same."

To her they might, which was why my student viola sat on display while my grandfather's remained stuffed into the eaves.

She added, "Yeah, maybe you should bring a copy to your father."

And then she turned back to Grandma with more about her aunt. Dismissed. I walked out, leaving my milk behind.

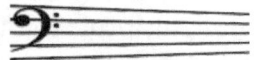

After practice, I parted ways with Josh at the door, but Shreya fell into step beside me. "How far are you going? I usually walk to 34th to get the F."

Ah, so she lived in Queens. "I'm going up to 32nd." And I messaged Dad that I was on my way.

As we walked uptown, Shreya said, "Why are you doing this? In my ignorance, I thought newspapers could be had in all parts of Manhattan."

I shrugged.

Shreya added, "And his office has no internet?"

I stared at the pavement. "Don't ask me to explain my parents."

It was odd being alone with Shreya. Normally practice ended and she took off, and we didn't hear from her again until next time. She wasn't on Facebook, hadn't provided a home phone number, told us nothing about her life. I'd never gone anywhere with her before.

Even the way we'd found her was bizarre. The night Peter left, Harrison with his typical insight realized that a string quartet with only one violinist is actually a "string trio," and, with equal insight, that we were screwed. He'd decided on the time-honored tactic of getting well-lit.

Three drinks later, he'd turned to the tall blue-haired Indian woman ordering a Long Island iced tea with a fake ID. He paid for her drink, saying, "I can play the violin."

That's not a bad pickup line, if you're wondering, and Harrison made himself look completely cute too. But Shreya only shrugged. "So can I. Thanks for the drink."

Not ready to give up, Harrison trailed her to a table and ten minutes later, because this was Manhattan, someone turned up a violin. Shreya made magic while Harrison stared. Then, dumbfounded, he exclaimed something to the effect of "Forget about sex—come join my quartet!"

That was us, thoroughly professional. I don't recommend recruiting that way, but Shreya sounded just as good when we were sober, and she seemed to think we'd do for now.

When we reached my dad's office, Shreya said, "I'll catch up."

I said, "You don't have to. I'm just going to drop this off."

Shreya said, "I thought maybe we'd get lunch. Do you have time?"

The response was automatic. "I have time, but no money."

She started. "Really? It's not Le Bernardin."

I ran through my budget, through the extra gigs we'd picked up. "Well, I guess."

"Then I'll catch up to you." And she went into Duane Reade while I headed inside.

The elevator took me to the ninth floor. In the greyest of grey waiting rooms, a secretary sat behind a tall desk with a potted tree towering on either side.

"I'm here for Zachary Mikalos."

The secretary glanced at her desk. "Do you have an appointment?"

"He's expecting me. I'm his daughter."

The secretary beamed. "Oh—Vivian! I'm sorry I didn't recognize you."

With a twinge in my throat, I said, "Actually, I'm Josephine."

A hesitation. The secretary dialed my father's extension, watching with suspicion, as if I were a rival executive assistant on a spy mission.

Shreya entered the lobby and took a seat. The secretary said, "I'll be with you in a moment," and Shreya said, "No rush."

After a long silence, the secretary cradled the phone. "He's not picking up. Was he expecting you?"

I hated that office, the grey-tinted windows, the over-stuffed low-backed couches, the coffee table with magazines scattered artfully across the glossy surface. I wanted to alphabetize them, arrange them so you could see all the titles at the same time.

I said, "Can you check again?"

She dialed a different number and asked where my father was, as his daughter "Josephine" was in the lobby.

Shreya wore a poker face.

The secretary hung up. "He's stepped out to lunch. He'll return in an hour."

"I'll leave something for him."

She pointed down the hall. "Third office on the left."

The secretary turned to Shreya, who stood and said, "I'm with her." She accompanied me like the Swiss Guard, both of us carrying instrument cases on straps over our shoulders. We should have joined the Mafia.

In my father's office, I took an extra fifteen seconds to fold back the page so our faces showed.

Shreya studied the framed photos. My mother. My mom and dad together. My sister. My dad and Zaden at Yankee Stadium. My dad and Zaden out somewhere in nature.

"You've got a nephew? He's a cutie." She glanced over the wall again but didn't need to say the obvious. Instead she said, "Your sister looks like your mom. She's older than you or younger?"

"One year older." I shrugged. "Irish twins."

We exited the sarcophagus-silent office, the secretary's eyes boring into my back.

Out on the street, Shreya said, "This is going to drive me nuts. Are you adopted? No, wait, you have your father's DNA because you look like your grandfather. Were you disowned?"

I folded my arms over my chest. "Maybe I shouldn't stay for lunch."

She looked me right in the eye. "No, you should. It's like a block away."

I trailed her to a hole-in-the-wall Thai restaurant where a server greeted her by name. We barely glanced at the menu before ordering.

Shreya leaned forward, her voice low. She didn't have to bother: we were the only ones there. "Are you the red-headed step-child?"

"Other than not being red-headed and not a step-kid." I traced a fingertip over my paper placemat with its indecipherable writing. "I was a hateful little kid. They never got over that."

Shreya scrutinized me, and I shrank back as if she'd see right through me. "What did you do? Set fires?"

And I couldn't think how to tell her—the thousand ways I never measured up, how I was selfish and how disappointed everyone always was. You don't need to set fires to be a rotten kid.

But to say it, when she dealt with me on a regular basis and could see for herself.... When I already had enough people who would never forgive me for everything.... So instead I said, "My sister needs them more."

Shreya squinted. "She's disabled?"

"No, but she needed them to pay for college first, and that meant there wasn't money for me to go to Columbia."

Shreya nodded. "And—?"

"Well, she left college to have the kid, so they needed to support her. When I turned eighteen, they said the kid needed my room, so I turned my grandparents' attic into an apartment and got a part-time job to pay rent."

Shreya's eyes widened. "Are you fucking kidding me?"

I shrugged. "That's what family does, right?"

She drew back. "You're not their family?"

I nodded. "Of course I'm family. That's why I had to help."

And yes, I was family. There had been that one day, the day I'd come home to find Mom sobbing at the kitchen table. "What's wrong?" I'd said, and she'd told me to sit, and made me tea, and said Viv was pregnant and she was so upset that

Viv was going to move in with the guy and try to make it on her own ("As if," she sniffed)—and then she'd hugged me. It was the first time in...in like forever, but she'd hugged me and said I'd always been such a good girl and she should have known I'd never disappoint her. For two days I'd walked on air, and Mom gave me gifts and told me secrets and asked mine, and on the third day I'd come home to find Viv and Mom at the table, all friends again. Mom had talked her into staying home, and she'd help raise the baby.

That was that. No more tea. No more secrets. The next year Dad had a baby boy to take to ball games and give sports toys, and everyone told me afterward how raising Zaden was "so good" for him.

Shreya said, "I think you should be pissed."

I bit my lip. "Look, I don't know. It's not like anyone trains you to be a parent."

Her voice rose. "I'm not a parent, and even I know you don't kick out one kid because another got knocked up!"

I shrank into my chair, but then our food arrived. I focused on my pad thai. It had firm texture, without the cloying sweetness of the pad thai in the discount freezer at Key Food. God, I liked it. And I didn't deserve it because this was what, ten bucks for one meal?

Shreya still looked grim. "Have your parents ever heard you play?"

"You want them to gate-crash someone's wedding?"

"But at recitals?"

I stared at the scar on my palm. It curved along the joint of my thumb, mimicking a lifeline. "It didn't make sense to sit for two hours just to hear me for five minutes playing something they heard at home." I bit my lip. "They'd come if it was a concert."

"Since when is a recital not a concert?" Shreya asked. "My hot-dog-selling father and my mother who's up at four AM making coffee both took the time to come to clubs and recitals. No one told them they had to. You know why?

Because they're *parents*. My parents sat through three hours of the Easter Vigil to watch me get baptized into a faith they don't believe—and your father couldn't delay lunch for ten minutes?"

I stared at my lap, my head down so she couldn't see me fighting not to tear up.

She said, "If you want some advice—"

"I don't!" Did she get a psychology degree all of a sudden? First she started an improvement project on Josh, and now on me? "Fine, you totally psychoanalyzed me. My parents are evil."

Then I couldn't talk anymore. I couldn't look up without her seeing how upset I was, and if she did, what would happen? She'd be just as pissed at me as everyone else.

But if she kept going— My mother hated the way I played, always made me mute the viola and said there weren't any world-class violists and it pained her to see me making a fool of myself, and I was a hypocrite to want attention. We had that damned CD, but I couldn't bear to listen because when it played, I heard my mother: embarrassed. I embarrassed her by being me.

Whenever I played, I played for strangers. It was better that way.

Shreya of all people should know how I sounded. Once I admitted it, it became an open secret. And she'd ask Harrison why he kept me, and he'd say he was wondering that himself, and poof, I'd be out.

Shreya sounded small. "I'm sorry. I shouldn't have said that."

I forced myself to take a bite, chew, and swallow. It was the same pad thai, but I was eating rubber bands.

She said, "They're your parents. I don't know the whole story."

My fist clenched in my lap. "No, you don't, and the fact that your life is perfect doesn't give you the right to go around judging mine."

Shreya choked. "My life is perfect?"

I nodded. "You've got everything. You just told me your parents think you hung the moon."

She opened her hands. "And? Let's see, you have the college education and the day job with medical benefits and a huge history with Josh and Harrison that I can't even touch."

I tilted my head. "Didn't you go to college?"

She shook her head. "I skipped college to be the violinist in a garage band."

My eyes widened. "Seriously? What does a violinist do in a rock band?"

She spread her hands. "Haven't you heard of the Dave Matthews Band? Kansas? 10,000 Maniacs? We made it sound awesome. The guitarist would have a solo, the drummer would have a go at it, and then I'd give them a solo to rattle the windows. I guess you'd call it a *cadenza*." She leaned into the word, and I offered a smile. "We did pretty good for a while."

I said, "Okay, so a violinist belongs in a rock band. Your parents didn't have a shit-fit?"

"Of course they did, but I didn't exactly give them a choice."

"My mother would have killed me." I shook my head. "Why are you telling me this?"

She leaned forward. "You said my life was perfect. But the band broke up, and it was the most painful, unnecessary, nasty thing I'd ever gone through."

I glared out the window, wondering whether they equaled out. Being an orphan versus being a violinist without a band. "You said bands are like family."

Shreya said, "Aren't we? Wouldn't it hurt like hell if we broke up?"

"Point." I frowned. "So what broke you up?"

"What breaks up any group? People doing shit to each other they'd never do to a stranger." Her words were angry, but her mouth trembled. "Eventually everyone's pissed at everyone else, and no one wants to meet in the middle." She looked so desolate. "You look for your cue and he says, 'What's your problem?' and when you don't look, he says, 'Just come in whenever you want, then.'"

I thought of Harrison saying, *It never ends well.* "What caused it?"

She flinched. "It doesn't matter."

"It does matter. You were the one who started this pissing contest about whether your life gave you permission to tell me how fucked up mine is."

"That's not what I said, and I'm not talking about your life." She looked up. "But I hate seeing you get walked all over."

"Like you're saving Josh from himself?"

"Telling him it's okay to be who he is," she said. "Why did no one ever say that before?"

My eyes narrowed. "So now I'm a lousy friend too?"

"Stop it!" Shreya's eyes were wide. "I apologized for messing in your family business, so quit taking everything so personally. It's not about you. And the last thing I want is for the quartet to break up because we went out for pad thai." She bit her lip. "I've been trying very hard with our group to make sure we don't have the same problems my other group had."

I frowned. "Yeah, because you can totally stop people from ever fighting again. Hey, World Peace, Shreya called— it's time!"

"As if. I can't even stop you from fighting with me, and I already told you I'm sorry." She drew half a breath, then grimaced. It was a look Josh got when someone mocked his stutter. "But the things that happened to us—I will not let them happen again."

I didn't respond. Finally she said, "Are you going to be mad forever?"

"No." I tried to eat. It started having taste again. "Just don't meddle."

"Done." She looked up. "What I told you about my band, would you mind not telling the guys?"

I ran my finger around the rim of my glass. "You realize if it was something big, if there's a public record—those attorneys might dig it up."

"There's no public record." Shreya shredded her napkin into little pieces. "It's just not something the guys need to know."

TWELVE

Tuesday was my day off, so I played until an alarm told me I needed to quit now, no really this time, and then cleaned. When I dropped off the rent check, I found my sister and her son chowing down on Grandpa's chocolate cherry chunk ice cream while the TV blared. Grandma and Grandpa weren't home, so I tucked the envelope in with their mail and went back upstairs.

"You should have some," Viv called after me. "I never got why you didn't eat every meal with Grandma and Grandpa. I certainly will."

"I'll keep that in mind." Even back in college they'd seldom fed me. They cooked for two because they'd been doing that for the past twenty-five years.

Besides, whenever Grandma did invite me, she wanted to complain about my mother. I'd listen and offer advice or an explanation while she rehashed some drama, and Grandpa kept his hearing aid turned off. Later I'd ask for an update and learn we'd moved to a new drama, and then Grandma would keep doing whatever she'd done for the past fifty years. I don't care how much chicken cost: it wasn't worth the price.

My phone buzzed with a text from Josh. "Are you around to IM?"

I opened up chat and found Josh online. "What's up?"

I'd figured because he buzzed me, he'd be ready, but it took so long. Had he crashed the taxi and needed me at the hospital?

Then his text appeared: "Since you're off tonight, do you want to go out for our birthdays?"

Oh, right. Our birthdays were a week apart, and for the last couple of years we'd done something together, kind of like when he brought cupcakes to school and said they were for my birthday too. It still felt like a novelty. I wrote back, "Coffee?"

A pause, and then, "How about dinner?"

I typed, "I don't know if I can." I added, "Money."

While the chat screen said he was typing, my mind raced through my checkbook register. I'd eaten lunch with Shreya. But we'd just been paid. The punctual groom of the late bride had coughed up a check (complete with a thank-you) and the corporate gig had paid right on time. There was money enough to cover dinner. It just felt wrong to blow a week's grocery money on one meal.

On the other hand, it was my birthday, and I ought to eat something. I typed, "Yeah, let's do that."

Josh's reply appeared simultaneous with mine, "I'll pick up the tab."

I replied, "Hah. Happy birthday, pay up." Smirking as I hit enter, I followed up with, "There's three checks clearing the bank. I'll make it work."

We figured out a place (a pizza shop with a restaurant in back) and a time (five-thirty) and when I asked if I should show up with decorative paper and a ribbon in my hair, he replied, "Just as long as you're present." Josh, making puns. All was good.

He was stuttering a lot when we met. Unable to look at me, he said it was because of the cold weather. I found myself looking away too, as if my silence could prevent him from speaking.

As we looked over the menu, I said, "So...did you want me to order for you?"

He snapped, "No." I flinched, and he apologized. "I'm just t-tense."

Tense? Why bother? Dinner at this place was as casual as you could get, with paper "tablecloths" setting the tone. And true to form, by the time our lasagna arrived, Josh and I were drawing on the table-top as if we'd never left first grade.

The waiter must have thought us insane, Josh because he stuttered and me because I was with him, but I forced myself not to cringe when Josh blinked or stammered. I'd never see this waiter again, and if he thought we were both mentally ill, well, what could I do?

Anyway, the stutter paled in comparison to Josh drawing a birthday cake in the middle of the table. He started putting forty-eight candles on it. "For both of us."

Quite an undertaking. "Should I set it on fire and make a wish?"

He shook his head without looking away from the candle-making ceremony. "Wait until www-we have a full p-pitcher of www-water."

Our meals were unremarkable, but I wanted to keep the paper with Josh's drawing of a cello plus a smiling face. His scribble of a cello and a viola surrounded by notes (which I amused myself by trying to read) and another scribble of hedgehogs nibbling tiny mites in my viola bow.

His hedgehogs were circles with spikes and a pointy face. I frowned. "When it comes to being an artist, you're a great cellist."

He twisted in his chair, pulled something from his coat pocket, and handed it to me. A box, wrapped in shiny red paper.

"But we don't do that!" I exclaimed. "I didn't get you anything."

Josh said, "I-i-i-it's not an eee-even exchange kind of thing." He forced a smile. "We c-could sw-wap twenties if you prefer."

Cheeks aflame, I opened the paper to find the Beethoven Duet for Viola and Cello in E-flat, sometimes called the *Eyeglasses Duo,* paired with the Hindemith duet for viola and cello. "Oh, thank you!" I hugged him. He smelled like cologne and Irish Spring soap.

He seemed flustered, so I focused on the CD. "You think these guys play better than us?"

He smiled. "How c-c-c-could they? We're pros."

At the end of the meal, I suggested bringing dessert home. Josh left a huge tip, and we trekked to the bakery to get a birthday something.

In line, I found myself following the radio and transposing the pop song into a violin solo. I'd begun doing that for the usually-hilarious results. This time, though, as I heard the opening of "Head Over Heels," I stiffened.

Josh frowned at me.

"Listen."

I could see him doing the mental arrangement as he listened. "It could be done," he said. "C-c-c-c-c—" He stopped, took a gasping breath, tried again and this time he blocked. I backed half a step away and looked out the window. He closed his eyes, and finally he forced it: "Could you c-c-c-ome back to my plll—"

I'd never told him how it felt watching him fight to finish a sentence when I knew what he was trying to ask, when others would turn and wonder what was his problem, and when I knew I could spare us both by interrupting and answering yes.

He switched words to "—apartment and work on it with me?"

My skin crawled as the baker stopped tying a box with bakery string to stare. With my voice a little too low, I said, "Sure—sounds great. I'll need to grab my viola."

The line moved to the bakery counter, and we selected slices of cheesecake. Josh got a cannoli for his father, working hard to get out those initial C sounds. Because Josh had picked up the check at the restaurant, I paid for dessert, struggling to ignore both the price and the heat in my cheeks.

Back at home, I dashed upstairs for my instrument, then refilled the cat food, amusing Josh by talking to the suddenly-appearing consumer of said food. The cat wore a death-eating glare: *Do not touch my kibble, tall one.*

Josh said, "He's got attitude."

I smirked. "Enough for all three of us."

"Has he g-got a name?"

By now it was a stock response. "What's the point of naming something that doesn't answer?" I touched his arm. "Let's go!"

On the bus, we discussed the parts. We practically ran the last block to his apartment and up the stairs. While I petted the hedgehogs in their cage and ended up getting quill-stabs, he downloaded the song from iTunes. A few minutes later, he had his cello between his knees, and we tuned to each other.

He decided what key it was and began picking out notes, then repeated them a few times. We back-and-forthed about what the keyboard was actually playing. It sounded weird in the cello's deep tones. Weird, but not bad.

He opened Sibelius and set down a framework of notes as a guideline.

Standing so I could see over his shoulder, I tried the guitar part. I missed horribly the first time, and we both flinched. He started over, and this time I nailed the opening.

"Good," he said. "I thought I was going to get a nnn-nosebleed."

"Hush, you." By now we could play something that resembled harmony, although the opening sounded distorted. Josh smiled as he played. I loved watching him do that, as if he'd escaped the world the same way I did.

"This will sound awesome." I leaned over his shoulder to get a better look at the screen, and he turned toward me. "Oh, that's what I'm doing wrong." I tried again, experimenting with a different position. "I think I can do it."

I counted us to start, and we took it slowly. The two lower voices of the quartet gave the passage a richness you didn't get with the violins.

When we stopped, I caught him looking up at me, his eyes alive, his smile broad.

My heart raced. "What?"

He looked away. "You're a good violist."

I pivoted away, because I wanted to believe he really believed that I was an equal partner in our group. I wasn't as good as him. I knew that, but he'd never hurt my feelings. So I only said, "Thanks. You're a good cellist." I pulled over a chair and sat near him, but when the silence went too long, I broke it. "You should get this arranged. It'll sound awesome on the violin."

Josh's mouth tightened. "I'm tired of Harr-rison getting all the good things."

I leaned forward. "First violin tends to hog all the cool stuff in a string quartet."

Josh didn't reply.

I picked up my viola, and after a hesitation, Josh joined me.

THIRTEEN

The next morning, I awakened to the creak of my apartment door.

Next thing I knew, my mom was in the kitchen. I hauled myself to my bedroom door. "What are you doing?"

"I'm visiting. Can't a mother see her daughter?" She went past me to my living room and studied the decoy viola.

As her gaze fell on it, I recoiled: when I'd staggered in last night, I hadn't hidden my grandfather's. It was in my bedroom. Right in front of my dresser.

"I need to get dressed." I fled to my room, slammed the door, and slid the viola under the bed.

No, no good. She'd look there. I shoved it into the dresser and piled underwear over the case, then pulled on some clothes. I came back out to find her looking in my closet.

Viv and Zaden had followed. "You should have spruced this place up," Viv said. "It's a pit."

I glared at her. "Good thing you're not living here."

Mom said, "I could have done wonders with these rooms."

Yeah, for her clients. "What do you want?"

"Oh, don't tell me you've turned into one of those girls who wants nothing to do with her own mother." Mom gave a pained sigh. "Come downstairs and let's catch up."

My mother hadn't "caught up" with me for two

presidential administrations. Maybe she'd had a fight with Dad and wanted to shore up an ally. But no, I'd bet Mom wanted me downstairs so she could prowl in peace.

Viv took my milk and turned on her toes. "I'll just grab this for Zaden."

Mom said, "You know, your grandmother's home is spotless. I've been supportive of your goth lifestyle, but is it really necessary to be a slob?"

My blood pressure soared. I could feel it in my ears.

She took my hand. "See? You even bite your nails."

I pulled back. "You have to keep your nails short to play viola."

"Oh, please don't lie just because you're ashamed. You always used to bite your nails." Mom sneaked a glance in my bedroom. "If you took a little pride in yourself, maybe you'd meet a decent man. Remember when all you had was that nice brain-damaged boy?"

I went numb, no floor under my feet. Everything was liquid.

Viv called upstairs that the coffee was ready. Mom left, saying to come and chat, and in her wake I felt like someone the newscast interviews after a tornado. *Tell me, how did it feel when the winds came?*

I went to my decoy viola. Moved, but not opened.

That nice brain-damaged boy?

Voices floated up the stairwell, helium balloons detached from their strings. My grandfather's viola used to sound that way, a voice wandering the walls until it lost all meaning and only let you know its presence with a muffled indistinction.

That was a comfort. This? This was—an infestation.

My eyes drifted toward my dresser, and two thoughts collided like cars rear-ending at an intersection.

First, that I needed to play right now.

And second, that my mother would have taken my viola.

If I hadn't been here right now, I'd never have seen it again. She'd have taken it and pawned it because it belonged to her by whatever logic she felt like using. Maybe someday I could replace it, but it wouldn't be Grandpa's.

In a flash, I pulled on my jacket and boots, then slung my grandfather's viola over my back. My keys and my cell phone went into my purse along with my wallet. And then, footsteps masked by their voices, I locked my door (futile) and sneaked to the street.

Around the corner, I ducked into the first store, a Hallmark, and surrounded by pastel cardstock for strangers to tell strangers how special they were, I struggled to get my bearings. I could go to the library.

But being alone right now—no. I pulled out my phone to dial *that nice brain-damaged boy.*

Immediately I hung up. I stood, phone in hand, eyes closed.

Damn it all. I hated that my mother broke into my apartment. I hated how she forgot I existed until she wanted something, and then I only wished she'd forget me entirely. I hated being an orphan while my parents were both alive. I hated it all.

I left the greeting cards and took the subway. Harrison taught all morning on weekends, and he'd keep my viola if I asked.

Even with the car pretty much to myself, I clutched my viola against my chest. As quickly as I'd left, I hadn't grabbed a book, so it was just me staring at a wall full of hemorrhoid removal ads. The rocking motion soothed, and I wished the world would disappear into the subway sound.

Half an hour ago, I was still sleeping. Damn it.

I let myself into Harrison's apartment to find a familiar scene: a girl by the windows, her half-size creeping note by note through a minuet from Suzuki Method 1, Harrison watching her bow technique, and a parent sitting on the couch. A parent who cared.

When she finished, Harrison circled one of the notes with a pencil, speaking animatedly about the things the student did right (according to him, plenty) and then suggesting changes.

That done, he turned to me. "Ah, my lovely bride!"

As the mother's head swept up, I said, "I'm not marrying you, Harrison."

"Oh, right. I keep forgetting," he said, and the girl giggled, "How could you forget that?"

He continued the lesson while I sat beside the fishtank. Harrison used the tank as a room divider, and the thing was huge. He'd told me all the fish in it once upon a time: discus fish, angel fish, German blue rams, a school of rummy nose tetras, and one zebra pleco to rule them all. None of it made sense to me, but I liked the bubbly sound of the filter.

Drinking the coffee I picked up on my walk from the subway, I absorbed his encouragement, the child's enthusiasm, his observations. Oh, those early lessons, the trepidation of a new technique followed by the triumph of mastering it. The days when, if only I practiced enough and learned enough, I'd play solos at Carnegie Hall and my parents would sit in the front row.

Ten minutes later, the lesson ended. The next student arrived, and the room busied with the sounds of setup and cleanup.

I stood as Harrison came over.

"I didn't expect you today," he said in a low voice. "Not that I mind, but did I forget something?"

"I had to leave my apartment. Visitors." I stared at the floor. "If I stay here—"

I couldn't keep going.

Harrison's eyebrows raised. "If you stay here...will I sell you into slavery? Will I make you teach?"

I forced out, "Will you not ask any questions?"

His face softened. "Sure. You might want to hang out in the bedroom, though. I have one more student after this, and it gets noisy."

That's how I ended up in a room I'd avoided for two years,

set up with a TV remote and an invitation to watch anything I liked. Yes, he had two TVs in a one-bedroom apartment, with an assortment of exploding-thing movies and some sitcoms on DVD. He wasn't a bookish person, but he had a few (two-thirds of them violin technique). There was also another resident: a single gaudy fish in a tank smaller than a bathroom bucket, its fins so drapey I wondered how it could swim at all. That hadn't been here last time. He'd made his bed and no laundry was in evidence, clean or dirty.

Then, before I'd decided what to do, I heard the sweetest sound in the world: Harrison tuned his student's violin. I couldn't help smiling as I remembered my grandfather tuning my viola long after I could tune it myself. That familiar twang, then the repeated smaller twangs up or down, then two strings bowed together for a perfect fifth, the whole process repeated three times until the instrument answered as it should, then everything rechecked (because invariably one string's adjustment threw another out of whack) and at last four bold bow-strokes before the instructor handed it back with the classic, "Show me what you've been doing."

I finished my coffee, then curled up on the bed, viola case in my arms, to stare out the window.

I didn't want to disrupt the lesson. But I wanted to play. I opened the case and moved aside the blanket to rest my hand on my prize, my purpose embodied in one and a half pounds of wood. *It's okay, Woody. We'll get through this.*

Eventually I scanned a hundred channels until I found a comedy I'd watched as a kid, the only thing that didn't make me want to vomit. With it playing, I stared at the fish in its tiny tank, swimming around its smooth river rocks and through a shattered urn in a glass apartment, never anywhere to hide and always completely alone. There were dozens of fish in the living room tank. Here was only one, so beautiful and so hidden.

Eventually the door opened, Harrison appeared, and I realized the apartment had gone silent. "Come on. I'll buy you lunch."

In the living room, he pointed to my voila. "That can stay. I won't make you sing for your supper."

Embarrassed, I locked the viola in the closet with Harrison's violins and Josh's practice cello. Ten minutes later, we sat half a block away in a Japanese restaurant, the same place he'd taken me the night before we broke up. Harrison recommended a platter of sushi to split.

I felt light-headed. I hadn't eaten anything today.

"I love these things." Harrison pulled apart his disposable chopsticks with a balsa-wood snap. "Okay, talk to me."

I shook my head.

He leaned forward, eyebrows arched. "You hid out in my apartment, watching TV of all things, acting like your life savings was in your viola case. Unless you're fleeing a mad scientist who wants to finish a personality transplant, I'm at a loss."

I forced a smile. "Am I that bad?"

"You're just so..." He paused. "I hoped if I put food into you, you'd feel better, but now I'm wondering."

I looked out at the street.

"The legal situation seems scary, but remember, sounding scary is their job the same way playing wrong notes in the low register is your job."

"It's not the lawyers." I couldn't focus. "I wasn't even thinking about them."

Dead silence. Finally, "Why did your viola come with you?"

"I didn't trust the people Grandma had over."

Harrison recoiled. "They'd damage it?"

"They'd take it."

"Lock your apartment!"

I bit my lip. "Grandma gives them the key."

His eyes widened. "Change the locks!"

Gaping, I wrenched my gaze inside. "My grandparents would flip."

He looked venomous. "Every landlord has to give reasonable notice before anyone enters."

Son of a lawyer. "Well, mine doesn't, and they'd steal my viola."

"That's when you call the police and have them get it back."

I flinched. "But they're relatives."

He rolled his eyes. "Oh, and relatives never steal from anyone?"

For an instant, the world fuzzed, and my ears rang.

Harrison grabbed my hand. "Are you okay?"

I whispered, "I stole it first."

He leaned forward. "Say that again?"

"I stole it. My grandfather died, and I knew my mother would never let me have it. But—it was his. So— It was the middle of the night—the day he died—and I still had the key, so I took the viola from his house, and I hid it."

Harrison frowned at me. "It wasn't yours?"

My mouth twitched. "He willed it to me, but my father was the executor, and he said I couldn't take anything until the estate was settled. I went in and got it anyhow."

Harrison clutched my hand so tight it hurt. "Joey, be clear here: your grandfather left it to you in the will?"

I nodded. "I told my parents he'd sold it to pay his doctor. But I stole it."

"You can't steal something that's yours."

He released my hand, and suddenly I could breathe. "What?"

"Your grandfather gave it to you. What do you think a will is? It's a list of gifts to be given on condition of someone's death. He gave you a gift, and you claimed it. How is that theft?"

I blinked, then whispered, "Really?"

"Really. You've lived with that guilt for how long? Well, I absolve you." Even as my brain whirled, he cocked his head. "Did he leave you anything else?"

"Some money." Harrison would have considered it pocket change, but Grandpa didn't have much.

Harrison only said, "Did you get it?"

I looked at my lap. Pocket change to Harrison would still have been a lot for me. Maybe four months' rent.

"I figured as much. You were right to take the viola. And if your parents take it from you, you produce that will for the police."

"I—" My eyes stung. "Everyone would hate me."

"So let's see." His eyes fiercened. "Your parents would steal your viola, and 'everyone' would blame you for wanting it back?"

"Because I'd be making trouble."

"No, they'd have made the trouble, and if they got arrested, tough luck. Why is that so hard to see?"

I blinked hard.

The waiter arrived with the soup. As he departed, Harrison said, "Do you have renter's insurance? Get it. It's something like ten bucks a month. I'll even spot you for it because a string quartet needs a viola." His eyes gleamed. "Although we could upgrade you to a chainsaw."

I smiled despite myself. "The difference between a chainsaw and a viola is that in a pinch, you can use a chainsaw in a string quartet."

He looked disappointed. "You heard that one too?"

"And," I added, "you can tune the chainsaw."

"I thought you could tune a lawn mower." He paid attention to his soup for a while, then looked up. "Okay. First, get renter's insurance. Then, when you file a claim for a viola, they'll wonder why they're shelling out twenty grand and do some investigating. Then your relatives can hate the insurance company."

Did Harrison have x-ray vision? His gaze was that relentless. "I'd have to file a police report. My family would still hate me."

His eyes clouded. "Look, your parents may be your

relatives, but you're talking about the antithesis of family. Anyone who would invade your apartment and steal your livelihood isn't family. And your dad, who didn't properly execute his own father's estate? Worthless as a father, and definitely not family. Neither, for that matter, are grandparents who charge rent while also requiring the tenant to clean. What are you? Cinderella?"

I recoiled. "My grandparents need me!"

Harrison looked unconvinced. "They go to a bowling league. They can push a vacuum cleaner."

I shook my head. "But they're all I've got."

"They're not all you've got!" He slammed his hand onto the table so hard that other diners turned. "They treat you well when they like what you're doing. Meanwhile we're not related, but we've got each other's backs even when we're driving each other crazy. That's what family does."

The soup bowls were cleared. The sushi arrived. My pulse slowed. People returned to their own food.

Harrison said, "My dad told me, 'Pick your family.'"

Yeah, because that was totally possible. "You can't choose your family."

"I had an aunt who pitched a fit whenever anyone disagreed with her. Four times a year she'd threaten my grandparents they'd never see the grandkids again, claim she didn't remember whatever nasty things she'd done, and flounce out. A month later she'd return as if nothing happened. Dad got tired of the show, so he cut her off. Even my grandparents aren't allowed to talk to him about her."

Was he really saying— "You want me to cut off my parents?"

"It was the best decision he ever made." Harrison pointed his chopsticks at me. "Pick your family."

I looked at my lap.

"You choose who you marry, right? That's the center of the family." Harrison gave a wolfish grin. "When you marry me, we'll start our own family."

"Thanks," I said, and then, "but I'm not marrying you."

He chuckled. "You hesitated that time."

My head swam. "But—cutting them off— My uncle did that. Uncle Bill and my aunt just walked out of my grandmother's one Thanksgiving. They—" I closed my eyes. "But that's selfish, isn't it? Doesn't family mean you can count on them?"

That's what Grandma said afterward. And Mom. Angry, always angry.

"You should be able to count on them," Harrison said. "My point is, it's not automatic. Take your mother. Does she treat you like family?"

Cold all over, I stopped eating.

"But Josh—does he treat you like family?"

Despite everything. Although I guess I had treated him the way my family treated me.

"My dad's right." Harrison was a judge rendering a verdict. "You can pick your family."

I pushed at a piece of sushi. "I figured friends were Fate's apology for our families."

He shook. "Except those people you chose as friends may have good families themselves."

When the check arrived, Harrison took it. "I invited you. In my world, the host pays."

I'd crashed his apartment, but somehow he'd invited me. "Thank you."

As Harrison slid his gold card into the plastic folder, he said, "Oh, I totally forgot! What do you think about performing at a music festival?"

What did I think? I thought, if I played at a music festival, that was a concert. Recitals had too many beginner students, and weddings were by invitation, but a festival—my parents would come.

With a flatness that belied my pounding heart, I said, "How would we manage that?"

"The recent publicity might score us an invite to one of

the summertime classical festivals. Shreya's for it, Josh too, so that leaves you."

I said, "Do they pay?"

He shrugged. "Not much."

As the waiter took the credit card, I said, "If we can wrangle an invite. And not just for exposure, because I'm not giving them slave labor. And not if we're already booked."

"I'm glad you're so flexible," Harrison deadpanned. "I'm eyeing one in Westchester and one in Poughkeepsie. I'll drop them an email. If they say no, we're no worse off."

And if they said yes, heaven only knew what Harrison would charge for the world-famous-performed-at-the-whatever-festival Boroughs String Quartet. But my parents might come. They'd hear us play.

The waiter returned. Harrison filled in the tip, signed it. He frowned, and numbers flashed in his eyes as he recalculated. I knew him well enough that if anything, he'd revise the tip upward. Sure enough, he did.

Out on the street, Harrison said, "Come back upstairs."

I shook my head. "I need to head home. I'm working tonight."

"Then I'll walk you to the station." Harrison's eyes were sad. "I'll keep the viola safe so you won't have to worry."

We walked three blocks in silence before stopping at the stairwell. I said, "It's probably a home-grown viola, you know. Not worth five figures."

"Regardless." His face tightened, his brows inverting. "I wish I could do something for you."

And then in a motion, he kissed me. My muscles melted, and with my eyes closed I inhaled the spice of him and pulled the warmth of him against me even as heat flushed through my body. I buried my hands in his hair. His arms, so strong. He smelled so good.

In the next second we both came to our senses and recoiled, eyes wide, breathing sharply in the chill.

"That wasn't professional!" I exclaimed even as Harrison

said, "I'm— I just—" He shook his head, like Josh clearing a block. "I didn't realize how hard it would be."

I couldn't tell whether he was going to back away or try again, but he stayed frozen, his eyes rooted to my face as if awaiting permission. Or a scolding. And as my heart hammered, I didn't know which I'd choose. Break his heart—or finish breaking my own.

"I'm sorry." He shifted aside, then repeated, "I'm sorry."

"Don't do that again!" I could barely see because of the wind, and all I wanted was to run. Leave behind my quartet, my past, my family, and the embarrassment of being not-quite-good-enough to be his girlfriend, but also not quite lousy enough to forget. "You told me it would destroy everything, and there's already enough destruction." He looked stricken. I tore my gaze from him. "Don't do that to me. Just—don't."

When he made some kind of affirmative motion, I fled into the subway.

FOURTEEN

Monday morning I made sure to arrive last, but even so, I hesitated before turning Harrison's doorknob.

Fortunately, the first thing I did on entering was burst out laughing: he'd secured my viola case to the couch with a Kryptonite lock through the handle and a bicycle chain around the coffee table.

Standing, Harrison laid a hand over his heart. "By God, Joey, your viola was safe with me!"

Shaking not just with laughter but with relief, I couldn't even unzip my jacket. It was okay: yesterday was just a glaring lapse in professionalism. Today we'd be professional again.

Harrison rolled his eyes. "Josh, go undress her. We need to get started."

Jerk.

Josh actually moved toward me. I waved him off. "No, really, I can manage."

As I stashed my hat and gloves in the sleeve, Josh lifted the jacket from my hands. Low-voiced, he said, "Wh-wh-wh—" He stopped. ""Wh-why is your viii-ola here?"

I looked at the carpet. "Harrison was keeping it safe."

Frowning, Josh took a step backward.

Harrison said, "Someone was looking for a five-finger discount."

Shreya crouched on the carpet, and a moment later she had the viola in her hand, the case open but still chained up. "Thank heaven for you, Harrison, safeguarding her most precious possession."

Josh said, "Viv?"

I shook my head. "Mom."

He sighed as he hung up my jacket.

Taking my viola from Shreya, I said, "I probably overreacted."

"If you could believe that at all, I doubt it was an overreaction." Shreya squinted at me. "What happened?"

I shot Harrison a helpless look.

"Oh, that reminds me!" Our fearless leader tossed Josh something off the bookshelf: a plastic package containing a locking doorknob and a set of keys. "Install this for her. She said she couldn't."

I snatched it from Josh's hands. "I know how to turn a screwdriver. It would be a bad move politically."

Josh followed me to the stands. "I www-would have kept it s-s-s-safe for you."

I met his eyes, but I couldn't very well say, *I started to dial your number, but—*

Josh said, "I was c-closer."

I said, "I'd pestered you late enough on Saturday night, and it was ridiculously early. You were probably still sleeping."

He accepted the lie. Great. Dig the hole even deeper.

Harrison, who never put down a shovel if he could help it, then handed me a key. "And this is so you can visit your viola whenever you want."

I blinked. "But—" Oh no, maybe we weren't being professional after all. "Um, thanks?"

"I've wanted one of you to have it for a while anyhow, in case you get here and I'm out." In two years, that had happened once. We'd waited five minutes. "You're the logical choice, since you'll need one after we get married."

I said, "I'm not marrying you. But thanks."

Josh, on the other hand, sounded like an arctic blast. "I don't get one so I can visit my cello?"

I tensed, but Harrison made puppy-dog eyes. "Jealous? I can make another copy if you want, but your good cello is home and I have the practice one. She's got it reversed." And then, without waiting for an answer, Harrison said, "Oh, about the CD, I have the studio reserved for Thursday. Show up there instead of here."

As if this wasn't enough of a trainwreck. Damn, damn, damn. We were going through with it. I busied myself sliding his key onto my key ring.

Shreya said, "That stuff we're recording? Are we sure we can use any of it?"

"We've got the rights to three songs."

I said, "Have we heard any more from the lawyer?"

Harrison glanced toward me, uneasy, then back to Shreya and Josh. "You won't hear from her again."

I cocked my head. "Your brother is handling things?"

Harrison grinned. "Joey, don't you know how a viola is like a lawsuit?" He waited a beat. "Everyone is happiest when the case is closed."

I said, "They dropped it?"

Harrison said, "Just don't worry. The *Voice* has lawyers getting rich off this stuff. With any luck, it's over."

That sounded strange, but before I protested, he pulled out his music. "Come on. We're string players, not attorneys."

Woody wouldn't tune, viola-esque punishment for not playing yesterday. Harrison scoffed until it wouldn't tune for Josh either. Finally I took the viola aside and explained about my mother. And whether it wanted attention, or whether my touch had warmed it, afterward it held its tuning.

When practice ended, Josh called his father to swap the taxi while I looked at the lock. Changing it would take five minutes. Dealing with the fallout, five hundred years.

As Josh shut his phone, I said to Harrison, "Josh and I worked on another fusion this Saturday."

Harrison brightened. "Have you got it with you?"

Josh turned from the window, uncertain. "It's nnn-not quite ready yet."

"I thought it was close." I offered a smile. "Could we get together and polish it up?"

Sounding puzzled, he said, "Sure. To-to-tomorrow morning?" Followed by, "Even if you think I'm sleeping, wake me up."

On Thursday, we met at a recording studio in Upper Manhattan. No more than a room with great acoustics and a zillion dollars in equipment, the place was large enough for us and four chairs. "Be careful," Harrison said. "They might squeak." We had music stands. We had music on the stands. We had Jenny.

Jenny managed the studio. She ran the equipment and performed sound checks, made sure everything recorded, and afterward propositioned the male musicians. Last year she nabbed Harrison.

Professional. That was us.

The first time we recorded, I would have sworn two women worked there. Behind the sound board, Jenny had all the humor of a safety officer in a nuclear power plant. From voice alone, I predicted a grey-suited woman with a bun so tight her eyes couldn't close.

Then I saw a woman with shaggy orange hair and a crop-top that showed off the Chinese dragon tattooed around her navel. She had "KISS ME" embroidered across the seat of her size-two low-rise jeans. She moved around the studio with a businesslike efficiency, bending over to attach this, wire that, check another thing, and at the same time allowing the guys to read the writing on the...well, read the writing.

Today, Sergeant Jenna issued headphones so we could

communicate with the sound room, and then Miss Jenny purred that Harrison's violin looked really hot.

Shreya stared open-mouthed. I never could bear to ask Harrison what happened with Jenny, but after a month he failed to mention her again. I assume she snagged some guy with a twelve-string electric guitar and forgot the violin. It never works out well.

Sergeant Jenna barked that we needed to get started. "Sound check!"

Josh announced, "My name is Joshua Galen!"

"Check!" said the drill sergeant. "Violins?"

The violins played G scales. Josh played a C scale. I did nothing with the viola, the sandwich instrument. Sergeant Jenna told us to hang tight while she adjusted the sound levels.

Josh said, "My name is Joshua Galen."

Déjà vu, all over again. "I knew that."

He beamed. "I know you know, but I wanted to say it while I had the chance. Hi, my name is Josh."

Hey, wait a minute. "You aren't stuttering!"

Harrison and Shreya stared as he tapped his headphones. "I can hear myself. It's creating a choral speech effect. I'm going to take this opportunity to say my name five hundred times. Hi, I'm Joshua Galen."

"Pleased to meet you, Mr. Galen." Shreya offered a handshake. "I'm Shreya Ramachandran."

Harrison said, "I'm sorry, but I didn't catch your name, sir."

"I'm Joshua Galen."

"People!" barked the drill sergeant into our headphones so we jumped. "I'm ready."

"Hey, Joshua Galen," Harrison said as he raised his violin, "let's see if you can play that thing."

"Of course I can." He watched Harrison for his cue. "Or my name isn't Joshua Galen."

Once the giggles ended, Harrison cued us.

You'd think after practicing a hundred times, we'd have sounded fluid, but then you'd be as wrong as I was. Instead we needed a dozen takes to finish the first piece. Playing a reception, of course, we never took do-overs, but then again, Harrison also didn't worry his pretty head so much about whether a note was slightly flat or a quarter of a beat late.

The lack of an audience, while off-putting, imparted more of a chamber-music feel. For a hundred years, chamber music would have been heard only by the musicians and maybe a couple of guests. The most spectacular performance ever, ever, ever was in 1785, with Joseph Haydn and Ditters von Dittersdorf on violins and Wolfgang Amadeus Mozart on viola, plus one Johann Baptist Vanhal as cellist. No wedding guests and no ticket-holders. Only one another and God Almighty.

So in a way, this was chamber music as it should be, played in a chamber.

And in another way, this was sterile and wrong, almost masturbatory.

Between takes, Shreya said, "You're self-conscious."

I frowned.

"Your vibrato is tense. Your wrists are tense. Your bowing is tense." She waved a hand to include the whole studio. "Forget this. Imagine a crowd paying attention to a bride."

"Musical wallpaper."

She pointed right at me.

On the second piece, I tried with my eyes closed, but whenever I checked the score, it was still the white walls and microphones which never voiced their opinions at the moment but expounded your sins later, when it was too late.

The second piece done, Harrison left to confer with the Drill Sergeant. Josh said, "Have we met? I'm Joh-joh-joh— Shit."

I shook my head. "What a strange name."

He took a few deep breaths like a diver, then blurted it all at once: "Joshuagalen." Head down, he swallowed. "Oh well. It was nice while it lasted."

Shreya checked the tuning on her D string. "Explain this again. You don't stutter if you hear your own voice?"

Josh shrugged. "I have no idea why. But when you recite in tandem, you get fluent."

Harrison returned. "We've got time for one more. Say, is there a Josh Galen here?"

"Why yes." Josh saluted. "I'm Joshua Galen."

"Thank God, because we're doing that piece with you in it." Harrison settled on his chair. "Jenny, you ready?"

"It'll be a couple of minutes."

Harrison said, "Time's money."

"Don't I know it? Cool your jets for about three dollars."

Harrison chuckled.

Shreya voiced my unspoken question: "Could you wear headphones and be fluent all the time?"

"And look like a dork, yeah." Josh grinned. "There's a device called a EchoChamber which does exactly that."

Harrison's head jerked up. "Where do you get it?"

Josh shrugged. "I guess at a speech therapy lab."

"Why don't you have one?"

"Well," and Josh rolled his eyes, "for starters, it's five grand."

"That's why you've got medical insurance."

"I've got—" Josh blocked, then gave a head-shake. "—catastrophic coverage, but even if it's allowed, it wouldn't come close to hitting the deductible."

"Consider it covered."

In three words, Harrison flipped the world over on its side. *Consider it covered.* He'd whip out the gold card and there it would be: fluency. A respectable, non-psychotic, non-brain-damaged, non-ashamed Josh.

Harrison leaned forward. "Make an appointment. Get the damned thing."

Josh drew back. "That's a lot of money."

Harrison opened his hands. "For something that would make your life so much easier, what the hell is five thousand dollars?"

Josh tried to speak, and he blocked.

"Look." Harrison flushed. "My grandfather left me a truckload of cash, and what am I doing with it? I didn't earn it. I doubt he earned it. I could buy a Bose sound system, or I could give you the ability to say your name five hundred times a day."

Take it, take it, take it!, I thought.

Josh wore a deer-eyed look. "I'm not your phi-fi-fi—phillll-lanthropy project." He shook his head, blinking. "I could have saved for it. I did the research. But some people aren't helped, and even if it does, it might stop working with h-habituation. It won't help blocks or soft syllables. And the biggest problem is, it amplifies aaa-ambient noise and distorts sound."

Crap. So much for Josh's verbal salvation. "And it's noisy in a cab."

He nodded. "Even worse, think about playing the cello, hearing a note in one ear at the right pitch and in the other a split-second behind and a semi-tone higher."

Shreya frowned. "That would suck."

"It would be crippling. So no. It's a nice offer," he added, gaze riveted to the floor, "but no thanks."

Jenna returned to the window. "Okay, people, we're ready."

Straightening his sheet music, Harrison said, "The offer stands if you change your mind."

For our third piece, we recorded a fusion of the Beatles' "Yesterday," the viola taking Paul McCartney's vocals, the cello playing the background, and the violins ornamenting. Josh had composed a phenomenal arrangement. He said it was just juggling the lines out of the score and assigning them to the different instruments, but if I did that it would sound like hell. He did and it sounded like a conversation: mournful, stark. With the violins constrained, the viola's mellowness resounded, and the cello provided a support that carried the piece forward.

We broke from "Yesterday" into the slow movement of a string trio Josh had intuited would mesh well, then circled back into the fusion.

In one take, we finished. Breathless I lowered the viola and found in Josh's eyes a brilliance I hadn't seen in ages.

"Wow, Josh Galen." I couldn't look away. "You're good!"

Abruptly he broke eye contact, and I hunched my shoulders, feeling like everyone in the world was staring.

Jenny bounded into the room and threw her arms around Josh. "That was awesome! You're amazing!" She braced her palms against his shoulders, forcing him to look her in the face. "How in the world did you learn to do that?"

Nonplussed, he said, "Practice?"

She laughed too loud.

Only Shreya's eyeroll prevented me from kicking Jenny in the embroidered behind.

Harrison called, "Give him some air, Jenny."

Ooh, jealousy?

She lowered her eyes and the pitch of her voice. "That deserves a medal of honor."

Josh said, "The viola carries the piece."

"I think it was all the cello." Wow—she knew what a cello was? She leaned toward him and said, "Can I touch your instrument?"

Beside me, Shreya murmured, "Smooth."

As Jenny ran her fingertips over the purfling, Josh removed his headphones.

She sat back on her heels so she looked up at him, and, coincidentally, gave him a view down her shirt. "How long have you been playing?"

Josh said, "Since f-f-f-fourth grr-rade."

She fell silent, her face blank.

Whoa. Her flirting was funny in a pathetic way. But then, right then, I wanted to kill her.

She remained silent as Josh set the cello in its case,

loosened the bow, and put away his music.

Harrison said, "So we're scheduled for next Thursday, same time?"

The charm returned: Jenny was all over Harrison and Harrison's violin while Harrison relished the adulation.

Stupid jackass. He'd kiss anyone. Anyone.

I yanked the zipper shut and followed Josh and Shreya to the lobby.

"You left Harrison alone with her!" exclaimed Shreya. "That's hardly fair!"

Right then I'd have left him alone in a tiger cage holding a violin case full of raw steak.

Josh said, "They w-w-w—" He stopped. "They went out a few times last time we recorded."

"Lucky him," said Shreya.

Josh laughed. "Harrison never lacks for a stream of sh-shallow women who want a quick ...thrill."

"Hey, watch it!" said Shreya. "He hit on me too!"

"Unlike some," Josh said, "you had the sense to turn him down."

He turned to me, and for the first time I wondered if Harrison and I hadn't been as discreet as we thought.

Shreya said, "Didn't you just want to spit in her face?"

Josh shook his head. "I stu-stuttered on purpose. I figured she'd back off."

I went cold. "You faked it?"

Shreya high-fived him.

But— Faking a stutter? That was wrong. He tested her. He was mocking her.

Josh said, "Why-why-why not? I've had plenty of practice!" Shreya gave him a shove. "Let Harrison have her. If stu-stuttering turns them off, then they're not worth my time."

I felt dizzy.

As Harrison and Jenny exited the soundproof room, she was gushing, "See ya!" while he looked smug. I couldn't figure out what he was thinking, whether about her or the recording session. But as soon as we exited the building, he made it clear: "This CD is going to rule the world."

"If anyone ever gets to hear it," Shreya murmured.

FIFTEEN

We hunched against the cold while walking to the subway.

"Oh, not that this is a bad omen or anything." Shreya handed me a CD wrapped in a plastic bag. "Enjoy."

In his best school-teacher voice, Harrison said, "You have to bring enough to share."

I peeked to confirm my guess. "It's a garage band she told me about."

Shreya's laugh sounded strained.

"No one we're going to cover?"

"Doubtful," said Shreya.

She took the subway to Queens. Josh, Harrison and I took the R downtown, with Harrison getting off in lower Manhattan. As the doors closed, I straightened. "Oh, crap! I forgot to give him my viola!"

Josh's eyes stood out in relief against the windblown red of his cheeks. "I'll keep it tonight."

Call me paranoid, but the last couple of days, I thought things had been moved. Usually if Viv had been through, my place was wrecked, but lately it was subtle. A drawer fully shut. The clothes huddled together on the closet bar.

"Thanks." My shoulders slumped. "I hate having to ask."

"I carried it for you in grammar school." He shrugged. "Not a p-problem."

Our voices varied in volume as the train slowed, sped up, stopped at a station. It was a New Yorker technique developed the day you realized you rubbed shoulders with millions, to be heard by each other but not everyone else.

I clenched the handle. I should ask about what he'd said, about women like me not being worth his time. A simple "I'm sorry" loomed like a brick wall I couldn't scale. Instead I said, "I would change my locks, but all hell's going to break loose if I do."

He said, "Why would you care? You'd be on the inside."

I snickered. "I'd need to leave eventually."

The train stopped in the tunnel between Whitehall and Court Street. I checked my phone for the time. "Why are we sitting here?"

"No clue."

We lurched forward three feet, and the lights blinked out.

A child shrieked. I turned, but I could see only shadows outlined by the yellow smudge of the tunnel lights.

An announcement: disabled train at the Court Street station.

"Terrific." It could take half an hour to clear something like that. Longer. My uncle once spent an entire night in a subway car. "I'm going to be late for work."

The sound of the crying child resolved into words: *it's dark, it's dark, turn the lights back on.* Her mother carried her to the door, but all the cars were unlighted, not just ours.

Josh said, "Ex-cuse me? Does she like mmm-music?"

The mother said, "What we need is a flashlight."

"I've got a ch—cello."

Josh opened his case. I had my viola set up in fifteen seconds, and I started "London Bridge" in my best imper-sonation of a first-year student. Beside me, Josh got the cello ready, and he joined me on the repeat.

The girl's cry subsided to whimpers and sniffles, a shade in the dark. I said to Josh, "Do you remember 'Freres Jacques'?"

I counted to start. Although we'd played like pros in the studio, while playing kids' songs in unison we sounded stilted.

Regardless, the girl had quieted.

I said, "I hope no one minds."

"Keep on," someone called in the dark. "It's not like we have anything else to do."

Except for the people wearing iPods. But they couldn't hear over a screaming child anyhow.

The mother whispered to the girl, "What else would you like to hear?" When the little girl said nothing, she prompted, "How about, 'If You're Happy And You Know It'?"

I said, "I'm not sure I know it—" before realizing how stupid that sounded, and Josh laughed. He experimented until he got a decent tune.

"Oh," I exclaimed. "Wait, Josh!"

We had a fun version of "Happy Birthday." Josh had whipped it up ages ago, turning the regular song into a canon (him four bars behind me) and then mixing it up. Because we'd done it often, once with beer involved, the rambunctious tune flowed easily. Although hardly in Shreya's league, I played this best on my feet, the viola's scroll dipping and rising.

The girl laughed every time we circled back around to "happy birthday to—" but cut it short. The mom settled on the opposite bench, daughter on her lap. Yes, we were stuck in the dark, but we had music. We had everything.

At the end of our demented birthday serenade came a smattering of applause. The girl asked, "Is it your birthday?"

I said, "It must be someone's birthday...?"

Josh called, "Anyone?"

From down the car, a voice: "My son's birthday is tomorrow!"

I replied, "Happy birthday to him!"

Laughter again. My heart swelled. I was working a crowd like Shreya.

Behind me, Josh started "Yesterday."

This wasn't a fun song, but we'd just played it in the studio. The dark enhanced its mourning, and I made my vibrato wide and slow so it reverberated off the car, making the space seem emptier. We couldn't see one another, but hearing was enough to keep us together. I could tell when he was about to slow, when he was poised to increase volume and overpower the viola, and again when he prepared to back off so the viola could melt out of the dark like dawn.

At the end of the fusion, rather than shifting into the classical material the violins would have played, Josh tapered into silence while I ornamented the final notes, and we closed.

In the momentary hush, Josh slumped against the bench. I stood breathless, bow poised over the strings.

This time, it sounded as if the whole car applauded.

Before we could start another, the train lurched and the lights returned. I lost my balance, caught it like a perfect New Yorker, and returned my viola to the case before we reached Court Street. A thousand people waited on the platform, refugees from the disabled train.

The mother brought her daughter to us. "What do you say?" Black-eyed, skinny, and with corn-rowed black hair, the girl thanked us. I handed the mother our flyer, and then three more people asked.

The girl asked to touch the cello, and Josh let her hold down a string to feel the vibration as he bowed. The girl's mouth opened; a light kindled in her eyes.

Oh, to bottle that moment: the instant the world births a musician.

The doors opened. I turned to Josh to find him beaming at me. Someone exiting the train murmured, "Only in New York."

SIXTEEN

As evening crept across my toll-booth, I slipped Shreya's CD into the radio.

The cover presaged stereotypical indie rock: blue-haired Shreya, three guys, and one other gal, all wearing a soulless pout. The male vocalist and the bass guitarist were brothers. An insert gave a long list of "the band thanks," something Harrison insisted we not include. Shreya thanked her parents, a crowd I didn't recognize, and God.

How odd: I knew nothing about her life, yet to her it was the world. We worked and lived in the same place, but each our own sphere, our private universe that collided with others' universes and bounced off unchanged.

Playing the CD, I couldn't pin down the style beyond *early garage band*, over-practiced and under-produced. Sergeant Jenna would have brought the treble down and enhanced the vocals. The two lead singers (one male, one female) had stunning voices. He had depth, and her sultry alto reminded me of Stevie Nicks. The lyrics were banal, but man, what they'd done with them.

Cars pulled in, paid up, pulled out. Bach and I toe-tapped with the fast songs, swayed with the slow. A pair of violin solos left me dizzy, but I analyzed her technique: a wide, fast vibrato you never hear in classical but which blended perfectly with the electric guitars. She'd put a lot of reverb into the violin, but I couldn't figure out how.

The final piece was a cover of "Come On Eileen," a song I never thought needed to be covered but which now, I realized, did. Needed to be covered by these guys. The track was eight minutes, five of them a shared-solo (a contradiction, so shoot me) where the lead guitar, the drummer, and Shreya kept trading it off like basketball players gunning for an open shot. Shreya took the song's violin line and turned it into a paragraph. Maybe several pages. I listened with my heart in my mouth.

The CD ended. I let it repeat.

I wanted to love it, but I knew the story's end. They didn't go into the studio intending to leave with a dead band and a dead-end album. They wanted to create. Instead they were left with nothing but a toll-booth operator dancing alone at the mouth of the Brooklyn Battery Tunnel.

I'd texted Josh my lane number, but he hadn't replied. He didn't owe me anything—he'd made that clear—and yet I wished he'd look up from the driver's seat to connect my universe to his for a moment.

Instead I looked out and groaned: The Gentleman.

I busted a roll of quarters into the register, and while he took his sweet time unrolling the window, I ripped open a packet of dollar bills.

With Shreya's CD playing, I leaned out to take his hundred. There was no one behind him. Good.

Blank-faced in response to his smile, I dropped his hundred into the safety box. Then, serenaded by a defunct band, I took one twenty from the drawer.

And one ten.

And two fives.

I counted dollar bills onto the shelf. I knew there were fifty. I counted out forty-two of them.

In my peripheral vision, I detected The Gentleman's concern. I had reached eighty-two dollars.

And now, at my leisure, I counted the entire roll of

quarters that the bank had counted already. Forty.

"Here you go!" I sing-songed. I poured out two pounds of quarters, then counted into his hand all forty-two singles, the fives, the ten, and the twenty.

Two songs later, he was all set. Beaming, I thanked him for visiting the Brooklyn Battery Tunnel, and have a pleasant evening. He did not look pleased. Poor baby.

No one came for a while, and I wished for a yellow cab. But then I remembered Josh laughing that stuttering weeded out the shallow women, and I thought about how he provoked Jenny to see what she was made of. He'd said to me I'd be surprised by the shit he could get past even though he remembered it just fine.

I hadn't thought he meant me.

This shouldn't have bothered me. Everything was exactly the same as before. If anything, he'd cleared the air.

I was sixteen when I'd gotten so self-conscious. It wasn't that I thought him stupid or psycho. It was that *I* was nervous. I never wanted people staring, and until he stuttered, they never noticed me. But then they did, and it hurt—it physically hurt—that awful moment when they turned from him to me and saw exactly who I am: a bad friend, a financial failure, an inadequate musician, and an all-around disappointment to anyone I ever loved.

And once they saw that, well, it was over. I could get people to tolerate me, but it was a testimony to their charity that they kept me around at all.

I tensed as a yellow cab emerged, but it went to another lane. Not Josh.

Harrison had made it clear I was replaceable. Shreya accepted me as a pre-existing condition. My family treated me like family. But I'd always thought Josh liked me. Losing that left me on a precipice without handrails.

And who could I ask for advice about something like this when the one I trusted most for advice was Josh?

I looked at Bach. "You got anything?"

No, no help there.

What sucked worst was how Josh must think I still felt that way. Back then, if Josh had asked me to marry him instead of going to that stupid dance, I'd have done it in a heartbeat. Back then he was my protector and confidant and best friend all together, and whenever he'd called me Mrs. Galen, I'd warmed with the thought that someday it would be real.

Slide open the window. Take a ten. Hand back change. Put up the arm. Put the cash in the register.

But this time after I took the toll, I left the window open. The chill swirled around me, and it stung.

I didn't have a choice, did I? Josh had never forgotten what I'd done. I needed to let him know I regretted it.

The CD ran out, and I hit stop before it played a third time.

A career in music was wonderful in so many ways, but it also highlighted the unfairness of a world that blessed some of its daughters and ignored the others. Barring a lightning strike, Shreya and Harrison and Josh would never become household names. Shreya and her improvisations, Harrison and his technical skills, Josh and his ability to hear the different voices of a piece. Shreya's defunct band with its powerful vocalists, its amazing bassist, and skillful compositions with juvenile lyrics.

I'd met people who played music so sad you'd cry, but they never got a contract, never went on the radio, never became known to more than a dozen other musicians. They taught kindergarteners who didn't practice and frazzled housewives who always meant to take up something. For twenty-five bucks a half-hour, they imparted wisdom gleaned over two decades filled with two or three hours a day of practice. Then the student went home and forgot it, and driving home they'd hear someone on the radio who lucked into the right connections at the right time and now played for millions, for millions.

Meanwhile, Shreyas and Joshes and Harrisons filled the country like so many troubadours, talent suffusing their universes without ever overflowing to flood everyone else's.

At a quarter to one, I was getting paid for reading *The Name of the Rose* while listening to Dvorak.

Josh interrupted the excitement with a text. "You want a ride home?"

I texted, "Sure. Why?"

His reply: "I'll be there when you get out."

By the time I'd hung up my stylish neon vest, a cab idled in the parking lot. I got in, and Josh punched the button to start the meter.

I laughed.

"Fine, you get a frr-reebie." He turned it off. "So listen—" He threw the cab into reverse, swung around so fast my vision darkened, and then launched onto the street. "Harrison called. Guess what?"

"We're going to court?"

"Yeah, because I'd pick you up to tell you that in p-p-p-person." He slammed on the brakes at a red light, cinching the seatbelt around my waist and shoulder. "We got ...invited to a music festival."

"Really?" My heart hammered, and not just because he pulled two-point-five Gs to start on the green. "Which one?"

"The one in May, in West...chester." He nodded. "We'll need to finish the CD right away."

I sunk back into the seat. Wow. Oh wow. We needed a playlist. Needed to know how long we had on stage. Needed to find accommodations. Needed to invite my parents.

Josh talked even faster than he drove. The crowds, the experience, how Harrison was beside himself planning our next step (What? Carnegie Hall? Or could we aim lower and start with Lincoln Center?)

Josh said, "I wanted to tell you myself, though. He'll have to c-c-content himself with sending ten emails."

When Josh pulled up by my house, I clenched my fists. No more dodging. Just do it. "I was thinking about what you said, back at the studio. About being shallow."

Abruptly I wished I hadn't started.

He frowned. "What about it?"

I ran my finger over the window button. "About avoiding you because of your stutter."

"Oh." He looked at the steering wheel. "Why are you still thinking about that?"

"Well... Yeah, I mean..." There was no air. I couldn't say it, not with his eyes devouring me. Instead I focused on the sidewalk. How do you apologize for something that happened a decade ago? "It was wrong."

The edge in his voice made my heart sink. "But what I did wasn't wrong."

I sounded plaintive. "It was a stupid mistake."

"That wasn't a mistake." His voice sharpened. "I recognize del...liberate avoidance."

I looked for my stray cat, but I couldn't see him in the streetlight. "How can you not hate that?"

"I..." I knew just how he'd blink and shake his head to clear the block. "...used to. But not anymore."

I was so cold. I couldn't speak.

Josh began, "I..." This didn't sound like he'd blocked. More like he didn't want to be having this conversation. Well, I didn't either. "I've accepted it. You of all people know how it is. Stu-stuttering filters out the people I wouldn't want to be close to anyhow."

Oh my God. I must have hurt him so badly. I must have gutted him.

He didn't look outraged. More like he was really shocked. I wound my fingers around one another.

He'd kept contact with me even though he'd never want

to be close to me. Why?

I said, "So...can people change?"

"Not really." He took a long breath. "People rrr-reveal who they are because I stu-stutter. You made me realize that."

Before this moment, I never would have thought I'd prefer one of Josh's detonations over him remaining calm. I pressed my thumb into the scar on my left hand, pressed hard enough to hurt.

He continued, "You don't need to worry. I'm not saying someone who does that is a bad person, but when it happens, I know what I can expect from them." A pause, then an uptick in his voice. "You're rrr-really rattled about this?"

Then his breath caught and his head raised. He stared right at me with what seemed like surprise.

"Jenny was just f-flirting!" He sounded urgent, and he reached for my hand. "I wasn't interested in her."

"It's not about her!" I yanked back. How could he stand to touch me? "But you said—"

I hurt him.

He leaned toward me. If I didn't know better, I'd almost say he looked happy.

I hurt him.

I looked away. No cat. No people. I'd ruined everything. Everything.

"Really?" His voice was raw with disbelief, but I couldn't face him. "So you wish things were different?"

"Of course I do! Don't you think I've spent the last eight years hating how I screwed things up?" I had to get out of the car before I suffocated. I shoved open the door. "I should have just left it alone. I'm sorry. Thanks for the lift. Don't wait for me to get inside."

He snorted a laugh. "Yeah, the extra fifteen seconds is a killer. See you t-tomorrow."

I raced up the steps and let myself inside without stopping to feed the cat. When I shut the door, I saw he had waited.

I held it together long enough to get into my apartment, but I didn't get all the way into my bedroom before I was sobbing.

SEVENTEEN

The next morning I marched into Harrison's apartment with my thermal mug of coffee, a list, and a calendar. By the time Shreya and Josh had arrived (Josh with both my viola and his cello) I'd commandeered the table and begun scrawling on March, April, and May.

"We need to be organized if we're going to pull this off." They stood in a row, agape, as if they'd never seen a schedule before. "Here's what needs to happen."

Using one color marker for each of us and a final color for the entire group (a quintet of their own with a heady smell) I filled in our performance dates and the dates for the studio. For the studio dates, I listed the pieces we'd record. Each of those pieces went into a slot for practice the two weeks prior. I arranged the ones with the rights secured first, the others for the end. "Hotel California" I omitted entirely. Finally I noted which pieces to review for performances.

Harrison folded his arms. "This is nice and all, but I didn't become a musician just to stare at a spreadsheet."

"And if you don't sometimes stare at a spreadsheet," I replied, "you don't get to be a paid musician."

Shreya pulled up a chair to point out flaws in the schedule, which I corrected. Harrison put in our drop-dead date for printing CDs to sell at the festival. We inserted final dates for

Josh's arrangements. I added dates to send press releases. I included time to keep the IRS happy by filing our taxes.

I asked about the lawsuit, and the others fell quiet. Right. You can't schedule a bomb drop, not when someone else is doing the fly-over. I wrote it into the side bar.

"You're giving me a headache," Harrison muttered.

Poor baby. "Better a little headache now than a larger one later."

Shreya said, "She's got the right idea. Be professionals."

Harrison sent a helpless look to Josh, who raised his hands palm-outward. Great. I'd upgraded myself from viola joke to unstoppable force.

"All these things would work themselves out," Harrison said, and I snapped, "But it's better if we work them out."

Harrison stalked to the kitchen, muttering, "Fine," and with that ringing endorsement, I finished planning our next eleven weeks.

When I snapped the last cap on the last marker, Harrison asked with a theatric sigh if we could finally, you know, play music?

As if he didn't normally waste that much time anyhow. "But don't forget, this afternoon you need to follow up on the rights to three songs."

Harrison herded me toward the stands with "Yeah, yeah, yeah."

He got his revenge because nothing was good enough. Either the dynamics were off or our timing was off or the phrasing was off or our interpretation was off.

"This is ridiculous," I exclaimed at one point. "You're saying Josh is interpreting his own arrangement incorrectly?"

"But it works better my way," Harrison replied, and once you reached that level, you could have had Hayden, Handel, and Don Henley in the living room, but Harrison would have kept repeating, "You have to trust me."

After ninety-five minutes, we still hadn't run through one entire piece, and I interrupted Harrison's argument with

Shreya about her entrance. "Look, we're recording the damn thing next Thursday. Let's run through it once, straight through, without you picking it to death."

"Sure, if you don't have a problem with sounding like crap."

"But we don't sound like crap, and the more you hammer on the stupidest details—"

Harrison rolled his eyes. "Didn't you waste the first hour of practice scheduling all the stupidest details?"

Half an hour. "Showing up on time isn't a stupid detail."

"But greatness is in playing the right note after you show up."

"I'm not looking for great." My eyes narrowed. "I'm looking for 'not about to rip out my fearless leader's throat.'"

Shreya stood. "We're done."

I kept glaring at Harrison like a junkyard dog straining at its leash.

"I said," and she dropped her voice, "we're done. Put away the instruments. I'm not having us break up over starting on an up-bow or a down-bow."

Harrison said, "We need to be professional—"

"I said enough!" She closed the snaps on her violin case like the lock of a cell door. "I've seen where this garbage ends. It's not worth it." She turned to me, eyes livid. "We need to cool it before people say things none of us will ever forget."

Easy for her to say. She wasn't the target of Harrison's sniping.

Harrison folded his arms and said to her, "Do you want the recording to sound awful?"

"If it keeps the band together, hell to the yes." She grabbed her jacket and strode out of the apartment.

Josh beside me whispered, "Oh my God."

The door slammed.

When Harrison looked at me, I stared back at him.

Josh stood. "She's right. We need a break."

The tension on Harrison's face left me unable to blink, as

if the first one to break contact would lose something. Finally he walked out of the room.

Josh touched my arm. I pulled away.

"Let it go," he whispered.

"This is how he drove out Peter!"

"Then don't let him do it to you."

Harrison reappeared in the living room. "Are you coming back tomorrow?"

Not this again. "Are you trying to get rid of me?"

"Don't be like that." He came closer. "I know it felt good at the studio. But we want to sound our absolute best."

We? As if he had the right to say what we wanted.

I chose a silent departure over saying something that would have gotten me ejected.

After a long elevator ride, we reached the street. Josh said, "What's wr-r-r-ong?"

"What do you think is wrong?" My voice came sharper than intended. Good job, Joey, pissing off the only quartet member who isn't actively angry at you.

My cell phone buzzed. Shreya had texted, "Can you talk now?"

I texted back, "Yes."

She texted, "Lay off Harrison."

What the hell?

I showed Josh, who said, "I agree. You're wound tighter than an A string."

"Why does Harrison have to go all picky on us when we have so much to do? It's only slowing us down!"

Speaking of slowing us down, I forced myself out of a speed-walk. What I wanted was to run.

"He wasn't that much wor-rse than usual."

"He's impossible! Quibbling over every note, everything, even when we did what he wanted—"

"Whoa!" He put a hand on my arm. I jerked away. After what he admitted last night, how could he bear to touch me? "C-c-c—" He blinked. "Calm down."

"How can I calm down when he's destroying everything?" I picked up speed again. "Look, I didn't get much sleep last night after— So much isn't done, and we may be sued, and now we've got this festival, but he's stuck on whether your phrasing is perfect on some passage no one will ever hear!"

With my hands shoved deep into my pockets, I blinked hard.

Josh said nothing more.

At the subway entrance, I turned to him. "See you tomorrow."

"If I'm lucky, maybe I'll see you at the toll-booth." He reached for my hands. I recoiled, but he took them anyhow. "G-get some sleep tonight. It's going to be okay."

As he touched me, the wind came up and I blinked at the tears. "It's not going to be okay. How can it?"

He leaned forward, squeezing my fingers. "It is. Tr-rust me."

He tried to draw me closer, but no, not after yesterday. "Don't." I yanked my hands from his. "Please."

Wide-eyed, he stared with a strangled expression.

"I'm sorry. I'm sorry about everything." And with nothing else I could say, I descended the concrete steps alone.

By next practice, it had blown over. Mostly.

Harrison and I exchanged non-apologies. That meant he said he was sorry if he had been too demanding (but thought he hadn't been) and I said I was sorry for losing my temper (but not for being frustrated with his frustrating behavior). We pretended that was fine. Kind of the way Josh pretended things were fine even though he thought I was shallow. Kind of the way Harrison pretended he wanted me around.

Of course, Harrison still jotted things like "blow nose" onto his calendar and then criticized everyone's playing, but it never again came to a fight. Shreya assumed the within-practice scheduling and switched us to a different piece if we got locked down, a relief after Harrison's policy of "hammer on it until it's good and dead."

On Tuesday night, I inhabited the toll-booth once again, my impersonation of the troll under the bridge, other than how I lacked a bridge and I wasn't a troll. *Trip-trap-trip-trap...who's that paying eight bucks to the MBTA?*

The unseasonably chilly night had surprised me without my space heater or gloves. Even Bach had gone dormant, too cold for his batteries to stay charged. I longed to do the same, but my paycheck required sticking my hands out the window.

Just after midnight, an SUV pulled up and the driver barked, "How do you get to the Port Authority Bus Terminal?"

Hello to you too. "It's on 42nd Street and 8th."

"But how do you get there?"

He still hadn't handed over his money. I'd seen that trick before, where they ask ten questions and then tell you they already paid. Fortunately, I was smarter than a violist. Oh, wait, I wasn't. But I was smarter than a viola.

I pushed the button for security. "Okay, so when you get out of the tunnel—"

The driver slammed his hand on the door. "I know I go through the tunnel!"

A yellow cab pulled up behind him. Awesome. Saying, "Hold on," I pushed the button on my cell phone to dial Josh. Looking confused, he picked up.

"How would this guy get to Port Authority?"

Need directions? Ask a cabbie.

Josh said, "He'll hang a right as soon as he gets out of the t-tunnel."

I said, "Hang a right when you exit the tunnel."

"That will be Www-west Street, which turns into the West Side Highway."

I repeated that. Angry Man glared while Walt took his sweet government-issued time ambling over.

"Take a right at Hubert Street, then take that four blocks to Hudson. Take a left and stay on Hudson until it turns into 8th Avenue. Port Authority is at 42nd Street."

Because I was repeating about four words after Josh, it slipped out automatically when he said, "And that's the porn district."

Angry Man recoiled. I glared at Josh, who was enjoying a great laugh at my expense. Thanks. Thanks so much.

As Angry Man's cheeks purpled, Walt finally arrived.

Flushing to my eyebrows, I said, "Eight dollars, sir."

Walt stood by, menacing in his ineffectiveness, as the SUV driver paid and left.

Josh pulled up, and reading his EZ Pass, the toll-booth raised the arm automatically.

He was laughing so hard he was crying. I muttered, "I'm going to kill you."

"T-totally worth it."

Walt said, "All set now?"

"Yeah." I thought about my front seat conversation with Josh, how he said the shallow ones were ashamed of his stutter, so without thinking, I blurted, "Hey, Walt? This is my quartet's cellist."

"Nice to meet you," Walt monotoned, then ambled away out of the cold.

Speaking of heat, my cheeks were a thousand degrees. "What was that crack about porn?"

A mischievous wink. "No one catches a bus at mmm-midnight. He wanted to pick up hookers."

I blew on my hands.

He said, "But you would know about that, as much time as you spend with that Woody fellow."

I grinned. "Of course I do! I'm a pro at standing out all night taking money from men in cars."

Chuckling, Josh pulled off his leather gloves. As he handed them to me, he said, "Does it have to be cash, or can you barter too?"

"What?" My head filled with questions. "What about you?"

"I have a heater." He extended them again. "Really. You need fingers to p-play the viola."

"You need them for the cello too." Why would he do that for me after what he'd said? "Thanks."

"No p-problem." He saluted. "See you tomorrow."

As he pulled out, I murmured, "Thank you."

Still warm from his body, his gloves felt supple on my hands. I remembered holding his hand eight years ago, remembered yanking my hand from his and sending him home. I put my face in my palms and wished I could go back in time and give myself a hard slap.

EIGHTEEN

We proceeded through my spreadsheets. Whenever Harrison and I butted heads, I'd reply with, "Blame the calendar." He blamed me anyhow, but we moved along.

Until Harrison lost his mind. He decided his violin needed to go to the luthier for a tune-up. Literally a tune-up.

Violins and violas do need TLC at the luthier, where an expert can adjust the soundpost, check the bridge, and look for cracks. But Harrison must have confused "luthier" with "pediatrician" because he insisted that after exactly a year, it needed its 50,000 note service.

Harrison's violin was out of warranty by about two centuries, true, but it wasn't a seventeenth-century Italian that required such a precise degree of babying. Regardless, I sometimes imagined Harrison spoke to it: "You poor thing! Here, have some peg compound." Josh joked that he tucked it in at night. To which Harrison only looked guilty.

In the end, with three against one, Harrison conceded: he'd take it in July, after we'd finished recording CDs, playing festivals, and serenading June brides. But for consolation, or maybe in a snit, he declared his intention to rehair the bow. For that I shut up because they guaranteed a 24-hour turnaround.

Besides, violin shops rock my world.

On our way to the Upper West Side, the sidewalks gleamed with melting snow piles, and the edges of the street had a gritty gloss from repeated salt application. It had rained, and I scented dirt on the air. Most cars were filthy, but sometimes I spotted one shiny, washed by an optimist.

In other words, springtime in New York.

Harrison shook his head. "You're just making sure I don't leave the violin."

I chuckled. "You'll never prove it."

While we walked, Harrison lobbed a few viola jokes in my direction. He bought a soft pretzel from a cart and offered me half. I thought about Shreya's family selling hot dogs to give her a good start in America. I thought about my sister, hanging around Grandma's apartment asking how many rent payments I'd miss before I surrendered. Thought about how I'd invited my parents to the festival and my father said he'd check with my mother. And how the same world could be so different for different people: the pretzel-sellers, the pretzel-buyers, and the recipients of someone else's pretzel-charity.

At one of a dozen row-houses, Harrison and I climbed a nondescript stairway to a second-story entrance where an apron-clad guy ushered us into a fantasy world.

A violin shop hits you with a scent you can't name but which is without imitation. The odor of animal glue, the spice of resin, the sawdusty smell of wood shavings: it's a dream. The sharpness of varnish contrasted with the staleness of sunlight filtering through closed windows. As a child I'd pressed my cheeks into the viola and smelled time, but this was the odor of joy.

I slowed my steps to gaze into the cases, the dozen violins and two violas upright in stands so you could admire the sunlight as it played with the woodgrain flaring across the back in a giant V. Oh, for one of these sweethearts, for a five-figure loan... Yeah, not happening. But someday. Maybe.

Beyond the showroom was a workshop, violins hanging

from the ceiling in various stages of building, repair, and disrepair. A mini crock-pot of vanish simmered near the back wall, alongside a metal case holding gouges, thumbplanes, and a dial gauge. With these we manufacture love.

The luthier himself was bent over a violin mid-autopsy. He had the belly off, and exposed to the world was the violin's heart.

Nothing. The empty space is what makes the music. A mute violin is solid wood.

The maestro removed his glasses with their jeweler's eyepiece. He shook Harrison's hand and then discussed Harrison's violin as if it were a child, noting its temperament and general health. I sat on one of the stools.

Harrison presented his bow for rehairing. "She won't let me leave the violin."

Damn straight. I glanced at the disemboweled instrument, the manufacturer's name fully visible on a bass bar that normally you could only see in the right light at the right angle. Violins sounded glorious; pieces of wood did not.

With a wink at me, the luthier assured Harrison his instrument would thrive until at least July. Then he turned to me. "Are you okay with temptation?"

My heart skipped. "Tempt away!"

In the showroom he leaned on one of the viola showcases, dangling a key. "Well...?"

Harrison got a look at my face and laughed out loud. A moment later, I was cradling fifty thousand dollars.

The luthier looked expectant. "What do you think?"

Its dark red-brown finish felt like a foretaste of its lowest registers. I tucked it under my chin and plucked the strings, then adjusted the D's fine-tuner a shade. "What do we have here?"

"This is a hundred-fifty-year-old Frenchman," said the luthier. "Survived two world wars and just underwent a neck reset."

I drew the bow across the strings, and the sound vibrated

right through me. I did a three-octave C scale and then brought it all the way back down.

I wanted to say, "Impressive," and act cool while handing back the instrument, but instead I yielded to temptation and launched into the Fantasia Chromatica, letting the melody climb through the strings and then sequencing the motive back down, down, down again to the low C.

"You're extremely good," said the luthier. "I played with it a bit just to make sure it talked, but I needed a master to make sure it would sing. Please, go on."

"She's amazing," I whispered.

"Ah," said the luthier. "It's a she? I couldn't tell."

Harrison said, "How do you sex a viola?"

The luthier said, "Violists know."

I did a repeat of the Kodály-Bach, and then abruptly, mid-sequence, I hit two wrong notes in a row. I knew they were wrong, but they felt right, right enough that I longed to continue.

The instrument kept humming against my throat, reminding me of nothing so much as my grandfather's viola fighting to recreate his songs.

I passed it back before I dropped it, my voice quavering. "Thank you."

That wasn't what I wanted to say. I wanted to say, *What the hell was that?* and then, *And why does it make me so sad?* But Harrison was mid-eyeroll talking about wrong notes in the low register, and the luthier locked it up again, thanking me for proving his "patient" had recovered. I struggled to remember the notes, but they wouldn't return.

Back in the workshop, the luthier ran Harrison's credit card, and I thought about a neck reset on a French viola and the disemboweling of that violin on the bench. These were the things you did for an instrument you loved.

If someone loved me enough to open my insides, what would they find? If my mother vivisected me on a table and slit me right down the sternum, while Josh set my heart off to one side and Harrison removed all the icky bits with hands double-gloved in latex, what then? They'd check the name stamped on my spine. It would probably be my grandfather's. Then they could open my brain and pass their judgment: "She tried." And after they'd emptied me out like an abandoned apartment, they could reseal the seams and try to figure out if there was still a song in that hollow space.

"Are you okay?"

I started. "What?"

Harrison's brows wore an inverted V. "Let's go."

I said nothing out among the traffic and the half-conversations of pedestrians with cell phones.

Harrison finally spoke. "If I'd realized the festival would upset you this much, I never would have tried to score an invite."

I wrinkled my nose. "Is this Non-Sequitur Theater? What are you talking about?"

He shook his head. "You're not yourself. You— Is this because—"

"It's not because of anything because nothing's different." I was never a great liar, but then again, Harrison was never a great lie-detector. "Have we heard from the nasty attorney?"

Harrison turned his head. "I haven't. No."

I frowned. "Isn't it odd they'd just drop it?"

"It's not about the lawsuit." As if I were a misbehaving puppy, he raised his voice. "The day after we got accepted for the festival, you marched in with the spreadsheet of doom, and you haven't geared down since. Josh said he'd tell you himself, but I thought he meant you'd be excited, not that you'd turn into a werewolf."

I hear werewolves lock their jaws and don't open until the prey dies. So too Harrison.

I said, "I'm not upset."

The light changed. We crossed, Harrison keeping pace with me.

He frowned. "You're lying to me. I may not be Einstein,

but I can tell you're lying. Is this because I kissed you?"

"I'd be lying if I said I didn't wish you hadn't done that, but no."

He bit his lip. "That's too many negatives. Rephrase, please?"

I shrugged. "I haven't thought about it since."

Proving he was lousy at picking up lies, Harrison only said, "Oh. Okay."

Let him be the disappointed one. For once.

He recovered fast enough. "Is it your klepto family? Did you change the locks and get renter's insurance?"

"No to the locks. Yes to the insurance. The agent even made me take pictures." I just felt tired of being wary. "Are you about to bill me a hundred dollars an hour for psychotherapy?"

Harrison muttered, "I figured since you were here, I'd at least take a stab at what's eating you."

"You are! You've sucked the fun out of the whole thing!"

Harrison said, "Thing? It's a career! It was never supposed to be fun!"

"Don't give me that—you sold it to me as something fun."

Harrison muttered, "Playing three-hour concerts for late brides is fun?"

"Yes. Being assaulted by a drunk bride was fun. Getting an irate call from a rabid attorney was even more fun. But what you're doing," I said, "is a musical frontal assault, and I want no part of your quest for perfection."

Harrison stopped. "You're leaving?"

I looked him in the face. He had the decency to pretend to be shocked. "Are you driving me out?"

"How can you even ask that?" He stepped closer. "No one notices quartets at a function unless there's a disaster. But they pay attention to a CD, and on a recording, the same errors get repeated for all eternity."

"Aren't those the same thoughts that made Peter leave?"

Harrison folded his arms. "So let me ask you again: are

you leaving?"

"I don't want to, but..." I hunched my shoulders. "It's not only on CDs that musicians repeat the same mistakes forever."

He sounded bitter. "I'm well aware of my mistakes."

Wow, was the great Harrison Archer admitting to a slight imperfection?

He stared at the ground. "Then what do you want from me?"

"What I want—" He'd tripped me up by asking for a list of demands I hadn't prepared, and yet he looked almost frightened. What did he think I was going to ask for? I ended up speaking staccato, "—is for us to function as a group. For you to be pleased with us, for Shreya to be comfortable, for me to sit in back and play a lot of wrong notes, and for Josh—"

I stopped.

"So just normal stuff." Harrison sounded relieved. "But you don't play a lot of wrong notes. Only when it counts. Ow!" (That was because I'd just given him a shot to the arm.) He rubbed his elbow. "I want not to sound like a bunch of amateurs."

"Do we?"

He didn't reply.

"Have we sucked for two years and you forgot to mention it?"

We stopped at the next corner. "Normally we sound amazing. But we should sound better."

Not good enough: a familiar feeling. "There's a limit."

He looked at me sidelong. "I'm not convinced we're there yet. I don't want to give up when there may be something holding us back."

I went cold. He meant me. Of course he meant me.

Because Harrison wanted a "real" album cover this time, not something rigged up with the free copy of Photoshop Josh found in a cereal box, we spent one morning at a photography studio.

Laden with bags as if fleeing the country, the Boroughs String Quartet gathered in a lobby enough like my father's that I wanted to hide. Josh arrived last, hat low over his eyes, lugging a cello and a suit bag. He immediately texted someone.

My cell phone buzzed: "I am never talking again."

"Oh, that sounds bad." I showed the phone to Harrison and Shreya. "Or looks bad."

Josh nodded.

"What happened?"

He pointed to my cell phone.

"Oh, right. You're never talking again."

Harrison rubbed his chin. "That might make things difficult."

As Josh sat on the couch, I said, "It's not even that cold."

Harrison took a seat across the room. "Cold makes people never speak again?"

"Yeah, it's called frigid mutism." I rolled my eyes "That's why Eskimos have twenty-seven words for snow."

Shreya raised a finger. "They don't. That's totally an urban legend."

I stared at her. "Is not!"

"Is so. Check it out on Snopes."

Harrison pulled out his phone. "Snopes, huh?"

While he played with his tech-toy, Shreya turned to Josh. "Is it a stuttering thing?"

How could she just say that? But Josh didn't mind. I mean, more than he minded the stuttering thing in general. Staring at the floor, he nodded.

She said, "Don't let the assholes get you down."

He pointed to himself.

"Don't let you get you down either."

He wouldn't look at me. Why would he? He said he knew what to expect, and I shouldn't ask him for more than he wanted to give. So I didn't do what I really wanted, which was to sit by his side.

Without looking up from his phone, Harrison said, "The offer stands to buy that EchoChamber thing."

Josh grimaced.

Harrison added, "But if you're not talking, you can't say no."

Josh flipped him the bird, but although I tensed for a fight, Harrison only laughed. "You communicated that just fine!"

"Not to change the subject," I said to change the subject, "but is that attorney ready to have us hanged, drawn, and quartered?"

Everyone got still, and then Harrison said, "A quarter of a quartet is one person, so if she quartered us—"

Ah, intentional stupidity. "You know what I mean."

Just then the photographer banged open the door. A squat middle-aged woman with a round face, she had a chin-length bob that reminded me of a mushroom cap and thick glasses with pink wire rims. "Let's get started."

What the waiting room was in terms of stale, the studio made up for in expansive. Imagine if a dragon swallowed a lighting store before the heroic knight sliced him open. Although the ceilings had fluorescent lighting, she'd stock-piled a thousand other lamps on tripods, peppered among backdrops and carts with props. It relieved me to spot at least one camera among the chaos.

At a partitioned area she told us to get changed. Harrison pretended he'd accompany me until Shreya and I shoved him out.

As we got ready, I asked, "You're photographing with the wig?"

She nodded. "At least for the cover. Gotta look dignified."

Per Harrison's instructions, we'd have two sets: one

formal and one casual. Five minutes later, Shreya and I reappeared in concert blacks, and both guys wore tuxes.

"You look awesome." I grinned. "Almost like professional musicians."

Josh flashed a smile and pointed toward me.

I winked. "You're going to have to say something."

Out came his phone, and he texted, "You look terrific."

"Cheater," I texted back.

The photographer whistled. "Let's get started!"

How did Harrison find these folks? Oh, right, his mother recommended them. His mother who allegedly liked us.

The photographer herded us and our instruments toward two bookcases and a leather couch. We'd look intellectual: wouldn't our "Hotel California" fans be surprised? As if we were store mannequins, she didn't hesitate to put her hands on our arms, heads, hips, shoulders, to position us. Then she'd snap a dozen shots, pose us again with her hands doing the talking, then shoot.

Finally she ordered, "You! Hold up that big violin!"

Ignoring Shreya's snicker, I raised the viola. The photographer positioned it on my lap so the scroll pointed up. She examined me from different angles, then came around behind to adjust my dress.

I was so used to her manipulations that she had two buttons undone before I realized she was undressing me.

With a shriek, I jumped away. "What are you doing?"

"You've got a good body," she said the same way I'd say, *That was a good dinner.* "I want you wearing your viola."

Retreating, I wondered if she'd lost her mind. Or, worse, whether Harrison had put her up to this.

"You need your album to stand out," she said, "and it worked for Lara St. John."

I held my viola with one hand while the other fumbled at my neckline. "I'm not doing that."

Harrison turned to her. "What did you have in mind?"

"Harrison!" I cried out, while Shreya said, "What are you,

nuts?"

"She's the professional." He looked curious, not scheming. "Let her talk."

That the idea originated outside Harrison's head didn't mean it was a good one, though. "She can talk all she likes. I'm not taking off any clothes."

Looking grumpy, the photographer explained her inspiration to the non-visionaries in terms simple enough for even a violist to understand: a stern-faced quartet with everyone dressed for the role except me. I would sit with my viola placed like Eve's fig leaves to indicate that our music had decorum, discipline, and sex appeal.

Harrison turned to me. "What do you think?"

"I think I already told you what I'm thinking."

Shreya said, "I don't want a naked woman on my album."

I said, "Aren't you the one who always spouts that garbage about being professional?" He shrugged. "If we start as we mean to go on, three albums from now we'll all be naked. Are you aiming for an uptick in nudist weddings?"

For a horrified second I could see into Harrison's head: calculating how much he could charge.

Josh stepped closer, I would hope to defend me and not to undo the rest of the buttons.

The photographer walked off with instructions to wait right here, as if we'd go play hide and seek among the lights.

Shreya redid my buttons. "Hey, Fearless Leader, did you ever look up Eskimos and snow?"

"Yeah, and I learned things about linguistics I never wanted to." He laughed. "But you're right. It's an urban legend."

"Busted," she said to me, and I held a hand over my wounded heart.

The photographer returned with a velvet drape. "We can achieve the same effect with this."

Was she channeling my mother? "This isn't up for discussion." Then like an idiot, I kept discussing it. "What I'm wearing is what you're photographing." Turning to Harrison, I said, "Would you pose nude?"

"If it got us attention, I believe I would." Only the honesty on his face prevented me from slaying him where he stood. "It wouldn't, though. Not the kind we want. She has a point about your body."

"Excuse me!" Shreya called out before I could tell Harrison to go to Hell. "We're not discussing Joey's physical qualities. Joey is wearing clothes. I will be wearing clothes. Harrison will be wearing clothes. Josh, you too will be wearing clothes."

Josh exaggerated the motion of wiping sweat from his brow. I giggled, and when he met my eyes, I relaxed.

Shreya turned to the photographer. "Let's get a move on. A professional should know how to photograph clothed people too."

"Your loss." The photographer glanced at Josh. "You don't talk much."

He nodded.

Despite her unnecessary fascination with nudity, the photographer had talent. She got some great shots, accounting for dead space for our name and album title. These photos cost half the earth, but the quartet could take the hit right now. Besides, if we got sued, the lawyers couldn't seize the photographs.

Next we changed into casual clothing, me on alert in case the photographer leaped around the partition with a snap/flash of the camera. *Surprise! Now go tune up because you've got a bachelor party in ten minutes and the spray glitter needs to set.*

While the photographer and Harrison conferenced at her monitor, the rest of us sat waiting, Josh on the couch and Shreya on the floor. Minus her wig, Shreya wore a silk blouse that accented her hair. She said to Josh, "Really bad day for stuttering, huh?"

She did it again. It totally didn't bother her.

He rolled his eyes, and then wonder of wonders, he spoke.

"It k-k-k-k-kicked my ass."

Shreya sat back on her heels. "What happened?"

"Sss-someone wanted d-directions to—" He struggled, then said, "—C-c-c-c-canal street. And I c-couldn't do it."

I bit my lip. "Ouch."

He nodded. "Fff-finally I pointed it o-out on a mmm-map. Where to ch-change trains. And then..." He flushed. "She looked em-mbarrassed and ap-p-pologized for asking."

"Double ouch."

His shoulders slumped.

Shreya said, "Don't feel you have to answer this, but what's it like?" She tilted her head. "Stuttering."

Shocked, I waited for a snarky comeback or a hurt look. You couldn't do that, couldn't go up to someone missing a leg or with two weeks to live and say, "What's it like?"

Josh thought a moment, then pointed to her violin.

A moment later, Shreya had her instrument tucked under her chin. Josh was saying, "You're the s-s-soloist. Everyone c-c-came to see you." He gestured. "Play something simple."

She started with "The Happy Farmer" from Suzuki Method 1. After three notes, Josh put a finger on the string, stifling the sound, then released it. She hesitated as she played. This time he depressed the string multiple times, so it trilled.

Cute: a violinistic stutter.

She shifted to the next lower string in a higher position to hit the same note. This time he pulled the bow so she dragged out the note.

Oh—prolongation!

He wrapped his hand around the neck and deadened everything but the G, then blocked her hand with his other so she couldn't play higher up the fingerboard. By now she knew he'd change things up, so she repeated that note until he let go.

Watching the pair of them in a "Sonata Against The Violin In G Major," I felt...well, that my focus was all wrong, that the opinion of the bystanders didn't matter.

But then I caught Josh's expression: a cat playing with prey. He pressed on the scroll so the violin tilted; her note came flat. She corrected only to have him deaden the A again. She tried the same shift, only now he deadened the D. She crossed to the G with her wrist cocked so she was all the way up the fingerboard.

He glanced at me: my predatory cellist needed me to re-enact the role I hated.

But I did it anyhow. "Violins, what the hell is going on? Just relax and play!"

She lowered the violin and looked Josh dead in the eye. "Dude, you live in a war zone."

Harrison returned with the photographer. "Shreya, I teach three-year-olds who play better than that." He took a half step back under the chorus of our glares. "Kidding! Geez. Let's get these pictures done."

I trailed them to the unforgiving cameras, the lights, the props...and a cellist who had recovered his voice.

NINETEEN

I stepped from the shower on Saturday to find a missed call. Figuring it was Harrison with another idea of brilliance, I rolled my eyes, only—

"Peter!" I exclaimed. After I'd emailed him so often and he'd never replied, I'd given up. But now here he was!

Although I guess he had kept hearing from me: being on our CD entitled him to royalties. Once per quarter, about as often as it made sense, Peter's bank account got a visit, so without fear it would be a legal threat, I played the message.

His long-ago baritone sounded just right. "Joey! It's been a while. I'm with a new show, and I can score tickets for you and Josh to see *Winter Branches* this week. Call me back."

Okay, so he was in the small minority who didn't hate me, but Harrison still capped the list of people he'd like to run up a flagpole. Peter knew about manners, and he'd clearly excluded his fearless-ex-leader.

While I phoned, I made coffee. There was the initial rush, the "I'm so glad to hear from you" and "How are you doing?" How cool to be talking to him again, to Peter-who-had-vanished. I didn't mention the quartet until he asked.

"You really want to hear about it?"

He sounded tense. "I never hated you. I just had to get

out."

I said, "We're recording again," and he groaned. I grinned.

"Listen, we could use a decent violist." He let that trail off. "If Harrison gets to be too much."

"We're managing him. Hey, have you seen our video?"

Peter laughed. "Was that The Archer's hare-brained scheme too?"

"No, the *Village Voice* did it, and it got us into a world of hurt." Good to know the entire musical world wasn't tracking our fiasco. I rested my feet on an open desk drawer and read Peter the URL. Momentarily Shreya played through the phone, and I closed my eyes. Oh, to be half that good.

"Holy cow," he breathed. "Where'd you find her?"

"Harrison picked her up in a bar."

Peter laughed. "He's so lucky he'd make a four-leaf clover jealous!"

You mean, Green with envy. I didn't say it. Violas are the jokes, not the jokers. "Enough about us. What about you?"

Playing in the theater pits was, according to Peter, much more crazy-fun than playing on stage in a tux. For five minutes, he entertained me with stories of pranks, mishaps, and the lunacy of life as a theater musician. "Plus, cozy up to management and you get free tickets."

Translation: the show wasn't selling out. For all that Peter was having a blast, the truth was that any musical could fail, and failure meant you were out of a job. I'd be a wreck thinking my gig could end at any time.

I leaned back. "Are free tickets okay? I don't want you to get in trouble."

"It's fine. Afterward, you and Josh should meet the music director."

A light-bulb shone over my head. "Ah. You're poaching!" And pretty damn desperate to be poaching me.

"I'm showing you an exit, but I can tell you won't take it. That's fine. I wanted to catch up anyhow." Peter paused, and then, sounding tense, "I know I left on bad terms. I didn't want to cut off you and Josh too."

My voice softened. "It's cool. We're talking now."

Peter said, "Speaking of Josh, have you two gotten together yet?"

"What?" The floor dropped out from under me. "He's not interested!"

"That's not how it was when I left."

Peter laughed, but my mother's voice echoed: *that nice brain-damaged boy.* And Josh's words: *Stuttering filters out the people I wouldn't want to be close to anyhow.*

So I said, "He's never had any interest in dating me." The finality in my voice was a closed cadence.

"Fine, fine. So, how about a Wednesday matinee?"

While he waited, I IM'd Josh. He was available, surprised I had Peter on the line, and agreed to Wednesday.

I hung up with an ache in my middle, looking at the notes I'd scrawled on the back of a pink envelope. I kept pondering Peter's roundabout apology: *I left on bad terms.* If you could leave on good terms, wouldn't you stay? For a year, I hadn't dwelled on how much I'd missed Peter's dark sarcasm, his sly eyes, his direct approach. There'd have been no point. He'd still have been gone, and Harrison wouldn't have let him return.

Speaking of which, Harrison might react any number of ways. For the past year, Harrison acted as if Peter never existed. Given what Harrison said about his father cutting off his aunt, it made sense. Flouncing out of the room meant you were dead.

The two of them had gotten along pretty well at first, respecting one another as musicians. But Harrison was someone either you loved or you hated, and over time Peter migrated toward the down side. Maybe that happened whenever two virtuoso violinists found themselves in close quarters. It's a wonder every string quartet didn't go down in flames.

So maybe Harrison would say, *Go meet Peter, see if I*

care. Or he might tag along for the chance to sock Peter in the jaw.

My computer chimed with an IM from Josh: "All set?"

"Wednesday," I typed back, "box office at 1:45."

During a minute-long pause, the screen only said "JoshGalen is typing." Finally his message appeared: "Would you like to do dinner afterward maybe?"

He wasn't trying to rub it in. He'd have to get the taxi from his dad anyhow, so he needed to kill time. "In Manhattan?"

"That'd be fine," came the reply.

I typed back, "Manhattan is $$$."

From him: "I'm good for it."

From me: "But I'll end up washing dishes?"

From him: "Not unless you want to."

My heart twinged. I typed, "Josh, I'm so sorry about being an idiot."

I imagined how he'd look while reading it, how he'd struggle to tell me it was better he found out who I was sooner rather than later.

Yeah, no. I highlighted the whole sentence. Delete.

Eventually he typed, "So—yes?"

It felt so odd having this conversation, knowing he'd put a black X over me. No, not odd. More like a punch in the gut.

"I'll think about it," I replied. Because there was lots to think about.

An hour later I walked out the door and bumped into my sister.

"Hey, I need your milk."

I held up my trash bag. "Just finished."

She opened the top to see the carton. "You're such a jerk. What's Zaden supposed to do?"

She followed me downstairs. Before I could get out the

door, my mom showed up. "Where are you going?"

"Practice."

"Without your viola?"

"I left it there. Should I lug it all over the city?"

She took the trash from my hand. "Come visit with Grandma."

I said, "I live here."

She said, "You know, you're young and have your health. She may not have many years left. You should hope you never have grandchildren who treat you as an obligation."

Viv said, "She didn't have any milk."

Mom *tsk*ed at me.

"I needed it for breakfast and coffee." It sounded lame. "Hey, have you thought more about the music festival?"

My mother said, "What festival?"

"The one my quartet is playing. In Westchester? In May?"

She said, "Oh, you did mention that. That's really not my thing."

If Viv were playing, she'd be camped out already. "It's kind of a big deal. And you said if we ever were in concert, you'd come listen."

She said, "It's not only you, right? It's a lot of groups?"

"But we'll be playing for half an hour, and you don't have to stay for the whole thing."

She shook her head. "Think how it looks if you walk out on another group."

Viv said, "Like Joey ever stuck around for anything."

In Grandma's kitchen, Grandpa was watching TV while Grandma put coffee on the table.

Mom said, "You never wanted to be with us. You were always gallivanting off on your own, doing your own thing, running off to your grandfather's—and then you moved here because you thought it would be more fun."

"Fun?" My cheeks flushed. "You kicked me out when I turned eighteen!"

Mom gasped. "Josie! How could you say such a thing?"

I rolled my eyes. "Because it's true."

"But it's not! You always wanted to leave." She shook her head. "Vivvy couldn't leave us because she could never live on her own, but when Vivvy had Zaden, you didn't want to live with a baby."

"You kicked me out!" Was I losing my mind? Was she? "You gave my room to the baby!"

Mom said, "That never happened."

That never happened? "You boxed up my stuff!"

"We were helping."

Oh dear God in Heaven... I turned to Grandma, who paid close attention to her coffee cup. "You remember this!"

Grandma said, "Don't be like your Uncle Bill. Your mother was so unselfish to let you live here, having you clean and help with your rent money. She doesn't deserve all this nastiness."

Speechless, I just stood there. They were lying to me. We all knew they were.

Mom said, "Honey, you need to be honest with yourself. Bill never thought he did anything wrong either."

"That's because I didn't do anything wrong," I said. "I remember what happened, even if you want to rewrite history."

Mom said, "You were always so stubborn."

"Good." I picked up my trash bag. "At least someone was looking out for me."

I ran upstairs to get my crappy viola. Mom would come snooping, and I couldn't have her thinking the thing was in two places at once. Of course, this had the ancient case with no shoulder strap, so by the time I reached Harrison's, my hand was cramped while my head still rang with protests: *Does she really think I wanted a life of indentured servitude in five hundred drafty square feet?*

My litany repeated all the way to Harrison's door: all the proofs that my mother had rewritten reality, that I wasn't insane, that Viv had no right.

I stormed into Harrison's apartment, where Harrison handed me a twenty and a ten. "Oh, I sold some CDs."

I so totally did not need this. "How many?"

"Two or three...? Take off your jacket and stay a while."

Whereas I already wanted to leave. "How can you not be sure?"

"Do I look like an accountant?" He cocked his head. "Why do you have that viola?"

Sure, when it came to things he shouldn't notice, he was a regular Sherlock Holmes. "How much did you charge? Was it fifteen each or ten each?"

He looked puzzled. "You know, I don't remember. I'd been thinking of cutting one guy a deal—"

"Yeah, that's such a hard detail to remember. It's not like we file taxes."

As I stripped off my jacket, he said, "You can count what's left in the box if you're so inclined, but as for me, I'd rather play music."

My blood pressure must have been sky high, and two hours later, after failing to get all the way through any piece without Harrison stopping us, I expected to blow an artery.

It wasn't just us he harassed. A quarter of the time, Harrison the Fearless Leader would critique Harrison the Violinist. "Note to self: *subito piano* doesn't mean *drown out everyone else*." (Which led to me playing with clenched teeth, and "Joey, you're bowing a bit tense.")

At the end of practice, with my jaw aching, Josh and Harrison both started speaking. Then they both told the other to talk. And while I rolled my eyes, Harrison said, "Yeah, we're a quartet all right. Josh, you first."

Josh, temporarily losing possession of his senses, said, "Would it be okay if we pushed practice to eleven on Wednesday?"

Harrison looked at Shreya, who shrugged. "Why?"

Josh said, "Joey and I are g-going to see a play."

So much for stealth.

Harrison's eyes widened. Shreya caught her breath and said, "Wait—what? Together?"

Why was everyone jumping on the Josh-dating-Joey bandwagon right after he'd made it clear he never could?

Josh looked a little too pleased. "P-p-peter offered us tickets to his show."

Harrison upgraded shocked to outraged. "Turn him down! Free tickets aren't a subpoena!"

Taken aback, Josh said, "I don't..." He blocked. Grimaced. Still blocked.

Stealth. Should have mentioned the stealth thing to Josh a bit sooner. I said, "I miss Peter, and he doesn't hate us. He even admitted we sound better with Shreya."

"What?" Harrison's voice sharpened. "Where did he hear us?"

"It's a run-down dive called the internet." Turning my back on Harrison, I strapped down my viola. "Remember that video the lawyer found interesting? As it turns out, Peter can view it too."

"But for God's sake, why give him the time of day?"

"Because despite what you think, he's still a human being."

Harrison planted himself in front of me. "Terrorists are human beings. We don't go to Broadway plays with them."

I rolled my eyes. "So now Peter's a terrorist?"

"He tried to blow up the group!"

"It was you!" I exclaimed. "You drove him out when he couldn't take your attitude anymore!"

Shreya's voice was low. "I've got an idea. Let's end this conversation."

I fell silent. Josh hadn't said anything since I interrupted him. And Harrison—

He said to Shreya, "You don't think only a total jackass would abandon his group?"

I shot a look at Shreya, who shrugged, but it was stiff. "There's a difference between leaving a group and destroying it."

Harrison shoved his hands in his pockets. "All the same in my book. I want nothing to do with him."

"He feels likewise." I zipped the viola case. "What is it with guys and never forgiving anyone? It's a play. I'm not going to marry him."

Harrison sounded stung. "You're supposed to marry me."

"I'm not marrying you either, Harrison." Ritual banter meant Harrison was defusing. "We won't even sit with him. What's the big deal?"

Instead of pouting, he focused a mistrustful glare on Josh. "Moving the practice makes me an accessory to treason." Then he brightened. "Afterward, there's a neat restaurant on Broadway that you guys will love!"

Back on solid ground, Harrison armed us with (as it turned out) five places we'd love, the last two added with an embarrassed explanation that they were "a little less pricey." Then Shreya asked what Harrison had wanted to say before he and Josh had their verbal head-on collision, and Peter blew off on the winds of conversation.

"We've all been tense," Harrison said, delivering the understatement of the week. "So how about a musical vacation?"

A musical vacation meant...what, we'd pick three locations to spend a weekend, and when the music stopped, one of us went back to work?

He went on, "My parents have a house at Lake George. It's sealed for the winter, but in late spring they open it up. We could do that for them, then stay the week."

That might be okay. I could swing some time off.

Shreya said, "I'd have to see how it works with my other job," and Josh added, "I'd lose income for the week. But it might be worth it."

Harrison said, "We couldn't swim yet because 'ice-free' doesn't mean it's much over thirty-three degrees. But there's touristy stuff, and we could take the boat, and it wouldn't cost anything."

Well, other than travel and food. I said, "How do we open a house?"

It turned out "house opening" meant turning on the utilities, doing a lot of laundry, opening windows, vacuuming months of dust, and straightening the grounds. With four of us, it should take a few hours.

Harrison started selling us on the amenities (cable, a boat) until I pointed out we weren't objecting because the place was a dump, but because of employment. "You don't need to convince us it's a nice idea."

"Although—" said Shreya, then stopped. "Don't take this the wrong way, but maybe it's better to have a break from each other." She sat on the arm of the leather chair. "If there's tension, we go four different ways when practice ends. But all together in one house, that's impossible."

Harrison's face tightened as he thought. "We're not that tense, are we?"

Shreya opened her hands. "We're tense enough that you're suggesting a vacation."

Harrison finally cleared his head. "It's a big house. We can peel off from one another so it won't be a problem. Trust me."

Shreya shrugged. "I'll look into it."

I pulled out the calendar and rearranged to clear the week before the festival.

Shreya hung around the door until I exited. "Can you come with me?"

As subdued as she sounded, I anticipated a lecture about the schedule. But who knew: maybe she wanted help getting Harrison's vacation off the rails.

Instead, she brought me to a "Grand Opening Boutique

Sale!" on a side street off Second Avenue. I squinted as I glanced through the glass storefront. "What are we looking for?"

She steered me toward a table full of sweaters. "Something perfect."

I picked up one and set it right back down. "I couldn't afford one of the sleeves!"

"Then you can afford the collar." Shreya selected a sweater in green and brown. "This would look great on you." She laid it in my arms. "I'll try it in red."

I leaned forward. "I'm not buying anything."

She whispered, "Me neither. But we're going to try on every single article of clothing."

Giggling helplessly, I followed her through the carousels, collecting jeans, tops, anything that caught our attention. Then, laden like maidservants of the queen, we received plastic hangtags from the dead-eyed woman counting our try-ons (thirty...six...thousand) and staked out the double-size changing booth with the three-way mirror.

I tried on the sweater and jeans, then examined my reflection.

"You look good." Shreya pulled on a blousy jacket and a thigh-length skirt. "This would rock with a pair of high-heeled boots." She turned around. "Try the blue one."

I changed tops, and she nodded. "Much better. You look less washed out." She tried on my brown sweater. It looked better on her. In other news, the Earth was still round.

I struggled not to feel self-conscious about the hole in my bra band. We swapped clothes, and we compared, and every so often I checked out a price tag feeling a keen despair.

Shreya pointed to one top. "You should buy that. It looks awesome."

My mouth twitched. I couldn't justify that amount, but the shape of it was just right, and the color too.

I said, "How'd you know this place was opening?"

She snorted. "They've been having a grand opening for

the past six years."

I laughed out loud.

"The banner's been up so long it's faded. Across the street, their competition's having their eighth annual Going Out of Business sale."

As she tried on a halter top, I noticed a tattoo on the back of her shoulder. In henna-burgundy, it resembled a ten-pointed sun etched in whorls and curves. I stood to get a better look.

In the center of the sun, the lines merged to form a treble clef, with just two eighth notes and then the end bar.

"Pickup notes," I said. It wasn't even a full measure.

She said, "What?"

"Your tattoo. When did you get it?"

"About a year ago." She pulled on a different shirt, one with sleeves, so I couldn't see it anymore. "Okay, talk to me. Are you and Josh dating?"

I sat myself and my illicit blue shirt back on the bench. "It's exactly what I said. Peter invited me and Josh to his performance."

"Really?" She pivoted so she was staring down at me.

I saw only a part of me in the mirror, a me too small and too poor, a me who couldn't make right the things she'd already botched. I studied the back of Shreya, less intimidating than the front. "Josh isn't interested. He said as much."

Her voice pitched up. "You talked about it?"

I glared at the carpet. "You think it would be unprofessional."

"Well…" A plaintive note. Had a relationship broken up her group?

For once she seemed younger than me, a kid playing pretend in her mom's clothes. I wrapped my arms around my stomach, hyper-aware of the buzzing fluorescents, the multiple mirrors, the industrial carpet with straight pins embedded near the walls.

Her voice was small. "Be careful."

"I am being careful." Wasn't I always? Didn't I budget things, plan things, protect things?

I picked up clothes from the heap, set them back on hangers with the tops buttoned so they hung right.

Shreya unzipped the jeans and slithered out, then studied herself nearly-naked in the mirror, hands on her flat abdomen. Such a perfect body. Such a gorgeous tattoo, only she didn't want me to know what it meant.

"Be careful," she said again, and got back into her own clothes.

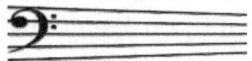

Returning my try-ons to the rack, I hesitated with the blue t-shirt.

Shreya said, "Buy it."

"It's so expensive."

"Well, hold onto it." She held up a gauzy skirt and blouse. "I'm deciding about these."

We browsed again, but subdued. Finally Shreya went to the registers with her outfit, and I stood holding the t-shirt, biting my lip.

She waved me over. She pointed to the counter. She paid for hers. Then, trying not to notice what I was doing, I paid for mine. My expensive, gorgeous, guilt-inducing t-shirt of concupiscence. But it looked so pretty, so pretty.

I followed Shreya to a Starbucks, where I went ahead and ordered something with whipped cream because I'd already blown the budget, so why not?

Walking to the subway with our loot, I said, "Is this an auspicious time to tell me how you learned to improvise?"

She frowned while sipping her coffee, then perked up. "Oh, yeah, that." She pointed to the hot dog stand at the corner. "Okay, so pretend it's summer vacation and that guy has no one to watch his nine-year-old. He brings her with him, tells her to sit where he can see, and that night has her dump out that disgusting water after the hot dogs have boiled in it all day."

I gagged.

She laughed. "If you ever wonder why I stayed vegetarian, that would be it."

"And when you realized you'd inherit the family business, you took up violin?"

"After I realized I'd be with that damned cart every day, I started bringing my violin for something to do." She rolled her eyes. "When I practiced during lunch hour, people gave me quarters. Some of them even bought a hot dog."

My eyes bugged. "You were busking!"

She nodded with a surprising earnestness. "I pulled down twenty dollars an hour."

Color me envious. "Because you were a kid?"

She cocked her head and widened her eyes, looking cute. "At that age, you can ask any adult for a quarter and he'll hand it over." She gave a wicked grin. "But last summer in Central Park, I could still get that much. So yeah, I had a little solo career courtesy of Suzuki Method 3."

I smiled at the pavement. "That's awesome."

"One day this guy asks if I do requests. I tell him sure, if you buy a hot dog." I laughed out loud. "He asks me for the 'Ave Maria.' Like I knew what that was. So I said, Sing it, and then I mimicked it."

I blinked. "Really?"

"Oh, I'm sure I fouled up the whole thing, but he applauded and asked for another. I told him to come back tomorrow and buy another hot dog. He actually returned with sheet music, so I played."

I sipped my coffee. Whipped cream. I should buy a can of whipped cream and do this at home. "You got your practice doing requests early."

She nodded. "Six hours a day! You get good in a hurry. Turned out this guy was a deacon. He gave me a Catholic hymnal, and they were all stupidly easy. I could sight-read by the end of the week. Then sometime in July, a guy selling knockoff watches started playing his stereo, so I'd stand there, figure out the key of any song, and improvise. Bach is awesome, but I got more bystanders for the Beatles."

I laughed. "You were fusing!"

She relaxed. "But you see how I got trained? That's why when you and Harrison and Josh start comparing Sibelius to Shostakovich I kind of sit there like, *Uh, yeah*." She shrugged. "I'm just a performer."

Abruptly she stopped speaking. As we waited at the corner, I finished my coffee, then tossed it into the trash can. Goodbye, five bucks. Long live the caffeine buzz. The light changed. I said, "There's nothing wrong with being a performer. Harrison performs."

"Yeah, but— There's more." She spoke slower. "In the middle of August, someone stole my violin." She stared off into traffic. "The next week, people asked why I wasn't playing. I didn't know who they were, but they knew me. They'd tell each other what a shame it was that someone could steal a kid's violin, and I realized that when I'd been playing, they'd stopped being a bunch of individuals and become a group."

I wanted to meet her eyes, but she kept looking down. I said, "It's like when we're taking requests and everyone sits forward, not just the requester."

She bit her lip. "Some people gave me a buck to put toward a new violin. But then—" I waited her out. "That deacon asked my dad if I could go with him. He brought me to Saint Francis at 32nd Street, and in the church office, on the desk, the staff had a sweet little half-size."

"You're kidding!"

She ran her finger over the lid of her cup. "Dead serious. There was even a red bow on the case. They'd raised money with a jar on the table."

I frowned. "That's not nice. The guy was grooming you to convert?"

Her eyes flew wide. "No, nothing like that. They never even asked if I was Catholic. That came later." She looked earnest. "The deacon said music was a gift from God, and that by playing, I spread the gift to everyone." She shook her head. "There were no strings attached, just go back and play on the corner. And one day I thought, I don't know if music is from fate or God or karma, but I shouldn't keep it to myself. I could sell hot dogs or make people happy, but maybe I could do something bigger."

I hummed. "Bigger how? Did you play for their choir?"

She chuckled. "Well, the next summer, yeah. Sometimes. On and off for years. But that still wasn't what I wanted."

"What did you want?"

She paused for so long I thought she wasn't going to answer, but then she said, "One of the stories in the Bible is about a guy who finds a perfect pearl, so he sells everything he has in order to buy it. What if music was my pearl? Would I be happier with all that other stuff, or should I just go all in and hang onto that one thing?"

"But you didn't know that story then."

She laughed. "No, but later on, when I heard it, I knew just what he was talking about."

I said, "Then why'd you become Catholic?"

Shreya shook her head. "That's a different story."

I said, "You're confusing me, then. What did you really want?"

She said, "I wanted to make people into more-than-people, strangers into friends. I..." It sounded like a block. "I wanted to give people something to care about together. A vision of something better."

She lost her words altogether at that moment, but I knew what she meant. Hadn't I felt that same impulse with my grandfather? Me with a lifeline-shaped scar and a viola like touching fire, her with a violin that could turn pedestrians into an audience and Fifth Avenue into a concert hall?

Eventually I said, "I still think it's pretty cool how you

trained yourself. Six-year-old Mozart was right. You don't need lessons to play second violin."

Her eyes flared. "Like hell you don't!" But then she saw I was laughing, and she joined me. "Yeah, and you don't need any to play the viola, either."

I grinned. "Only two lessons. One on how to sit in the back, and one on how to play all the wrong notes."

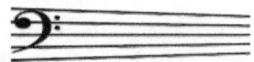

Shortly after he dumped me, Harrison told me to come to Carnegie Hall for the Emerson String Quartet. I was stupid: I wondered if he'd decided professionals could fall in love, and I hadn't decided whether I'd say 'yes' or 'fuck you.' When I found Peter and Josh waiting, that answered me: business. Once again I'd been filed to the back of someone's life like an old receipt.

Harrison had reserved seats close to the front, sub-optimal from an acoustics perspective but ideal for scrutinizing how you perform when you're the best of the best. Watch the way they cue each other, he said, and the way they adjust mid-play. During intermission and then for an hour at a Starbucks afterward, we combined observations and planned our tactics.

Over the next two years, we heard twenty-five string quartets, many of them free performances. We'd gone as critics and returned with data. Needing mentors, instead we found examples.

By now, I was a damn good analyst, so I analyzed Peter's play.

Winter Branches was a youngish Broadway musical which got great reviews and languished on the vine. You can describe the storyline of most musicals in one sentence, and you leave the theater humming the final chorus. Not this one. The plot was complex, and the powerful ending had an undercurrent of sadness.

In other words, it wouldn't have enough word-of-mouth to sell out for five years running. Not even five weeks. You'd dwell on the story all the way home, but you'd never call your friends to say, "Hey, you've got to see this!" Peter would be looking for work in a month.

Keeping my verdict to myself, I accompanied Josh backstage to meet thirty musicians. The music director adored Josh, handing over his card with "Look me up!" By contrast, his eyes glazed when I said I played viola, the vegetable on the orchestral buffet. You kind of need it, but why go out of your way to get one?

Peter brought us to a glorified deli that hadn't made Harrison's list. Josh seemed a little off-balance, but at least it didn't look like a date.

"The music for these things isn't all that tough," Peter said. "I practice a lot so I don't lose my edge."

"You could start your own chamber music group," I said.

He shook his head, and I felt storm clouds: a topic to avoid.

Josh looked the waiter right in the eye and stuttered while ordering, and I braced myself in case anyone snickered, but no one did. The one getting attention was me. When I looked up, I found the waiter staring down the front of my shirt. I had to tell him twice to put oregano on my sandwich.

Peter turned to Josh as the waiter left. "What happened to you? You're totally different."

Josh said, "H-h-how?"

"You don't wear that baseball cap like you're being dive-bombed by pigeons. And you used to point to the menu or ask for whatever someone else had."

Josh said, "I'd had en-n-n—"

"Enough," Peter said, "right, but it's like how you talk isn't a big deal anymore, and that's cool."

I adjusted my shirt so the waiter would have a harder time getting his thrills.

Josh shrugged. "It's st-still a big deal, but I'm not letting it st-stop me from getting what I ...want."

Peter laughed. "Good for you!"

Josh averted his eyes. "It's tough, though."

Peter turned to me. "And now your turn."

My head snapped up. Did he know what I'd done eight years ago? My turn? "For what?"

He raised his eyebrows. "Don't panic. Just tell the waiter to shove off." He leaned forward. "Or should Josh do it, since he's all empowered and stuff?"

I struggled to regain my composure. "You want me to make a scene?"

"Why should that dude treat you like his personal peep show?" Peter grinned, and Josh flushed.

I unwrapped my silverware from the paper napkin. "So when he brings the food, I should stick my fork in his eye?"

Josh laughed out loud. "It'd st-stop him from doo—"

"Doing it again," Peter said. "Yeah."

Josh turned to him. "Knock it off."

Peter stiffened.

Josh looked away. "Quit finishing my sentences. I can finish them m-myself."

The look on Peter's face made me flinch and laugh simultaneously. Peter gestured to our companion. "Case in point. But he did it without putting a fork in my throat." He turned back to Josh. "Sorry, man. That wasn't cool."

Peter had done that for an entire year straight. Josh had never objected.

When the waiter tried again to help himself to the view, I clasped my hands under my chin, forearms blocking my chest, and met his eyes with my stray cat's territorial stare. For a moment the guy didn't even set down the plates, and as soon as he did, he left.

"Oh, poor thing," I murmured. That worked better than I expected. "He forgot to say we should enjoy our meal."

"No one better want dessert," Josh replied in a voice

equally low.

Peter shot me a grin. "Remind me not to piss you off."

As predicted, the waiter didn't give a drive-by to ask if everything was okay, and with empty plates we sat while he failed to bring a check. Big deal. He only punished himself by not turning over the table. Finally we put on coats, and then the waiter appeared.

On the street, Peter told us to keep in touch, as if he hadn't been the one who disappeared. He shook hands with Josh and then gave me a hug.

I kept my eyes closed against his wool coat, forehead to his shoulder, wishing my friends didn't all have to leave and that somehow we could have a string quartet with three violins. But then he vanished into his theater, Josh went to meet his father, and I returned to Brooklyn.

TWENTY

In mid-April, Harrison dropped a bomb. "We're having a baby shower!"

I was barely in the door, Shreya still in the hallway, and I couldn't step further for wondering whom Harrison had knocked up.

Josh was already on the couch, looking pleased. I choked out, "What?"

"Sunday!" Harrison glowed. "I arranged things with the hostess about five minutes ago. We'll play for two hours. It's at a restaurant in—"

"Hold on." My brain spun as I sorted the information. Okay, not Harrison's baby, but still chaos-making. I got inside, and Shreya followed. "There's no time in the schedule."

"With all due respect," Harrison replied, leaning against the kitchen counter, "fuck the schedule. This is a paying gig. I don't remember your calendar cutting us a check."

I folded my arms. "We have a schedule, just to remind you, to keep from cramming in so much that we sound like idiots."

Shreya's voice cut through mine. "What do they want us to play?"

"Mozart. Lots and lots of Mozart. Only Mozart."

Josh echoed my thought before I even said it: "Mozart

has gr-gr-groupies?"

Harrison nodded. "Among the infant demographic."

Shreya set her violin on the couch. "Some scientist said babies who listen to Mozart have higher IQs."

Harrison looked me dead in the eye. "Must be why I'm so stupid. Mom loved Beethoven."

I slammed the closet door.

Shreya said, "So we won't play 'Take Good Care of My Baby'?"

Harrison nodded. "Or 'Baby Hold Onto Me.'"

Josh said, "She Must Be Somebody's Baby."

"Don't Worry Baby," Shreya added solemnly.

Harrison breathed, "That is so deep."

"Look." I raised my well-creased schedule. "We're done recording, but we needed that day."

"We'll burn the midnight oil." Harrison got our instruments from the closet. "It's what, four quartets?"

Shreya said, "Not even that many if they play games."

Harrison did a double-take. "Games? What kind?"

"Stupid games. That's what they do at a baby shower. Plus gifts and maybe a craft."

Harrison looked at me, horrified. "You won't have one of those for our kids, right?"

"No, because for the five hundredth time, I'm not marrying you." I took a seat. "If you're dead set on this, we might as well get to work. I'll rearrange the schedule later."

"I love your upbeat enthusiasm." Harrison sighed. "Schedule enough time to cash the check."

But then a miracle occurred. For the Mozart, Harrison was a gem. Comment at the end of the third movement was, "Sweet!" and not, "Fifteen measures ago, you were sharp on the B. Let's do the whole thing over."

So although I wanted Harrison's head on a pike, for five days the music became a joy again. I looked forward to practice, as one per day we reviewed quartets for the Mozart-ensmartened baby, and afterward we practiced the festival playlist.

On Sunday, we showed up to a medium-sized function room at a Kew Gardens club where servers were straightening tables and arranging bouquets. The airy room had music stands in a corner. Two violins, a viola, and a cello could make a lot of noise, but the carpeting and table linens would absorb most of it.

Guessing from the decorations, Mom expected twins, one of each variety.

Harrison leaned toward me and Shreya, whispering, "I didn't realize 'rhyme disease' had spread to baby showers," and he pointed to the opposite wall.

"Rhyme disease" had been discovered by Doctor Harrison Archer when he'd requested clients send an invitation for our scrapbook. It seemed like a good idea until we realized half the couples included a shakedown for gifts right on the invitation. It was our fifth client whose invitation broke the camel's back. Harrison had shoved it into my hand right at his door, saying, "I just learned it ennobles greed when you say it with poetry. Check it out."

After Mr. and Mrs. Whatever requested the honor of your presence, was this gem:

Boxes and ribbons have plenty of flash,
But save all the trouble, and just gift us cash.

And before Harrison would play anything that day, he required me to change our client contract so it requested the program instead of the invitation.

Now Harrison pointed to three tables with signs. I couldn't read the first or the third, but the second faced me.

Think of a tip, good or bad
On how to be the best Mommy or Dad.
Please share your wisdom, but leave off your name
And then we'll play a guessing game!

Rhyme disease at its finest.

Shreya didn't respond. Actually, she looked sad. I said, "Hey, you okay?"

She looked up. "Huh?" Then, "Oh, I just never understood the point of showers." She forced a smile. "It seems like they should have it after the kid's born, to be sure everything's okay."

Harrison snorted. "That's grim."

Shreya stared at her violin as if testing the strings with her eyes. I said, "She's got a point. And it would save a lot of hassle if the ultrasound was wrong about the sex."

Harrison shrugged. "That's why you give gift receipts."

We were in full Mozartian swing when the Guest of Honor arrived with enough camera flashes to simulate D-Day, and then we played Mozart after Mozart in an attempt to boost the babies' IQ by as many points as possible in two hours.

After two quartets (and fifty minutes) the guests broke from eating their cream cheese and cucumber sandwiches (no kidding!) to watch the Mom-To-Be open a hefty pile of gifts. Our contract specified fifteen minutes for lunch, so as soon as the servers brought our vendor meals, we clustered around a back table and feasted. The babies were losing their chance to attend Harvard by the second.

We got burgers and fries. Harrison must have been in testosterone withdrawal from all the pastels because he started a fight with Josh about the Yankees.

Choose one: which is the true Yankees fan?

Harrison: *This year! This is the year they'll take it all the way! They've got hitting, they've got pitching—*

Josh: *Are you out of your mind? Management sucks, they have no bullpen, and they sunk all their money on a one-year contract for a center-fielder who's already injured. They might as well pack it in now.*

The right answer would be "Josh." Harrison would cheer for the Mets too. For Josh, there were only two teams: the Yankees and whomever the Yankees played. For two years now I'd watched them engage in the Yankee Fan Dance, with Harrison's part staying the same year-round, but Josh's changing with the season. March: *This is the year! This year they go all the way!* April: *They suck! Someone should fire them all and call up a Little League team.* June: *They had a slow start, but they're going to pull it out!* August: *If they win every game from here out, they'll make it!* September: *Next year! Next year they'll take it all the way!*

While they argued, a waitress brought us cake. "Would you like anything else?"

Josh said, "Actually, I'd like a c—"

I'm not sure how to describe what happened next, although I could write it in music notation. The cello part is marked "solo" and repeats that C for two million measures while the first violin is at rest and the viola's part is marked "blush." The second violin is supporting the cello, with little "nod" marks, while the waitress, who I guess is our audience, stays stock still.

Josh managed to get out "Caa—" before blocking, and then he burst out laughing.

Shreya said, "Should I get you a menu so you can point?" and he laughed even harder.

Harrison looked worried. "I'm not sure if I should be laughing."

"You mmm-might as well." Josh grinned. "I'll try again."

I tensed in anticipation of the waitress's disgust, except she maintained a poker face while Josh stammered very hard over, eventually, "Cap-pu-cchi-no," a word I'd never realized consists entirely of booby-traps for the stuttering brain.

Shreya gave a restrained, "Yay!" and Josh, inexplicably, beamed. "I knew you could do it."

The waitress bent close. "My cousin stutters." Then she fled to the kitchen.

Flushed, Josh wore a satisfaction I hadn't seen in...well, I certainly hadn't seen it in the first grade cafeteria, where he'd brown-bagged it rather than try telling the lunch lady he wanted a hamburger instead of a hot dog.

Harrison said, "Mind sharing what that was all about?"

"Two words every stu-stutterer has problems with,"

Josh said, then paused. "Three. First is that it's unfair that 'st-stutter' begins with S-T. Second is his name. And third—" He looked up, and yeah, that was pride. "Third is ca—"

He blocked again. Shreya broke up in giggles, and I hid behind my hands.

The waitress returned with Josh's hard-won cappuccino and a coffee pot, from which she refilled everyone else's.

Harrison glared at her retreating form. "I hate that. I get my coffee with the perfect balance of cream and sugar, and without asking, they refill it right to the very top so I can't fix it."

"My God, I'm sorry," Shreya whispered. "That's terrible."

"It's such a pain. Oh, you're making fun of me." I wasn't sure what tipped him off because Shreya had her hands clasped and so help me, tears in her eyes. Harrison's eyes crinkled. "Say, Josh, if you want a cappuccino every day, I hear there's this device."

Josh's eyes flashed. "I hear I t-t-t-turned it down, too."

"Hey, guys!" said an approaching figure.

The only other male in the room averted a fight by introducing himself as the father-to-be, "solely necessary to lure in the mom!" Heavy-set and dressed as if for an afternoon wedding, he smiled easily and often. Perhaps desperate for a testosterone boost, the guy seated himself between Harrison and Josh.

"You guys are awesome." The dad pulled out his checkbook. "My father-in-law recommended you."

Antennae up, Harrison said, "Where did he hear us?"

"At his retirement dinner. He said one of you was ready to die."

Harrison raised a hand guiltily.

The man handed the check to Harrison, who passed it to me. I glanced at it, then handed it back. "You didn't write in the memo line."

The guy laughed. "Should I write 'amazing performance'?"

"You should always write the memo. That way you can

prove what it was for."

The guy grinned. "Would you do that even to your mom?"

I rolled my eyes. "My mom was the one who argued until I had to write two checks for the same thing. So yeah."

Silence fell around the table with everyone looking uncomfortable, as if someone had farted. Finally the new dad said, "Well, I trust you."

I pocketed the money. You just can't save some people from themselves.

Conversation stayed stopped until Harrison realized the guy had checks left. "If you want Mozart, there's some on our group's CD."

The man nodded. "I know. I copied my father-in-law's," and Harrison gave a wounded look.

Shreya had been staring distractedly around the room, but now she gestured to the side. "Is that your mother-in-law?"

I pivoted to look behind me, only then realizing that while most of the women clustered up front for the present-fest, one remained at her table: the woman we'd played for at the retirement party.

I said, "Was she in a wheel-chair then?"

Or on oxygen? Because she certainly was now.

The new father shook his head. "She has emphysema. My father-in-law retired because the company got hostile about him taking intermittent leave when she went on hospice care. Called it an 'undue disruption.' He told them no job was worth that."

"Oh my God," Josh whispered.

Shreya rose and went to the woman's side.

That made no sense at all. Who wouldn't give a guy time to care for his family? Wasn't that what you had family for? God knows I'd be expected to quit my job if my grandparents needed care. What executive thought this guy's work was so important they couldn't get along without him?

And well, they were getting along without him now, weren't they?

The new dad was saying, "Stacy's aunt was supposed to sit with her, but I guess she went to watch the gifts."

Shreya spoke to the woman while the other guests ogled a stroller more complex than the space shuttle. I stood to join them, but unlike Shreya, I couldn't think of what you say to a dying woman, so instead I wandered over to the rhyming placards. They had a station for decorating a baby t-shirt, some projects already spread out to dry. How many shirts did two babies need?

Beside that were several cards in a glass bowl, along with the sign asking for advice.

As I glanced over the display, violin music stopped me. I turned.

Alone at the table with the new mom's forgotten mother, Shreya played "Danny's Song," the same one requested a month ago.

The women at the front kept watching the gifts, but for me, I could focus on nothing else.

Even seated, Shreya moved with the music. The woman in the wheelchair wore a broad smile as Shreya serenaded her, only her.

With the song finished, Shreya lowered her violin, and the woman leaned forward to lay a hand on her arm. It was clearly thanks. Shreya bowed her head, a reply that was just as clearly, "It was nothing." But it wasn't nothing, was it?

I turned back to the display, and with trembling hands, I printed on one of the index cards, "Love them both the same."

I stuffed the card down the side of the bowl, then rushed back to the fortress of music stands.

TWENTY-ONE

Invading Canada would have taken less preparation than vacationing at the Archer lake house. Harrison goaded me to create a spreadsheet. I didn't. I should have.

First problem: we needed to get there. The only car among us was a beat-up Jetta, too small to hold four adults, their instruments, and their luggage. And while Amtrak had a station fifteen miles from Lake George, we needed transportation after arrival.

Harrison, therefore, rented an SUV without consulting us, then insisted on paying because it was his idea. And then because the rental was from a Westchester agency, he decided Josh, Shreya, and I would meet him at his parents' home in Chappaqua.

"Shreya will have to meet you guys in Brooklyn," he said.

Josh said, "It makes more sense for me to get J-J-Joey and then swing by Shreya's. Queens, right?"

Harrison said, "It's better if you all start in one place."

Harrison figured if Josh picked up me and Shreya at the same time, he could just take off for all parts North, whereas if Josh got me first, we'd have to (brace yourself) *get off the highway* and *find Shreya's place*, and somehow in doing this we'd lose an hour.

Josh said, "Why should Shreya have to haul her stuff on

the subway?"

Harrison said, "It'll save an hour." He turned to her. "Can you get a ride to Brooklyn?"

Josh was glaring by that point. "I do know how to drive."

And Harrison just blew onward with hurricane force. "At that time of day, you'll want to take the Saw Mill Parkway."

Josh said, "I'm taking the Sp-Sprain Brook."

Harrison shook his head. "It's not worth it. Take the Saw Mill."

Josh said, "You know, since you're such an expert, maybe you should drive a cab? Like, every day?"

Harrison said, "Just do it, okay? Why are you arguing?"

It turned out the reason for Harrison's obsession with the extra hour was that the roads in Lake George wouldn't be lighted (seriously?) and we needed a plumber to turn the water back on. Two half-days for travel, three full days for practice. Chappaqua to Lake George would be a three and a half hour drive, although Harrison did add, "That's not factoring in the way Josh speeds," to many protests from Josh that he wasn't actually a maniac.

It was harder to pick clothes than I thought. Actually just one particular article of clothing. In the end, I took the plunge and cut the tags off my pretty blue shirt.

On D-Day, Josh and I (and my blue shirt) waited in my apartment for Shreya. The self-nominated Snack Master, I made sandwiches while he puttered around.

From the next room I heard, "You s-s-saved this?"

I turned to find him holding our grammar school yearbook. I was about to reply that of course I saved it when I saw what he was holding: a slip of paper.

The one he'd passed me on the last day. The one saying, "Will you be my first kiss?"

I flushed right up to my eyeballs. "Um...yeah."

He blocked.

I turned back to the counter. Damn, damn, damn. Him finding that—either he'd think I was pathetic for saving it or he'd be angry at himself for wasting his first kiss.

I heard the book touch the table, then felt him behind me. I couldn't face him. He rested a hand on my shoulder, then guided me around toward him. He put his other hand under my chin so I was looking right at him.

He said, "Could I have another?"

He leaned forward, and I stretched toward him. He kissed me on the lips.

Unapologetic, so strong. Unexpected, and over so soon.

He withdrew, half-smiling, a little breathless.

I stammered, "I'm sorry." My cheeks burned. "I didn't— I mean, I figured—"

"Thank you." Josh averted his gaze. "It's s-sweet that you sss-saved it."

I closed my eyes so I wouldn't cry, hunching my shoulders and fighting the feel of his hands.

He drew me closer as if he to kiss him again, and I clenched my jaw, afraid I might cry.

Footsteps in the hallway. Blinking rapidly, I backed half a step into the kitchen counter. Josh moved toward the table as the door opened, and in sauntered my sister.

She studied Josh like someone scanning merchandise at the secondhand store, a look she'd given me all too many times. Nope, not up to par. Josh must have fit the décor because without saying hello to him, she handed me three beat-up paperbacks. "Here. These are for you."

I edged toward her. "Thank you?"

She shrugged. "Grandma said you were going into the wilderness, and I thought, hell, she should at least have something to do. You always liked those."

Still with hand-printed $1 stickers from the used book shop, the books were each two inches thick, women sprawled across the covers with bosoms and ruffles. Each woman's goal would be to land the richest nobleman so she'd be happy forever. It figured Viv wouldn't know the difference between historical fiction and regency romance. "Thanks."

She finally acknowledged Josh. "Are you from the quartet?"

Josh nodded.

Viv looked back. "I know I've been pushing you about the apartment. But Zaden and I need to get out of there. Mom thinks I'm totally incompetent and treats me like a child."

"I'm sorry to hear that." I folded my arms. "But that doesn't mean you can move in here."

Viv pointed to the closed door off to the side of the kitchen. "Why don't you use that room?"

"No insulation. It sucks out the heat."

She shook her head. "That's just ridiculous. Grandma and Grandpa should have fixed that."

Josh glared at her under the brim of the ball cap, but I was shocked that my sister cared whether I was cold. "Well, that's another reason you don't want it. It's not big enough for you."

As she said, "And what about the—" the door opened behind her. Shreya blew inside, her cheeks flushed. "Josh-man, I need your keys so I can load up your trunk." She looked Viv up and down. "Have we met?"

Viv stared at our blue-haired willowy sylvan. "Who are you?"

"I'm the second violinist." She flashed a smile while catching Josh's keys out of the air. "Thanks, dude."

Shreya took her cue from Josh, who still eyeballed Viv with caution. She didn't leave even though she had Josh's keys in her hands and, presumably, someone waiting in a car outside.

Viv looked from one to the other, and then to me, annoyed. As if she had something to say to me? Why was she even here? "Well, you guys have a good trip. You'll be back on Tuesday? Tuesday evening?"

I said, "Yeah," and she left.

As Viv went down the stairs, Shreya looked at me, her expression one big question mark. "Look, I don't know," I muttered, and she rolled her eyes.

I turned back to Josh, only he had picked up my bag. "Let's g-get the car packed," he said, and he went downstairs with Shreya.

Last to leave, I paused on the landing, dizzy from Josh's kiss and my resulting bewilderment. Then, with a firm click, I locked the door and left it all behind.

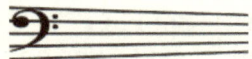

Harrison's parents had not been timid about using their money to buy a home. Although not quite a mansion, it sat well back from the road on a landscaped lawn, and my mouth went dry just beholding it.

Josh hesitated before making a left onto their property. "Do you think they'll b-b-ban my car from their property?"

Shreya snickered. "They'll just throw a tarp over it."

Unreassured, Josh pulled up alongside their garage.

Harrison met us on the driveway and grabbed Josh to pick up the rental (and maybe keep Josh's Jetta from infecting the asphalt). I watched Josh leave, wondering whether I felt disappointed that I couldn't pull him aside. Disappointed... or relieved.

Harrison's father invited me and Shreya into the kitchen. We sat at the table while Mrs. Archer prepared lunch and Mr. Archer "mingled."

I'd met the Archers at the quartet's earliest functions. We'd booked our initial weddings only because Mr. Archer, who knew half of New York, promoted his son's quartet with a doggedness that made Harrison seem like a second-century hermit. This might have been the first time either of them saw me in jeans. Or Shreya in blue hair.

While a grey-muzzled golden retriever sprawled treacherously across the tiles, Mrs. Archer started the coffee maker. "Harry wanted to order a pizza, but I said that was ridiculous."

With a covert glance at me, Shreya mouthed, "Harry?" I stifled a giggle.

Mr. Archer leaned back in his chair. "Make sure to take time to relax. You've been under such pressure lately with the festival, the recording, and your regular bookings, not to mention needing a lawyer to deal with that record label."

"And what's the problem with involving a lawyer?" said Mrs. Archer, Esquire. Dr. Archer laughed and flashed her a very-familiar demurring smile.

"It's not that bad," I said. "She only called once."

Shreya said quickly, "You're an attorney, right, Mrs. Archer?"

"Please call me Allison."

Mrs. Archer said she normally worked on Saturdays, but she'd wanted to give us a proper sendoff. And aww, she was Harrison's biggest fan. She loved our first CD and looked forward to the next.

As soon as Harrison set foot in the door, the golden retriever padded out of the kitchen. Harrison got down so the dog could be all over him, tail wagging like a hurricane fan on a movie set. "What a good girl!" He roughed her fur. "Yes, you missed me. You've totally forgotten I was here half an hour ago. Good girl!"

Shreya said, "I didn't know you had a dog."

"Of course I had a dog," he baby-talked. The dog couldn't get enough, flopping onto the tiles. "Who wouldn't want this dog?"

Mrs. Archer said, "Harry wanted to take Sherbet with him into Manhattan, but that wouldn't have been fair. She loves it here."

Harrison grinned as he stood. "Yeah, Dad gave me the same cock-and-bull story about how she needed the space to run, when really he wanted to keep her."

Josh stood behind him, avoiding everyone's gaze, "everyone" being "me."

The dog stayed for lunch. Mrs. Archer had made subs, and

for Shreya there was hummus, a tabouli salad, plus a bowl of fruit she could graze on for a week. Mrs. Archer pretended not to notice Harrison slipping tidbits to the dog.

"Thank you so much for letting us use your house," I said. "What will we need to do?"

"Harry's done it a thousand times," said Mrs. Archer— surely hyperbole unless Harrison was seven centuries older than his violin. She gave a rundown (during which Harrison looked bored) and finished by rendering special instructions about the quilts: they must not ever, under any circumstances, be slept under. They must be removed from the beds and enshrined.

I started taking notes.

Harrison rolled his eyes.

She pulled out a checklist. "Joey, you're my kind of woman."

Despite the fact that any one of the kitchen tiles cost more than a week's groceries, the Archers loved us. Harrison's dad was...well, like this:

"What have you planned for dinner tonight?"

Harrison shrugged. "Chinese takeout."

With Josh's dad, the conversation would have ended there. Mr. Archer's conversation continued:

"You should take them to the Inn at Erlowest."

"Chinese is fine."

"What's wrong with the Inn? They have the region's highest-rated wine cellar."

"We'll be tired."

"The view will restore you to life!" Dear Old Dad then told Shreya that the restaurant was set in an old castle, with a fireplace large enough to roast a cow, plus a grand piano, triangular plates, entrees you'd remember for fifty years, and dessert coffees prepared right at the table.

Next he turned the sales pitch on me, asking had I ever dined in a place like that, and then back to Harrison with the offer of his credit card. "I'll ask the maître d' to reserve a table by the window. What time would you like the reservations?"

Harrison, irritated, muttered, "We'll figure it out when we get there."

Shreya was smothering giggles. Someone could out-Harrison Harrison.

Mrs. Archer turned to Josh. "You've been quiet. Is everything fine?"

Josh nodded.

The six of us had taken a family configuration: Mom and Dad on either end, Shreya and Harrison on one side, Josh and me on the other. Until Mrs. Archer pointed it out, I hadn't noticed Josh's silence; he hadn't asked us to pass anything because all the platters had either gone around the table or were within arm's reach.

"Did you have enough to eat?" said Mrs. Archer, and this time, Josh forced a soft, "Yes, th-th-thank you."

"Oh, do you stutter?" Mr. Archer said it the same way I'd have said, "Oh, are you Italian?" He reached for the salad dressing. "*The Journal of the American Medical Association* just printed a study of hundreds of stutterers, and there may be a genetic connection."

Josh looked the same way I'd feel if Mrs. Archer had noticed holes in my socks and started recommending places to buy socks on the cheap.

Harrison leaned forward. "It's genetic?"

His father shook his head. "The sad truth, Harry, is we don't know. It's multifactorial, although these researchers narrowed their study to a specific polygenic mutation in three genes, two of which are associated with fatal childhood diseases; in their opinion, having all three mutated genes offered a protective effect."

This was wild. How could someone just whip off a sentence like that? Maybe we could talk about me next, and Mrs. Archer would say, "Oh, toxic family dynamics? According to recent studies in triangulation—"

Harrison had gotten excited. "Oh, like how the gene for

sickle cell anemia stops you from getting malaria."

When did Harrison learn to talk genetics? Oh, maybe at the table with a father who discussed medical journals rather than other family members.

Shreya looked at Josh in awe. "Dude, you're a mutant!"

Josh grinned. "I'll be on the X-Men. The St-stutterer."

"But not all the time." Harrison looked so damn cheerful. "When you had those headphones on, you talked like a pro!"

In a string quartet, it's imperative for the violist to read the first violinist's mind. Because the viola is less responsive, the violist needs to start half a second before the violinists for the instruments to sound at the same time. Right then, I read Harrison's mind. Read it just like one of Viv's cheap paperbacks.

Harrison's Dad, played more expertly than any violin, said, "Oh, the choral speech effect! Did you know there's a device that mimics it?"

That was the moment Shreya, our graceful and poised second violinist, knocked over her glass of water.

Conversation stopped as we donated our napkins. Shreya apologized, appearing chastened, while Mr. and Mrs. Archer reassured her all was fine, no harm done. Comfortable in the spotlight, Shreya took center stage while Josh fixed on Harrison a look that could have fried bacon.

Trembling, I handed out new napkins while Mrs. Archer replaced Shreya's water. Paging a diversion to the lunch table, stat! I said to Mr. Archer, "Where do you work?"

"Saint Francis Hospital in Port Washington," he said.

That was why you don't put the violist in the spotlight: I didn't know how to prolong the diversion, and by the time I thought to ask what his specialty was, he had returned to Josh. "I could look into a prosthetic for you."

"I don't mean to interfere," Shreya said, giving the world's most ironic preface, "but are you a speech pathologist?"

Mrs. Archer said, "St. Francis is a cardiac care center. He's a surgeon."

Ha-ha, I got jitters when the worst I could do was hit a wrong note, and this guy resectioned aortas with a knife.

Mr. Archer plowed through two theories about a neurological basis for stuttering, something about the *Lancet* saying the left hemisphere had low activity in the speech areas and high levels of dopamine... and while it was nice not to hear Josh treated like an idiot, this felt intrusive. Dr. Archer wanted a world-class neurologist to scan Josh until he lit up like a Christmas tree.

Harrison said, "It's too bad musicians can't get employer-based health insurance."

Shreya sounded icy. "As I recall, *Harry*, it wasn't about the money."

Mr. Archer said, "Not a problem. I know a neurologist who does quite a bit of pro-bono work. I'll find out where he's working now that St. Vincent's closed."

Harrison looked across the table. "Isn't that great, Josh?"

Josh shot me a look. Helpless. And my brain dial-toned. Change the subject. Somehow. Anyhow.

I said, "Those are both Catholic hospitals, right? That's why they do charitable work?" I looked right at Shreya, and her eyes went wide. "Did you know Shreya became Catholic last year?"

Based on her glare, the next glass of water was heading right in my face.

Mrs. Archer said, "Oh? I assumed you were vegetarian for religious reasons."

She forced a laugh. "You mean if you'd known it was only dietary preference, you'd have slipped me some chicken?"

"Of course not," she said, as if my mother didn't brag about crap like that. "Did you become vegetarian in college?"

Shreya looked like she'd make an exception for my still-beating heart. "I've never eaten meat."

Harrison's mother said, "That's wonderful. I'd be lost if I had to remove meat from my diet, but you didn't have to habituate."

"I wish I could convince all my patients to try vegetarianism," said Mr. Archer. "It's so much healthier for their hearts."

We never got back to Josh. Shreya praised the increase in vegetarian restaurants, and Mr. Archer reassured Harrison the Inn had veggie entrees. Good. I could hear Josh sweating.

After lunch we transferred our stuff into the SUV, which Harrison's mother worried might be too much vehicle for Harrison to handle. I kept unpacking the dog from the trunk, so I didn't notice right away what Shreya had brought: a double-violin case.

Harrison said, "You play two at once?"

Shreya seemed subdued. "It was supposed to be a treat. If we're jamming."

Josh exclaimed, "And an amplifier!"

I rushed over. "I can't wait to hear!"

She turned away.

Josh said, "Can we amp the c-cello?"

Harrison said, "If we amp the viola, maybe we can hear it," and I shot him a filthy look.

Harrison's mother said, "Harry, show them your little violin."

His eyes flared. "Uh—they've seen those before."

She returned a moment later with a tiny coffin-style case. "Eighth-size?" I said.

"Quarter." She opened it with flourish. "He bought it with his tooth fairy money."

Josh murmured to Harrison, "Dude, you had a hhh-hundred teeth?"

Shreya had to turn away or die laughing. I'd never seen Harrison this red, not even last year when a bride flashed him.

"He knew exactly what he wanted," Mr. Archer said as Harrison slipped it away from his mother. "He paid for it himself, and then we had to drive him right to his instructor."

About-facing, Harrison said, "Thanks for the trip down

memory lane. We need to finish packing."

"Can we take the little violin?" Josh sing-songed.

Harrison stalked away. "No."

The hilarity over, we loaded the SUV with a cello, three violins, an amp, and my viola. Josh fixed his EZ Pass to the windshield and dropped his iPod onto the console. Harrison went afterward with his own iPod and plugged it in.

Mr. Archer had boxes filled with cleaning supplies and liquids that would have frozen in an unheated house. When I bent to get one, Josh grabbed me around the waist. I shrieked as he lifted, then carried me over his shoulder and set me in the trunk.

I stared up only to find him grinning. I gulped.

His eyes glinted. "Sorry. M-mistake."

As I slid out of the SUV, I noticed Harrison open-mouthed. "Just a misunderstanding," I called, darting back to the boxes.

Harrison thrust a crate at Josh's chest. "You need to work on your aim."

Josh smirked.

Right, just a misunderstanding. This was Josh on the move, and it made no sense, no sense at all. Harrison thought it too—and he didn't even know Josh kissed me.

Mrs. Archer brought out a cooler. "Things for breakfast."

Harrison seemed startled. "We'd planned a grocery run tonight."

She kissed him on the cheek. "Now you can wait until tomorrow."

I looked away.

At noon, Josh took the keys from Harrison. We hadn't even gotten out of the driveway before he said, "You'll need to dirrr-rect me to the highway... Harry."

"Don't even," he muttered. Thus began our musical vacation.

TWENTY-TWO

O n the highway, the universe inverted. Josh turned into a good driver.

Once we entered the Saw Mill and weren't turning left, merging, or stopping for lights, Josh settled into one rate of speed. He didn't insult the other drivers; instead, he talked to us. He had his arm resting on the door, with the beginning of a driver's tan, and he was wearing the hell out of a pair of sunglasses. He was speeding—of course he was, or I'd have checked for a pulse—but not enough to make me curl into a fetal position and find religion.

In a white Ford Expedition with leather interior and surround sound, he'd taken the Cabbie out of the Cellist. He was comfortable. Happy.

Meanwhile, I wasn't. I mean, the seats were cushy, the temperature fine, and the engine less noisy than my fridge. Harrison and Shreya chatted while Beethoven played. But my brain itched.

Hadn't Josh said we could expect only a certain level of friendship? Forever? I'd figured Harrison would start gunning for a friends-with-benefits arrangement. Not Josh.

Yet he wasn't leaving many options. Kissing me might have meant, "Since we'll be sleeping in the same house, maybe we can get some action." It might have been rubbing my past in my face. It might have been "On second thought, maybe I can tolerate you."

Harrison and Josh began ranting about last night's Yankee game. Harrison had watched it; Josh had listened in the cab. It was a barn-burner but hardly a pitcher's duel, with a final score of twelve to ten in extra innings. Josh and Harrison had reversed roles in the Yankee Fan Dance. Harrison had decided management and all the pitchers needed to be tried as war criminals, while Josh crowed that this was the year they'd go all the way, that of course they wouldn't choke *this* year.

"Never underestimate their ability to snatch defeat from the jaws of victory," Harrison said. Then, "Joey, know anything that rhymes with 'direct deposit'?"

Josh laughed. I said nothing.

He turned all the way in his seat. "You okay back there?" I nodded. "For a minute I thought we'd forgotten you."

Shreya stared out the window.

Harrison said, "You don't get car-sick, do you?"

"I'm fine." Fine being a relative term. "Just thinking."

Josh checked me in the rear-view mirror, but I couldn't see his eyes through the dark lenses.

Harrison said, "Want to share?"

And because I didn't want to share, I said, "Did I tell you? About eleven o'clock last night, a driver asked me to marry him."

All three burst out laughing. Harrison said, "No kidding? Doesn't he know you're supposed to marry me?"

"I guess not, because he paid his toll and proposed. Said he'd been admiring me for weeks."

Harrison looked baffled. "You don't know who he was?"

"Not a clue." I rolled my eyes. "I hope he didn't have a ring."

Josh said, "Was he drunk?"

Oh, good call. I never thought to have the boys in blue pick him up at the other end of the tunnel, assuming the guy even got there, and then he could weave all over the same roads as Josh. Damn.

Harrison snorted. "Are you jealous because no one ever hopped in the cab and proposed marriage to you?"

"One very dr-runk woman did." He laughed. "I rrr-replied to her in Spanish. She left me alone after that."

Shreya picked up her head. "Hablas español?"

"I said '¿Dónde está el m-museo, señorita?'" He grinned. "I can stu-stutter in two languages."

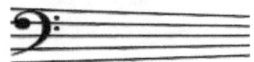

The trees thickened, and then the mountains swalllowed us. I-87 ran parallel to the Hudson River, and every so often we crested a rise that drew an "Oh, wow!" as the valley and all the Earth's grandeur opened before us. Although not from Harrison, who after Fleetwood Mac ran out of greatest hits took the opportunity to play "Guess the Soloist" with five versions of the Tchaikovsky violin concerto.

By the fourth one, it became apparent: the host for our working-weekend-musical-retreat felt the pressure crescendoing like the mountains putting pressure on our eardrums. His great-grandparents might disapprove from the grave when he didn't serve tea as the clock chimed four.

Past Albany, Harrison latched onto a new topic: *Are you sure you can do the driving?* And every time, Josh replied, *Yeah, I drive for a living.* We heard advice about speed traps, or whether Josh was too slow or too fast, and Josh mm-hmmed but kept doing whatever he wanted.

By the time we crossed the Hudson, the river was narrow like Park Avenue. Harrison suggested we stop at the Glens Falls rest area because the water wouldn't be on in the house. We took turns baby-sitting the car, and Harrison phoned the plumber to meet us.

At that point, inspired either by male bravado or by

concern that we arrive in one piece, Harrison insisted on driving the final fifteen minutes. He took us up the west side of the lake and showed us Millionaire's Row, but (he laughed) we would just drive right past that.

At what was barely a gap in the woods, Harrison made a right, and the SUV dipped down an inclined driveway so steep Josh must have been slamming the imaginary brake pedal. I leaned forward for the first glimpse of our destination, a two-storey white house with red trim and a wraparound porch. The windows were larger than our SUV.

"Whoa," Shreya breathed. "You spent your summers here?"

I wouldn't have asked questions while Harrison crawled our vehicle down the slopes of doom, but Shreya never struck me as risk-averse.

"Only weekends, although some years we got summer jobs."

The woods closed around our car. We descended until the house dominated our field of view, and then the driveway opened out into enough pavement to park five cars. The lake side of the house was windows, windows, windows, and beside the house a wooden walkway led to a dock.

I pointed to where the driveway continued to the lake's edge. "Do you sometimes park underwater?"

He snorted. "All the time. Or maybe it's a boat ramp."

Josh laughed.

Flushed, I hopped out of the car and put some distance between us. Sure, because where to park my boat is one of those questions I consider on a regular basis. That and how to polish my gold.

I stopped at the edge of the grass to zip my jacket and shove my hands in the pockets. Well, maybe it was a dumb question. Dozens of boats dotted the lake.

After a moment, I spotted a hawk circling. The water sounded so still, but the air clamored with birds. The trees had the tiniest light-green leaves, which confused me until

I realized these were buds, barely erupted. The rare pink or white tree was covered in flowers. We'd come to open Harrison's house, but nature was opening house too. New branches, buds, seeds pushing their heads from beneath leaves that had fallen four months ago.

I'd expected the brochure of a resort. But this...? Maybe they had houses like this in heaven. I couldn't imagine owning this and not living here all the time, certainly not in favor of New York.

It was too much, too much. A symphony of greens had assaulted my world of grey and black. Instead I retreated to the porch where Harrison wrestled a lock last bolted in October.

It clunked open, and we stepped inside to stale air in a huge open space. The foyer had a twenty-foot ceiling and a window where there should have been a second floor. Shreya and Josh followed my lead, gaping in the cathedral entryway.

Harrison let down his bag and flipped on the lights. "Cool. Power's on. It's always a trick when they forget." He rubbed his hands together, then adjusted the thermostat. In the basement, a heater huffed to life. "Let's unload the car. Then I'll give you a tour."

Following him, Shreya murmured, "Yeah, I think we'll do okay this week."

In came the instruments, the bags, the cleaning supplies. In came the cooler, which Harrison would have unpacked right away, except I shut the refrigerator door and turned it on. "We need to leave things in the cooler until this gets cold."

He looked surprised, but then Josh entered with a man in his late fifties. Harrison greeted the man by name and went with him to whatever mysterious equipment would get the water turned on. Shortly after, the thrum of the heater was joined by the whirr of a shop-vac.

Shreya opened all the ground-floor windows, then looked at me on the white leather couch. "Was I the only one who had no clue how posh this place would be?"

I chuckled. "You don't live like this?"

"Somehow, no. Will your apartment ever be featured on a reality show?"

"Not unless they start one called *Dumps*." I glanced at Josh. "How are you doing?"

He joined me on the couch. "T-t-t-t—" He stopped, collected himself, then tried again. "Ti-red."

Shreya said, "I thought you drive for a living."

I gave Josh a little push. "This wasn't even combat driving."

He shifted so he was closer to me, and the hair stood up on my arms. "This was lon-ng and steady. No breaks."

Josh then told his own tale of woe: knowing he'd lose five days' income, he'd picked up one last passenger at LaGuardia after he'd ordinarily have gone off-duty. Of course she wanted a ride to Yonkers, so he got home after four, then was up again at eight to pack and get us.

Harrison called up the stairs to test the sink, and a minute later, he bounded up from the basement with the plumber-guy. As the guy pulled away, Harrison shook his head. "We could do that ourselves. In October he filled the pipes with antifreeze, and now he vacuumed it out. Big deal." He turned to us. "The faucets need to run for a bit, so let's have a tour!"

We began exploring Casa Archer on the Lake, a house with no name but which really needed one. Harrison started with that amazing foyer, gesturing left toward the living room with white leather couches and bookshelves. Passing through that, we reached the formal dining room at the back corner, featuring a china cabinet and sideboard, plus a shiny table that seated twelve.

Harrison led us through the kitchen (directly behind the foyer) and past a breakfast nook to a sunken family room that took up the right half of the house. Under the cathedral ceilings were a pool table, home theater, and stereo. It had a fireplace, but I couldn't imagine Harrison's family doing anything as pedestrian as burning wood.

Harrison had us bring our bags up the curving staircase to the second floor, although he left his downstairs, maybe waiting for his butler. Upstairs was quite a bit smaller because (Harrison said) they'd knocked out two bedrooms to remodel with the cathedral ceiling. He stopped at the first bedroom ("Josh") which had a blue wallpaper theme and a view of the lake.

"Don't sit on the Sacred Quilt of Doom," I said, and Josh mischievously touched it while Shreya gasped.

The next bedroom faced the woods, neutral beige and with a star on its sacred quilt. "Shreya." At the bathroom he turned on the faucets, and then we stepped into a master suite larger than my apartment. It had a king-size bed, a checkerboard Sacred Quilt, a window seat in a bump-out window, and its own bathroom.

I wasn't the world's best mathematician, but we'd just run out of bedrooms. Harrison put his arm around my shoulder. "You and I will stay here."

I twisted out from under his arm and bumped into Josh, who'd come up behind me. "What are you talking about? I'm not marrying you, Harrison!"

Shreya got right in Harrison's face. "For God's sake! Did you plan this whole trip just to proposition her in front of me and Josh?"

I wrapped my arms around myself. "How is that professional?"

"I'm kidding!" He shot a look at Josh, but he might as well have asked for help from the National Organization Of Women. "I screwed things up. I forgot the air mattress. I was going to camp out on Josh's floor."

Josh said, "I'm f-f-fine with a couch."

Shreya said, "This is a huge bed. Joey and I will stay right here, that way you and Josh each get a room." She folded her arms. "But cut the bullshit. We're all tired and hungry, and that's not improved by the addition of sexual harassment."

Harrison's eyes flared. "That's not sexual harassment!"

"Why don't you call your attorney brother and ask what happens to a CEO who informs his direct report she has to put out on a business trip." She stalked out of the room, only to return momentarily with her bag. She dropped it on the bed.

Harrison had gone white, and his voice was stricken. "I never thought about it that way."

She glared at me, and I set my bag beside hers. "Let's go back downstairs, okay?"

"You go." Harrison's voice was thin. "I need to run the water."

Minutes later, Shreya all but spewed smoke from her ears as she paced the living room. "When he does that, tell him to fuck off. Why do you let this go on?"

Good question, and my only answer was, we began as we meant to go on, only we never really knew how that was. "It's a game. It's just a game."

"And when did his little game start? Back when it was you and three guys, and he wanted to secure the alpha male position by staking claim to the only female?"

My cheeks burned.

She folded her arms. "You need to look at reality. It's a game until the minute he tells you to get in bed with him. It's a game until he threatens your job. You know what? Call his bluff. Say yes and see what he does?"

I had no idea what he'd do. I wasn't sure if he'd laugh it off or plan a fancy wedding.

Josh put his hands in his pockets and leaned against the wall "Or you could cut to the chase and t-t-tell him to go to hell."

"And while we're on the subject of being inappropriate," Shreya said, her voice dangerously low, "what was that at lunch?"

I dropped my head and closed my eyes.

I could feel her in front of me. "I told you we weren't

discussing why I became Catholic. I'll tell you whatever you need to know, and when I say something is not for conversation, that means it's not for conversation."

My eyes stung. "But— You wanted to distract Harrison's father from attacking Josh!"

"And you improved matters by attacking me?" She dropped onto the couch, arms folded. "If you wanted to distract him, why not tell him about your mysterious vanishing father and your bitch-whore sister?" Her eyes bored into mine. "That would have changed the subject every bit as well, and you know what? The man might have floated you the cash for your own fucking house so your sister could have your grandmother's attic."

My mouth trembled. "My sister isn't that bad! She just got knocked up. And my Mom is helping her out—"

"Don't waste time defending your family," Shreya snapped. "They're not the ones I'm angry at. It's not noble to betray your friends. "

Josh had fallen silent. I wrapped my arms around my waist. "I'm sorry. I was wrong."

She didn't respond. Finally I said, "You think so much faster than I do, knocking over the water."

She chuckled. "I screwed up. I wanted the thing to land in Harrison's lap."

I bit my lip. Yeah, that would have changed the subject.

The first of the faucets shut off upstairs. Not wanting to see Harrison yet, I went into the kitchen, eyes stinging. Awesome. Just in case Josh teetered too close to believing I wasn't a shitty friend, I'd just proven I was.

The fridge was finally chillier than everyone's attitudes, so I unpacked the cooler. Milk and orange juice, butter, bagels. There was even a cake. His dad might be bull-headed, but hey, who'd argue with a strawberry cheesecake?

I looked up from fridge to find Harrison. The first thing he did was apologize, and I told him it was all right. We both ignored the dark looks Josh shot at him.

With that swept under the rug, I retrieved his mother's checklist and settled down with the laptop. I opened a spreadsheet.

"You've got to be kidding!" Harrison leaned over me and shut the lid. "We've got four solid days, and we're highly motivated. I'm not going to consult the computer for permission to sit on the couch." He interrupted my protest with, "We went through a lot of trouble getting here, therefore we'll go through the trouble of gathering in the living room to practice."

I glared at him.

"It's called spontaneity. Give it a try."

Hearing the bickering, Shreya reappeared, her eyes haunted.

I said, "Your mom's list has twenty items."

He snapped the list with a sound like a firecracker. "Half of which are done." (A gross exaggeration: even in Harrison's universe, two was not half of twenty.) "Power's on. Water's on. There are four of us, and there's only one house. Trust me that we can wrestle it into submission."

Shreya said, too loudly, "I feel like playing. Anyone up for practice?" She folded her arms. "As in *right now*?"

Harrison looked at me in mock surprise. "Wow! Almost as if that's why we came!"

I didn't follow at once. Trying to get my brain back in groove, I stayed in the kitchen examining the list and estimating the time it would take to knock off a few items. Organize things, organize the world. Item 15: "Wash sheets." What would that take, a couple of hours? But we could do other things at the same time. Fuse the chores. We'd get it all done. We had to.

Jittery, I reached into the laptop bag and plugged it into the charger, then pulled out my phone to charge it too, except— No charger.

Terrific. I'd meant to grab that before we left, but after Josh...and then after my sister...I totally forgot. It was in my kitchen, charging nothing.

I pulled out my phone: battery at half life. We'd been calling and texting all morning to coordinate the trip. Well, nothing for it. I powered off the phone and shoved it in my pocket.

That's when I heard Harrison exclaim, "What the hell is that?"

I snickered. This couldn't be anything but good.

In the living room I found Shreya holding the skeleton of a violin. It was the violin equivalent of a hard-body electric guitar, in a cobalt blue that glittered.

"It matches your hair!" I bounced on my toes. "You never said which violin!"

"Oh, this is just a little something." She plugged it into the amplifier and swiped her bow across the strings, creating a shocking whine.

Even as Harrison's eyes popped, I squealed.

She dialed up the distortion and, Cease and Desist or not, went to town on the riff from "Hotel California." Despite the cord running down her chest and into the amp, she danced as she played, her musical power under loose restraint.

We stood open-mouthed. She turned to Harrison, eyes wicked, and extended it to him.

He grimaced. "I'm going to hate myself for this, aren't I?"

Harrison picked what else but Bach? After a few measures he stopped, as though afraid of the thing in his hands. "This is a travesty."

"Didn't sss-sound like that to me." Josh took it and flipped it over, examined the mechanism, then handed it back. "There's no vibration other than the str-strings? The amp does the rest?"

She nodded. "For the right song, it's tremendously cool."

Harrison tried again with the adagio from *The Hunt*. He restrained his vibrato to let the violin itself make the distortion.

I said, "Can I?" and then regretted it. But Shreya didn't

glare as he handed it to me.

First difference: the sound didn't emerge from under my ear, but from the amp. Second difference: in addition to being a lot lighter than a viola, it was ergonomic. I could have played for hours. The sound felt alive, a little out of control with the volume, but even so, I found myself smiling as I played.

As I handed it back to Shreya, I noticed Josh smiling too. At me.

Shreya said, "They have electric violas and cellos, you know."

"Great. An electric quartet." Harrison gave a mock shudder. "What do you do with that monstrosity?"

Shreya then treated us her defunct band's solo from "Come On Eileen." It was like listening to Eddie Van Halen if the world's greatest living guitarist had picked the violin instead. Beaming, I tucked in for a concert.

That's what we'd needed all along: a musical vacation. A chance to set aside the work of music and just...play. What did people do at a resort? Because I didn't imagine they went to beaches or mountains to be the same uptight selves they were in real life.

But Harrison looked baffled by Shreya's performance. Baffled and more than a little uptight. Sure, he complained about my schedule, but to him it wasn't a vacation after all as much as a business trip. And a trip to do things on his parents' house. And maybe a trip to shore up his position as our fearless leader.

Shreya finished and bowed, and I applauded. She grinned, then said, "Okay, now we can do Mozart."

As she put away her electric violin, I peeked into the case. She had a sparkly blue teddy bear fastened to the handle, and inside was a picture of an Indian couple (her parents?) and a hospital bracelet. Before I could look closer, though, she clicked it shut, saying, "First let's run through the festival playlist."

Smooth. That would keep Harrison from stopping us every five notes.

Harrison nodded. "Good idea. That will make sure everything fits into the time-slot, and we'll hear the transitions."

Um, yeah. That too.

We played for approximately one minute and seven-point-three-five seconds before Harrison stopped us...and Shreya produced a recorder. "Let's run through everything. Afterward, you can analyze it."

Give the woman an award. Give her two.

And shortly, after five festive fusions, I sat, dazzled. "That cannot have been half an hour."

Shreya clicked off the recorder. "Twenty-seven minutes and forty seconds."

I surprised myself by laughing. "It didn't feel nearly that long!"

"The recorder disagrees." She handed it over. "This, Fearless Leader, is for you to critique at your leisure."

Harrison said, "Actually, before we listen, I want to review measures fifty to seventy-five—"

Those words served as the pickup notes to the *Harrison Sonata*, twenty minutes of him and Shreya bickering about nine measures of Mozart's String Quartet in A Major. Nine irritating measures during which Josh would play seventy-three E notes in a row (I counted them) and I struggled not to die of frustration. Eventually I laid down my viola and left.

In the sunken living room I gazed out the window at the lake. It really was an amazing view. Kind of a shame to waste it by having me looking at it. The window should have been occupied by the Queen of Sweden, who would have appreciated it.

Josh appeared. "We're ready to move on."

Just like that, we were alone. "Um—" I should have prepared a speech. "Later...when you get a chance...I want to talk to you."

He stepped nearer, grinning. "I c-c-can't imagine why."

He stood so close his breath brushed my forehead. My pulse did a tremolo.

Harrison called, "Josh, is she lost?"

"I'm on my way!" I glanced at Josh, but he was looking right into my eyes, and I had no idea what to say, so I returned to Harrison.

TWENTY-THREE

After practice, Harrison said, "Anyone else want dinner?"
I said, "Um, that place your father suggested? I didn't bring my evening gown."

Harrison snickered. "Like I'm going to drag all of us over there. That'll be a great place for when we get—" He stopped short. "Tonight let's order Chinese."

And that was Harrison's lesson on how to deal with Harrison's tactics. Ignoring the bulldozer was a legal maneuver.

Harrison rooted through a kitchen drawer for a takeout menu, then muttered to himself, "Oh, I forgot: we live in the internet age." Instead he found their menu online with my laptop. Of course Harrison also had to check his email, and then with his phone he sent four texts. I just felt lucky they weren't to me. *Joey, I had a great idea about chicken lo mein!*

Josh took the notepad with our choices, dialed his cell, but then stopped. His face tightened, and he started breathing hard.

Harrison took the list. "I'll call."

Josh slumped at the table, head in his hands.

Shreya sat beside him while Harrison got out his phone. "You okay?"

"I c-c-can't do it." Josh pressed his fingers into his temples. "I hhh-hate ordering food."

Harrison paused. "Really? You've done it the last few times."

"B-b-because I ...hate it." Josh waved him off. "Just c-c-call."

While Harrison placed the order, Josh just looked beaten. So, a little risky, I played cello to his viola: standing behind him, I rubbed his shoulders. He tensed at first, then relaxed his head into his hands.

Harrison looked up to make a wiseacre remark, and then stopped cold.

Josh said, "I'm s-sorry. I should be able to do that."

"You get a pass." As I rubbed the bands of muscle, he melted. "You drove up here on only a few hours' sleep."

Stung, Harrison set down his phone. "I did offer to drive. I wouldn't have let you try to order if I'd realized you hated it."

"You're not my mmm-mother." The tension returned to Josh's shoulders. "I don't nnn-need you to look out for me."

Harrison said, "Get a EchoChamber. You won't need anyone to look after you."

"I don't need it now." Josh's voice sharpened. "Prr-roblem solved."

Harrison picked up the car keys. "Whatever. If you guys could find some plates before I get back, that'd be great."

In the cabinets I found every item double-bagged in plastic, and moments later had a dishpan full of sudsy water. Meanwhile Shreya and Josh picked a task off Mrs. Archer's list and walked the fence line to check for downed tree limbs.

Washing crystal water glasses, I watched Josh climbing the hill, the movement of his long limbs and his sharp-eyed profile with the jacket and baseball cap. The pines were just putting out new growth at the tips, slender green bits that stuck straight up, as if Nature were giving me the finger a thousand times over. If I'd been smarter, I'd have had Shreya wash dishes while I walked the fence. On the other hand, I considered Josh's shadowed eyes and how hard he was stuttering. Putting him on the spot while exhausted wasn't fair.

With the table set, I moved the laptop to the island, and it woke. Harrison hadn't logged out of his account, and as I was about to close the window, my eye caught the words "re: Hotel California rights."

It was the subject line of several emails from one Amy Aitken, Esquire. All marked read.

An attorney?

I clicked on the thread. It asked for a password, so I couldn't read it, but I didn't need to. Harrison's father said we'd involved an attorney; he hadn't meant the Eagles' attorney. Our fearless leader had lawyered-up in secret.

The front door opened, and Shreya was saying, "—yeah, I never saw anything like that—"

"Guys?" My voice wobbled. "Guys, I need you."

They came into the kitchen, Josh unzipping his jacket. Unsure how they'd respond, I said, "Harrison hired a lawyer."

They exchanged a look.

I recognized it. Like when my grandmother looked at my mother because she knew something, something I should have known except—I don't know, except they just never said.

Shreya spoke, the information building in my head like storm clouds. "Harrison's brother said it would be stupid not to have our interests protected." She looked down. "We couldn't count on the paper's attorneys. His mom recommended a lawyer who works in the entertainment industry."

My fists hurt. "Who's paying her?"

She said, "Harrison paid the retainer himself."

Of course he did. I shouldn't have bothered asking. "Why didn't you tell me?"

Josh looked away.

"He said you were upset," Shreya said.

"I'm more upset now!"

Shreya stared at the floor. "It seemed like a good idea when he sold it to us."

I stalked back to the table, unable to speak. Damn it, this was my group too. Was I five years old, that we can't tell Josie the things that might disturb her pretty head?

I set up for dinner. Napkins. Plates. Knives—and be careful not to insert this elegant serrated knife right into Harrison's elegant treacherous heart.

I still hadn't said another word when Harrison returned with a bag of MSG in five forms, two bottles of soda, and two six-packs of beer. Good. I'd need it.

Remember how quartet members could read each others' minds? Josh and Shreya vanished.

While Harrison unpacked, I said, "Amy Aitken."

His head jerked up. He didn't breathe.

"You left your inbox on the screen." I took the bag from his hands and distributed paper cartons, fortune cookies, and packets of soy sauce. "The nicest thing I can say is don't ever cheat on your wife, because you have the stealth of a hippopotamus."

Harrison edged back from the table. "Are you mad?"

Only the way the ocean was wet. "I had a right to know." I stepped toward him, and he inched backward again. "Why didn't you bother to tell your business manager? I'm not a child."

He said, "You were upset."

"Because it's upsetting to get sued! Why would defending ourselves upset me more?"

Harrison couldn't respond. Without his words, I could only judge from the flare of his eyes or the pitch of his brows, the shape of his mouth—and he was frightened. In his world, I'd never have found out, and he hadn't realized how much of a betrayal it was until after I had. Bastard.

I glared into his face. "Well?"

"You weren't just upset. You were crazed." He spoke faster. "I'd checked your voicemail like you told me to, and she'd left two more messages. That couldn't go on, so I deleted them and told her to call our own lawyer."

I trembled. "Are we going to court?"

He sounded hesitant. "She thinks they'll drop it as long as we don't do anything stupid. Which she's advised us not to."

That's good. If you hire an attorney, she ought to tell you not to be stupid. "How much are we paying her?"

"I took care of it."

"Then how much are we reimbursing you?"

Harrison started to speak, and I held up my hand. "When an attorney defends a business, the business pays."

He nodded.

"Get me the exact amount after dinner, and I'll transfer the funds. Now let's eat."

The food was hot. Good. Go was my temper.

If I weren't furious with everyone, it would have been comical how no one wanted to sit near me. Even Josh forgot about that kiss and sat at the opposite end. Shreya put herself cater-corner to him, leaving Harrison the choice of sitting at my side or directly opposite. He chose opposite. Let's glare. It added spice to a dinner conversation that otherwise consisted of "Can you pass the soy sauce." Eventually Shreya forced a subject-changing (subject-starting?) question about tourism, and Harrison, tentative, talked about Fort William Henry. He said you could hear the fort fire their cannons all summer, but given my pounding heart, I could hear them now.

A thousand days later, dinner ended with Harrison snapping open his fortune cookie. "Get this, guys: 'You are the crispy noodle in the vegetarian salad of life.'"

Josh said, "That should have been Shh...reya's."

Shreya intoned, "That is so deep," and then read hers. "Your everlasting patience will be rewarded sooner or later."

Even I laughed. Josh's said, "Pray for what you want, but work for the things you need."

Shreya said, "That's usually *Trust in God, but tie your camel*."

Harrison said, "*Trust in God, but keep your powder dry.*"

"That too," she said.

And I opened mine to find this: "When the heart can't speak, it sings."

Harrison snorted. "Wholesale theft. Victor Hugo said it first: 'Music expresses that which cannot be put into words and cannot remain silent.'"

Shreya rolled her eyes. "I doubt they have actual mystics writing these things."

Plagiarism or not, I tucked the fortune into my pocket and ate the cookie.

While we cleaned up, Harrison handed me a number on a yellow sticky note. Four figures. We hadn't been sued, but already lawyers were taking our money. Letting Shreya stacked dishes in the dishwasher, I logged into the bank account and reimbursed our very own son-of-a-lawyer.

As I took a screen shot of the confirmation page, Josh handed me a sticky note of his own: the circle with spikes (his hedgehog) curled into a ball and shedding sweat drops in front of a viola. A cloud hovered over the viola, raining a cluster of profanity symbols.

Grinning, I stuck it to the side of the laptop screen.

Then it hit me like a body blow—Josh had gone along with the deception. Josh would kiss me, but then he would deceive me. What had happened to my world?

When I heard a buzz, I thought it was my head, but Harrison glanced at his phone and beamed. "Great news, Josh! My dad says the neurologist can see you next week!"

I exclaimed, "Are you out of your fucking mind?"

Shreya said, "Who said your father could book an appointment?"

And Josh? Josh just stood open-mouthed.

"No, this is great!" Harrison beamed like a toothpaste commercial. "This guy has a waiting list for months, but he worked you into a cancellation before he goes to a conference in Germany."

Paging Dr. Steamroller to the kitchen. Harrison must have spent half the day coordinating this. Via text, so no one could overhear.

Josh shook his head. "I don't www-want an appointment. I'm fine."

"And now you'll be better than fine." Harrison started texting back. "It's in Manhattan so it's not a huge inconvenience, and it'll be free. How could you possibly object?"

"And yet he has," I snapped. "Several times."

Harrison looked up. "When did you become Josh's mouthpiece?"

"When did you?"

He shrugged. "Look, I'm not a doctor. Let the doctors figure it out."

Josh said, "I'm not g-g-g-going."

Harrison frowned. "My dad pulled strings for you."

"I didn't ask him to pull st-strings!" Josh said.

"But this guy is world-famous!"

World-famous neurologists being slightly more famous than world-class violists.

Josh folded his arms.

Harrison said, "Dad says it doesn't have to be a device. There's also drugs that can help stuttering."

Josh shook his head again. That wasn't a block. He was speechless.

Harrison frowned. "My father's going to be hurt."

Emotional blackmail. If you can't bulldoze them, wring them out to dry.

Josh, to his credit, said, "He has my s-sympathies. Tell him to cancel."

With a theatric sigh, Harrison texted again. Time for a subject change. Maybe someday I'd get good at those. "Guys, can we stop bickering and have dessert? Harrison's mom sent us a cake."

Shreya chuckled. "That's sweet."

Literally, yeah. Harrison went to the cabinets, I figured to get cake plates, and thirty seconds later set a box on the table in front of Josh.

Josh glared lasers. I couldn't figure out why until I registered what Harrison had produced. A cappuccino machine.

Harrison leaned forward and dropped his voice. "Here's a thought. Get the right equipment, and you can have whatever you want."

Josh stalked out of the kitchen.

Shreya turned from drying her hands. "I have a brilliant idea, Harrison." Her voice was a taut whisper. I wouldn't have bowed that overtightened string for fear it would snap in my face. "Shut the fuck up."

She left too.

For a moment, Harrison and I stood alone in the kitchen, and the only things I could think to say would have started a fight—a satisfying, necessary fight I should have started months ago. Years ago. Except now I stood in a stranger's kitchen, breathing another family's expensive air, and I had no idea how to start. *Begin as you mean to go on.*

Above my head, I heard the throaty vibrations of the cello warming up. Scales. Up up up two octaves, down again to the home note, then up again. Josh, accounted for.

Harrison walked away, into the living room, he turned on the TV.

Alone, I wondered how we'd gotten to this point: a quartet, quartered. Wasn't the point that we were supposed to stick together, each in a role?

Not wanting to be alone, I joined Shreya in the parlor. She stared out the window at rows of lights above the lake surface. A dinner cruise.

I said, "Are you still mad at me?"

She waved her hand with an *eh*. "You're in luck. Harrison pissed me off more. Him and his superhero father."

My mouth tightened. "What a jackass."

She blew out her breath. "Substitute 'jackass' for 'rich powerful guy who saves the lives of the less fortunate who don't know how to ask for themselves.' How could he pass up the opportunity? Don't we see Harrison doing that too?"

"Yeah, our fearless leader." Fearlessly watching TV. "Saving us by retaining a lawyer."

"I'm sorry," said Shreya. "I should have told you."

I rested my chin on my knees. "And I should have shut up."

It's not noble to betray your friends.

Shallow.

Terrific. The more things changed.

Shreya's mouth twitched. "Look, I'll get over it. But you need to talk to Josh." The cello sang through the ceiling, the benefit of an instrument that touched the floor. "You're his touchstone."

I shook my head. "I'm the last person he wants to talk to right now."

Even as Shreya asked why, I heard, "Mind if I join you?" Harrison entered without waiting for an answer. "You guys okay?"

I refused to look at him. "I was asking Shreya if she knew why second violinists never suffer from hemorrhoids."

Harrison knew the rest of the joke: all the assholes become first violinists.

Instead of retorting, he dropped into a seat near the windows. "Josh will come around."

I snapped, "How's he supposed to 'come around' when you keep hammering on a non-topic?"

"Yeah, funny that," Shreya murmured.

I ignored her. "And what was that about Josh taking drugs? He doesn't want to stick a thing in his ear, but he'd take medication?"

Shreya said, "Or conversely, were you leveraging the drugs to make a thing in his ear seem palatable?"

Harrison said, "The neurologist told my dad that dopamine antagonists can help."

Harrison would know about antagonists. I said, "It's not

your decision! Josh is fine!"

"Josh was too wiped out to order dinner! Is that fine?" Harrison cocked his head. "At the top of our game, we're going to play four weddings every weekend. What will clients think when he can't talk after that?"

Unsteady, I said, "You promised you'd do the talking for him."

Lowering his voice, Harrison leaned toward me. "But Joey, I get that thing plugged into his head, and effectively, I am!"

Shreya made a strangled yelp. "For your own sake, don't ever say that again. He shouldn't be beholden to you for his voice."

"He could have everything he ever wanted if he'd just take it. He doesn't want to be my philanthropy project. I can respect that." His eyes were as bright as when he'd pitched the fusion mixes. "It wouldn't be from me!"

Shreya said, "And Josh's refusal? That means nothing?"

"Doctors live for this stuff." Harrison pretty much glowed. "My dad's friend would die happy if he could give Josh a voice."

"He's got a voice!" My hands clutched the throw blanket. "He's doing fine!"

"He'll do even better!" Harrison nodded. "You have to trust me. I've done a lot of research."

Taking my shock for agreement, Harrison turned to Shreya. "I don't mean to divert a good dogpile, but I'd assumed you were vegetarian because you were Hindu."

Shreya shot me a look, and I shrank.

She said, "My parents are Hindu, and they raised me vegetarian."

I looked up. "Wait a minute—?"

Chuckling, she sat back. "You're going to ask why my vegetarian parents sell hot dogs?"

Harrison sounded baffled. "Your parents sell hot dogs?"

She gave a sigh that would have impressed a silent movie

actress. "It's a sordid tale of woe and lachrymation."

"That's a pretty big word." Harrison made himself look serious. "You'd better lay it on us."

"Actually," she said, "that's something I consider private, kind of like how you never mentioned the tooth fairy dropping by with Benjamins."

Harrison's gaze sharpened. "You know—"

"Yeah," I muttered, "this is great for our stress level."

He and she both fell silent. Finally he got to his feet. "Come outside for a bit. There's something you need to see that'll make it all worthwhile."

A Stradivarius, the selection team from Carnegie Hall, and a winning lottery ticket? "What?"

He grinned. "You'll just have to come see."

Shreya shook her head. "Too cold for me. You want me to get Josh?"

Harrison shrugged. "If he comes down, send him. But for now he's getting in some good practice."

Outside, Harrison picked his steps down the unlighted walkway to the dock, me following. At the edge, he stopped.

"Isn't this amazing?" Harrison kept his voice low. "It's not like this later in the summer, when everyone comes back."

I waited for his cue as to what he expected.

First I noticed the stars. In the cloudless sky, the moon had reached a crescent-phase, and under so little light, the lake lay like a moment out of the apocalypse. In the chill, I craned my neck to pick out constellations, but I couldn't. Maybe I'd never seen stars, swallowed by streetlights as I kept my gaze grounded.

We stood surrounded by water and overarched by spangles. Harrison's voice was like a breath. "I love the silence. If we played here, it would carry the whole length of the lake." A wry chuckle. "I've always wanted to perform something from Handel's *Water Music* right out there on the boat, but then I think about tipping over and my violin getting wet, and I can't bear to try."

He was right on about the acoustics. With us totally still, I could hear voices from other homes in different directions, mingling like one conversation.

The faint sounds held power. The plips of water in the lake, the soosh of wavelets against the pilings, the distant hum of men's voices. Sometimes I'd hear a car. Overhead, a plane. I could pick out the notes of the cello, but muffled.

I sat on the dock, then stretched back on my hands. "I hope this works out."

Harrison sounded shocked. "Of course it'll work out. Trust me for once!"

"Trust you?" I struggled against the edge in my voice. "Sure, I'll forget you lied about that attorney."

"I never lied. I acted to protect the group."

"Protect it from me?"

"Regardless, everything's going to be fine. Tomorrow we'll get up, have coffee, and buckle down to the music. Everything's done now except playing together."

I shook my head.

Harrison said, "Hey, how do you stop a violist from drowning?"

"You take your foot off her head?"

"I was thinking you peel the stickers off the bottom of the bathtub."

"Ooh," I whispered. "Sparkly stickers?"

He chuckled. "Anything you want."

I pointed into the darkness. "I want an island. Could we maybe get the kayaks and visit one of those?"

"We could hit Diamond Island, but the nearby ones are privately owned."

Wow, your own island. Just sail off and if anyone follows, you tell them it's private. No one banging at your door, no one saying you're a goth who solicits from men in cars, no rich guy solving problems you don't have.

I could no longer hear traffic, only water slucking beneath the dock. "I still don't know."

"Trust me."

"But Josh—"

"He'll see reason." Harrison sounded breezy. "I wear contact lenses. People use hearing aids and crutches and insulin pumps all the time. You're supposed to use a device if your body isn't working right."

"Do you even hear yourself?" My voice dropped. "You're saying he's defective."

Harrison said, "He is defective. If his car had a flat tire, would he ride around on the rim?"

Conscious of the night, I kept my voice low. "He communicates fine."

"Haven't you ever wanted to reach down his throat to pull out whatever word's stuck this time?" Harrison shifted behind me. "I've seen how you want to slink away when someone stares."

Crap. Well, *now* I wanted to slink away.

"Why are repeating low notes so gorgeous in music and so awful in speech? I hear how he could be speaking, the same way I heard the way we could be playing." I heard a shuffle behind me as Harrison folded his arms, either stubborn or freezing. "Don't you ever hear what he isn't saying?"

My eyes stung. A month ago, I had. And ever since, I'd wished I hadn't.

He laughed. "We'll fit him out like the Bionic Man, and he'll tour the country telling kids about the cello and giving them taxi tours. Don't worry. I'll win him over."

"Of course you will." I sighed. "You know what's best for everyone. You're rich, charming, good with kids and good with dogs. What else is there?"

Harrison sounded hurt. "You left out my incredible good looks."

"I also left off your world-class ego."

"Touché!" He laughed out loud, and it carried over the water.

I couldn't get over how night could feel without thousands

of cars passing by. I tried to memorize the moon, the black smudge of the trees. Harrison wasn't the one I wanted on the dock, though. That one was ensconced on the second floor, playing his cello and smoldering. Although come to think of it, I could no longer hear the cello, so maybe he'd played himself into calmness.

Harrison said, "He'll regret it forever if he doesn't seize this opportunity."

Wisdom from the Great Harrison. "How would you know? You've never regretted a thing."

"I wouldn't say that." He drew out the final syllable.

His hand closed on my shoulder. Oh, no.

"About upstairs. I shouldn't have done that."

"You already apologized."

"Yeah, but—"

I didn't turn to him, instead focusing out over the water. Not this. Not now.

"I'd be lying if I said I didn't want to. I never thought of it as sexual harassment, and I'll stop. But—" His voice was very low. *Subito piano.* "Maybe I'm having difficulties with the professionalism thing."

I wanted to run. "Why bring it up now?"

He hesitated. "Maybe I've been looking for a halfway point, when there can't be. So... If I were to say it again—?" I braced myself. "Would you marry me someday?"

I didn't give myself rein to think in case I second-guessed. "I'm not marrying you, Harrison."

Other than the lapping water, Harrison's quiet spread to quell every sound around us.

I turned, and my night-adjusted vision could make out his face. Even I could barely hear myself. "If anything, these last weeks proved you right. It wouldn't end well. We work great together, but—"

"Spare me the 'you're a great guy' talk." Harrison glanced away. "I wish you didn't always have to make sense."

I made a strangled noise. "I make sense?"

"You know what I mean."

I couldn't have explained the layers of his thoughts, but I didn't think he regretted breaking up, not in general. Right now he did, and until the moment passed, it would eat him alive. Then he'd set it aside and we'd move forward. Friends. Partners. Players. But never lovers.

I looked over the water. "You'll do best with some classy chick who speaks French and never shopped Goodwill."

Harrison chuckled. "No one outclasses you." He waited. "Are you and— And who would you end up with?"

Not a cabbie cellist who looked coy when he averted his eyes or who had a characteristic smirk when starting trouble or who had told me to my face that he'd never trust me again because I tossed my friends to the lions. And who'd been right. Right about me.

I whispered, "I've never been much for predicting the future."

"Okay." He sounded relieved. "That's why you should trust me, see? Because I can." He stood. "Let's go back."

I started trailing Harrison up the path, but then I stopped to steal one extra moment with the nighttime. The low lights, the lake, the expansiveness. The silence.

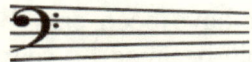

Inside, the TV babbled pitching statistics. Josh stared through the screen, and based on his scowl, the Yankees were getting their asses kicked. Grabbing my book, I joined him and Shreya in the family room. She was painting her nails blue. I curled up in a throw blanket.

Harrison flipped a switch on the mantle. Within moments, a fire flared in the fireplace.

I gaped at him.

"Oh, it's a gas log. We installed it during the remodel."

The room warmed nicely, but not the residents. Harrison

half-sat on the arm of the couch, commenting on the game. Then Harrison shifted to a seat, and Josh went to the pool table.

Over the course of the next hour, I moved in front of the fire and read eighty pages, Shreya went to bed, and Harrison finished a beer. Josh played pool the whole time. I couldn't tell if he was trying to annoy Harrison, but the "klok" of numbered balls gave the baseball announcer some competition.

When the game ended, Harrison showed us how to switch off the gas log. Then, about to leave, he looked at Josh, then at me. "Maybe you two should call it a night. It was a long drive."

Josh said, "I don't need another father."

When Harrison seemed worried, I said, "I'm good. At home, I'd still be working."

Harrison yielded. Over the next few minutes, I heard running water, footsteps, the click of a door. More clack and tok as Josh cleared the pool table.

Lying on my stomach, I buried myself back in my book, but I started when I felt his hand on my shoulder. He apologized, and I sat up.

I was one ball of tension. We were alone. And while my questions wouldn't have been easy before, after tonight it would be impossible because I'd seen in myself what Josh knew all along. I couldn't say, "But back then I was only sixteen," because now I was twenty-four and making all the same stupid mistakes.

He started to speak, but he blocked. I extended a hand, and he took it, then wrapped his arms around me and rested his forehead against mine.

Was he drunk? He ran his hand up my hair, tucking his face close so I could feel his breath against my neck, and as I closed my eyes, he pressed me against his chest.

The rhythm of his breathing fell in with mine. I reveled in the sound of him, the warmth, the scent, the fire before us. Wasn't this a scene I read in romance novels? What was I doing in one? But reluctant to lose the moment, I kept him cocooned around me.

He nuzzled my throat, and I snuggled closer. He laughed, a combination of surprise and thrill, and I slipped onto his lap. "You think they're both asleep?" I whispered.

"I don't care," he murmured.

He sat back and gazed into my eyes, rapt but disbelieving. I drank in the look, conscious of just how quiet the house had become. Even the fire made no noise. With my nerves alight, I traced my fingertips down his cheekbone, over his jaw, over his lips, and he kissed them. I inched closer. He kissed my hand, then my wrist.

He guided his hands up behind my neck, gentled my head toward him. I leaned forward, and we kissed.

This time he lingered, his fingers in my hair, and I moved closer so we were pressed pounding heart to pounding heart. This was not a mistake and not a tease. This was a kiss, two kisses, more.

I leaned back, as breathless as Josh. "You weren't kidding."

"Of course I wasn't k-kidding," and he drew me close to prove it.

Intoxicated, I murmured, "What are you thinking of?"

"Anything you w-want." He kissed my throat, my neck up to my ear, then back to my lips. "Right now, I'm just glad to be rrr-right here."

So was I. Shocked, delighted, and more than a little afraid because there was no way I deserved this, and as soon as Josh came to his senses, he would do what Harrison did, would do what my mother did. And then how could we work together, play together, even just be together with my heart raining down in pieces and him seeing right through me and knowing—knowing—

He ran his hands down my back, over my legs, then back up again to my shoulders. He put his hands behind my hips, shifting me so I was straddling his lap. He leaned back against the couch to take my weight against him.

I settled on his chest with my cheek pressed to his shoulder, eyes closed, breathing with him. Encircled in his arms, I struggled not think about what happened next.

My eyes stung, and I clutched Josh's arms.

"W-what's wrong?"

My throat closed. How could I ask him? But how could I not? Because if he was screwing with my head, if he was thinking he'd cleared it with me that I was shallow and that meant we could have a no-strings-attached roll in the hay... that I couldn't do. I couldn't do it for Harrison, and then Harrison had dumped me. And if Josh had me, all of me, and then made it clear he didn't mean it, I couldn't bear that. Harrison got rid of me when I didn't do what he wanted. And what would Josh do to me if I did?

Without looking up, I said in a broken voice, "Before we go further, I need to know...what changed your mind?"

"Nothing's ch-ch-changed."

Clearly something had.

He said, "I've wanted this for ten years."

I traced my finger over a shirt button. "With a little break in the middle."

"No, the ...whole time." He squeezed me. "You have no idea how often I dreamed about you. And now you're here."

I sat back, squinting at him. That drew him up short, and he flushed. "Uh-oh. Did I just rrr-ruin the mood?"

Had I fallen into an alternate universe? "How many beers did you have?"

He shrugged. "Just one."

Okay, then. "Didn't you say you couldn't date someone like me?"

He raised his eyebrows. "When did I say that?"

"After Jenny hit on you, when you said...we were talking in your car, and you said..." I swallowed hard. "You couldn't count on me." I ducked my head and hoped he didn't see my eyes water. "You said that's how you weeded out the shallow ones."

He tilted his head. "I n-never said *you* were shallow. I said—"

There's a joke that there's no difference between a bomb and a viola solo. By the time you hear it, it's too late to do anything about it.

And by the time I realized what he'd been saying back then, he realized what I thought he'd said.

He got that wide-eyed strangled look he had back when he wanted a trombone and received a cello. Exactly the same.

There, right there, ended the harmony, and we replaced it with silence. Josh and Joey's D-minor symphony, third movement, scherzo. Don't hang around for the fourth movement because it's over.

I climbed off his lap, and he tucked back his knees as if to keep me from returning. "W-which was it? You're d-dating Harrison? Or are you ash-sh-shamed to be seen with me?"

I looked into the fire, blinking in an attempt to stare myself back into self-control. "It isn't like that."

Naked shock. "You were?"

"No, but—" I closed my eyes. "Back when we went to that stupid dance, and everyone was staring at me, and you wouldn't look at me, and you kept twitching, and I couldn't deal with it. I'm sorry. I just— I thought you realized. I thought you hated me for it. I loved getting your letters."

"It's just me you couldn't stand." He angled his body away from me.

"You stopped writing me!"

"I thought you www-wanted to do the just-be-friends thing and you were upset that I'd put my arm around you!" Josh shook his head. "I didn't think you were..."

His face reddened as he fought the block. I knew which word had gotten away: "humiliated." The soft *H* an EchoChamber couldn't fix. You can't cure humiliation. Or hurt. Or a hollowed-out heart.

His eyes narrowed. "And you st-still think I'm *defective*?"

The room went airless. "No! I was sixteen! What the hell did I know when I was sixteen?"

But I could see him tallying up the times I'd looked away or couldn't meet his eyes while he stuttered, and what it added up to... I couldn't argue with the math.

He got back up on the couch while I stayed on the carpet. It wasn't a recoil as if he'd touched something hot. It was calculated, like a hiker avoiding an animal carcass.

Josh looked into the fire, a real fire shooting from a fake log. Then he closed his eyes and kept them closed, his whole face screwed tight. Finally he looked over his shoulder. "You're not dating Harrison, right? He didn't b-bring you outside to p-p-pro—"

I couldn't let that go on. "No, not tonight." I stared at the carpet. "We dated for a few weeks back when we started the quartet."

He whispered, "Really? And you didn't say?"

My eyes flared. "You wouldn't have joined?"

"I mmm-might not have." His eyes fixed on me for a long moment, but it took effort, and then he returned to letting me see the brim of his cap.

"Then we were right to break it off, because we need you."

He looked nauseated. "W-when did you break up?"

"Ages ago. The group didn't even have a name yet."

"Then why did he th-think he could bed you again this weekend?"

"Because he's a jerk?" My voice trembled. "So when you kissed me—? You meant it?"

He jerked to a stand in one motion. "Well, that was a mistake, wasn't it?" He glared right at me. "I'm sorry to have forced my presence on you."

My mouth quivered. "I'm sorry."

He turned away.

"Don't do this!" I scrambled to my feet. "I loved you. I screwed up. Don't go to bed mad."

He avoided me when I tried to touch him. "I'm not mad." His shoulders dropped. "More like—devastated."

He left me there in the living room, this gorgeous house, the cathedral ceiling, the fake fire, and me alone.

TWENTY-FOUR

I muted the viola and played for three hours.

With the fire at my back and my eyes closed, I played all the Bach in my repertoire, did scales until my head ached, and then played past the pain, blurry-eyed and unable to think. Go the hell away: Harrison on the dock, Shreya on the warpath, Josh upstairs with his heart bleeding out into the darkness.

That left me and Bach, so I did injury to Bach by playing too quickly with a rubber stopper across the bridge, played until pain shot up both arms and down my spine and across my shoulders.

I did what Shreya said, guessing at key signatures and improvising tunes I'd heard all my life. I did my own version of "Eleanor Rigby." All the lonely people. Who cared if I got it wrong? Why should my music be different than everything else?

Finally I struggled with shaking hands to slip Woody's centenarian body back into the slot, and I strapped everything down and locked it into place because at least I could keep one thing safe in a cushioned coffin where no one could hurt it. And with my hands pressed to the floor, half-kneeling, I screwed up my eyes and struggled not to fall apart.

With only the light slanting in from a hallway nightlight, I fished my pajamas out of my bag, dropping my clothes like a puddle around me and changing in the middle of the floor. I looked back at the hallway and hesitated.

Harrison's door. Josh's door.

Keeping silent, I crept toward Josh's door. I tested the handle.

Locked.

I tucked into the bed I shared with Shreya, wishing I could wriggle under Josh's thick covers, wake him by wrapping my arms around him, have him hug me and then tell me right now, in the dark, that he could forget what I'd done. He'd never forgive me. No one ever had. But maybe when the sun rose, he'd see I was no different than before, and he tolerated me then, so he could tolerate me still.

I barely slept before Shreya slipped out of bed at 5:15. Light split the room as she moved the curtains covering the window seat.

I pushed to sitting, and she turned, saying, "Listen."

I squinted at the shard of light and then I heard what she had. Birds. A thousand birds, singing for the sunrise with that same cacophony as a symphony orchestra getting in tune.

She whispered, "That makes everything worthwhile."

"I'm not sure." My voice wobbled. "I've messed everything up."

Dropping the curtain, she returned. "I'm over it. We're cool."

"We're not cool. I fucked up."

She tucked up her knees. "When did you get to bed?"

"Three-thirty."

"Go back to sleep. It'll look better when you're rested."

My throat tightened. "It'll never be okay."

She hugged me. "We'll be fine. Don't make me drag Harrison out of bed to tell you to trust him."

Shreya watched the sunrise over the lake while I lay with self-hatred gnawing at my heart and my stiff hands fingering some wordless tune against my pillow.

At ten I forced myself downstairs to breakfast. Harrison read his email while I choked down a half-bowl of cereal.

"Where's Josh?" I sounded raspy.

He shrugged. "Out on the porch, drinking coffee."

I stood.

Harrison's head snapped up. "I'll get him. We need to practice now."

I said, "Actually," and he said, "No. We came here to practice, and I don't want you to dig out that schedule again."

Aching, I set my bowl in the sink while he fetched Josh.

With no eye contact at all, Josh tuned his cello, drawn and pale. Harrison fussed with his A string while Shreya debated what we should practice first.

Harrison tried his A again and adjusted the fine-tuner.

"Dude, no one cares," Josh muttered.

"I care."

I figured we'd wait it out, but Josh said, "Seriously, it's fine."

Harrison ignored him until his A was vibrating at 442 rather than 441, then made sure endlessly tuning the A hadn't thrown the other three out of whack. We started.

The piece Shreya suggested we practice was, in fact, awful. The viola wasn't loud enough, the cello too loud, and the violins were in competition. After the tenth failure, Shreya said, "Let's give this a rest and try something else."

Harrison said, "We need to get this right. Josh, play it softer."

"I'm barely pl-playing as it is."

Harrison shrugged. "We can't hear the viola."

"Maybe I should just not pll-lay."

"Or, maybe you should play softer." He picked up his violin. "*Subito pianissimo*."

We played two bars before Harrison exclaimed, "For pity's sake, Josh!"

This time, Josh stared Harrison right in the eyes.

"Are you trying to drown out the viola?"

"Are you tr-rying to be a world-class asshole?"

Harrison stood, and then Josh was standing too.

"What the hell?" Harrison's hand tightened around his violin's neck. "Do you think I like stopping because you won't follow simple directions?"

Shreya jumped up. "Guys! Cool it!"

"I d-don't need your defense," Josh snapped.

I got out of my chair and backed away.

Harrison rolled his eyes. "By all means, then, explain. If you're playing softly enough, why can't I hear the viola?"

"Maybe the sound of your ego got in the way?"

Harrison raised his chin. "I'm talking about the music. We can discuss our personal greatness over lunch."

"I'm sick of you patronizing everyone just because you're the rich brat with the rich friends and the rich violin!" Josh stepped closer, making Harrison look up at him. "It's not all about the money!"

Harrison's face hardened. "Which one of us brought up the money? It wasn't me."

"You've got everything!" Josh shouted. "You're the one who's privileged and good with kids and good with dogs! What's left for the rest of your defective quartet?"

Shreya pushed between them. "Enough!"

I couldn't breathe. Because those words meant Josh had overheard us outside. And there was no way around that.

Harrison hadn't put it together, apparently, because he took a stab at the problem and missed. "Look, you can be pissed off all you want, but you're the one being stubborn."

Josh folded his arms. "And all should bow before the altruism of Harrison Archer?"

Harrison said, "It wouldn't be from me."

Josh snorted. "Yeah, I forgot. Fix the defective st-stutterer courtesy of the Jackass Medical Consortium."

Harrison's eyes blazed. "That's my father!"

"And apparently the one who gave you all your asshole

lessons. You were a great student." Josh put the cello in its case. "I hope this is quiet enough."

He stalked up the stairs. He wasn't halfway up before Shreya said, "Nicely done, Harrison."

Overhead, Josh slammed his door.

"He needs to get a grip," Harrison was saying, and Shreya shot back, "And that wasn't the way to do it. What's wrong with you?"

Biting my lip, I went to the bottom step. Because I wanted to go up. And I knew I should stay down.

Shreya put away her violin. "You saw he was tense. I told you to drop it. This whole trip was a mistake."

A wonderful house. A beautiful lake. I wanted to go home. I wanted these two days never to have happened.

Shreya came up behind me. "You need to talk him down."

"I talked to him last night." My eyes stung. "It didn't go very well."

Harrison said, "He needs time to cool off."

I went into the kitchen and hunted until I found a kettle. I set it to boil, but then I couldn't turn up any hot chocolate. It would have to be tea instead. Josh did that for me when I was upset. If I did it for him, would he acknowledge the peace offering? Would he listen long enough for me to apologize?

Defective.

Had he heard Harrison's half-baked question about dating again? Had he heard my answer?

While I waited for the kettle, I strained to hear cello vibrations through the ceiling. I could catch urgent conversation from Harrison and Shreya in the next room. Nothing from Josh.

In the dining room, the sun gleamed on the tabletop. Did the china in the curio cabinet ever see something as normal as lunch? Did apologies taste better in fragile tea-cups?

The kettle shrieked, and in the next second, so did Shreya. "Joey! Get over here!"

I dropped the kettle back onto the burner and rushed to

the entryway. Josh stood with his duffle bag over his shoulder and his cello case against the wall.

Shreya yanked me by the arm. "Talk to him! Stop him!"

Josh dumped his bag by the front door, his mouth tight, his hat low.

I tried to touch him, but he jerked away.

Harrison said, "And how exactly are you leaving? You plan on walking to New York?"

He pulled on his jacket. No answer. Of course not. Why open his mouth and sound defective?

Harrison put his hand on Josh's wrist, and Josh pushed him back.

"You can't get anywhere from here. This isn't the city. Get your ass inside and quit the dramatics."

Josh's eyes narrowed. "Amtrak. Car service. I have a phone."

Harrison was breathing hard. "If you leave, don't bother coming back."

"Harrison!" I got right in his face. "No!"

Josh zipped the jacket all the way to his neck. "Why would you want me to c-come back? I'm defective."

My ears rang. "Josh, don't. He didn't mean it that way!"

"Not good with dogs, either."

My voice cracked. "Please. We can work this out. Give it a chance!"

"I did." Josh looked outside. "I'm done."

I stepped right next to him. "I'm going with you."

Josh looked me in the eyes. "No." And he left.

Shreya followed him out the door.

I made my way to the steps and sat on the lowest, face in my hands.

Harrison watched at the entrance. Then, "What happened last night?"

I lowered my forehead so I leaned on my knees. Oh my God. Just like that, it was over. Seventeen years of friendship, done.

I whispered, "Go apologize before he's gone."

"Car's here already." Harrison narrowed his eyes. "I don't beg people to stay."

Shreya returned alone. I looked her in the eyes, and for a moment, all our voices were silenced.

TWENTY-FIVE

Harrison and Shreya talked at the kitchen table. I wanted them to shut up, and at the same time, I hungered to hear it over and over. My hands shook, so I pressed an empty mug in my palms. I'd never made Josh's tea.

The post-mortem felt like ants crawling all over me, but they reconstructed his timeline. Shreya confirmed he went to find us on the dock but returned before we did. She'd asked him why, and he'd said it was too cold. Absolutely he overheard Harrison.

During the vivisection, Harrison's eyes bored into me. I could feel it even when I wasn't looking. I shrunk. It never ends well.

I went upstairs. Let them keep looping the past.

At Josh's blue bedroom, I stepped into the still-life: the dormered windows, the motes in the sunlight, the unmade bed, the towel cast across the closet door. He should have walked in any minute now. He wouldn't. Harrison and I had pushed him to where he was waiting for "just one more thing." And this morning, we'd handed it to him on a sterling silver platter.

Curling on the bed, I hugged his pillow. It should have

smelled like him, but we'd wash the sheets and even that bit would be gone. Gone.

Mrs. Galen.

Mr. Galen.

I powered on my cell phone and texted Josh. Only, "I'm sorry."

I texted his father next. "Josh is going home. Let me know when he gets in."

I powered down the phone. I told myself it was to save the battery, but in reality, I didn't want to hear the silence of Josh never calling me again.

After lunch, we opted to drive back.

In the SUV, Harrison played four symphonies in a row. The same discussion had circled for hours, but the facts hadn't changed. We had a dozen event bookings, five in June alone. We had a festival in ten days. We had no cellist.

Harrison wanted one of our backups to play the festival. Shreya wanted to cancel. I wanted them to shut up, but when they asked, I said, "We have to play it. No matter what it takes."

Harrison decided to drop us off at the head of the 1 line in the Bronx so we could take the subway into the city. He'd go back north for dinner with his parents and spend the night.

Shreya, so damn practical, said, "What do you want to do about practice tomorrow?"

Harrison said, "We should take a day off."

I shook my head. "We need our equilibrium back, and fast."

Shreya frowned. "Another day will give Josh time to cool down. Then I'll call him and let him know he's still welcome."

"He's not." Harrison pulled up at Van Cortlandt Park and set the car in neutral. "I don't put up with that pretty-princess crap. Flouncing out the door isn't a perpetual ticket to getting your way."

"He has the right to change his mind."

"I have the right not to change mine."

I shook my head. "I know, I know, you never forgive anyone. You'll have to call our backups. Alex is the best able to catch up in time for the festival."

Shreya stayed slumped in her seat. "You can call anyone you like. I'm taking tomorrow off."

"No." I looked right at her. "We need to keep playing. I don't care what else happens."

Five minutes later, Shreya and I sat in an otherwise-empty train car at the first stop, and I tucked my duffle bag between the seat and my legs to divert the heat from the blowers.

She stared at the platform. "Just so you know, the oldest trick in the book is crying in the shower. And if you scream into a pillow, no one can hear."

I blew at my bangs. "Even if they did, who'd care?"

Just get home. Get into my crappy little apartment and take the world's longest shower. Curl up in bed with whatever book happened to be on my nightstand, maybe even one of Viv's paperbacks. Crawl into my nest and make the world go away.

Shreya kept up her thousand-mile stare.

I muttered, "Hooray. I save some vacation time."

She said, "Yeah, there's probably still time for me to get back on the schedule."

I frowned. "You need to get on your parents' schedule?"

"What?" Then her eyes widened. "No, I'm assistant manager at a grocery store. I help my parents in the morning, but after practices, you can usually find me making a schedule or overriding mistakes on the registers."

I blinked. "Oh. I didn't realize."

We returned to silence, and when it lasted a long time, I traced a toe over the scuffed floor. "Is this a total fucking nightmare for you? Seeing it happen twice?"

"At least it's not my fault."

I stiffened. "You're saying it's mine?"

"No, I mean last time, it was my fault. Kind of."

Silence for a minute.

Finally I said, "What did you do?"

She wove her fingers together. "Remember the tall guy on the cover, the guitarist?" When I nodded, she said, "We were dating, and I got pregnant." She flipped the handle of her violin case toward her, away from her, toward her again, a rhythmic tok against the hum of the idling train. "He didn't want the baby, and I kind of did."

Why was she telling me this not twenty-four hours after she'd called me a snake?

And then I remembered my mother at the kitchen table after Viv revealed her pregnancy. With Josh out, maybe Shreya wanted to shore up an ally, payment due in confidences?

Not sure what she expected, I said, "Did your parents make you get rid of it?"

"Right before I planned to tell them, I started bleeding." She closed her eyes. "Like a period times fifteen. But we had a gig. I was passing out, but Trevor told me to wear black and play through."

My eyes went huge.

"Between songs I staggered off stage and curled up on the stock room floor. I think the club manager called a cab. Somehow I ended up in the ER at NYU."

I said, "You lost the baby?"

Biting her lip, she nodded. "I didn't know yet. When they asked if I had a religious affiliation, I realized we were so close to St. Francis Church, so I asked them to call Deacon Cullity, the guy who gave me the violin, and for whatever reason, he came."

She stopped flipping the handle to trace her finger along the seam of the case. At that point, the inbound train rolled into the station, and our doors slid shut.

I said, "Weren't you worried he'd hate you because you

weren't married?"

She shrugged. "He stayed with me during the ultrasound. They found a ten-week pregnancy with no heartbeat. He asked permission to pray for me, and I said sure. They wheeled me back to the ER for a transfusion, and while I was waiting for a D&C, the baby came out."

I wanted to vomit. "Oh my God."

Her mouth quivered. "It hurt like the Incredible Hulk punched me in the stomach, and it was just this tiny thing, the size of a rosin cake. I didn't think I'd see it. Deacon Cullity rang for the nurse and then asked if I wanted the baby baptized. He was crying too. I don't think he knew what to do. So I said sure. I mean, I had to do something for it."

I put my hand on hers as the train lurched into motion. A life never lived. A song never started, only the pickup notes.

"I called Trevor to get me. And he yelled that I'd screwed up the whole gig. And that—" Her voice cracked. "—that was the real end. Even if he never wanted the kid, he didn't— He was just—"

The doors opened and closed at the next stop, but no one entered. As we lurched into motion, I said, "And later you became Catholic?"

She forced a chuckle. "I figured, since we baptized the baby, I should find out where it went. I stuck around." Then she looked to me. "But maybe Josh felt like that, like you killed his baby and told him he didn't matter. Then Harrison did his dominance display, and Josh just couldn't suck it up anymore." She clenched her hands. "But I don't know. Maybe with all these secrets, we were doomed from the start."

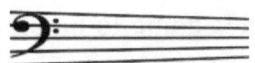

The instant I reached home, it was all wrong. Lights blazed in my apartment, and cardboard boxes lay strewn near the trash cans. I steeled myself for mayhem because clearly my mother or my sister had been through my apartment, taking my milk and opening my mail and hunting for my viola.

Which was on my shoulder.

Oh. That was sobering like a cold shower. With another look at the lights, I hid my viola behind a trash can, noting as I did that the stray's bowls had been knocked aside. What was going on?

Carrying only my duffle bag, I hiked up the steps to my apartment, where I found my sister leaving with a cardboard box.

"What are you doing here?" she exclaimed.

I yanked the box from her hands to find my books. "These are mine! This is my apartment!"

She tossed her head. "You've been evicted."

I thrust the box back at her and stormed downstairs to my grandparents' kitchen. I banged open the door and rushed up against the kitchen table. "What are you doing? Why are you letting her pillage my apartment?"

Grandma and Grandpa both looked up. Grandma looked uneasy. "But Joey, you weren't paying the rent."

"What are you talking about? I have never, not once, missed a rent payment!"

Three thoughts crashed into one another all at the same time. At my back, my sister entered Grandma's apartment. In my head, I pieced together why all spring my sister had been hanging around come rent day. And in front of me, my Grandmother said, "But I haven't gotten a check since January."

I whirled toward my sister. "You fucking thief!"

She smirked. "Prove it."

"Your signature is going to be on those checks!" I knew every one of those checks had cleared the bank because when every penny counts, you count them. "You want to explain to the police how you stole from your grandmother?"

My grandmother said, "Girls?"

I turned to her. "Why didn't you say anything? I live right

upstairs!"

Grandma said, "I told your mother to ask you why you weren't paying."

"And it's 'Lived,'" said my sister. "I'm moved in. Possession is nine tenths of the law."

My grandmother said, "Joey, please don't be mad at her. Think of your sister."

My pulse beat a staccato, and if I'd tried to speak, I'd have started screaming because I couldn't believe—except I could believe every word. This was my life right here.

My eyes stung, and my throat closed up.

"You can't be so selfish," Grandma said. "I need a tenant who pays on time."

You had that. You fucking had a tenant who paid the rent on time, and I don't for a minute think my sister will unless she gets Mom to do it, and you're telling me not to get upset because she's family, but why am I not family?

"But you still have a home," Grandma said, "You can go back and live with your mother."

I couldn't breathe. I shoved past Viv into the hallway.

Viv said, "Come back tomorrow to pack your other shit because I don't want to keep climbing over it."

I grabbed one of Viv's regency romances from my bag and hurled it at her head. I had the satisfaction of her ducking as it smashed into a shelf and knocked a metal bowl to the floor with a clang. I couldn't hear anything else as I ran for the front door.

I grabbed my viola from behind the trash cans. Beneath it I found a cockroach, four inches long and flat on its back, skinny legs in the air. I jolted back from the thing in disgust.

I pivoted, only to find my stray cat with his head poking out between two bars of the stair rail. Hungry.

"I'm sorry." Blinking hard, I couldn't manage more than a whisper. "I have nothing to give you."

TWENTY-SIX

I had:
- one viola
- one bag with toiletries and clothing
- a cell phone with an hour's charge
- ten dollars but no credit card and no ATM card

If this had happened last week, I'd have fled to Josh's. Even if Josh weren't around, Ed would have taken me in. But now? Now I walked until I lost myself, as if anyone back home would have bothered pursuing.

No, not back "home." Back "there."

I stopped at a Wendy's. Although I couldn't eat, I needed a place to triage my life.

The upshot: I could survive a couple of days. Owning nothing and living nowhere made it easier to walk away. But it was pretty damned hard to survive without money.

The first thing I did, the very first, sitting with a rapidly-cooling cup of burnt coffee, was to spend some of my remaining battery calling my credit card company. Five minutes on hold never bothered me so much. I reported the card lost and they froze the account. Next I called the cell phone company and had them note the account to verify any changes by calling me back at my phone number. I then used the Wendy's WiFi to access the Post Office website and hold mail delivery. I put a fraud alert on my SSN.

I tried to freeze my checking account, but the bank was closed. I'd call again in the morning.

Finally, my hands shaking, I checked voicemail. Five missed calls.

Josh. Oh, God, let it be Josh.

But no. All five were from my mother.

First call: urging me to call her right back. Second call: call her right now, something was happening. On and on they went. Actually, one was from my dad, telling me I was worrying my mother by not calling back, but that was effectively her anyhow. By the last, she was furious, demanding I call her right-this-instant-young-lady.

Right. What was she going to do? Tell me to sleep in my old room now decorated with footballs and with chewing gum stuck to the closet door? No, probably I'd be on the couch. And then what? I'd get to listen to what a failure I am because, you know, successful people's sisters don't steal their checks and their apartments.

I'd sooner die. That wasn't hyperbole.

I stared at my coffee, trying to imagine calling Shreya. And I couldn't. Not that she wouldn't have helped, but what she would say, her reaction. She said my parents were evil, but...were they? It's not like I had no place to go. I didn't want to go to my parents, but it wasn't like they wanted me on the streets. Shreya would tell me, "I told you so." Harrison had told me to cut them off, too, but how could I be that selfish? And... And who cared?, because it really didn't matter now.

Josh would have let me crash on his couch without pushing for a game plan. I'd have been okay. I needed okay.

When it got good and dark, I walked to the subway, not thinking too hard about my next move. Viv had stolen my apartment. Time to pay it forward.

One train-trip later, with the spare key clutched so tight it hurt my palm, I collapsed onto Harrison's couch.

Curled beneath a tasteful red and black throw I'd never seen unfolded, I covered my face in my hands and whispered, "Grandpa... Grandpa, I have nowhere to go."

Dawn. I awakened on Harrison's couch with music cycling in my head. Only two measures, but in their murmur I detected the hint of a tune. I hummed them as I forced my limbs to unlock. Ten notes. My fingers imitated them, and I wondered where this orphan passage fit into the world and what song it called home.

I struggled not to panic as I checked the clock. Six AM. Harrison shouldn't return before nine. He had nothing waiting, so why cram into a train with a thousand commuters?

I didn't know when or how I'd get a shower again, so I rushed through, making sure to leave the bathroom immaculate. Using his phone, I called mine to pick up voicemail. My mom had left more messages, pleading with me to come home. Not that she wanted to know where was I, or how was I doing, just...come home. Delete, delete. Dad and Grandma, too, "You're upsetting your mother!" There was nothing from Josh. I used the phone once more to call my job, leaving a message that I'd work today, then cleared out.

Okay. So until the afternoon it was me, myself, and nowhere.

Commuters encroached on the streets like a rising tide. With some of my remaining money I got a coffee, but I needed an infusion of cash. And soon. I was hungry.

Viv had my apartment and all my important papers, and Josh had my soul. But I still had my grandfather's viola. Pyrrhus would have been proud.

The viola and my bag and I camped out on a bench at Tompkins Square Park where I finished my coffee. Those two measures of music, what were they? They felt old, like something played in an early recital, only they didn't "feel" baroque or classical...more folksy. Finally, figuring I'd already endured every humiliation, I got out my viola to work out those notes. Familiar, so familiar. What key was that...?

I played them again, and suddenly I remembered the next measure.

I ran through those three, and then I had a song. A whole song.

My grandfather's song.

I got to my feet and played through, starting from those two measures mid-refrain, then pushing through as I remembered the ascending sounds, the call in the middle that always reminded me of a bird of prey, how Grandpa crescendoed, and how a near-hush followed which made the house become bigger and emptier.

Oh, Grandpa, Grandpa...

With my eyes closed, I reached through time to resurrect his song, and I let it unfurl its wings like a bird caged for five years.

I finished with my eyes burning.

A small cough started me. A short woman in a brown jacket looked nervous as she handed me a dollar. "I would have put this in your case, but it wasn't open."

I took it, my throat too tight to respond.

Thank you, Grandpa. Thank you. Thank you for a song. Thank you for a way out.

I took the train to Union Square where the L, the R, and the IRT lines intersected. I paced the uptown R platform before choosing a niche under a stairwell. Laughing at myself, I scattered change in the case. I couldn't get any lower down the musical totem pole, but hey, if I got arrested for busking, at least the police would put me up at the New York's Finest Motel.

A train thundered into the station, overwhelming my opening notes. Then, after it pulled out, I restarted my grandfather's song.

Self-conscious, I hated how the stairwell distorted the sound. But as I stepped forward, I realized how few people watched. And if no one paid attention, why be afraid? Sometimes you just had to make a noise. So I made a lot of it.

The trains came every three minutes. I had only that long to capture someone's attention and their spare change. Bach was good, but I heard more coin-jingles for "Eleanor Rigby," so I changed my repertoire to match my audience. Between trains, I cleared the bills from the case. And once I warmed up, I started to move.

I channeled Shreya with a half-dance, then extemporized for the slate-faced commuters, bestowing a little intrigue on their trip. I played "Hotel California." I was nowhere near as good as my role model, but nevertheless thrilled to be playing at all, and later relieved when an outgoing train swallowed my mistakes.

The platform regularly crowded and cleared, like a pulse of people. The trains belched heat onto the platform, and next came the drafts. My poor viola. When I had only a couple of watchers, I wondered if something had happened to the L line. Maybe the police were shunting people aside, the better to arrest me.

Then I checked my watch and discovered the reason: nine-fifteen. Wow. Wow!

Ten minutes later in Union Square Park, I smoothed the crumpled bills: eleven bucks. At the bottom of the duffle bag, my hand probed for quarters in the sea of change. Shreya said she'd cleared twenty to forty dollars an hour. She'd failed to mention it would weigh ten pounds.

I rubbed that scar on my hand, queasy. I hadn't eaten since yesterday. A deli turned up a loaf of bread and a jar of peanut-butter. At the counter, I asked the sullen clerk for a plastic knife, and she thrust one at me.

It took half a minute to make a sandwich, and I devoured it on a bench, wondering when was the last time a sandwich had left me filled. I thought about making a noise, making money, making joy.

At nine-forty-five, I finished an interminable call to get my bank account locked tighter than Fort Knox. I'd missed a call from Harrison, so looking with sadness at the fading battery indicator, I called back.

"What's up?" I'd separated ten dollars in quarters into one of the side pockets, and they gave a metallic grind as I moved.

"I'm home. Were you serious about practicing today?"

"Sure, before I go to work. I—" As I looked around Union Square Park, my voice caught. I imagined playing under the sun, not for the spare change but for the music. Why did it feel so long since I'd truly played?

Harrison said, "You okay?"

"I'm fine. I'll be there at ten-thirty."

"Where are you?"

Practically under his window. "Just go ahead and call Shreya and our replacement cellists."

I powered off the phone to preserve whatever battery remained.

I strolled in Harrison's general direction, no longer surrounded by speed-walking office workers, and held both my viola and duffle bag on straps over the same shoulder. Manhattan in the daylight seemed like a wedding hall with the tables stripped. I could make music here. It was a stage with no props on it. Yet.

I walked past Only Strings, and with nowhere to go, I stopped inside. At the counter, Arvin explained to a woman that he didn't sell rosin, Only Strings. Next he answered the phone, paused, and said, "No, sir. Only Strings."

The person in front of me: "Full set of strings for a hurdy gurdy."

"Vielle a roué?"

"Yep."

Smooth as gourmet coffee, Arvin pulled six square packets from an unlabeled drawer. The man paid.

Arvin turned to me. "Corelli Alliance mediums? Already?"

I shook my head. "Have you got an empty apartment and a new quartet?"

He squinted. "Sorry. Only Strings." Then he paused. "You look like hell."

The hurdy gurdy man left. I said, "Josh quit the group."

He stopped cold. "I thought you two were buddies."

I dug my nails into my palm. "I guess we weren't."

Arvin jutted forward with his elbows on the counter. "What happened?"

"He got tired of being treated like crap?" Light-headed, I closed my eyes. As it turned out, peanut butter wasn't the best breakfast. "I don't know. Harrison dogpiled him, and I said something stupid, and he blew up."

Arvin sighed. "Why'd you let that happen?"

My eyes flew wide. "Let it?"

He stared off sideways, maybe at the bulletin board. "Yeah, doll. It sounds like you treated him badly."

I stared at the floor.

He said, "That was wrong. So he changed what was wrong."

I said, "He changed everything."

"Tell me," said Arvin, glancing at my face and then back at his countertop, "if you bow the C string by the bridge, doesn't the whole string vibrate?"

I breathed sharply.

"And doesn't the G string vibrate too, even though you didn't bow it?"

Damn. Damn. Damn.

"When you tighten one string, it can put the other three out of tune." Arvin frowned. "Sometimes yeah, you have to change everything, even if it means losing something you love." He leaned up close, an eye-to-eye I rarely got from Arvin. "And sometimes you need to fight real hard for something you love too."

This time I was the one who turned aside. "You're full of wisdom today."

"No, doll." He rested his smooth hand on mine. "Only Strings."

A customer entered, and I left as Arvin explained that no, he sold Only Strings.

Tuning a viola. Tuning a cello. Tuning a quartet.

Half an hour later at Harrison's, I found him on the phone, pacing. A lot of mm-hmms. Then, "Okay, what time?" "Have you got a song list?" "No, don't worry about that." And finally, "I'll call back after I check whether everyone's available."

That didn't sound good. Add in his downcast eyes plus the way he clutched the phone, and it sounded totally awful.

The last thing he said was, "No, thank you for calling us. I'm sorry."

He hung up the phone with a dark, "Josh, you idiot." Then he bit his lip as he met my gaze. "We need to play a funeral."

All the strength drained from me.

"Oh—no, not Josh's. God, Joey, sit down." He grabbed both straps off my shoulder and pushed me into a chair. "Josh is fine. I mean, I think he is. Remember the guy from the retirement party? His wife was sick? She died yesterday. He wants us to play her funeral."

I rubbed my temples. Breathe. Breathe.

Harrison shook his head. "The funeral's Tuesday. But without Josh, I'm not sure how we'll sound."

Letting off a long breath, I shook my head. "Okay. Um—" Why was it so hard to think? "Josh hasn't contacted anyone?"

Figure it out, Arvin said. Fight for what you need.

"Will you play with him if he shows up?" I lowered my voice. "Because this bullshit about him being gone for good because of one fight? It's stupid."

"It's as much your fault as it is mine."

"I'm not assigning blame, damn it." *Think like my mom. What can I use for leverage?* I stood. "Get his practice cello."

Harrison's eyebrows shot up. "What are you doing?"

"That's a four thousand dollar instrument. He'll talk to me for four grand."

Harrison produced the cello, then fished in his jacket for Josh's EZ Pass. "He left this, too."

With my viola case like a backpack and my duffle bag over my shoulder, I grabbed Josh's cello case by the handle and tested the wheels. I couldn't hike a mountain this way, but to Brooklyn I'd manage.

As I left, Shreya walked in. "What's going on?"

"I'm going to solicit Josh. Get the details from Harrison."

"And practice—?" said Harrison.

"If I wait, he'll go to work, and I need him face-to-face." I smirked at Harrison. "You don't need me anyhow. I only sit in the back and play the wrong notes."

Thirty minutes later, I stood on Josh's stoop. It was easy to sound brave in Harrison's apartment, where the scariest things were the tropical fish. The facing of Josh was another matter.

Why does a violist stand in the street? Because she can't find the key, and she doesn't know when to come in.

Yeah. Go me!

I pushed the doorbell.

With cunning that would impress a Navy SEAL, I propped Josh's cello behind the hinges of the outer door. To get the thing, he'd have to come out long enough to talk. That was a trick I'd learned from living with my mother: if they might not listen, make sure there's no choice.

Josh answered through the intercom. I said, "I'm here

with your cello."

Silence.

I could have counted out the steps to the front entrance. How many seconds it should take. But the time passed, and that was the loneliest feeling in the world, knowing that even with his cello on his doorstep, he wouldn't face me.

Screw this. If he didn't come, I'd take it with me. Maybe he'd chase me down the block.

But he did open the door, and then I could say we both looked like hell.

I held the EZ Pass at arm's length, and he took it, careful not to touch me. When he stepped out to get the cello, I slipped between him and the door. "We need you to play one more time."

With shadowed eyes, Josh glared under the brim of his baseball cap.

"Remember the retiree's wife from the baby shower? She died. They asked us to play the funeral. There's nothing on the playlist you'd need to practice ahead of time. You'd only have to show up."

"Th-tha-that's what it's come down to?" About to step forward, Josh realized I was blocking the door, so he held position. "I j-j-just have to show up?"

"No, you were my friend, and I screwed up badly." If I met his eyes, he'd see tears, but it was time to quit channeling Mom and do the right thing, so I stared at his sneakers. "I want you to reconsider, but I have no right to ask. I hurt your feelings. I'm sorry."

Josh said nothing.

Still looking down, I said, "Will you do it for them?"

"I'll th-think about it."

"They need to know by this afternoon."

It was so tense. Where was the rapport? How could one stupid disclosure change everything?

Josh said, "If I 'just sh-show up,' do I have to keep my defective mouth shut so you won't be ashamed?"

"I'm sorry for being an idiot. That was my issue, not yours."

More silence. Then, "For the last month, you rrr-really thought I'd never...forgive you?"

"I was right, wasn't I?" No one ever forgave me. "You said I was too shallow to trust. I thought you had good reason."

"I always trusted you." He paused. "That's why this stinks."

This was going to be it, wasn't it? I had only one weapon left.

I handed him the creased paper square in my pocket. He unfolded it to find a blank music sheet with my attempt at a drawing, neither improved nor hampered by the lurching of the subway. At the top I'd put a bass clef with no notes. Below that, a viola and a sad face on one side of a slash, and on the other, a cello with some hedgehogs and a question mark.

He didn't fold it back up, nor look at me, nor even crumple it. Instead he looked for a really long time.

I had nothing left. Rather than keep him trapped, I went down the steps.

As I reached the sidewalk, he said, "I'll play."

TWENTY-SEVEN

That night in my toll-booth, Bach grooved to Rachmaninov.

The woman with 1985 hair handed me her toll and a chocolate bar, smiling when I exclaimed in surprise. She thought it was a snack. I'd call it dinner.

I turned on my phone to check messages and found a text from Josh: "Hey, genius, when/where is this gig anyhow?"

Oh, yeah, that detail might be important.

Ten minutes after, he'd sent a second: "Not an insult. Sorry."

On eggshells. I hated it.

Someday, maybe ten years from now, I'd see Josh again. Maybe I'll hail a cab in the rain and climb in, drenched, with my instrument and my umbrella, and the driver will say, "Oh, are you a mmm-musician?" When that happens, I'll look up, and he'll recognize me. He'll say, "Joey?" and I'll say, "Wow—" and we'll be awkward. I'll tell him, "Grand Central Station." He'll ask what I'm doing, and maybe I can apologize again, and just like Peter he'll tell me he's over it. And I'll be scared he'd get upset if I tip him high, but...well, I might never see him again after this week; there was no point in anguishing over what to tip when I did.

Arvin was right. Bowing one string vibrated the whole instrument. If you dampen that vibration, the instrument wouldn't sound. Tightening one string would cause the other three to shift, but then you retuned, and you kept at it until all four strings sang together.

But if the fourth string snapped, could we get it back on the instrument?

We brave warriors of the MBTA were keeping it down to a steady five cars in line as it grew dark. Well, relatively dark. Out at Lake George, it had been truly *Dark*, but here we'd tamed the beast with fluorescent bulbs, traffic lights, and the radio.

I thought of my viola safe in my locker with my duffle bag, visualized playing Mendelssohn's *Viola Sonata in C-Minor* to the incoming traffic, imagined everyone sailing through while I gifted their world eight extra dollars and music.

I'd make the paper, and any publicity was good publicity. Of course, I couldn't afford to lose my mind now, but somehow that made insanity more attractive. I flexed my fingers in an approximation of the notes.

The radio changed to Tchaikovsky's *Serenade for Strings*. A black Cadillac pulled into my lane, and I smiled until I realized who it was.

The Gentleman lowered his window. "Pleasant evening to you."

He held out his hundred.

The viola vanished from my mind. How much longer would this guy keep jerking around the toll-booth operators? How long would I keep hitting my knees in the face of his ego?

I pushed the security button, then shut off Tchaikovsky. Herr Bach paused mid-bop. "I'm sorry, sir. I can only accept denominations under twenty."

He extended it. "This is all I have."

This life was all I had. "I'm bound by the regulations of the Metropolitan Bridge and Tunnel Authority."

A hardness came to his eyes. "You have to take it."

Good. I'll see your anger and raise you a ream of

paperwork. "You can be billed. Please hand over your driver's license."

I wouldn't want to be on the sticky side of that red tape. You probably had to fill out a form to request the application you needed to acquire the paperwork so you could send in your check.

He put ice into his voice. "I demand to speak to your supervisor."

Ted would have suspended me. Walt, our on-the-spot security dude, approached instead. I leaned out when he stepped between me and the Cadillac.

"He says he can't pay." I gestured to The Gentleman. "I've requested his license so we can bill him."

The Gentleman said, "She's refusing my legal American tender."

Back to me, Walt.

I pointed to the "No Bills over $20" signs the MBTA helpfully installed all over the toll plaza.

Walt seemed unamused. And I realized—he wasn't going to back me up.

Inside me, a volcano rumbled. Had Josh felt this way, facing Harrison as a self-styled King of the Mountain? Because if so, he deserved a medal for not punching him.

Or rather, punching me, because the problem here wasn't the King of the Mountain. It was the loyal backup who suddenly was neither loyal nor a backup. Maybe Ted was going to suspend me after all. But I didn't care any longer. I couldn't keep lying down and taking it.

Then, unbelievably, amazingly, Walt said to The Gentleman, "Do you have another bill, sir?"

The blood rushed to my head. That—that right there—should have been a fanfare.

The Gentleman tilted up his chin. "If I don't, she has to accept this."

Think like Josh. Hold silence. Just hold silence.

Walt shrugged. "If you don't have a smaller bill, we'll

charge you the unpaid toll plus a processing fee. Please hand me your driver's license."

Relief gushed through me as Walt took the spotlight of The Gentleman's rage squarely on himself. Which yes was his job. But he'd done it for me.

The Gentleman removed a ten from his wallet.

They don't throw parades for this. They don't throw parades for ten dollar bills the same way they don't throw parades for ordering pickles or taking an Amtrak home. Sometimes you're the only witness to victory.

The Gentleman left. As Walt turned to go back to the office, I whispered, "Thank you," and he shrugged: "Nothing at all."

But it wasn't nothing, was it?

For five minutes, I fought giggles. In honor of the triumph, I opened my celebratory "dinner" of chocolate and pirouetted to Tchaikovsky with Johann Sebastian Bach.

My shift ended. Exhausted and hungry to the point of shaking, I hung up my orange reflective vest and slipped into the dark conference room. I dropped onto the couch at the far wall and scrunched down under my jacket until I fell into a light sleep, the kind when you're in a place you shouldn't be, where if caught you'd need to explain. Footsteps, voices, doors slamming—anything startled me.

When the janitor flipped on the lights, we frightened each other. I apologized, grabbed my jacket, and staggered to the kitchenette for whatever I could scrape out of the coffee pot. Eventually a plastic cup held artificial sugar and powdered creamer, plus a liquid strong-smelling as gasoline. I choked it down, the acid burning a trail to my uneasy stomach. Using bread and peanut butter from my locker, I forced calories into my body. I'd need another food source. Maybe a bag of apples.

I checked my cell phone and learned it was six-thirty. Josh had texted two hours ago.

"You're not shallow."

He'd be asleep right now.

I finished my sandwich wondering what this overture meant and whether Josh wanted a response; what might soften him up and what might lure a skittish cellist back to his quartet. Back into a friendship.

No. It was all too much thinking. I sent, "I miss you."

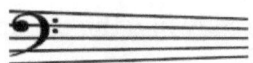

On the subway, I fought jitters and grins, my body alight with anticipation. Time for busking.

At the same time as the text from Josh, I'd gotten one from Harrison: "Practice is extra early tomorrow. Come at nine." Maybe. If I went at nine, I'd lose the last part of the rush hour. Maybe Harrison could just cool his jets until whenever I happened to show up. My phone had so little battery now that I didn't respond.

I opted for Tompkins Square Park over a subway station. I played for an hour and a half, alternating Bach with extemporized songs, smiling at anyone who tossed in change—until a square-shouldered cop my father's age asked if I had a license.

I did what Harrison would have quipped was second nature to a violist: I played dumb. "You need a license to play?"

He nodded. "You might cause a disturbance."

Yeah, the crowds surrounding my viola would rival Bono shooting that video on an L.A. rooftop.

I set my instrument back into its case, him watching every second. I should have tossed him twenty nickels to buy a donut. Jerk. He was earning money while stopping me from doing the same.

When he said, "You're free to go," I stopped myself from replying he was free to go to hell because I shouldn't get arrested. To raise bail, I'd have to do the thing he'd just arrested me for.

Without anywhere else to go, I walked toward Harrison's. At a coffee cart I paid for a small coffee in dimes and nickels. The Pakistani vendor snapped, "This isn't an ice cream truck, and you're not six years old."

What was it The Gentleman said? "You can take my legal tender."

Good thing I already had the cup in my hand. He told me I could fuck myself.

I checked my phone in case Josh had texted, and instead, there was a missed call.

And it was from that damned attorney from the Eagles. The one Harrison had said would never bother me again. And here she was again, bothering me.

With all sorts of profanity ringing through my head, I punched the button to retrieve her voicemail. Nasty crap, right? I still hated her clipped voice, and she said they were still having to deal with our nonsense, and I been snakey enough to organize some kind of social media war?

Snakey? We'd done everything we were supposed to! We'd pulled money out of our ass so we could have an attorney to trade latinesque phrases with her and argue what the meaning of *is* is. We hadn't spoken to the media, hadn't recorded their precious song, hadn't screwed them over, which was better than they'd done. What the hell was her problem?

Unable to choose which horrible thing I'd say first, I pushed the callback button. And wonder of wonders, she answered her own phone. Maybe at this hour she hadn't unchained her slaves yet from the dungeon. I said, "This is Josephine Mikalos, and you just called me. Aren't you supposed to be harassing my lawyer?"

"Miss Mikalos, I have some questions."

"You're supposed to be talking to Amy Aitken."

"You're the business manager of the Boroughs String Quartet, so I'm talking to you."

I said, "As the business manager, I know we pay our attorney a shitload of money to listen to your nonsense."

"I want to know—"

"I'm done with you." What a bitch. "Our cover wasn't going to harm a world-famous group," I said over her protests. "It was fair use, and in fact, I just finished playing it in public."

"You're going to court," she said.

"Take me." I stopped in a throng of pedestrians at the corner, raising my voice without caring who heard. "I'd love to see the judge's face when you ask her to overturn a hundred years of legal precedent." And then, "You know what? Come to the Westchester County Festival of Concert Music a week from Saturday. Because so help me, we're playing it just to piss you off."

She said, "Not only will I be there, but I'll have enough important people with me to haul you off that stage in handcuffs."

"Go ahead and try," I said.

Well, I said most of it. My battery died. She probably got the gist.

I don't care anymore. My eyes burned, and I shoved my dead phone into my pocket as I reached Harrison's building. *I just don't care.*

Upstairs, I opened the door to find Harrison at the table with Shreya. He gestured for me to sit.

They both looked serious. That meant one thing.

I should have fled. My brain kept urging my legs to run, but my knees refused to respond. Numb, I had only one thought: *Fuck them.* I wouldn't make it easy. To get rid of me, they'd have to work like fishermen scouring barnacles off the bottom of a boat.

Without budging from the doorway, I said, "What's going

on?"

Shreya said, "Why don't you tell us?"

Pulse skyrocketing, I looked from her to Harrison. This was it. The only reason they'd kept me was to anchor Josh, and now that I'd failed to bring him back, I was a liability. And I'd already lost everything else.

Even as my eyes clenched, Harrison's voice went plaintive. "What's going on? Because you aren't right. Today, yesterday—you still had your bag from Lake George, and you were exhausted. When I called, you were on the street, and today you look even worse."

When remembering it later, I had the impression of darkness, as if they'd turned down the lighting like an interrogation. I quivered, starting with a tentative, "I—" and then my strength ran out. I covered my face in my hands and struggled to breathe because I couldn't say it, couldn't imagine choking out the words or what Shreya would tell me, someone whose parents were rock-steady no matter what, or how Harrison would react when he learned my family had done what he'd wanted to do for two years now.

Shreya tried to take my viola, but I clutched it back.

Harrison said, "Is this about Josh?"

Shreya said, "I've got an idea. Let her tell us what it's about. Joey, sit."

For a minute, I couldn't. Shreya guided me from the door to the table, giving a self-conscious chuckle. "It can't be worse than what I told you, can it?"

Harrison said, "Girl-talk?"

Rubbing my shoulder, Shreya glared at him. "You mean woman-talk?"

Harrison said, "How about I just retract the question?"

I hunched over my viola, awaiting the guillotine.

Harrison said, "Joey?"

I whispered, "They kicked me out."

A sentence at a time, to their expressions of outrage, my story emerged. Harrison was on his feet, saying, "For God's sake, why didn't you call me?"

"But—" I fought the tears. "I don't want you guys to get rid of me too!"

Harrison said, "What's that got to do with anything?"

Shreya said, "Why would we get rid of you? We don't need your apartment."

Shuddering, I recoiled from her arm on my shoulder. "You needed me to keep Josh, but I sent him away, and I'm not a good musician, and I've never been good enough for you, and now I'm just a liability."

Harrison had gone white. "What the hell are you talking about?"

Shreya said, "You are too a good musician!"

"Do you think I'm stupid?" Harrison's voice carried an urgency. "Why would I have suggested the idea of a string quartet if I didn't think you were an amazing musician? You were wasted in that orchestra! No one would ever have heard you!" Harrison leaned forward. "More than that, you're our business manager."

I tightened up. "Anyone can do that!"

"I could have hired someone to do that!" Harrison looked horrified. "You happen to be amazing at keeping all the balls in the air! We'd never have gotten this far—oh, God, I'm sorry." He shook his head. "You're good enough. You're better than good enough."

Shreya said, "You do great on that thing. I've never had a problem with your playing."

She didn't look like she was humoring me. Harrison, whose poker face had yet to be invented, was flat-out stunned.

Shreya said, "It never crossed my mind to get rid of you."

Harrison bit his lip. "I...can see why you might have thought that. But unless you want to leave, you're here for the long haul."

I put my face in my hands.

Shreya gave a squeeze. "Where have you been staying?"

I couldn't stop shivering. "There's a couch at work."

Harrison said, "What have you done to get the apartment back?"

"What can I do? She's moved in."

He raised his voice. "You call the police, that's what! You press charges. You get an attorney."

Gulping, I looked up.

"Even without a lease, they need thirty days' notice to evict you. And eviction proceedings can take months." Harrison folded his arms. "What did they do with your stuff? I know every attorney in Manhattan. How about your sister gets an eight-by-eight apartment courtesy of the state? Maybe right next door to your grandparents."

I looked from him to her, cold. "But it's my family."

"Joey—" Harrison looked desperate. "Criminals have family too."

Head bowed, I wrapped my arms around my stomach.

Shreya hugged me from behind. "No, don't think about the police yet. That's huge. First get your bearings." She sighed. "You need a place to stay."

"I don't know where to start." Busking wasn't going to bring in first and last month's rent plus a security deposit.

Harrison said, "Were you planning on sleeping at your job forever? Tonight, come here."

"Or stay with me," Shreya said. "I'm closer."

As I breathed through my palms, their words sank in. "Really?"

"Yes, really!" Harrison exclaimed, but Shreya just kept her arms around me.

"Of course we'll help. Don't ever think we wouldn't have your back." She gave a squeeze. "Have you had a decent meal in the last two days?" As I raised my head, she turned to Harrison. "Make her something to eat and a pot of coffee. Then we'll figure out what happens next."

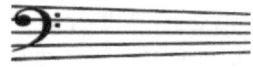

Two years ago, a bank manager explained everything I needed to know about business banking. Luckily we weren't exactly Fortune 500 material, so "everything" got covered in twenty minutes. We'd spoken once more when the bank account needed an upgrade, and again when a transfer got lost in cyberspace.

Today, after trading in two rolls of quarters, six penny rolls, twenty bucks in dimes, and five more in nickels, I recognized her even if she didn't recognize me. She glanced at my viola case and said, "Didn't mobsters used to walk into banks with guns in their violin cases?"

I made myself appear worried. "This is worse, because I have a viola in there, and I know how to play it."

Laughing, she escorted me to her desk. "What kind of help do you need?"

When I explained about Viv and the rent checks, her face hardened. "How about I freeze your accounts? Oh, you did that already," followed by, "Let's set you up with different account numbers while you fill out this Affidavit of Fraud," and five minutes of silence later, broken only by the click of her typing, she said, "Now, give me the check numbers."

With my laptop on one side of the desk and hers on the opposite, we tracked down four checks Viv had endorsed and deposited into her own account.

"Give me the January check number," said the manager, and then she laughed out loud. It was the best sound in the world. "We've got her nailed. Your grandmother's signature is loopy and pretty." The manager sighed. "You're such a sweetheart too. You wrote 'rent' in the memo lines."

Where was that victory fanfare when I needed it? I resolved that with my dying breath, I'd scrawl "funeral expenses" across my last check.

Mom had started both our accounts, so Viv and I belonged to the same bank. For the first and last time, Mom had made my life easier.

The manager stamped the form. "You'll get your money

back in a week. I just need the police report, and we're good to go."

Hey, wait a minute— "Police report?"

"Yes." Her gaze felt like the crosshairs of a rifle. "I've frozen her funds, but I need that report. What your sister did was a felony."

TWENTY-EIGHT

I couldn't stop smiling when Josh pulled into the church parking lot. He was ten minutes late, and he was wearing a tuxedo and his Yankees cap. Then Harrison muttered how stupid it looked. Way to mend fences.

With the tension cranked, we didn't chat during setup. My chest ached. It could be the last time we four played together, appropriate enough that it was a funeral. When the pastor ran down what we'd play, Harrison handled it. He hadn't so much as looked at Josh since that "remove the hat" glare.

Josh said nothing at all. Not to the pastor, and not to the family when they thanked us for playing on such short notice. As if you could schedule a death. He shook the hand of the bereaved husband, but wordlessly.

Shreya breathed into my ear, "Do you hate this? I do."

We played Mozart's D Minor Quartet for twenty minutes prior to the scheduled start, written in the same "key of death" he'd used for the *Requiem*. Afterward we turned Harrison loose with the third movement of "The Hunt" and its soulful adagio until the casket arrived.

A wedding, this professional will tell you, is boring. The happy couple may pore over every detail, but after the first fifty, weddings lost their charm.

But funerals? No matter how many I would attend, I doubted they'd lose power. A funeral is the end. People cry at weddings, but it's not the same.

After two readings from the Bible and one from Shakespeare, we played again.

Midway through, I realized how smooth we sounded. I tried not to get self-conscious, but I could hear the transitions and the melody and the harmonies flowing together. We were mind reading like we used to do: here, when it counted, we'd done it again.

People gave statements about the woman: her community involvement, her skill as a mother, and her struggle to hang on long enough to become a grandmother. They say everyone is a saint at her own funeral, but she did sound classy, like the head of a family I'd have enjoyed a lot better than my own.

Her husband spoke last, and I steeled myself in case he started crying. He talked about thirty-five years together, the rough patches when one or the other of them wanted to walk out, but how they'd persevered.

"We knew we were worth more together than apart." He did cry, and I struggled not to join him. "We started as two people and came together as one family, creating something more important than ourselves."

I wondered how many people on the benches were ex-coworkers, maybe even the bean-counters who thought it cost-effective to deny a man time with his dying wife.

We played as the pallbearers carried the coffin to the hearse, and then the funeral director chased us out so we'd get to the cemetery ahead of the procession. We dashed to the parking lot.

At the door, Josh said, "You guys n-n-need a ride?"

"Brought my own," said Harrison. We took off in opposite directions.

At the cemetery, Harrison parked a distance from the open grave, and a funeral home employee escorted us to a tented area. Harrison checked his tuning compulsively until a procession of cars arrived, and we got our signal to begin.

The casket arrived. The pastor opened in prayer, and at that point, our work ended.

Harrison, Josh, and I put away our instruments, but Shreya slipped into the crowd holding hers. It was probably more cheerful there than between Josh and Harrison.

As we walked, I asked, "What time is it?"

Harrison checked his watch. "We've got time."

Josh said, "What he m-meant to say is, it's eleven-fifteen."

"Thanks." Halfway to the cars, I turned. "Shreya's still there. Should I get her?"

"Like I said, we've got time."

Josh frowned. "What's with the c-c-cargo van?"

Harrison said, "We needed it."

Josh said, "To carry your ego?"

"To move Joey."

"What?" Then he looked at me, wide-eyed, and I realized what conclusion he'd jumped to.

I tried to sound amused. "I don't know where I'm moving, actually."

Harrison said, "But hey, a van functions as short-term storage."

I rolled my eyes. "And an apartment too. We'll have to make sure we put my bed flat so I can sleep on it."

Harrison chuckled. "If it only fits vertically, you've got a few bungee cords."

Josh said, "What h-happened?"

He looked right at me, and I went cold. Not because he was angry, but because telling him would be worse than telling Harrison and Shreya. Worse because he knew me, knew all my flaws and every embarrassing thing my mother had seen right from the start.

Harrison had no such issues. "Her sister committed check fraud and got her evicted. At one o'clock, we're going to invade, retrieve her stuff, and find her a new place."

I turned away rather than see Josh's reaction.

The sky curved with a blue made all the starker by the bulbous clouds, and they traveled eastward on the same wind that swayed the trees. Every ninety seconds, a plane skirted the horizon and vanished near Kennedy Airport. Behind us, the murmur of a highway swallowed the voices from the funeral.

Josh took pity on me and didn't respond. He knew who I was.

As the mourners started to break up, Harrison picked up his case, and Josh took his.

That was when Shreya's violin sounded.

The mourners paused. Turned.

Carried on the wind came a final blessing to a woman we never knew. Momentarily I recognized the tune: "Danny's Song."

"I didn't know she planned to do that."

Harrison's voice was low. "I didn't either."

High and sweet, then mellow and deep, the song played until it modulated keys and transitioned into a song I couldn't name.

"Londonderry Aire," Harrison murmured.

Josh said, "No. It's 'D-Danny Boy.'"

My heart thudded.

Shreya had forged a perfect blend of the songs once she'd bridged the gap, the marriage into the funeral, a musical gift to a husband and wife at their parting.

Behind me, Josh sang, "Oh Danny boy, the pipes, the pipes are calling, from glen to glen, and down the mountainside..."

I stepped closer to the crowd and willed the wind to carry their voices in my direction because I knew others had to be singing. Yet I heard nothing other than Josh behind me and Shreya before. It was Shreya and a violin. It was Josh and a voice of his own. It was tears and it was a group of kids running up the road past parked cars and gravestones.

And I shall hear, tho' soft you tread above me,
And all my dreams will warm and sweeter be

If you'll not fail to tell me that you love me,
I'll simply sleep in peace until you come to me.

Shreya transitioned back into "Danny's Song," then closed.

I expected applause. The song deserved silence. For once, I got what I wanted.

But people didn't leave, either. It was as if the gift of her song had fixed them in place, and after that, they could no longer bear leaving.

Endings. Leavings. I turned to Josh where he stared into the ground. "Are we going to see you again?"

He said, "I don't know," and he left.

Just like that, he left. I didn't chase him. I didn't give him one last hug. Goodbye. Goodbye and goodbye.

Shreya unblended from the mourners, her violin back in its case, her head high. Harrison put an arm around my shoulder and gave me a squeeze. "Let's go. We'll grab some lunch, change out of funeral clothes, and then get the fireworks started."

Fireworks indeed. I still had my key, but I rang the bell as a warning. There were four of us: me, Shreya, Harrison, and Officer Randall from the NYPD.

And a darned good thing about Officer Randall, too, because as soon as I stepped inside, my sister flew across the kitchen to grab me by the shoulders. "You disgusting bitch!"

I backed to the wall while she screamed a dozen names into my face. Officer Randall got between us. "Calm down, Miss! Don't force me to charge you with assault."

I'd been warned to let her hit me if she tried. He'd have had her cuffed and out the door, and I'd only have to worry about the bruising. I was more concerned about not bursting into laughter. My sister was waving a FedEx envelope and shouting that I had ruined her life.

Yeah, she stole checks, but *I* ruined everything.

My grandmother had knocked over her chair getting to her feet. "Josie! Why are you causing all this trouble? Why did you involve the police?"

The officer said, "I'm here to investigate charges of fraud and theft, and to ensure Josephine collects her belongings without harm."

Grandma turned pale. Viv loomed as close as Officer Randall allowed. Maybe she really would risk jail time to rip out my throat. Harrison yanked me away from her and toward the door, between him and Shreya.

The officer produced some paperwork. "Vivian Mikalos? Hazel Edmundson? I have an Affidavit of Fraud from Josephine's bank stating that rent checks made out to Mrs. Edmundson were unlawfully cashed by Vivian."

Harrison had cautioned me to say nothing, but it was so hard when Grandma turned to me. "How could you?"

Not, "How could your sister steal your money?" Not even, "How could I have thrown my own granddaughter out on the street?" Just, how could I have dared object?

The officer handed Grandma the police report, which she stared at as if in Swedish.

Zaden came into the kitchen. Grandma's voice wobbled. "Zaden, honey, go upstairs."

He said, "Why should I?"

She said, "Please, sweetie."

Viv said, "Let him see what an asshole his aunt is."

I said to my grandmother, "Where's my stuff?"

She said, "Viv put it in the basement."

"Don't bother," Viv snapped. "I locked the door."

Fortunately, locks worked both ways. "Unlock it."

"It's Grandma's property now to make up for back rent!"

The officer turned to my grandmother. "Well? The signature on the checks. Forged?"

She looked at Viv, then looked at the check copies. Then

at me.

In my peripheral vision, I saw Harrison glance down the hall and do a double-take.

That had to be my mother. Viv would have phoned Mommy the minute the bank notified her.

As I grew dizzy with that stared-at feeling, Shreya whispered, "Josh?"

I spun, and it was Josh. Josh and his father filled the doorway, arms folded, mouths grim, glaring from beneath the brims of their matching baseball caps.

It had been Viv who charged at me, but it was Josh's presence that knocked me back into Shreya. What was he doing here? Hadn't he made it clear he hadn't forgiven me?

The officer said, "Mrs. Edmundson, I need an answer."

Shreya nudged me.

My voice broke. "Grandma? I only want what's mine."

What was mine. What should have been. Things like parents, a family, a childhood. I couldn't carry those out of here, but I could take a futon, a dish rack, and my silverware.

The officer said, "Is that your signature?"

Come on, Grandma. Make a choice. For once.

In the end, she didn't give me even that. She trudged to the cabinet and pulled a key from a decorative vase, then handed it to the officer. "Tell her to take her things."

With an outraged shriek, Viv stormed from the kitchen.

The officer turned to me. "Start getting your property together."

I forced myself to meet Josh's eyes. I choked out, "Why are you here?"

He looked away. "I th-thought you could use someone to hhh-help do the heavy lifting."

Harrison said, "Right now I need help moving that van. I'm going to put it into the spot with the hydrant, but it's a barge."

"I'll direct you," said Shreya, and took off with him.

Viv had thrown my belongings into her assortment of

open-topped boxes and stacked them all over the basement. Good thing I didn't own much.

On top of one box was my cell phone charger. My crap viola was there too. I wanted to hug the ancient case, rusty hinges and peeling vinyl and all.

I struggled not to start shaking with relief. "This is some. But there's more missing, as well as my furniture."

Upstairs Viv had rearranged all the furniture and put new drapes and new area rugs. I walked through ticking off the things she'd stolen. "My dresser. My futon. My shelves. My coffee maker." Viv could keep my thousand-year-old mattress and bed frame. It wouldn't be good enough for her or her kid, so I'd leave her the headache of hauling it out.

She'd opened the sealed-off room because, well, it was May. Come November, she'd be first in line for wool socks. Or maybe she'd run portable space heaters and burn the place down. Not my problem.

Shreya raced upstairs with boxes and a roll of packing tape. "Let's get this party started!"

Her usual go-getter self, Viv had moved only my books and clothes. She'd kept my CDs, although for the life of me I couldn't imagine her listening to Dvorak. I retrieved my Visa and ATM cards, the first time in history that money had been safe in the hands of Mozart.

While Shreya and I became packing machines, Viv argued in the doorway with the officer, but he pointed out that I had an itemized list and photographs, courtesy of when I'd acquired renter's insurance. Did she have receipts? No? Then it sucked to be her.

She called Mom from her cell phone, whining about how she needed help and I was being unfair and please don't be mad (*What?*) and making sure the officer heard her calling him a pig.

With a purring sound, Shreya's packing tape sealed another box. Then she said, "Wait, I'll grab that," and helped Ed carry my futon.

Josh said to Harrison, "Help me with this," and they lifted my dresser. I followed with the empty drawers.

Josh said, "You knew you were m-moving furniture, but you dressed like that?"

Harrison had changed out of his tux into khaki pants and an oxford shirt, with a blazer no less. "It's for the camera crews." He grinned. "A bit to the left."

Two minutes later, the guys were still sending conflicting instructions about how to clear the stair rail.

Yeah, that was totally workable in a quartet. "You know, I got it for five bucks at a garage sale," I called. "If it falls to pieces, no big deal."

"I'm trying not to b-b-b-bang up the railing," said Josh. "Lift, Harrison! It needs to clear the knob."

"Easy for you to say." Harrison looked up. "I've got the heavier end."

Josh snorted. "I thought the difference between f-first and second violins was you could get things higher. I should have asked Shhh-reya to carry it."

Harrison heaved, and Josh pivoted it to clear the railing. Harrison staggered and then caught himself.

"So hey," he said, "does this mean you're playing the festival on Saturday?"

Wow, bad timing much?

Josh said, "You want a d-d-defective cellist?"

Harrison glanced behind to keep descending. "I told you, I shouldn't have said that, and you didn't hear the whole conversation anyhow."

Okay, apology, but...really? What was he doing? "You've got three more steps," I called.

Harrison went on, "Thanks. It's not like I came out and said, 'Now Josh, he's defective.' I had a good idea and you weren't listening. It never occurred to me it wasn't a good idea."

At the landing, Harrison started micro-maneuvers to slip the dresser through the doorway, which Ed had bungee-corded open.

Josh said, "Ap-pology accepted. It's not like you were being any more of a jackass than usual."

"Hey!" I shouted, but Harrison only said, "Gee, thanks."

Josh said, "But b-before I agree to anything, we need some ground rules."

Agree?

There were so many things I wanted to say that they all piled into one another and none of them got out, for much the same reason my dresser had trouble getting down the staircase. But there was Harrison, doing the impossible, doing it fearlessly—and succeeding.

Harrison had reached outside where the stone staircase descended to the sidewalk. He checked over his shoulder. "Like a ground rule that I shouldn't ever mention a specific coffee-and-steamed-milk-drink that begins with C?"

He looked at Josh with that deliberately-cute expression, as if unsure whether Josh were going to laugh, or give that dresser a push and send him to his death.

When Josh appeared unamused, Harrison added. "And as for me, I don't ever want to hear you say my father gave me asshole lessons. I'll have you know," and he tilted his chin, "that's one hundred percent natural talent."

Josh burst out laughing, and then Harrison did too.

"Guys!" What was going on? "You're going to drop the thing!"

That set Josh off worse, and Harrison looked behind again to get his bearings. "Anyhow, I majored in music. Jackassery was my minor."

With Josh still laughing, they got it down to the sidewalk and over to the van. I tried to meet Harrison's eyes, but he wasn't looking at me, wasn't being coy, was just being... honest. This was him. And there was Josh, even after he'd taken a knife to the back, listening.

Josh finally said, "I'm tired of being prrr-rotected."

Harrison said, "The deal when you joined was you

wouldn't have to talk."

Josh said, "I don't w-w-want that anymore."

Harrison said, "Then you've got to make up your mind, because how do I know when you want to talk to the pizza guy but not the reporter?"

Josh's mouth twitched. "Good point."

I propped the van's doors. Ed and Shreya had already put the futon into the back, and I climbed in to move boxes so they could get he dresser inside. Harrison and Josh fit the drawers back in, then lifted it into the cargo bed, Josh pushing and Harrison guiding from inside. I scrambled over the front seat to get out of the way.

Harrison's phone sounded with the third movement of *Eine Kleine Nachtmusik*. "Hey, Joey, grab that?"

I pulled his phone from his back pocket. "It's— Oh my God!" I answered the call. "*Peter?*"

"Joey? I thought I called The Archer himself, but hey, good enough. Listen, I got you an apartment."

"What?" My vision went spotty. "How did you know?"

"Harrison asked. I guess he already phoned everyone else in Manhattan and decided he'd give me a shot."

I gaped at Harrison, who ignored me. My voice wavered. "I had no idea."

"Well, there's a piccolo player who's moving back to Indiana and needs to sublet her studio. It's in Brooklyn Heights. You can take a look tomorrow."

"Yeah," I whispered. "Tell her I will."

"And hey, don't worry. It'll work out. If you need someplace to crash for a few weeks, call me."

I said goodbye, then looked at Harrison.

His shoulders dropped. "I called everyone, Joey. I called ex-clients. I called our replacement players. I had Arvin search the bulletin board, and he's calling his friends. I even called that reporter." He chuckled. "You know a lot of people, and a lot of people want to help."

Upstairs again, Shreya had disassembled my shelving

and Ed was carrying out the pieces.

Officer Randall said, "What else is there?"

I could have taken the shower curtain, every light bulb, and the little rug in the living room. There was some stuff in the cabinets, but Viv had already moved in her oddments, and I didn't want to bicker over the Ritz crackers. "I'm done."

As Shreya and I stacked the final boxes in the van, my mother pulled up in her silver Accord and left it there in the street.

Shreya breathed, "Wow, double-parking right in front of a cop."

Josh laughed. "It's fine. She put on the h-hazards."

Harrison said, "Not so loud. I'm parked illegally too."

My mother marched up to me, her face one giant fury. For the second time that day, I thanked God for the presence of a police officer.

She put her hands on her hips. "I can't believe how much trouble you're making. I called you eleven times and you never answered! All this could have been prevented if you weren't so stuck on doing everything for yourself." She lowered her voice. "You march yourself back in that house, young lady."

I blinked at her. "What?"

"You get right back in there and apologize to your grandmother." She turned to the top of the steps. "Viv? Get down here right this instant. Now!"

I'd never heard her angry at Viv. Not once in twenty-four years.

Viv came down. "She called the cops!"

"Do you want to be arrested?" Mom folded her arms. "Well? What have I been sacrificing for all these years if you're just going to run away? Is that any kind of gratitude?"

I stared, open-mouthed.

Viv said, "But I want to be on my own!"

"You *can't* live on your own! Look what happens when you try. I let Josie come here because your grandmother could use her, but you? You wouldn't last fifteen seconds." She pointed to Viv. "In the car. You're going home."

Viv's eyes glistened. "But—"

"Do it, Vivvy!" Mom returned her glare to me as Viv slunk to the car. "Now you unload all your furniture and get everything back upstairs where you belong. You can't just turn tail and run from your family like that. You owe it to your grandmother."

My breath came jerky. I trembled.

Behind me, Shreya squeezed my shoulder.

Mom took a step forward. "Now, Josie!"

Shreya's hand tightened.

My throat hurt. "I'm not going back."

She got right in my face. "Then you owe me. Think of all the things I've done for you."

I squared my shoulders. "I don't have to pay you back for raising me. We're just going to have to live with an uneven score."

She cocked her head. "Where are you going to go? Who else except your family would take you in?"

I opened my hands. "Who's my family?" I gestured to everyone around me. "The ones who care about me, who accept me, who help me, they're my family." I faked a smile. "I think I'm going to do okay."

She folded her arms. "There's a police officer right here. Do you want to go to jail?"

I smirked. "For running away from home at age twenty-four?"

Mom said, "You're a thief, and I can prove it." She pointed to the battered viola case in the back of the van. "That's not your viola."

I said, "That's the viola I've had since fifth grade."

"Does this case look new?" She yanked it out of the van, unsettling the topmost boxes. "Your grandfather brought that viola from Europe. It's a family heirloom over a hundred years old, and you stole it out of his house while he was dying."

I turned to the officer, who said, "Ma'am, if you'd like to file a report, we'll investigate."

I said, "Actually, let's investigate now." I removed the viola and pivoted it until the sunlight shone through the F-holes. Thank you, bass bar, for having what I needed. I said to the officer, "Can you please look in here and tell her what it says?"

Any luthier would have laughed after one glance at the finish, but why argue when we had facts?

The officer squinted. "What am I looking for? Oh, there!" He snickered. "Ma'am, it's stamped with 'Eastman And Co, 1988.'"

White with fury, my mother hurled the case at my feet, and the bow popped out along with the rosin. I bent to reassemble everything. With any luck she'd kick me in the face and then no one would ever have to wonder how she felt about me. But my luck had run out. She took a step toward her car.

Harrison said, "Mrs. Mikalos? Did you know that once it's probated, a will is public record? Among all the officer's paperwork is a copy of your father-in-law's will."

She stopped mid-exit.

"Failing to fully execute that will was a felony." He gave a disarming smile. Now I realized why he'd gone for a button-down shirt and a blazer: he looked like an attorney. "You're still within the statute of limitations, so you may want to think twice before filing a false report."

I bit my lip as I reassembled the viola case. Give a violinist a spotlight....

He added, "Hector Mikalos' will specified a cash inheritance for Josephine in addition to the viola. Since those funds were never dispersed, I strongly suggest you use that money now, to make good on the stolen rent."

"I hope you're happy." My mother towered over me, and I stood because on second thought, a kick in the face wasn't an attractive option. "You've been nothing but a disappoint-ment. You are no longer a part of my family."

She stalked back to her car, gunned the engine, and took off with a jump that should have impressed both Josh and Ed.

And that... That was how I became an orphan.

I buried my face in my hands, inhaling hard. Ed gripped my shoulder, and I backed into him, letting him take my weight.

Behind me, Shreya said, "*Harry*? Is any of that legal stuff true?"

Harrison seemed amused. "Who knows? I told you I know every lawyer in Manhattan. I didn't say I consulted them."

The officer said something about everything being finished, and Ed told him he could go. I thanked him, and he shook my hand.

Ed said, "That was a long time coming, sweetie."

Shreya said, "So...time to go apartment-hunting?"

I said nothing for a long time, only let my chosen family surround me.

TWENTY-NINE

"**A**nd now, please welcome to the Westchester County Festival of Concert Music... The Boroughs String Quartet."

Polite applause. It turns out a music festival is more like a big wedding than Yankee Stadium greeting the Rolling Stones, but hey, we'd promised to give them a show, and we were going to do it.

We took the stage and set ourselves up, Harrison for once not double-checking his tuning because he'd already checked it fifty-eight times. Although all four of us were nervous, there really wasn't any need to be. The organizers had sandwiched our bandshell performance in between two chamber groups of equal caliber: no record deal, no performance in Carnegie Hall this season, and not looking too good for the next one either.

As we got settled to start with our fusion of "Baker Street," I glanced at Harrison for our cue but instead found him staring into the audience with surprise. I followed his gaze to find several nasty faces among the couple hundred picnic blankets. These business-suited folks had foregone their sandwiches and juice boxes in favor of recording devices.

Ah. The legal eagles.

Shaken, Harrison started us, and shortly we had Shreya

dancing.

So far I'd had a blast: speaking to other musicians was cool, but I spent my time wandering through the tents, stuffing their promotional material into a canvas bag. Josh called it my "reconnaissance mission." But let's be practical: some of these guys had paid a lot of money for professional publicists, so why not learn?

And yes, we were still a quartet.

After moving me out, Harrison and Josh had gone to war, exchanging email and text salvos over the bylaws of the Boroughs String Quartet. Shreya and I haunted the group chats with increasing trepidation as the four of us hammered out rules one or the other hated (such as "All group-related expenses must be distributed equally" or Harrison's snarky, "notifications of personal upheavals that render one homeless").

Once Harrison got onboard with the idea of bylaws, though, he'd embraced it with an enthusiasm usually reserved for animal activists attending a dog fight. He was lobbying hard for monthly "state of the quartet" meetings. After the first day, with a blizzard of texts suggesting possible guidelines, Shreya blessed us with her own suggestion: "Messages on a single topic will be capped at one hundred per day." But despite the arguing, bickering and bantering, and the occasional jibe of "The floor recognizes Josephine Mikalos," we were still here.

After our first fusion, the audience applauded; well, all except the legal nasties. Harrison and Shreya looked at me, and I stood.

"I'd like to thank you for coming to hear us," I said, "except you didn't come for us. You're staking out spots for the Arturo Delmoni String Quartet." That drew some laughter, although none from the suits. They were three men and a whip-thin woman, and bet me that woman was the Witch Lawyer I spoke to.

Well, now she could darn well listen to me. "Just so you

know whose captive audience you are," I said with a smile, "we're the Boroughs String Quartet. Harrison Archer is our illustrious first violinist and commander-in-chief. Shreya Ramachandran is our second violinist, although as you can hear, she's second fiddle to no one." I pointed them out as I went along, and I kept my eyes on the legals. They were definitely recording us, and I'm pretty sure that was forbidden in the rules for the venue. But hey, if someone's going to break the law, who better? "Josh Galen is our cellist, but there isn't anything funny to say about him." This time it was Josh who laughed as I met his eyes. "And I'm Josephine Mikalos, your violist."

Shreya said into the other mike. "Joey, why do so many people take an instant dislike to the viola?"

I grinned. "It saves time."

Then we played our fusion of "Yesterday."

I'd moved on Thursday. My new landlady? The late bride. She'd forgotten until, oh, last month that she'd need to unload her Red Hook condo, so Harrison sweet-talked her into renting it to me: a studio in a refurbished factory, a whole fifteen-by-twenty feet. My three-quarter bathroom fit a toilet, shower, and sink so tightly they interlocked, and the sole window gazed on a continuous traffic jam. My kitchen table was a cardboard box, and at night, I unfolded my futon to make a bed.

Was it okay? I loved it.

I loved it not because I could lock the doors or because I had a lease, but because it used to be the factory's executive meeting room. The *soundproof* meeting room. Walls that once kept out the clangs of a metal press now kept in the song of a viola. The first day, I blasted my stereo and strained in the hallway to hear even the high notes. This was a musician's apartment.

I'd gotten calls and texts from my mother and sister, all of them threatening, plus emotional blackmail messages from my grandmother and a cousin I hadn't heard from since

2006, until I blocked every single family member. My money reappeared in my account hours before I needed to write a check to pay for the new place.

I only returned to the old house once, at midnight with Josh's dad and a borrowed humane trap. An hour later, we raced across Brooklyn with a furious, nameless caged cat, Ed demonstrating where Josh got his driving skills.

When I'd asked, "Is Josh ever going to forgive me?" Ed only replied, "Well...I wouldn't say *never*."

When we finished "Yesterday," the audience was silent at first, followed by applause louder than before. Looking at the crowd, I found people drawn to the outskirts of the field. The legal team, of course, remained completely out of place where they were getting their illicit video.

Harrison started the intro to our newest mix: Boston's "More Than A Feeling" wrapped around a Beethoven string trio, with the cello voicing the bass guitar part and the second violin handling the vocals. But while he did that, I locked eyes with the Witch Lawyer. Her face, so tight she might have been wearing a document clamp on the back of her head, showed no expression whatsoever.

And that was a shame. You know, if you're going to work with world-class musicians, even as their bulldog, you should at least like music.

We played, but I kept glancing at her, and that's when it all made sense. Josh and Shreya and Harrison had kept telling me this the whole time, that we'd always have our music. This woman, without a soul and without any kind of appreciation for anything, she couldn't steal our music because in some respect she couldn't even hold it. So while I played, I moved in my seat, and then I took to my feet and joined Shreya in her dance because this was freedom.

We were motion and love and yearning. We were two melody lines singing words the heart could never speak.

We ended. Everyone was applauding.

Before Harrison could introduce our fourth piece, I put

my bow back to the strings and unfurled the riff from "Hotel California."

Witch Lawyer glared at one of her minions, and I grinned. Sometimes you just had to make a noise.

Harrison shook his head, and Shreya looked startled. He put his hand over the mike and whispered, "Are you out of your mind?"

I looked him in the eye. And I grinned.

I started playing again. One phrase later, Shreya joined me, and we went through the "Hotel California" riff in a round. Then I repeated a phrase and we caught up to one another to play in unison, at least until Harrison broke in to begin the Mozart section.

The string fusion: forged to appease a drunken bride, the force that tightened the first of the strings on the instrument that was our quartet. Our second CD, our first news coverage, our first lawsuit, our second fight.

The Witch Lawyer had grabbed one of her minions by the arm and was stalking up to the stage. This was about to get truly interesting, so I kept playing.

We reached Shreya's solo, and she took off, doing her own riff and then sending it back to me. She and I had never played it this way before, so I repeated it. (The musician's credo: when in doubt, repeat.) She repeated. We played in unison. She took it over again and improvised.

Our fusion turned into a game of tennis, the violin and the viola throwing the line back and forth, sometimes modulated, sometimes ornamented (and a violinist like Shreya could ornament the hell out of anything) and at one point inverted.

We passed play back to the guys. The four of us together brought it to the next riff, and then Shreya took it over again, this time solo.

Harrison signaled to cut all our repeats. Shreya unleashed every bit of love into her violin, so alive that it looked like the bow was flying, and she was deaf to everything other than her song in what amounted to a public jam session.

At some point, Shreya grabbed that cadenza by the heart and finished. Everyone was on their feet, the crowd cheering.

I turned, and the lawyers were positioned alongside the emcee in the alcove, humorless as a coconut and twice as soft.

The blood went to my head, but I bowed alongside Shreya. Maybe I'd pass out, but the more I listened to the applause, the more I just let it work through me. We were alive. We were music.

Harrison and Josh also bowed, and then Josh took my elbow to guide me toward the back of the stage. The audience was still clapping, and I turned for a last wave back at them before we got out of sight.

With so little room in the alcove, the Witch Lawyer was practically breathing in my face. I forced a smile.

She glared at me, arms folded.

I gestured toward the crowd, still applauding.

Staring into my eyes, at last she said, "Fine. You can have your rights. Have your attorney call my office on Monday."

She turned, and all the men in suits and holding recording devices followed in her wake.

That's when it came to me what she'd just said: this was permission. Permission to play it now, play it forever, put it on our album, cut them a royalty check—it was official. We were good to go. Sorry for the inconvenience of demanding your head in a bag.

Josh guided me out of the back, and I blinked in the sunlight. Permission. We'd done it. People loved it, and the lawyers had caved.

The oncoming group said something like "Gee, thanks." The festival's photographer started taking pictures of our blue-haired violinist, and I just wanted to set my viola back in the case. My body was shaking with a delayed reaction.

"Hey! You guys did great!" Josh's father rushed up to us. He slapped Josh on the back, then bear-hugged me. A minute later, Shreya's parents were with us, and also Harrison's. Josh's brother ribbed him about finally playing something worthwhile.

My family wasn't there. But then again, this was my chosen family, and they were all around me.

"Um, excuse me?" Someone tapped me on the arm, and I turned to find a reporter. "I'm Tom Ethan from the *New York Post*. Would you mind answering a few questions?"

He faced Josh, who at first backed away, then squared his shoulders. "We'd l-love to." Standing beside me, he picked his words with care. "B-but first, I nnn-need to tell you that I stu-stutter. It might take me a few s-seconds longer to say something, but don't feel you need to st-stop me or finish my sentences."

The reporter started asking questions. Josh answered. The man bought a CD. We ended up at our tent talking to other excited musicians who wanted to try the same thing, one who propositioned Shreya to join his group (or maybe was hitting on her), and someone who recognized Shreya from her previous band (with Shreya telling a confused Harrison she'd explain later).

Josh came to stand behind me, and I tensed.

He said, "Did you name the cat?"

I didn't turn. "There's no use in naming something that doesn't come when you call it. But yeah, I named it Tiger."

While Harrison sold CDs (had his pupils formed actual dollar signs?) and Shreya traded war stories with another musician, Josh bent over our table to write something. I leaned over his hands to watch what he drew.

Under his pencil appeared a hedgehog and a tiger-like cat with a viola and a cello, the instruments leaning against one another. The notes above them formed a G chord.

He wrapped his arms around my shoulders.

I wove my fingers through his and pulled him closer, my back to his chest, and there I stayed in silence, secure and surrounded, no questions, no doubts. Harmony and hedgehogs. I closed my eyes. This was permission. This was forgiveness.

Thank you so much for reading *Pickup Notes*! This was such a fun book to write, and I hope you had fun reading it too.

So many people helped out along the way with this book, but I need to give a special shout-out to the online stuttering community who helped make Josh authentic: Daniele Rossi of Stuttering Is Cool, Greg Snyder of the Stuttering.Me podcast, Heather Baier, and Pamela Mertz of Make Room For The Stuttering. Daniele and Heather were also early readers, and because I didn't realize different stutterers use different stuttering patterns, Josh (it turns out) stutters the same way Dr. Snyder does. Thank you so much, guys.

And the music! Holy cow, the things I needed to learn about classical music, string quartets, violins...I can't even begin. Well, I'll try. Thank you to Jane Eady Gitter of Festivo Strings, musician Sue Holcomb, and musician Marnie Hall. I may be forgetting others. I'm sorry.

If you have a couple of minutes, please leave a review over at Amazon or Goodreads. It doesn't have to be a five-part essay like the ones you learned to write in fourth grade. Just a star rating and a couple of sentences works fine, and it helps the writer and other readers a lot more than you realize.

If you enjoyed this story, I've got other ones you might like. Go ahead and sign up for my mailing list at http://eepurl.com/bcnCNX, and you'll get a free copy of the Seven Angels Short Story Bundle.

Honest And For True

29-year-old Lee has a Park Slope apartment with easy access to Manhattan, loves her job as an auto mechanic, and can see her guardian angel (a wisecracker with a fascination for the Rumours album.) That's kind of a full life for a kid in the world's biggest playground. Despite what everyone thinks, she doesn't need, or want, a romantic relationship.

Far more comfortable in blue jeans and flannel than in heels and satin, Lee finds herself lying to every man she dates. To the physical trainer, she's a preschool teacher; to the guy at the bowling alley, she's a secretary. The lies keep romance at arm's length even as they drive the angel to distraction until the day she realizes she's fallen for a straight-laced accountant who's exploring his dark side through bizarre foods (please note: sea cucumber is not a vegetable). But after her lies, he thinks she's someone she's not.

Now she's got to turn those mechanic skills on herself to diagnose and repair the most important relationships in her life. And just think, she used to find it tough repairing a transmission!

www.ingramcontent.com/pod-product-compliance
Lightning Source LLC
Chambersburg PA
CBHW050917250626
47155CB00001B/269